THE
MOUNTAIN
GOAT

A NOVEL

JIM TRAINOR

**UpNorth
Press**

By Jim Trainor

Grasp: Making Sense of Science and Spirituality (2010)

Waverly's Universe (2012)

The Sand People (2013)

Up North (2014)

The Mountain Goat (2017)

THE MOUNTAIN GOAT

The Mountain Goat is a work of fiction.
Characters, places and incidents are the products of the
author's imagination, and any real names or locales used in the
book are used fictitiously.

Quotations from the Book of Common Prayer, including the
Psalms, are taken from the 1979 version.

For information contact
UpNorth Press
www.JimTrainorAuthor.com

Cover photo by Jim Trainor

ISBN-10: 1539455122
ISBN-13: 978-1539455127

For Mary
and all those who love
to wander.

The Trip

Prologue

Target at 6 p.m. was a zoo. Especially the checkout lines, which were long and slow-moving.

But she wasn't worried about how long the lines were. The longer the better. She had just a few items, but she was in no hurry.

The man in line behind her also had just a few items in his cart. She knew he was there. He was supposed to be there, but she didn't look at him. Instead, she busied herself examining the different flavors of chewing gum available in the rack next to her. She picked up a pack of Orbit White and examined it, then placed it back in the rack and picked up a pack of Orbit Mint.

"The customer is not happy," the man behind her said to no one in particular.

She didn't look at him, but she heard him. Now she handled a pack of Freedent, turned it over in her hand, studying the ingredients. "The customer should not worry," she said.

The man rearranged a few of the items in his cart, then pulled out his phone and scrolled like he was looking at emails. He didn't look up as he said, "It doesn't matter what the customer should do. What matters is that the customer is not happy. You need to take care of that."

"It will be taken care of," she said, now gazing off toward the cashier, busily working her way through a massive pile of items on the moving belt.

"When?"

"Soon."

"Will the customer be satisfied?" The man continued to scroll through his phone.

She hesitated for just an instant before saying, "Yes."

"You should have seen this coming." There was an uncomfortable edge in the man's voice now.

"You're overreacting. This incident is harmless. And we're taking measures to see that it doesn't go beyond that."

"Your solution had better satisfy the customer."

"Just tell them to cool their jets, okay?"

"If the customer is not satisfied, there will be consequences. You know that."

The woman continued examining the gum, but said nothing.

"And the old man?"

"Yes," she said. Now she looked down, as if momentarily troubled. But she quickly gathered herself. She looked at the chewing gum again. "The old man. That is a problem. Something will have to be done."

Chapter 1

It didn't feel any better the second time he got fired.

Instead of facing the question he'd just been asked, Ryan closed his eyes and took himself to the corner of the court, where he was open and where Dickson hit him with a quick pass. *The ball felt hard and pebbly in his hands as he went up for the shot, a smooth integrated motion in which the release was a continuation of the jump. As the ball left his fingertips on its high arc toward the bucket—*

"You freaking idiot," she said, her voice cracking. "Answer me." Evelyn Rockville stood behind her desk, leaning over it toward him. He wanted to stay on the court. He wanted to lose himself in the moment of the game.

But he could no longer avoid her glare. Now Rockville stepped from behind the desk and came toward him. Shaking, her arms rigid at her sides, fists clenched. Her fury was barely contained.

He looked away toward the window and the sunny day on the other side of the pane and a world getting by just fine. Moving along, seemingly unconcerned about what a colossal ass he was.

"Answer me," she shrieked.

"Because I had to," he said, and maybe that was actually true.

"Because you had to," she said, her voice now softer, but seething. He thought she might take a swing at him. "Well, here's what I have to do. At the very least you are fired, starting right now. And if I have anything to say about it—and you can be sure I will—you creep, you'll be rotting in jail."

He turned without looking at her—he couldn't—and headed toward the door, trying to take it slow and nonchalant, but his knees felt weak and wobbly. *He was in the corner again and Dickson drilled another pass, chest high, toward him. He was wide open and went up for a long three. But it felt all wrong. He watched its trajectory toward the hoop, willing it in, praying for it to bend its arc down—it was too long. It clattered noisily on the rim and—*

He heard the door slam shut behind him.

Chapter 2

The Roadtrek was the only thing his mom had left him when she'd died last year, because it was all she had. The large Chevy camper-van sat in the driveway of Ryan Browning's house in Lawndale, California, and Ryan had taken to hauling his laptop out there in the evening, swinging the tall captain's-chair driver's seat around to face the rear, pulling out the little table that folded out from under the sink, grabbing a couple Blue Moons from the fridge, and settling in.

After his dad had left, ten years ago, Ryan's mom had sold the house in Garden Grove, put everything into the Roadtrek and hit the road. She'd lived in it full-time and once told him she had been to every state. He suspected she'd still be going strong if that Peterbilt hadn't backed over her, while she was walking across a truck-stop parking lot outside Carson City.

The Roadtrek—Ryan recalled she'd said it was a '96 (she'd gotten it used)—had everything you needed to get by: a propane two-burner stove, a small refrigerator, a couch in the rear that folded out into a bed, and even a tiny bathroom. The van was not only his wheels—his broken down '91 Escort with 200,000 miles sat in the garage—it was also his office.

It was a much more cheerful environment than his dreary dining room and provided just the right ambiance to work on his new blog. That is, it would be his new blog once he came up with a name for it and decided what it would be about. This much Ryan knew: he wanted it to be about something important, about the challenges of life, because you don't get to be thirty-four without learning something about disappointments and setbacks. At least he hadn't, and he suspected a lot of other folks hadn't either. Anyway, writing the blog entries—and he had at least a dozen of them stockpiled already—was cathartic. That and the Blue Moons helped a lot.

And when those weren't enough, Ryan would lean back and study the dozens of travel magnets that his mom had plastered on every available metal surface in the van. Small magnets from everywhere, it seemed. Mostly little squares with the names of the places she'd visited, like Bozeman and Acadia National Park. But some were other shapes, like one shaped as a wine bottle from Sonoma County and another shaped like a saguaro from Tucson.

He could picture his mom in each of those places, taking it all in. She'd never been much of an adventurous sort, but after Dad had run off to Florida with that woman from work, she'd seemed to come into her own. He originally thought it was a bad idea—in fact a dangerous one—for a woman to head out across the country alone. But after a year's worth of photos from her texts—usually a selfie of her smiling confidently in front of a glacier or a beach or a city skyline—he came to realize how this was what her life had needed. In almost every text she invited him to join her: "Meet me in the Great Sand Dunes next month," or "I'm headed for the

Smokies, come join me." Ryan always replied that he was too busy with work, and the last thing he needed was to drop everything and head off to parts unknown.

The magnets gave him a sense of peace, and they transported him to those places where she had been. And he was there with her. A mother and son—all that was left of this family—living life and laughing and sipping pinot noir by the Russian River.

But now, of course, there was only him.

Chapter 3

"Lots of people lose their jobs, but to get fired and have to leave immediately—not even wait until the end of the day—that takes a special talent." Ryan laughed, a little too loud and too hollow, as he emptied his mug of Leinie's Summer Shandy.

The Wednesday-night crowd hadn't yet made its way into Lydia's. Doug Bartles, who he'd gone to grad school with at Irvine, sat next to him at the bar, while behind the bar a panel of sports experts pontificated away from a huge flatscreen above shelves of backlit booze bottles.

Doug seemed irate. "They can't just fire you like that, can they? Haven't they ever heard of employee rights?" He rested one arm on the bar, turning more toward Ryan to show his empathy. With one index finger he pushed his frameless glasses back up on his thin nose, raised one side of his unibrow, and eyed Ryan hard. "Unless there's something you haven't told me, of course." A thinly veiled prompting for more information.

Which he wasn't going to get. Not yet. Doug loved to share juicy little tidbits of gossip to show what an insider he was. And this would certainly fall into the juicy category. Ryan circled his hands around his mug and peered into its foamy emptiness, then lifted it toward the bartender, signaling the need for another Summer Shandy. After a moment of silence, he said, "Well, they probably felt justified in—"

"Justified? That's BS," Doug said, almost shouting and punctuating his outburst by hammering a fist so hard on the bar that it made Ryan jump. Then leaning forward, he said, almost in a whisper, "Here's what I'd do. I'd call up the state labor relations board or whatever they call it, and I'd lay it all out for them. Then I'd sit back and watch the axe fall on those bastards." He now sat back, looking satisfied, like he'd just claimed some deep victory over all the evils of the world.

Even in his sorry state, Ryan almost laughed. He began to speak, but then his cell rang. "Evelyn Rockville," the caller ID said. "What the—?" Ryan blurted. He clicked the phone off. No way was he taking a call from her now, or at any time. He looked up at Doug. "Can you believe it? That was the woman from Lightyear who fired me today." He chewed on this for a moment, then added, "And why the hell would she be calling after hours?"

Doug shook his head, as in disbelief. "Probably wants to rub it in some more. I tell you, Ryan, let the axe fall."

The idea of watching the axe fall on Lightyear wasn't all that unpleasant. In his two years there, Ryan had never really been treated like a scientific colleague—not the way a physicist was treated back at Los Alamos. His research at Lightyear was only a small piece of the company's mission, a mission never explained to Ryan. Apparently, Nils Robie, the senior scientist and founder of Lightyear, was too involved in things like schmoozing customers to ever spend much time with Ryan. Ryan had long suspected that the only reasons he'd been hired were that his Ph.D. from UC and those years as a staff scientist at Los Alamos looked good on their contract proposals.

Doug wasn't done yet. "And, anyway, it's not like you were working on the frontiers of science. Hell, back at UCI we were working on cool things like plasmas and advanced fusion energy for the world, and you're working on—What was it again?"

"Flow properties of powders and aerosols for agricultural applications," Ryan said without much excitement. This wasn't, after all, the discovery of the Higgs boson or some cutting-edge technology breakthrough that would send Apple stocks plummeting. And it wasn't something he wanted to talk about now. Like Doug had implied, that's not what he'd gone to graduate school to study, but Lightyear's offer was the only one he'd had in the year following his layoff at Los Alamos.

"Yeah, that's it. Dr. Ryan Browning, plasma physicist from the University of California and Los Alamos, now working to improve crop dusters," Doug howled. "And, furthermore—" He paused and pursed his lips together like he was pondering something profound. "Furthermore, maybe now you can get a decent job and move out of that dump." He gave out a cynical chuckle. "I say getting canned was a blessing in disguise."

"Actually, it isn't the worst thing that could have happened to me. I've got some writing projects going, and this will give me more time to bring them—"

"Writing projects?" Now Doug's entire unibrow was raised, signaling maximum incredulity.

"Yeah, I'm working on a blog." Ryan said it just a bit too defensively.

"Blog? You're kidding me. Like passing along cupcake recipes or waxing on the beauty of the weeds in your backyard?" Doug was on a roll now. "Damnit, Ryan, a blog is nice, sure. But what are there, about ten billion blogs in the world?" He drew in a long breath and blew it out with force. "So okay," he said with a resigned voice, "what's your blog about?"

Ryan chose to ignore the sarcasm. "Well, I'm not exactly sure yet, but I want to talk about important things, like the challenges of life that everyone has. You know, relationships, failures, figuring out the meaning of life, and so on." Okay, so he'd put it out there. Let the potshots begin.

But Doug apparently wasn't in the mood for potshots now. Maybe he sensed how serious Ryan was. "Yeah," he said. "Sounds good, but are you going to focus on something specific? I mean, everyone has the kinds of issues you're talking about." Doug ran a hand through his thinning hair and sighed. "And, don't take this the wrong way, Ryan, but what makes you so qualified to talk about these things?"

Ryan decided to treat this as an earnest inquiry and not a putdown. "It's because everyone has those issues that I want to write about them. And it's exactly because I'm not special that I'm the guy to write about them. Everyone can be inspired by some poet or psychologist or whatever, but maybe who they really want to connect with is an ordinary person just like them, who doesn't have all the answers, but like them is struggling to find them. Does that make sense?"

Doug shrugged. "How the hell would I know if it makes sense or not? But I say, if that's what you want to do, then go for it." He looked down for a moment, as if gathering his thoughts about what to say next, then locked eyes with Ryan. "The problem with all of us—just two guys sittin' in a bar here, so factor that in—the main problem is not the crazy things we launch out and try. It's the things we don't do, the chances we don't take. You know, all that deathbed crap about regrets and whatever." He hoisted his mug high in a toast, looking around like others in the near-empty bar might want to join in. "So here's a toast to the first blogger I've ever known. Here's to Ryan Browning, blogger deluxe."

An hour later, Ryan pushed open the front door of his house and, as always, almost gagged at the stench of dog urine. He was convinced the previous tenant had had a dog with a urinary tract infection. Maybe Doug was right. The place—all nine hundred and eighty square feet of it—was a dump. The flat roof leaked, tufts of weeds poked up through the plentiful cracks in the driveway, and the garage door closed crooked, leaving a six-inch gap on one side. But it was Ryan's home, and it was the best he could do for nine-hundred bucks a month in a low-end suburb like Lawndale.

Even this late, there was the din of traffic outside on 147th Street. The noise never seemed to subside. This didn't make sense to Ryan, because Lawndale—although technically located in the happening South Bay area of LA—was a place where in fact very little was happening. It was a town that was more or less forgotten, even though it was only a few miles inland from Redondo and Manhattan Beaches, and for years it had been on a slow downhill skid. The town now had a large and growing population of the elderly—here, like Ryan, for the relatively low rents—leading one local pundit to quip that its major industry was Meals on Wheels.

Ryan stepped inside, but held the front door open for a while to air out the place. The living room—just twelve by twelve, with a low ceiling sprayed with a cheap popcorn finish—felt claustrophobic to a guy six-two. The blank white walls didn't help. Although he'd been here for a year, he hadn't hung anything on the walls. He should, he knew. After all, he owned a pro-level Nikon and an impressive collection of lenses, and he had thousands of his photos stored on his computer. He wasn't even certain where the camera was—off in some closet gathering dust.

He flopped onto the sagging old sofa—the only furniture in the room other than the two folding chairs—then leaned over to scoop up the basketball that lay on the floor nearby. It was an official NBA game ball he'd paid nearly two hundred bucks for and had gotten Kobe Bryant to sign at a Lakers game. Sometimes he'd shoot the ball against a hoop mounted in the small backyard, one of the features that had led him to rent the place, and often he just carried the ball with him around the house, taking comfort from the feel of the leathery ball in his hands.

Would Lightyear really prosecute him? Could there be jail time? What he'd done certainly wasn't criminal in his mind, although it did technically violate the nondisclosure agreement he had signed when he'd joined the company two years ago. He knew he was going against company policy, and yes, he had violated that policy—twice—and, yes, he had known there would be consequences. He had felt like a rebel at the time, like a crusader. But now he was not so sure. What was it Doug had said? We really only regret the things we didn't do?

He grabbed his laptop and headed out to the Roadtrek.

Chapter 4

Amanda had the second-most-popular name of girls born in 1984. That's what her mother had told her. The most popular name was Jennifer, but that was the name of her father's high-school girlfriend, so that was off-limits. Still, second-most-popular was an ID that had resonated with Amanda Seward for most of her life.

Adam was still *liking* her Facebook posts, and that infuriated and troubled her. Why would he do that if he was shacking up with that twit from work? Breaking up with him was the smartest thing she'd done in a long time, and she should be getting an injection of new self-esteem from being so strong. So why did she still feel like crap? Sure, she could unfriend him on Facebook, but she couldn't—not yet. Second-most-popular strikes again.

Amanda had everything going for her, and she enumerated her assets to herself frequently these days. A successful career—well, on the path to a successful career. Probably on the path. And she still had her looks. Thirty-two and she looked like twenty-five. At least that's what her friend Katy had said the other day. But now she leaned in closer to the mirror for a better look. She ran her index finger across the crow's-feet and rubbed them, as if she could make them disappear. But you had to look closely to see them. And last week she'd plucked a gray hair from the brown roots of her blonde-tinted shoulder-length hair.

Tonight she'd go out with the girls—Katy and a couple of others from work. Margaritas at one of the trendy bars in Manhattan Beach, then a long supper at Chez George. It would be a nice break from the hectic schedule of get-acquainted dates that Match.com made possible for her before and after Adam—an endless chain of coffees, drinks, tapas and other one-evening outings that never led to anything. Oh, they each could have led to a one-night stand, but Amanda would not let this happen. She was looking for more: a spark, something with promise. All of this was exhausting. Uneventful. Depressing. She'd report to the girls tonight that she'd dropped out of Match, ready for a break. Yes, maybe she was just a few months away from becoming one of those old women with ten cats, but she needed a break. And if anyone said one more word about biological clocks, she'd be walking away nursing a black eye.

She had thought Adam might be the real deal. Stockbroker at age thirty-three. Good looks. Oh hell, not just good. He was a real hunk. Loved sailing and backpacking and stand-up paddle boards. Knew how to cook and dance and pick out the best wines. They'd been going out for three months, and just when Amanda was thinking she might be moving in with him, Adam had suddenly taken up with Bree, that giggly tart who must be no more than twenty-two and wore those sexy tank tops and short shorts—she could do that with that skinny little body. Adam had laughed at Amanda when she'd confronted him about Bree, said some crap about why can't we just be a little more open and modern and she shouldn't get all jealous and intense, that it wasn't very attractive.

She had fallen for Adam. Is this what a broken heart felt like? Or was she more discouraged because once again she was second-most-popular?

She examined herself from the rear in the full-length mirror on the bathroom door. She smoothed down the tunic over her hips, grimacing, then sat on the bed to pull on her high black boots. It would be good to be away from the computer-dating scene and out laughing with her friends tonight. Otherwise she'd probably just look for more gray hairs in the mirror, check for more of Adam's likes on her posts, and cry her eyes out.

Chapter 5

Ryan pulled the bottle from the cabinet underneath the small sink, grabbed a plastic cup from the dishes that his mom had stocked in the Roadtrek, and settled into the driver's captain's chair. It was an eighteen-year-old Oban Limited Edition single-malt Scotch that his uncle Wil had smuggled home from his last trip to Scotland. Tonight he had left the Blue Moons in the fridge and would concentrate on some hard stuff. Ryan didn't know if Uncle Wil had really smuggled in the Scotch, or if he'd legally carried it in his suitcase, but *smuggle* was the word he had used and it made the fine Scotch even tastier.

He flipped open the lid of his laptop and began a new blogpost. Perhaps he'd publish this someday, but for now it just felt good to write. He took a healthy swig of the Scotch, which he was drinking straight, and thought about a suggestion—allegedly made by Hemingway—to write drunk and edit sober. So this was just good prep work for writing. He almost laughed out loud at the thought. Maybe he'd write about why bad things happen—he had something to say about this, didn't he? Or maybe he'd write about something else, he wasn't sure.

But an hour later, he still hadn't finished his blogpost. In fact, he'd started over several times, still uncertain about what the topic would be. He lowered the lid of the laptop, leaned back, and scanned the interior of the camper van. Again, the magnets caught his eye. There must be a hundred of them. He wondered if his mom had somehow known that one day he'd be looking at them and that, even though he'd never joined her on any of her trips—which he now regretted—the magnets might help share her journeys with him.

He looked away and felt tears begin to grow in his eyes as he thought how his mother must have had a lonely life. He had been unaware of it too long and ultimately had done so little to alleviate her loneliness. For all of Ryan's early life, his father had worked as a national sales representative for a large company. His position required much travel, and he was often gone for weeks at a time. Ryan had always accepted this as part of the realities of his dad's work, but he had since come to wonder just how necessary those long trips had been, or if his father had wanted to be gone. He even considered whether his father might have been one of those men who led a double life, with another family somewhere. But Ryan couldn't remember his mother complaining.

His dad was just a man he knew from his youth, a man he saw occasionally, a man with whom he had a cordial if not close relationship. He didn't know how to expect any more. And so it hadn't been a big surprise when he'd received that letter from his mom announcing that his dad had left. Maybe he should hate his dad. But hate is akin to love, and since there had never been enough of a relationship for there to be love, neither was there enough of a relationship for there to be hate.

But he had survived it intact. Or had he?

One of his mom's magnets caught his eye tonight. It was from Glacier National Park. His mom had been there several times over the past few years, and she'd said it was one of her favorite places. He'd never been there. He'd heard it was a great place to hike, but then so was California, and he'd done a lot of hiking and backpacking in the Sierras of California. Why would he want to go to northern Montana?

But it wasn't the idea of the national park that struck him now. It was the simple black-and-white image on the magnet. A mountain goat stood atop a rocky crag, in silhouette against a bright sky. Its head was raised slightly, as if it were looking off into a great infinity. Ryan tried to put words to his feelings, but they came up short. The mountain goat looked free and majestic and wild. Self-sufficient. Above the cares of the world. Or was it something else that moved him so deeply? Something else entirely?

Chapter 6

New Blog Entry

For much of her life my mother seemed to have a broken spirit. My dad was gone for long periods of time, but my mom never complained. She put up with a lot of poor treatment from him, and for so long she never stood up to him—she just took the path of least resistance.

But somehow her broken spirit was replaced by a spirit of adventure—I mean, she traveled the country by herself. I find this intriguing because my life certainly hasn't revealed a spirit of adventure. Sure, I went into physics, which some people claim is one of the most challenging fields of study, but that had always been easy for me. So, when it came time to go to college, I also took the path of least resistance. Headed off to UC Irvine, the school closest to my home in Garden Grove. When it came time for graduate school, I should have done something more adventurous. Like enroll at Glasgow University or some such exciting place. But I just stayed at Irvine. A bolder person might have taken a year off from school to wander, or maybe join the Peace Corps or the Marines. But not me.

Even my job at Los Alamos was my grad-school advisor's doing. So it would seem that, unlike my mother, I've never had much of a spirit of adventure. But I did stand up to Lightyear, even though it cost me my job. Why did I do that? Sorry if you're reading this post looking for answers, because I seem to only have questions.

Chapter 7

After Amanda had pulled off the high boots and rubbed the aches out of her feet, she padded into the kitchen and poured herself a tall glass of Chardonnay from the half-full bottle in the fridge. Maybe this was over the top—she'd already had that huge margarita at the bar and two glasses of pinot noir at Chez George, and she wasn't that much of a drinker—but what the hell.

She was glad to be home. Sure, the apartment was only one bedroom and bath, with a small living/dining room combo and the kitchen that was no more than an alcove in the corner of the living room. It was tiny and the rent ate up half her salary, but it was only ten blocks from the beach. Not that Amanda went to the beach often, yet knowing it was close somehow comforted this Midwest girl. Yes, the apartment was claustrophobic, but she had done what she could to make it look tasteful and comfortable, with a few sleek pieces from IKEA and accessories from Target. She kept the furnishings sparse to create an open look and avoid overfilling the small space. In fact, she had very little stuff, and Katy had once remarked that she could probably load it all in the back of a station wagon in a half hour. Adam said it looked empty, and remembering that remark now made her bristle.

Amanda flicked on the Pandora app on her phone, and it quickly paired to the Bluetooth speaker on top of the fridge. The Indie folk music was soft, romantic, and edgy. Yes, maybe it was also sad, but that seemed to fit her recent moods.

Sipping the Chardonnay, she let the music enfold her as she danced slowly toward what she laughingly called her gallery, extending the wineglass in her right hand, as if it were the hand of a partner. Her gallery was one wall where a dozen art prints she'd purchased from various museum gift shops were mounted. She stopped at the first print and studied it, even though she'd had these prints for years—since before she dropped out of college—and knew them intimately.

The first print was a favorite, Breton's famous *Song of the Lark*. Amanda had read much about this well-known work and always spent time with it on her several visits to the Art Institute of Chicago. Yet, she remained mystified and mesmerized by the painting. Was it sunrise or sunset? Most said it was a sunrise scene, but the woman looked tired and disheveled and there was dirt on her face. And what was that expression on her face? Awe? Surprise? Mourning? Whatever it was, it came across as authentic and true, and maybe the ambiguity was like the ambiguity in Amanda's own life.

A sip of Chardonnay and one step to the next print, of a painting from the Tate in London—although she'd only seen a commissioned replica in Chicago. It also portrayed a woman: *Beata Beatrix* by Rossetti. Apparently inspired by the artist's dying wife, it showed a woman near death, and, like in the *Song of the Lark*, there was mystery in her expression. Her eyes are closed, her lips parted, her hands opened in prayer. What was it about her face? Was it peace or was it pain? Or was it simply resignation and surrender?

What was it Katy had said at dinner? It was just after the bruschetta had been delivered to the table and the waitress had taken pictures of the laughing group with their pile of iPhones. While everyone was uploading her photo to her Facebook page, one of the girls had said something like, "Yet another party picture of all of us laughing and being wild little divas." That had prompted Katy to say, "Yep, you'd think all we do is laugh." Each of their faces, although masked in laughter, held just as much mystery and ambiguity as anything Rossetti ever created.

Amanda turned and walked to the window. A few lights were still on in the other apartment buildings along the boulevard, even though it was nearly midnight. Only an occasional car sped by, its headlights shimmering off the sheen of a light spring rain that glistened the streets.

Back home in Wausau it was snowing, not unusual for central Wisconsin even in May. Even though she hadn't been home in over a year, Amanda kept Wausau as a favorite on her Weather Channel app, and she even had it send her alerts when weather advisories were issued. She wondered if her dad would have to snowblow the driveway tomorrow morning.

She downed the rest of the wine and made her way to the bedroom. On the way, she checked her phone one more time. Twenty-two likes on the picture from Chez George. None of them was from Adam.

Chapter 8

The lobby of First Federal was a tasteful mixture of glass and oak paneling that screamed prosperity and security. The bank was exceptionally busy on this Thursday morning. Eight people were queued ahead of him between the velvety ropes that defined the zigzag path to the tellers' windows. Ryan had been using First Federal for, what, two years now—ever since he got his job at Lightyear—but since he did all his banking online, this was probably only the second or third time he'd been inside the bank building.

Ryan turned around to see that several more people had joined the line. He laughed and said to the man behind him— busy writing in a notebook—"Looks like we might be here all day."

"No problem, buddy," mumbled the man, without looking up.

Ryan turned forward again and looked down upon the white hair, formed into a tight bun, of the small lady ahead of him. She wore a long blue wool coat, even though it was late spring and in the mid-sixties outside and at least seventy degrees inside the bank. Apparently she sensed his eyes upon her and turned to look up into his face. Clear blue eyes set into a deeply wrinkled face seemed to penetrate into him.

"Slow line this morning, huh?" she said. Her thin lips formed a slight smile, a look of serenity. "Hope you're not in a hurry."

"Oh, I'm okay."

"So what's a young guy like you doing here? I thought it was only old fogies like me who actually came inside a bank building anymore." She had a gentle and welcoming way about her, and Ryan could envision her serving him scones and tea on the shady porch of an old Victorian.

"I just had something I need to do in person."

The woman considered this. "Hope they can take care of it for you. Must be important."

"Yeah, I think it may be."

"You can call me Rose. You're not in some kind of trouble are you?"

Ryan noticed one of the customers leave a teller's window, so there were now only seven in line. He looked down again at Rose, who was waiting for an answer. He thought about his abrupt firing at Lightyear, how he'd brought most of this upon himself, how he might in fact be facing prosecution. He'd laugh his way out of this. "You know us young folks, Rose. We're always in some kind of trouble." He followed up with a carefree laugh that probably didn't come across as authentic.

Rose didn't laugh. She squinted like she was sizing him up. It made him squirm. "You really are in trouble, aren't you?"

Ryan needed some air. Rose was prying, and he didn't like it. Still, she seemed like a truly caring soul. He couldn't just blow her off. He looked beyond her at another customer concluding her business. Only six in line now. "The truth is,

I'm looking to make a fresh start. I've been stuck in the mud in my life, and for too long I haven't done much about it." He wanted to kick himself for letting this stranger draw this much out of him. "So what are you doing here?" he said, with a phony lilt in his voice.

But Rose wasn't buying any of it. She closed her eyes like she was trying to connect into some vision, then opened them again and looked hard at Ryan. "Look, I know you probably think I'm just a nosey old lady who ought to mind her own business, and maybe I should, but I've been like you. Too often in my life I also haven't done much about being stuck in the mud. And so I've changed. I say what I think. I mean, what are they going to do to a ninety-year-old woman, anyhow? Throw me jail?"

Ryan laughed at this, but Rose wasn't done yet.

"So I don't know anything about the mess you're in, and I don't want to. But what I've got to say pretty much fits any situation. And it's this. Don't be afraid to change." She paused as she noticed Ryan was checking out the line ahead of them again. "Did you hear me? Don't be afraid to change. But do not let fear drive anything you do. Or anything you don't do." The serene smile returned to her face. "Okay, that's the end of my sermon."

Only five left in line now. Ryan looked back down at Rose, crafting what he should say, but she had turned toward the front.

Her comments had rekindled an image of afternoons when he was fourteen, playing basketball in Tyler Jansen's driveway down the block. They'd play for hours, firing up shots at the old netless rim above the garage door, pretending they were various NBA superstars. Ryan had perfected a shot that Tyler and the other b-ball adversaries from the neighborhood called floating death. He'd get the ball at the top of the key, fake left, then drive right, across the top of the key, parallel to the free-throw line. Then, in motion—floating, you might say—he'd spin and release the ball while off balance. He was deadly with this shot, and it was hard to defend. Floating death.

When Ryan got to high school and tried out for the basketball team, one of the first things the coach did was break him of the floating death. Ryan still remembered his words. Leaning over him and wagging a finger in his face, the coach had barked, "You do not shoot a jump shot when you're off balance. You must first plant your feet before you go up for the shot. Got it? I don't want any more of those off-balance antics. Okay?"

Ryan never shot the floating death again—his most powerful weapon had been taken away—and consequently he was consigned to mediocrity and spent the next four years warming the bench. "Do not let fear drive anything you do," Rose had said.

"How can I help you today, sir?" the matronly teller said without looking up as she counted through a stack of twenties. She was dressed in a sensible and conservatively tailored suit and reminded Ryan of his geometry teacher in high school. Miss Jenkins had been all business, her passions apparently channeled into isosceles triangles.

"I'd like to withdraw all the money from my checking and savings accounts and then close those accounts."

The Miss Jenkins lookalike now looked up, placed the stack of cash into a tray off to the side, raised an eyebrow and was silent for a moment, as if considering the nature of this request. Then she said, "Why don't you step over to one of our customer service reps across the way?" She gestured toward a row of desks on the other side of the lobby. "One of them can help you with that."

Ryan sighed—so that long wait was unnecessary, when he could have just stepped across the lobby in the first place. He made his way across the plush carpet to the desks, which were aligned parallel to an oak-paneled wall and adjacent to a glass-enclosed office, where a well-dressed man worked intently at a computer. Only one of the customer service desks was occupied. A young woman studying her phone seemed unaware of his approach. Ryan cleared his throat and she looked up, quickly pushed her phone under a stack of papers, and gave him a pasted-on smile. "I'm sorry, sir, how may I help you?"

"Uh, yes, I'd like to withdraw all the cash from my checking and savings accounts, then close those accounts."

She continued to smile, flashing perfect white teeth, unfazed. "Sure, I can handle that for you. Why don't you have a seat, Mr. ..., uh, ..."

"Browning, Ryan Browning." He slid into a plush upright chair across the desk from her. She was a blonde, probably in her late twenties, with a good complexion. Probably worked out. Looked like a lot of women in west LA. He noted the small plastic name plate on her desk: Amanda Seward.

"Give me a moment to look up your account." While she typed a few strokes into a computer, she said, "While I'm pulling this up, might you share why you are closing your account with First Federal? We strive for the best customer satisfaction here, and when one of our clients leaves, we are of course concerned." She glanced up from the keyboard briefly to give him an earnest look.

"Oh, I have no complaints about the bank. Everything's fine on that score." Ryan cleared his throat again. "It's just that I'm in a bit of a transition right now and I want to have maximum flexibility in my life." Transition, sure. Maybe complete collapse would have been a better way to describe it.

"Mr. Browning, I want you to know that you can still leverage your flexibility while you keep your accounts open at First Federal. I'm sure you know that with our Ready-Cash ATM card, you can make withdrawals no matter where you are and still retain the security and earning power that we offer here at First Federal." Another white-toothed smile.

Leverage your flexibility? He sighed. What he really needed to do was remove a means by which the cops could trace him— like through ATM transactions—in case Lightyear planned to really nail his ass. "Thanks, but I think I'd like to stick with my original plans and just close the accounts."

"Certainly, Mr. Browning. Transition, you say? I hope everything is okay." Ms. Seward gave him a concerned look that he wasn't sure was sincere. She was still entering keystrokes into the computer.

Ryan looked up at the wall behind her, above a window, at a huge clock that looked like a gigantic old-time watch face. He saw several seconds tick off. Then he looked back at Ms. Seward. "Well, you might say I'm sort of out of options around here." He paused and looked up at the clock again. A few more seconds clicked by. "Truth is, I'm in between jobs right now and I've inherited this RV from my mother. So it would seem like a good time for an extended road trip." He paused, then added, "I haven't really travelled much."

Now Ms. Seward lifted her fingers from the keyboard and stood to remove a printout from a printer a few steps behind her. She wore a gray dress that looked like wool. It came down to a few inches above her knees. The dress was dignified and businesslike, but couldn't hide the fact that she had a shapely body. Ryan took this all in quickly, so that he wouldn't be found to be gawking at her when she turned back toward the desk.

When she returned, she laid the printout in front of her, then clasped her hands together on the desk and looked at him. For the first time he noticed her eyes. They were green and warm, almost misty. They had a bit of a mysterious look, as if she had a few secrets stored away. "Where do you think you might go?"

He looked to his left, then his right, as if someone might be eavesdropping on them, gave out a nervous little chuckle, then leaned forward toward the desk. "Okay, this probably seems a little crazy to you. You see, my mom has these magnets in her RV—you know, the little touristy things you see in gift shops? Anyway, she has—had—this one magnet with the silhouette of a mountain goat on top of a jagged peak. It looked so free and majestic, I guess it just inspired me." She seemed to be following his comments closely. Her mouth had fallen open slightly. "It's from Glacier National Park. I've never been there."

Ms. Seward nodded, her mouth still open slightly, but she didn't speak for a moment. Then she looked down at the printout and said, "So, Mr. Browning, I think we're all set here. You have three hundred and forty dollars in your checking account and a little over nine thousand four hundred in your savings account. Would you like a check for the total?"

"I'd prefer cash."

She gave Ryan a brief penetrating look, then nodded and said, "I'll send that over to the cashier right now." She typed more strokes into the computer. "They'll have it ready for you in a few moments." Then she clasped her hands in front of her again and said, her voice quieter than before, "Actually, I don't think you're a little crazy at all." She gave him a more genuine smile this time. "It's hard to not admire someone who has the courage to leave a situation that isn't working out. I hope you have a good trip." Then she stood and extended a hand to shake. "I wish you the best of luck, Mr. Browning."

Chapter 9

After Mr. Browning left, Amanda checked her phone again. Forty-four Facebook likes on the photo from Chez George last night. She clicked on the likes to see if Adam had liked it, chastising herself as she did. Yes, his like was there. The bastard. Was he trying to torment her?

She heard the click of the door to her left and quickly pushed the phone beneath the stack of papers again. She looked up to see Mr. Osborne, the bank president, emerging from his office. As always, he had a big smile on his face.

"Amanda, it seems to be a quiet time, so maybe this would be a good time to talk." He took the chair that Mr. Browning had been sitting in a few minutes earlier.

Amanda put on her brightest, model-employee smile. If this was going to be news about a promotion, perhaps senior assistant to the president, then the timing couldn't have been better. "Certainly, Mr. Osborne. What's up?"

"You know, Amanda, how highly we value you here at First Federal. You've been here, what, two years?"

"Three, actually, Mr. Osborne."

"Yes, three. In that time, you've made yourself indispensable, and I'm not sure how we'd get along if you ever decided to up and leave us." He leaned back and gave out a nervous laugh. Amanda continued to manufacture a bright smile. Craig Osborne wasn't much older than Amanda, and he'd obviously made it big in a short time. It hadn't hurt that his dad, Craig Sr., was the former bank president. He had a polished, self-confident look that his days at Dartmouth had no doubt helped perfect. His wavy hair, coal black and tossed in a slightly carefree way, was probably the product of a three-hundred-dollar haircut. Though, when you spend three hundred bucks, they probably don't call them haircuts.

"Anyway," Osborne said, then paused. He sat back casually and crossed one leg over the other, looking relaxed and carefree. "Anyway," he said again, "you know how we always seek to synergize our human resources at the bank to optimize our organizational productivity." He paused again to let Amanda ponder this. This wasn't sounding like the intro to a promotion.

"So …" Again he paused. His right foot, beautifully encased in those nine-hundred-dollar Ferragamos, made a little tapping motion now, betraying just a bit of nervousness. "So, I've concluded, and the board agrees, that going forward we need to work a little harder to synergize our team." Amanda noted that this was the second time he'd said *synergize* in the last two minutes.

Where was all this BS leading? It didn't sound good. Amanda nodded while maintaining the bright smile. She felt just a hint of perspiration above her upper lip. She gave Osborne a peppy nod.

"So, what this means, Amanda, is that starting at the next pay period—I guess that's next Monday, right? Starting at the next pay period, you will be working as a team with Cynthia

Smith to staff this customer services position. How does that sound?"

How does that sound? She'd like to tell Osborne and his Ferragamos just how it sounded. She cleared her throat, then said, "So you're saying, Mr. Osborne, that I'll now be working part-time? Is that correct?" She laid her hands out flat before her on the desk, willing them not to tremble.

Osborne gave her a knowing nod. "Yeah, I guess that's one way of putting it. Like I said, Amanda, you know how indispensable you are, so I really hope you'll be able to get behind this."

She was speechless. She did her best to maintain her cheery smile as Osborne stood and gave her a thumbs-up as he returned to his glass office.

Amanda was shaking now. Lord, she'd never seen that coming. She swiveled her office chair to stare out the big window behind her onto a crowded parking lot backed by a slate-gray sky.

"Excuse me." The voice from behind interrupted her bleak thoughts, and she swiveled back around so fast that she almost toppled her chair. It was Mr. Browning again. She appraised him as he stood there at her desk. Tall and slender, his face bore an uncertain look. He appeared to be reserving judgment, uncertain how to interpret his surroundings, cautious—that's it: he looked cautious. Except for his eyes that betrayed his aloofness—they were dark and passionate, full of longing, eyes that appeared to be seeing and not just looking. His beard was short and well-trimmed, but his shaggy hair gave him a scruffy, natural look. There were many guys in the South Bay who were paying big bucks to achieve this same wild-and-free, slightly tousled look. His sweater, hanging loosely over blue jeans, looked worn and comfortable and made him look huggable. Or maybe it was that she just really needed a hug right now.

"Yes, Mr. Browning," she said in her most professional voice, quickly pulling herself together. "Was there something else I could help you with?"

Browning shuffled a bit, his eyes darting left and right. She noted how he had a prominent (but not large) patrician nose—did she hear that term used in an art history class? It was dignified, and it made him look noble.

He looked at her and said, "Um, I was wondering." He licked his lip, and she could see his Adam's apple move as he swallowed. "I was wondering. Have you ever been to Glacier?"

Chapter 10

Ryan immediately regretted his boldness. Miss Seward scooted her chair back a few inches from the desk, like she was putting some distance between herself and him. She placed her fingertips on her neck, like she was feeling flushed. He confirmed again that she wore no wedding ring. "Are you inviting me to go with you?" she said.

"Maybe—I think so, but this isn't some romantic thing, I mean—I was just trying to be spontaneous, haven't always been very good at that." He realized that he was stammering.

"Maybe you'd better sit down," she said, nodding toward the chair he'd occupied earlier.

He continued, "It was probably a silly idea. I mean, you don't know anything about me."

She laughed. "I do know how much money you have." Then she added, "Not much."

He shrugged. "Well, now I'm afraid I'm looking like some kind of a predator, but that's the last thing I—hey, I thought I'd give it a shot. Probably a stupid idea, you probably—"

She gazed over toward the glass office, where the well-dressed man leaned back in his big leather chair. He was talking on the phone now, laughing, while he fiddled with a golf ball in one hand. She looked back at Ryan. "You know, I'm also kind of out of good options around here."

An elderly couple now appeared behind Ryan, waiting to see the customer service rep. She smiled up at them and said, "I'll be with you folks in just a few minutes. Why don't you have a seat over there?" She inclined her head toward some couches off to the left. Then she returned her attention to Ryan. "How long will you be gone?"

"I don't know." He fidgeted in the chair, feeling suddenly awkward. "I haven't thought about that part."

"But you are coming back?"

"Probably, but you could come back any time you want. I really don't mean to—"

"I could help with the driving," she said, matter-of-factly.

Chapter 11

Ryan was discovering that being spontaneous requires some planning. He'd already taken care of the bank business, but then he'd had to worry about what to do with his car and his house. He was able to get the old Escort down to Larry's Limo Lot, where Larry himself assessed the vehicle and handed Ryan $400 cash, about half of Blue Book, but a good deal for Ryan, considering the work the car needed.

Inside the door of his house, Ryan had piled some clothes, his old backpacking gear, the camera equipment, all the beer from the fridge, the laptop and his basketball, all to be loaded into the Roadtrek. The only other thing of value was his wall-full of physics books, which he loaded into cardboard boxes and dropped off at the library. The rest—the few used pieces of furniture he had were all junk anyway—he would leave behind.

He planned to leave the key under the mat at the front door and send an email to the landlord, telling of a family emergency that necessitated his move—getting fired and facing prosecution qualified as a family emergency, didn't it? He had little confidence that he'd get his last month's rent and the security deposit back, but it was worth a try. His email would ask the landlord to send his refund to his current address, as the post office would be holding his mail for a month, and by that time Ryan hoped to have another address to which the mail could be forwarded.

And then there was the girl. He leaned back on his sofa as he contemplated Amanda Seward. All the other stuff was easy in comparison. Talk about spontaneous. If he hadn't had that conversation with Rose in the bank line, maybe he'd have never had the balls—or was it plain insanity?—to ask her to go with him. And he certainly almost fell over when she didn't say no.

His cell rang. Oh God, it was Evelyn Rockville again. This time he answered. "Hello, Ryan. It's Evelyn." Ryan could almost hear the pinch in her harsh, even severe features. Her calm, steady voice—part of her usual façade—was like a hand grenade wrapped in a cashmere sweater.

Evelyn Rockville was both the CEO and CFO of Lightyear. Why would she be calling? He checked the time on his phone—9:20. And why would she be calling so late? Probably another threat. He struggled to sound calm and objective. "Yes, Evelyn. What can I do for you?"

"I'm inviting you stop by tomorrow to see Dr. Robie. He'd like to do an exit interview with you."

Nils Robie, the senior scientist and founder of Lightyear, who stayed out of the day-to-day operations—Evelyn mostly took care of that—wanted to see Ryan? Now?

"What does Dr. Robie want to talk with me about?" Ryan was pleased at how calm he remained. If it was about his two infractions—the violations of the nondisclosure agreements—then he'd pass.

"I think he doesn't want you to leave under a cloud." She paused for a moment. "He's concerned that some things were said over the past few days, and he'd like to conclude your relationship at Lightyear with a higher-level conversation." She paused again. "A conversation between two professionals."

Ryan wanted to puke. Rockville's persona was like a thin sugar coating on a bitter pill. *Some things were said?* Why, yes, Evelyn, he wanted to say, some things were definitely said over the past few days, and you were the one saying them. It sounded like Robie had not been pleased with the way Rockville had handled his termination—he hoped maybe she had gotten a good chewing out, but that probably hadn't happened.

Ryan pictured Rockville sitting behind her desk, still wearing her tasteful, tailored business suit this late in the evening. He actually preferred the Evelyn Rockville he had encountered during his final meeting yesterday—it was a more honest person, the real Evelyn Rockville. Usually she was polite in a perfunctory way around him—he was not worth her wrath—like the big game hunter not wanting to waste her ammo on a ground squirrel. "I'm sorry, Evelyn," he said. "I'm afraid I'm tied up for the foreseeable future." One thing for sure: he would never darken the doorway of Lightyear again.

"Ryan." Evelyn Rockville's voice now reached a slightly higher decibel level—was the real Evelyn Rockville about to make another appearance? "You should reconsider this. Dr. Robie does want to speak with you, and I highly recommend you accept his kind invitation."

Kind invitation, sure. Ryan was now becoming convinced that there was something else that Robie wanted, but he was not curious enough to find out what it was. "I'm sorry, Evelyn, but that won't be possible." Then he clicked his phone off. He had handled this beautifully.

It was easy to put Rockville's call behind him—he needed to put it behind him. He was moving ahead with his life. Evelyn Rockville and Lightyear were now part of his past. His thoughts quickly returned to Amanda Seward. Tomorrow he'd be heading out on a long trip with a woman he didn't know, if she even showed up, once this all sunk in. He hoped she knew he wasn't a dirty old man, but in fact he couldn't be sure she wasn't some Lizzie Borden type, who would slit his throat in the middle of the night and make off with his ten grand. But in truth, he was less worried about being murdered than how he would make conversation with this good-looking stranger while they were plying the endless miles across I-15.

He wondered what Amanda Seward would do once she realized how crazy and complicated their plan was. He figured it at about 80-20 that she would not show up tomorrow in front of the Johnny Rockets next door to the bank. At this point, part of him was hoping she wouldn't show. That would be a lot simpler. But what about the way her mouth had parted slightly when he told her about his plans?

He tried to banish these thoughts and the path down which they were leading him. But God she was so lovely, and she seemed so engaged with his story, and there was something in her eyes that was inviting him to invite her. He struggled to remember her face. Beautiful? Yes, she was. The long blonde hair and those puffy lips had hooked him right away. But what color were her eyes? Blue, he thought, but he wasn't sure. He had been too nervous to make much eye contact. He wondered how old she was. Twenty-eight was his guess, but she could be five years older or five years younger. All he knew was her name: Amanda Seward, a pretty name.

And now he was heading out on a long trip with this girl—er, woman. They hadn't even discussed things like sleeping arrangements in the RV. Yeah, she probably wouldn't even show up. And that would be best. He blew out a nervous breath.

Ryan scooped up his basketball from the pile next to the door, studied the Spalding Official Game Ball logo and Kobe's signature scrawled large with a Sharpie. He encased the ball in his hands and took himself mentally to the free-throw line for a one and one. *There was one second left in regulation, the team was down by one. If he missed the first shot, the game would be over. If he made them both, the team would win. He bounced the ball a few times, then calmly sank the first shot. The crowd went wild. Ryan was unfazed. He turned and high-fived two teammates behind him, then returned to the line. The arena was now completely silent as he focused on the rim. He sent a high, soft arching shot toward the bucket, his eyes following it all the way.*

Swish.

Chapter 12

Amanda stood outside the Johnny Rockets, where Katy had dropped her off, at nine a.m. It didn't open until eleven. Her former employer, First Federal, where she had quit just yesterday, would open in another hour. Rush-hour traffic still clogged Rosecrans Boulevard. A thick coastal fog had lifted in the past hour so that ground visibility was now good, but it still cloaked the city like a wet gray blanket.

Beside her were a big roller bag, two large duffels, and three long mailing tubes containing the prints from her gallery. She grimaced as she surveyed her luggage; she'd brought way too much stuff, and Mr. Browning—should she call him Ryan?—would no doubt be appalled. She had no idea how long she would be gone—and this lack of knowledge excited more than frightened her. Maybe just a couple of weeks, but maybe months—maybe, who knew, forever. That's why she had come prepared, why she had brought the prints from her gallery.

She reviewed her morning's attire. Getting dressed had been a balancing act. She looked informal enough in her Banana Republic jeans with sequined designs on the hip pockets; a conservative green turtleneck covered by a Patagonia down jacket; and lime-green Skechers that matched her turtleneck. Just like she was headed out for a hike with friends. Casual and indifferent, with just a hint of sexy; that was the look—the challenging balancing act—that had taken her so long to achieve as she laid her clothes out last night. So why had it taken her so long to pick them out? This wasn't a date. Or was it?

She had jogged three miles this morning, the first time in a month, and her legs ached, but it was just what she had needed. The endorphin high energized her for the uncertainty and adventure that lay ahead.

Why was she here? That question kept raising its ugly head, but she kept stuffing it back down with images of Adam and Mr. Osborne—in fact, images of the whole eight years she'd been here in southern California, which now seemed like a complete waste of a prime time in her life. Perhaps saying yes to Ryan was her repudiation of that period, her clenched fist thrust into the air—her rebel victory cry.

But was this the answer? Was she just running away? Was this the irresponsible act of a woman with the emotional maturity of a repressed thirteen-year-old, running away from home? Amanda paced in front of Johnny Rockets, pausing to take in a banner that promised hot wings served the way you want them. She could cut this thing off any time she wanted. She could hop out of the car and say sayonara at the first gas stop. She was in control, calling the shots. Wasn't she?

The logistics of the trip were actually quite simple. Amanda loaded her car and left it in Katy's garage. Katy would help get the apartment sublet—there was huge demand for low-end rentals close to the beach. She'd be in touch with Amanda later about details.

They'd worked it all out last night over sunset cocktails at a window booth in the bar at Kincaid's, by the wharf in Redondo Beach. First, Amanda told Katy all about Ryan Browning, which didn't take long, as she knew almost nothing about him.

Katy's long red hair swirled as she shook her head, open mouthed, like Amanda was reporting that pregnant space aliens had landed in her back yard. "Holy crap, Amanda," she almost shrieked, while giggling at the same time. "Are you freaking serious?" Then she leaned forward and took Amanda's hands in hers, and said, "But as long as the guy's not Ted Bundy, I guess I'm all for it. I should be telling you how stupid you are, because that's just what a responsible and prudent friend should say. Well, you're lucky—or maybe unlucky—that I'm neither responsible nor prudent." She let out a great laugh. "So I say, go for it. Your parents will, of course, want to have you committed."

Amanda laughed. "They've wanted to do that anyway, ever since I dropped out of Madison to follow that jerk Richard out to UCLA." She didn't need to dwell on that sorry chapter in her life right now. Richard, her live-in boyfriend at Madison, gets a partial scholarship to UCLA to complete his masters; Amanda drops out of school a year shy of her BA to follow him; works for four years in a local bank, then Richard says he needs a new start and splits. She didn't date for two years, then hit the dating scene again for a year or so before Adam came along. Enough of that crap.

Katy said, "Personally, I think this may be exactly what you need to do. And maybe I'm just a little jealous."

Katy was the only person Amanda would miss in LA. Oh, she had already been missing Adam, but she was convinced that she had now set into motion the means to put him behind her for good.

A camper van turned into the Johnny Rockets lot. That would be Ryan.

Chapter 13

For the past mile, as he approached Johnny Rockets, Ryan had been trying out various opening lines for when he'd first see her this morning. The fact that he knew almost nothing about this woman he'd just invited on a long road trip was settling into his gut like a bowl of wet concrete. He gasped when he saw her standing right where she'd promised to be, in front of the restaurant. So much for the 80-20 that she wouldn't show.

Ryan lowered the passenger-side window and asked, in a carefree voice he'd worked hard to perfect, "Anybody here going to Glacier?" He cringed a bit, realizing how lame he sounded. She gave him a big customer-service-rep smile. Ryan hopped from the Roadtrek and busied himself getting her luggage into the rear. *God, she brought a lot of stuff,* he thought, but said nothing about it. He began to open the passenger door for her to climb in, but then didn't, thinking this gesture might smack of a chauvinism that Amanda Seward might not appreciate or that would show he recognized she was a female and he was a male. While this was obvious, it felt more comfortable to treat her for the time being as just his traveling buddy. Even though he couldn't take his eyes off the sequin design on her hip pockets as she climbed in.

As Amanda began to slide onto the passenger seat, and before she closed the door, she turned toward Ryan, still standing behind her. "Okay, there are a couple of things I need to know about up front."

"Of course," said Ryan with an air of confidence, while shuffling from one foot to the other. "Shoot."

"Are you married?"

"Appropriate question." He generated a laugh. "Nope, not married. Never have been married." He could have added that he hadn't even had a serious girlfriend since he moved to LA two years ago—not since Melissa back at Los Alamos—and for the past year, since his mother died, he hadn't even had a date. "And, oh, I should add," he said, "I'm thirty-four. What else do you need to know?"

"Probably lots." She laughed. "So I guess I should say that I'm not married either. Never have been, and I'm thirty-two."

As he climbed into the Roadtrek, he said, "So I guess we're actually going to do this thing." Ryan manufactured another laugh, although he wasn't yet convinced she wouldn't hop out at the next corner, and the last he'd see of her would be in the rearview mirror as she went stomping down Rosecrans Boulevard, dragging her mountain of luggage behind her.

As he busied himself with starting the vehicle, she spoke. "What route are we going to take?"

This took Ryan by surprise. He had assumed that he'd just plug Glacier National Park into the Google Maps app on his phone and take off. He turned and looked at her and almost had to catch his breath at her stunning looks. She was running her hands through her shoulder-length blonde hair, like she was gathering it into a ponytail. In the few seconds he could examine her face without leering, he tried to take in everything. Her large green eyes sparkled; they were truth-seeking eyes that made him squirm a bit, eyes that looked like they were probing to see what was beneath the surface, what was real, as opposed to what she had been told. They also betrayed a trace of vulnerability, as if she expected you might be getting ready to say something that would hurt her.

Her high cheekbones and her smooth, white, almost-pale skin made him wonder if she was of Scandinavian descent. She didn't need to wear makeup, and if she was wearing any, it was subtle. She did wear lipstick—*or do they call it gloss?*—a soft pink that enhanced the natural color of her full lips and made them look moist.

Then there was that award-winning smile, like she should be waving from a float in the Rose Parade. Her teeth were perfect and ultra white—she looked like a toothpaste commercial. That smile alone would guarantee success in a job where she'd meet the public. A job like the one she'd just walked away from.

Forcing his eyes away from her, he noticed a Rand McNally Road Atlas wedged in between the front seats, and said, pulling it out, "Why don't we check out the maps and see how we want to go?"

The atlas had seen a lot of use. He opened it to a map in the front, showing the whole United States, and was immediately taken aback. Notes had been scribbled in the margins around the map—some in pen, some in pencil. His mother's handwriting. Ryan flipped quickly through the book and realized that notes had been written in the margins of almost every map. He remembered that his mother had been to every state. He began to tremble, considering the treasure he held in his hands, but quickly got himself under control.

"Are you all right?" Amanda asked.

"Sure." He forced a laugh. He focused his attention back to the map, realizing that with no time constraints, they did not have to take the most direct route. "I'm thinking there are two places I'd like to visit. Santa Fe. I've always loved that place. It's close to where I used to work in Los Alamos. Then, I'd like—"

"You worked at Los Alamos? The place where the bomb was invented?"

"Oh, yes, I worked there for several years, but not on bomb stuff." This wasn't the time to tell her he'd been let go from the Lab. He'd been RIF'd; RIF stood for Reduction In Force, a nice term for laid off. "I worked on plasma physics with the—"

"You're a physicist? Do you have a Ph.D.?" She appeared genuinely impressed.

"Yeah." He shrugged like it was no big deal. "Went to UCI, undergrad and grad school. You know, Irvine?"

She nodded, then looked back toward the road atlas that he had spread open between them. She grasped the right side of the atlas in her hands and leaned toward him slightly as she did so, enough that he could take in her soapy-clean scent. "And where else did you want to go?" she asked.

Ryan traced his finger along a route generally north from Santa Fe. "I'd also like to stop in Bozeman." He added, "In Montana."

"I know where Bozeman is," she replied quickly. He hadn't meant to insult her intelligence.

"That's where my uncle lives. It would be good to see him." He paused, then asked, "So what about you?"

She pulled the map a few inches closer to herself and pondered it for a while, seeming to take it all very seriously. Then she said, showing him another of those incredible smiles, "You know, I've never been to the Grand Canyon."

"Geez, I haven't been there in years. In fact, that might be a good first stop. Let's do it." With that, Ryan closed the atlas and placed it securely beneath the seat—he would study the notes from his mother at a more quiet time. Then he entered Grand Canyon into the Google Maps app, which told him that it was 511 miles and eight hours away. "It will be a pretty long drive, but I think we can make it today," he said.

As he began to shift into drive, he noticed Amanda looking toward the rear of the Roadtrek. "Oh," he said. "Sorry. I should've offered you a tour of the camper."

"It looks kind of small," she said, with a note of concern. "I thought you said it was an RV."

"Oh, it is an RV," he said quickly, probably sounding too defensive, as he turned to survey the Roadtrek also. Well, it was pretty much just a van, but it was much more than a van. It had started out as a commercial-sized Chevy van, but the motorhome company—he thought he'd seen it was based in Canada—had replaced the upper body behind the front seats with a taller, wider body. Behind the front seats, a narrow passage way ran to the rear. Even though it was narrow, it still was high enough that a six-two guy like Ryan could stand up. On one side, a galley contained the sink and two-burner stove, the compact refrigerator and even a microwave. Other than keeping a stock of Blue Moons in the fridge, Ryan had not yet used any of this stuff. On the other side of the passageway there was a small marine-style toilet and sink inside a tiny closet. In the rear, a vinyl-covered sofa folded out into a full-sized bed. There was even a TV mounted above the sofa. To make the space even more usable, the driver's and passenger's captain chairs could be turned to face the rear, and a small table could be unfolded from beneath the sink area—this is where Ryan often sat and worked on his blog. All in all, it was a cozy space. Perhaps cozy was euphemistic—but it contained all the necessities for living—indeed, all the features of a much larger RV, in a compact form, while being only a little larger than an ordinary van.

"I guess I expected it to be much larger," Amanda said, a hint of alarm in her voice.

"Sorry if I misled you," Ryan said. Maybe she'd leave even before they pulled out. "It's got everything. Here, let me show you." He rose from the captain's chair and began to move toward the rear, but Amanda stopped him with a hand on his arm. "That's okay, we can tour later. Let's hit the road. I'm looking forward to getting out of Dodge."

This was the first time, he noted, that she had touched him. "Me too," he chuckled, then pulled the Roadtrek out into the morning traffic.

They drove in silence for the first few miles, Ryan focusing on the driving—he didn't have much highway experience with the big van. He should be making small talk, he realized—nothing heavy or too personal—but maybe they both needed the quiet for now. Occasionally, he'd sneak looks at her, busy with her phone, her practiced thumbs speedily tapping away. With her head tilted down toward her work, her blonde hair fell forward, and he could not see her face.

Somewhere beyond El Monte, Amanda held up her phone and smiled, "How about some music?"

"Sure," Ryan grinned.

"Does the van have Bluetooth? I've got a portable speaker buried in one of my bags, but I'd never be able to find it now."

"I'm pretty sure not. This is like a '96 or something."

"Hmm," she nodded, then began exploring the dashboard area. "Is there a USB connection?" Then she answered her own question. "Guess not."

Ryan looked down from his driving, grimacing. "Sorry. Looks like all we have is a CD player."

"And no CDs," said Amanda.

"Don't you have some earbuds?"

"I thought we could listen together." She shrugged and turned on the radio and scanned through the stations. The only one that came in strong was a country station, AM 1480, from who knows where. Amanda turned her body away toward the window as Kenny Chesney sang, "You and tequila make me crazy ...."

Chapter 14

"To tell you the truth," Ryan said, once they'd been on the interstate for a while, "I haven't driven this thing on the freeway very much."

"I think you're doing great," she said. She studied him in profile as he concentrated on maneuvering the big van on the four lanes of busy eastbound traffic. He wore an old wool half-zip pullover, with the zipper open to reveal a dark plaid shirt. He looked like an ad for the REI used clothing department, if there was such a thing. His hair was a bit too long; he'd need a haircut if he wanted to fit into the Marina del Rey crowd, which she suspected he didn't. It looked like he probably had a hard time keeping it under control. Not like Adam or Richard for sure. And the beard—it was dark, trimmed short and well-groomed. She'd never dated a guy with a beard before, actually never even kissed a guy with a beard. *What is that like?* Good God, why was she even thinking such things?

It didn't bother Amanda that the little conversation they had for the first hour or so was cordial and superficial: topics like what they would see at the Grand Canyon, how it was a beautiful day for traveling, how they would have to stop along the way to store Amanda's things into the closet compartments of the Roadtrek, whether to buy food and cook in the RV or eat out. They never mentioned why Ryan was out of a job or why Amanda had been so ready to walk away from her employment; they didn't discuss current or former relationships. There seemed to be an unspoken assumption that these topics would be addressed in due course and that there was no need to rush them.

They left the I-10 near Fontana, just west of San Bernardino, and headed north on the I-15, which would take them up over the Cajon Pass to Barstow, where they would split off to the east on I-40 toward Flagstaff and the South Rim of the Grand Canyon. Despite Ryan's openly stated concerns about how the Roadtrek would handle the ascent, the old RV climbed up over the 5,000-foot-elevation Cajon summit without a problem. Soon they descended into what locals call the high desert, that strip of the vast Mojave Desert along the northern flank of the San Bernardino Mountains. Stately, angular Joshua trees and spiky yuccas dotted the arid landscape, giving it a surreal beauty.

Just beyond Hesperia, they exited the interstate and drove a mile or so to the Stater Bros—located in a strip mall—where they could stock up on groceries and other supplies. They had decided that most of the time they would eat in the RV to minimize costs, and perhaps eat out once a day—probably breakfast or lunch, which would be cheaper than dinner. Amanda had created a shopping list from their brainstorming during the past hour of shallow chit chat.

She now read from the list as Ryan pushed the shopping cart through the aisles. Anyone observing them would naturally assume they were just another married couple doing their weekly shopping.

They stopped in the deli section to get cream cheese. Ryan scratched his head and said, "Geez, I didn't know this stuff came in so many flavors." He laughed. "Do you want the plain? Or the strawberry? Or the chive and onion? Or the jalapeño?"

Amanda had not shopped for groceries with a man in almost four years. "Hmm," she said. She placed a forefinger on her chin, as if deeply pondering this important question. "Let's get one plain and one jalapeño. That okay?" This felt good. Safe. Domestic.

In the parking lot, Amanda asked Ryan to move in close, then took a selfie with him in front of the Roadtrek. Although they did not touch, she sensed him raise his arm to place around her for the photo, then drop it to his side. She immediately posted the photo on Facebook with the message, "On the way to Grand Canyon and beyond with Ryan."

They loaded the supplies into the fridge and cabinets, then packed away Amanda's luggage. The long tubes containing her art prints had to lay out on the rear sofa, next to Ryan's basketball—some things, Ryan laughingly confessed, just don't fit into a narrow RV closet. He also pointed out the amenities of their living space. Two items were of immediate concern to Amanda: the bathroom and the sleeping arrangements.

"Not to worry," said Ryan, sounding optimistic and worry-free. "The back folds out into a big bed—and notice, there's even a TV. This is all yours. The passenger seat folds back into a single, and that's where I'll bed down." He apparently saw the look of apprehension on Amanda's face, and seemed eager to dismiss any incorrect assumptions. "It'll be like camping. I'll make sure you have plenty of privacy and take a hike when you want to change." He looked at her for affirmation.

Her uncertainty must have been pasted all over her face. "Well," she said with hesitation, "let's give it a try and see how it works." Looking around, she added, "Maybe we could hang a sheet between the front and back?"

"Sure," said Ryan, with a no-big-deal air of confidence. "That should be easy."

The bathroom was something else altogether. It was a tiny toilet crammed into a narrow closet, no larger than a small food pantry. Yes, she could squeeze in there, but it was so close to the passenger compartment, and the thin door would provide little privacy. With hands on her hips in a decisive stance, she said, "Okay, so this just isn't going to work. No way am I going to use that thing. And I hope you don't either."

Ryan grinned. "I'm in full agreement on this one. I figured we'd always be stopping in campgrounds that have bathrooms and showers," he said, and she could tell his comment was made more out of hopefulness than absolute confidence.

Amanda nodded slowly with a tentative acceptance. "Okay," she said and shrugged.

"So," Ryan said, "on to the Grand Canyon?"

She looked around at the beautiful high-desert landscape stretching to infinity just beyond the blacktop parking lot of the supermarket. She made her best attempt at a big, reassuring smile. "On to the Grand Canyon," she said.

They stopped for lunch at an In-N-Out Burger across the street from the supermarket. Standing in the long line for fast food, out here in the desert, among a crowd—most of whom were probably, like her, enroute to somewhere far from here—

gave Amanda the sense that she was indeed on a road trip. Grabbing a gut bomb in the middle of nowhere, then heading off into the unknown. She felt her pulse quicken.

As they took their seats in a white molded plastic booth, Amanda was ready to talk, ready at last to start getting to know Ryan. But then his cell rang. He glanced down at his phone and shook his head in disapproval. Then he looked at Amanda, gave out a big sigh and said, "I'd better take this." He left his double cheeseburger on the table and went outside.

Chapter 15

Ryan paced outside the In-N-Out. "Hello?" he said into the phone, as if he didn't know who it was.

"So, Ryan, I was hoping we'd be able to sit down and have a conversation." Nils Robie, chief scientist of Lightyear, didn't bother with introducing himself. He sounded calm, almost friendly.

"About what, Dr. Robie?"

"About expectations. I understand academic freedom, but this isn't academia. Some things are secret and sensitive for good reason."

Ryan could picture Robie's stern face, rough and red like a Swedish fisherman's, and his wavy sandy-gray hair. It was said that Robie had been a head honcho at the Naval Research Laboratory in Washington, but he'd found himself in a power struggle with an admiral, and Robie was out. His revenge was to start his own company. Rumors were that Evelyn Rockville and Robie once had a thing going between them, but that could have been just office gossip.

"But none of my work was classified. Look, if it were, I'd have respected that, and—"

"Maybe not classified, but sensitive, nonetheless. We need assurances that you will honor that. You've been quite a loose cannon, Ryan." His voice remained calm and fatherly; he was playing the wise mentor dispensing advice.

Oh, give me a break, thought Ryan. *The last thing I am is a loose cannon.* "Look, Dr.—"

"Maybe you've heard of people like Julian Assange and Edward Snowden."

Ryan rolled his eyes, but said nothing as Robie continued.

"You've shown a tendency to, shall we say, step out of the box. To treat sensitive information in a reckless way. How can I be certain this is not just the beginning of something truly harmful?" An uncomfortable edge had now appeared in Robie's voice.

"Hold on, Dr. Robie. What I did was just be true to the universal ethic of being open with scientific information. I submitted two short abstracts to a national science conference. That's what hard-working physicists do—you should know that. I never disclosed anything that was classified—because I don't know anything classified or even proprietary. In other words, Dr. Robie, I have done nothing wrong!"

"Ryan, must I remind you that after you sent that first abstract in, we spoke about this." Actually, it had been Evelyn Rockville who had chewed him out about it. "And then, as if you were intentionally working against Lightyear's best interests, you submitted a second abstract." That was true. The second abstract had been in protest to Rockville's narrow attitudes toward a scientist being able to publish his research results. "And that left us little choice." If his voice was still fatherly, it was not the voice of a kindly dad, but of a harsh disciplinarian.

"I repeat, Dr. Robie, I did nothing wrong."

"That's exactly what Assange and Snowden said."

Ryan felt heat in his face. "So what am I supposed to do?" he said. "You've already fired me."

"I'm considering what to do, Ryan. What you've created for us is a problem. It's important that we talk before this escalates."

Ryan looked over at the Roadtrek sitting nearby in the parking lot, and this somehow gave him the boldness that he needed. He said, his voice steady and firm, "We have nothing to talk about, Dr. Robie. If you're running an honest business—and I assume you are—then you have nothing to fear from ethical scientists like me or anyone else. So excuse me, Dr. Robie, but I think this conversation is over. Please do not call me again." Ryan terminated the call with a decisive tap on his iPhone.

He felt good for being in command with the senior scientist. So why were his hands shaking? What was it he had heard in Robie's voice that troubled him now? Was it fear?

Chapter 16

Amanda was waiting in the molded plastic booth when Ryan returned, sipping from her tall Diet Coke. "Is everything okay?" she asked.

"Just an annoying call from my former employer. Nothing to worry about. And nothing worth polluting our trip with." He was ready to put this behind him.

But in the parking lot, there was more trouble. The front driver's-side tire was low. Very low, but probably drivable, at least for a short distance. Ryan groaned as they both stared helplessly at the tire for several moments. Then he checked his phone for the nearest tire dealer. "Fortunately, there's a Chevy dealer just up the road, in Victorville."

Amanda looked concerned. "Will they be able to fix it?"

After the stressful call from Robie, Ryan had to work to keep a positive attitude. *He had to act quickly. It was a tight man-to-man defense, and he was being guarded by a consensus All American. Ryan gave his opponent a head fake, then drove to the right, leaving his man in the dust. Ryan spun as he went toward the bucket, moving the ball to his left hand, as their big center was now all over him. Fully extended, Ryan's outstretched left hand laid the ball in softly for two.*

But his fantasy was shattered by the memory of a real basketball event. He was a freshman, trying out for the team at

UCI, the Anteaters. The head coach, Roger Sperling, was tough and knew the game. At one time he'd been a starting guard for one of Johnny Wooden's great UCLA teams. In the scrimmage that afternoon, Ryan had gone up for a rebound, only to have the ball plucked from behind him by a leaping teammate. Coach Sperling had jumped to his feet on the sidelines and hollered, "Browning, it would be great if you could add a couple more inches to your jump. That would make four inches altogether." Ryan was cut from the team the next day.

He turned toward Amanda with a phony confident smile. "Let's go find out. Probably won't be a big deal. I'm hoping we can still make Grand Canyon tonight."

Indeed, it wasn't a big deal. The Chevy dealer found a nail in the tire and repaired the leak easily. But because the service bays were full when Ryan and Amanda arrived, they had to wait almost three hours to get the tire fixed.

The claustrophobic waiting room—which smelled of new tires and stale popcorn—was packed with customers, so for a while they wandered among the new cars in the showroom. Laughter helped the time pass. Amanda comically draped herself against the hood of a big red diesel Silverado and gave Ryan one of her great smiles. "Here's the one I think you should get, Ryan." She was now calling him Ryan.

"That looks perfect," he said, nodding to confirm her choice. "And for you … hmm." He rubbed his chin with his thumb, seeming to struggle with the decision. "Maybe this little baby." He pointed toward a tiny Spark, the least expensive model on the floor. He let out a big laugh as Amanda grimaced, then said, "Nope, not even close." He sauntered slowly over to a silver Corvette, stroked the sleek roofline, and smiled. "Ah, yes, here it is. Got your name written all over it." He leaned down to check the sticker. "Only sixty-seven grand. Maybe we should get two."

They amused themselves this way for a half-hour before returning to the waiting room and finding a spot on a worn-vinyl sofa, with so little space that they had to sit shoulder to shoulder. When she turned her head to check the wall clock, Ryan felt her long blonde hair brush against his neck. She was pretty tall, probably five-seven, and sitting, she was just a few inches shorter than him. Her scent—still soapy clean, but mixed with perspiration—was intoxicating. Amanda was now checking her iPhone, and Ryan could see she was scrolling through Facebook.

He surveyed the other customers in the small, windowless room: a white-haired old man staring blankly at the far wall; a burly young guy with a shaved head, in a muscle shirt, flipping impatiently through a tattered hunting magazine; a mother looking exasperated, trying to keep an overactive toddler under control.

Amanda pushed her phone into a pocket of her down jacket, now bunched on her lap in the overly warm room. She turned her head toward Ryan and said, "So your mom left you the camper? How long has she been gone?"

Ryan looked straight ahead; if he turned to face her, their mouths would be distractingly close. "Just a year."

"Oh, my," Amanda said. "I'm so sorry."

Ryan let out a long sigh. "Yeah. I'm not sure I've really processed it yet."

"How did it happen?" Her face was still turned toward him.

"It was a pedestrian accident. Hit by a truck in Carson City, Nevada."

"That's terrible. Was she killed instantly?" Then she added, "I'm sorry if I'm probing into painful territory."

"That's okay." Ryan now turned his head toward her, willing himself to remain calm this close to her face. "Actually, she lived for two weeks. It was terrible."

"Oh, God. Did she suffer?" Her eyes were large and looked on the verge of tears.

"She was unconscious the whole time, so I don't think she suffered. For a while, we—my uncle Wil, the one from Bozeman, and I—thought she might make it. There were several operations, but in the end she'd just been hurt too bad." His voice faltered a bit. "Then she died."

"Oh, Ryan." Amanda placed a consoling hand on his arm. What he didn't tell her, because it seemed relatively unimportant now, was that his mother had had no health insurance, and the medical bills had more than depleted his mom's and his savings—over $100,000. In fact, until just a couple months ago, he'd been making monthly payments on the balance. The $9,400 he'd withdrawn from First Federal two days ago was what he'd been able to sock away in the past year by living a miserly life: replacing his 4Runner with the old Escort and renting that dump in Lawndale. There would be time to talk about these things later. Now, he was more interested in the warm hand on his arm.

"And where's your dad?" she asked.

Another painful topic. Ryan looked away toward the old man, who was still staring at the opposite wall as if lost in a parallel universe. Then he looked back at Amanda. Her mouth was open slightly, as if anticipating his next words. "He split over ten years back. Headed to Florida with some woman from work, and no one's heard from him since. I don't know where he is, or even if he's still alive." He could have said more. He could have told her about the father that was never there to play catch in the back yard, help him with algebra homework or build the pinewood derby car with him for the Cub Scouts. In fact, his dad had missed his high school graduation. He tasted something bitter in his mouth—this wasn't his favorite subject.

Amanda seemed troubled. She shook her head slowly, then said, "Have you tried to find him?"

"No."

Amanda nodded, but said nothing, obviously realizing that she shouldn't push this any further. She pulled out her phone again as Ryan turned his attention to the opposite wall, seeking the same parallel universe the old man apparently had found.

Chapter 17

To Amanda, the Mojave Desert beyond Victorville bore a strong resemblance to the lunar surface. The Joshua trees and yuccas of the high desert gave way to endless miles of low, drab green sagebrush, some of it dried and turned into tumbleweeds. Ranges of rugged mountains, treeless and dry, gray and brown and shadowy, lined the horizon. The only indications of civilization were the blacktop stretching to infinity in front of them and the rows of tall electrical-transmission-line towers, carrying power to LA, marching across the desert, as if out of an invasion scene from *Star Wars*. Occasionally, they saw a freight train, groaning along tracks parallel to the highway but several miles away—it was hard to judge distances out here—like a long string of multicolored pearls. Several times they crossed bridges that spanned dry washes—parched beds of sand—or passed a dry lake, which emphasized how waterless this terrain was.

They crossed the Arizona state line at seven, with Google Maps showing it was still nearly five hours to Grand Canyon Village, where the national park campground was located. By the time they made it to Kingman, at eight, they were hungry and tired. They pulled off I-40 for gas, across the street from a Walmart.

When Ryan climbed back into the driver's seat, he said, as he pushed the key into the ignition, "We can press on and probably make it by midnight." Then he looked over at Amanda. "What would you like to do?"

Amanda could see that he was tired, despite his best efforts at a gung-ho attitude. So she said, "I'm hungry and it's been a long day. Maybe we could find a place to stay around here?"

"There must be some RV parks around here," said Ryan, pulling out his iPhone to check.

"I've heard that RVs can park at Walmart," Amanda said, nodding toward the big parking lot just across the street.

Ryan seemed to consider this for a moment. "No hot showers," he cautioned.

Amanda had been on camping trips before. She could rough it for one night. "I can wash up in the restroom in the store." Then to add reassurance, as she saw the concern in Ryan's face, she said, "I'll be fine."

They parked the Roadtrek at the outer edge of the lot, not far from where two big rigs and a large fifth-wheel had also settled in for the night. After a half hour sorting through the cabinets of dishes that Ryan's mom had stocked and locating various food items they had purchased, they set a pot of water boiling for pasta, and washed and dressed the greens for a salad. They took a moment to sit back in the two captain's chairs—turned to face the rear—to relax.

"Ah," said Amanda, raising a finger, "I have something I think you'll like." She jumped up and rummaged through one of the rear cabinets, where her belongings had been stowed. She returned with a small Bluetooth speaker and set it atop the counter. She soon had Pandora playing her favorite Indie folk music. "Here," she said, extending a hand to Ryan, "let's dance."

For a moment, Ryan seemed uncomfortable with the invitation, but then he stood and extended his arms toward her. She moved in close to him and they swayed more than danced in the tiny space of the camper van. When the piece had ended, Ryan said, "That was very nice. Thank you. Now I have something I think you'll like." He invited her to sit back down while he pulled the Oban Limited Edition from one of the drawers, along with two glasses. "This is from my uncle Wil. Hopefully, you'll get to meet him in a few days." He poured healthy amounts into the glasses, adding only a splash of water to each.

As they settled back into the deep captain's chairs, Ryan said, "You've heard about my parents. I want to hear about yours."

"Umm, not a whole lot to say. They're both alive and well. They live in Wausau, Wisconsin. That's where I was born. My dad works in a factory that makes custom wood windows, but he's thinking about retiring. My mom stayed home to raise my brother and me. Now she does a lot of volunteer work. My older brother, who still lives in Wisconsin, works in insurance." She looked at Ryan, as if saying *that's it*.

But Ryan had more questions. "So you grew up in Wisconsin?"

"Yep. Went to Madison to study art history."

"Art history? Cool. So how come you were working in a bank?"

The Scotch was smoky and powerful. Amanda was not much of a Scotch drinker, but this was good. "Well, that's a long story, so maybe—"

"I've literally got all night," he laughed. "I'm all ears."

She took another sip of the Scotch, let it finish in the back of her throat, then said, "Okay. So my father was always opposed to me being an art history major. He insisted I do something practical, something that would lead to a job offer." Her eyes met Ryan's, and she recalled her first impression that his penetrating eyes were seeing and not just looking. They seemed to be seeing at this moment. Her gaze travelled beyond Ryan to the counter area behind him and the array of his mother's souvenir magnets. Her eyes fell upon the Glacier magnet with the mountain goat. "Oh my," she said, "this is the first time I noticed the mountain goat." She smiled.

Ryan turned and looked at it and nodded. "Yes, that's it." He seemed somber for a moment, then quickly recovered. "I wonder if it ever had to spend the night in a Walmart parking lot." They both laughed. Then he leaned slightly closer to her and said, "So how did you deal with your father's disapproval?"

"I was pretty clever, I think. I kept my art history major, but minored in accounting. In fact, I only took a few accounting classes, but my dad thought I had an accounting minor, and he was okay with that. Actually, those accounting classes came in handy when I had to find work in banking."

"But what did you do with your art history degree?"

Amanda looked down briefly, then took another sip of Scotch. "I never finished my degree. Dropped out after three years to follow a guy out West. Thought he was the love of my life, so I was more than happy to put my education on hold to support him while he finished grad school. Then, after four years, when he had that new diploma in hand, I learned that he had someone else in hand also." Amanda grimaced. "Pretty stupid, huh?"

"I don't think so," he said softly, then leaned forward and kissed Amanda. It was a gentle, light kiss on the lips. He pulled back and looked at her. She felt glassy-eyed. He leaned in again and kissed her more deeply, and this time she moved against him.

Then she pushed him away, gently but firmly. Smiling, she said, "C'mon, Mr. Browning, we haven't even made it through the first day yet." Then her brow furrowed, she pursed her lips, and she looked down. "I need to take things slow."

"I'm sorry," said Ryan, drawing a deep breath and leaning back in his chair.

She looked up. "Don't be sorry," she said.

Chapter 18

After Amanda left to wash up in the Walmart bathroom, Ryan settled back into the driver's chair and stared out into the darkness. It was after ten, and the parking lot was now nearly empty. There was only the occasional red flicker of a tail light off in the distance on I-40. He'd only had one glass of Scotch, but it had been enough to leave him with a warm glow. After the kisses, he'd put the Scotch away and tried to get the evening back to normalcy, and Amanda had been a supportive accomplice. She'd switched the romantic Pandora station to something classical. They'd eaten dinner among light banter and laughter, then washed the dishes and left the counter spotless. By then, things were pretty much back to what they had been before Ryan had leaned in and kissed her. Those kisses. A bad idea. Maybe. Or maybe not, he wasn't sure. Those luscious lips. He tried to force his thoughts away to other things.

He hadn't had a real kiss—one from responsive lips like Amanda's had just been, albeit so briefly—in over a year. And it had been what—two years?—since he and Melissa had broken up back at Los Alamos. That was right after he'd gotten his RIF notice, the hard news that he had been laid off. Melissa was a chemist he'd met at a seminar on the interface between chemistry and physics, and then for a couple of years they had been quite an interface themselves. Their initial friendship—the conversations at Starbucks about the direction of American science research and the ever-popular topic of Lab politics—quickly turned to passion. She was just coming off a divorce and was, so she had said, just getting back on her feet. It ended when Melissa told him—he still shook his head in disbelief about this—that the chemistry just wasn't there. By that time she'd been promoted to the job of group leader, with supervisory responsibility over a group of twenty or so staff scientists and technicians. She was clearly on the way up, and Ryan clearly wasn't. Melissa apparently perceived herself to be in a new world now—one that didn't just gossip about Lab politics but actually shaped it—and that world had little room for Ryan.

Los Alamos was a challenging place to find someone to date. Very few physicists were female, and anyway, most people who moved there were already married. For the ones who weren't, there were few social outlets where you could meet someone. Only the Starbucks or a few bars. Other than that, there were the scientific seminars, hardly hot spots for romance to blossom.

Ryan stared out onto the dark Walmart parking lot. Then he picked up the road atlas from between the seats and turned to the Arizona map. He had already decided to be deliberate and methodical; he would read his mother's notes only for the state they were currently in. After the conclusion of his trip, he would read the entries for all the other states. He studied the map of Arizona for only a few moments, noting how isolated Kingman was out in western Arizona.

Then his attention turned to his mother's notes in the margins. Almost every blank space was filled with her writing, the familiar small and neat cursive he had not seen for so long. It was so rare today to see much handwriting. *A lost art*, thought Ryan, even though he was a product of the computer age, when creativity in writing style meant selecting an appropriate font. But what he saw before him, the almost-miraculous coordination between her brain and the nerves and muscles of her fingers, was as unique as her face. Just seeing her writing now brought forth old images of his name written on his school lunch bag in the second grade, the long letter—filled with hope and love—she wrote him when he graduated from high school, and the shorter letter she wrote to notify him that his father had left.

He set the atlas down for a moment to collect himself.

Then, starting at the top, left-hand corner of the map, he read every note. Many of them were logistical entries: *Plan to make it to Bisbee by Saturday, 2/11* and *Is two days too long to stay in Prescott?* But there were other notes that expressed her views, hopes and observations. One that he read twice said, *You already have everything you need. Last night, I learned about a tiny owl that makes its home in the giant saguaro cactus. In the middle of the desert there is such beauty. Even here, there is everything you need.* It was like he could hear her voice saying these words to him.

His mother—who saw beauty in the stark desert, provision where there was scarcity, whose unique handwriting was before him now, as if it had been written yesterday and just for him—was dead. The atlas fell from his hands, and he looked off into the empty night again, trembling.

Chapter 19

There were only a few people shopping in the Walmart this late. Probably some of them were stopping by after working the swing shift. And likely there were some who just didn't want to spend the evening alone at home. For a year after Richard left, Amanda had been one of those people. She knew about pushing her cart slowly and deliberately up each aisle, making herself linger to examine the manager's specials in detail, carefully comparing the nutritional data on cans of soup, and trying to be spontaneous about spoiling herself with a special treat.

She made her way into the empty restroom and did her best to wash up using paper towels, water that wasn't very hot and came out only in intermittent spurts, and the soap dispenser that oozed a gooey pink gel that she couldn't be sure was really soap. In front of the mirror, she brushed her teeth, then worked her brush through her hair. Her expensive Balayage streaked highlights were a tangled mess. She groaned out loud, then laughed. Apparently Ryan didn't think she was such a mess. She turned to view herself in profile. She'd been wearing the turtleneck out all day, but maybe it looked better tucked in. Didn't matter now. Soon she'd be enveloped in the loosest, most modest flannel pajamas she could find and trying to sleep, just a few feet from the guy—the pretty good-looking guy—who'd made a move on her just a couple of hours ago.

After she'd packed her toiletries back into her small kit bag, she checked her iPhone once more. The photo in front of the RV with Ryan had garnered sixty-eight likes. She scrolled through the list. Adam's name wasn't there. She smiled, relishing the image of him recoiling at the photo, frowning as he considered her romantic getaway with another man.

Just inside the front sliding doors of the store—next to several rows of shopping carts and beneath a bulletin board with sad posters that read, "Have You Seen This Child?"—in the near-darkness, a woman sat on the floor against the wall. Her legs were pulled up in front of her, her head was buried in her knees, and her hands were on top of her head, like she was shielding herself from a beating. It was her sobbing that got Amanda's attention.

"Are you okay?" Amanda leaned slightly toward the woman, but did not approach too closely.

The woman looked up, her face tear-streaked. She was probably in her early forties, with dark skin and coal-black hair. She wore the blue smock of a Walmart employee. In her right hand she clutched a small crucifix. She was silent for a moment, then rattled off a string of sentences in Spanish.

Amanda looked to her right, then her left, hoping there might be someone there to help, but there was no one. She held a hand up toward the woman, as if asking her to stop, then said, "Mas despácio, por favor. No hablo Español." This was just about the full remnant of her vocabulary from two years of high school Spanish.

The woman drew a deep breath, then was quiet for a while before saying in halting English, "I do not know what to do. I do not know what to do."

"What do you need?"

"My husband. He come to pick me up after his work, but today he no come." Her sobbing threatened to return, but she quickly got herself under control. "He works today in Flagstaff, with the—how you say?—construction crew. But now he is in hospital. They said he maybe had a heart attack." This caused a great burst of sobs, which lasted for some time. When she could speak again, she said, "I cannot get there. I cannot be with my husband." Her sobs returned.

Amanda said, "What is your name? I'm Amanda."

"Cepi." The woman now clasped the crucifix with both hands.

"Are you supposed to be working now, Cepi?" Amanda had now stepped closer and leaned down toward her.

"Yes. I stock the shelves."

"Is your boss here?"

Cepi looked toward the customer service center, just inside the door. "Mr. Caldwell," she said.

"I'll be right back, Cepi." Amanda reached out toward Cepi but did not touch her. She hurried toward the service desk, where a portly, balding man in his fifties stood, going through some papers.

"Mr. Caldwell," Amanda said.

The man sorted through several more papers, then said, without looking up, "Can I help you?" He appeared to be annoyed by the interruption.

"Mr. Caldwell, your employee Cepi has a family emergency. Her husband is in the hospital in Flagstaff. Is there someone here who can take her?"

Mr. Caldwell sorted a couple more papers, then adjusted his horn rims as he looked up at Amanda. "Oh, is she still here? I thought she got a ride."

"She has no one to take her."

Caldwell shrugged and gave Amanda a pained look. "I wish there were something we could do, but everyone here is busy. Can't she find some family member to take her?"

Amanda frowned, then abruptly turned away.

She returned to where Cepi still sat, her sobbing having returned.

Amanda went down on her knees in front of Cepi, and extended a hand. "Cepi," she said. When the woman looked up, she added, "Come with me."

Chapter 20

Ryan had begun working on a new blog post when Amanda opened the side door of the Roadtrek.

"Ryan," she said with urgency, "can we go to Flagstaff? Now?"

Ryan's mouth fell open, and he was about to say something—although he didn't yet know what—when a second face appeared in the doorway, that of a Hispanic woman. He fixed Amanda with questioning eyes.

"This is Cepi," she said, all business, "and her husband is very ill in a hospital in Flagstaff, and she has no way to get there."

"But ..." For a moment he could find no other words. Then he said, "We're kind of settled in for the night here." His fake objectivity was probably not masking his growing irritation that Amanda would even consider them driving a stranger to Flagstaff in the middle of the night. "Anyway, it's over three hours away. Best to wait until morning, don't you think?"

"Ryan," Amanda said, with an edge to her voice. Even in the poor light, he could see the fire in her eyes. "Ryan," she said again, "Cepi's husband may have had a heart attack. She needs to be with him. She has no other way to get there."

When he didn't respond, she said, "Ryan, this can't wait."

Ryan's mouth suddenly felt dry. He started to stand and then sat back down. He took a deep breath and tried to center himself. "Sure, I guess we can go," he said. Then he pulled out his iPhone and brought up Google Maps. A moment later, he said, "It says here the main hospital is the Flagstaff Medical Center, and it's 210 miles away. We can be there around two, if we leave right now." He looked up at her to see if this new information might have caused her to waver, but her eyes were locked onto his. He said, "I just need to turn off the propane supply and get these chairs turned around."

Amanda got Cepi settled into the one other seat in the Roadtrek, right behind the front passenger seat. Ryan started the engine and, with no further conversation, they left for Flagstaff.

"Thank you, Ryan," Amanda said, reaching over to lay her hand on his arm. "I didn't know what else to do."

"It's fine." Actually, as he got his mind wrapped around the idea, it was more than fine. He now felt a surge of adrenalin to be pulling out into the night on a mission of sorts—at least, compared to hanging out in the Walmart parking lot—and his admiration for the generous thing Amanda had done was replacing his initial irritation.

Amanda had now turned in her seat and was speaking to Cepi, who was mumbling in Spanish. Perhaps she was praying. "We'll be there in three hours, Cepi," Amanda said, "Ryan knows right where to go. What is your husband's name?"

"Rey. Reynaldo Gomez," Cepi said. "He is a very good man."

"Can we call the hospital and see how he's doing?"

Cepi nodded. "I do not have a phone." Then she said, "Please, you call. My English ..." She gave Amanda a pleading look.

Amanda found the number for the hospital and called. She glanced over at Ryan—who was focused on navigating the darkness of I-40—as if he might be able to help her with the conversation. She then asked to be connected with someone who could tell her how Reynaldo Gomez was doing and was put on hold for a long time. "Yes," she finally said, "I'm calling about a patient, Reynaldo Gomez, who was brought in earlier. He may have had a heart attack. I'm with his wife now. She doesn't speak English well." Now she listened for a while, shaking her head. "Look, I understand your regulations, but we're three hours away. His wife needs to know how he's doing." She nodded impatiently as the person on the other end obviously refused to tell her anything. She put the phone into speaker mode, then held it out toward Cepi. "You need to say something to them."

Cepi looked wide-eyed, then said in a loud voice, leaning toward the phone, "Mi esposo ... my husband ... Reynaldo Gomez ... is he okay?" Her voice broke on the last words and ended in sobs.

Amanda now spoke. "Look, we're on our way to the hospital from Kingman now." She looked over at Ryan, as if seeking confirmation that she'd said the right thing. "I see," she said. Then again, "I see." She gave Ryan an exasperated look, then said, "Okay, thank you."

She shook her head slowly, then turned toward Cepi in the rear. "They still haven't admitted him, but they apparently did give him some emergency care. And they still don't know for sure if he's had a heart attack or if it's something else." Amanda let out a big sigh, like she wished she could provide more specific news. She rested a hand on Cepi's knee and said, "We've just got to hope and pray that he'll be okay."

"Oh, I am praying. All the time. I say, 'God, please take care of Rey.' I say it over and over again. Then I say, 'Thank you, God,' because God has been good to me, and I know he will help us." She held up the crucifix that she'd been clasping.

"That's beautiful, Cepi," Amanda said.

"I hope you pray for him, too," Cepi said.

Amanda nodded but said nothing.

"And you pray, too, Ryan."

Ryan also nodded and smiled at Cepi in the rearview mirror.

This seemed to raise Cepi's spirits. "Amanda," she said, "You have very nice husband. You must be very happy."

Amanda shot Ryan a mischievous smile. She said, "I …," then stopped and just nodded toward Cepi. It wasn't clear to Ryan if she was about to say "I am very happy" or "I just met this guy two days ago."

By the time they reached Williams, with still an hour to go, Amanda and Cepi had both drifted into sleep. But Ryan was wide awake, and he was now free to shoot long glances at Amanda next to him, her head drooped to one side against the seat back, facing toward him, breathing softly through her mouth. Her face was dimly illuminated by the instrument lights, and the occasional splash of headlights from the oncoming traffic. Who was this lovely woman he had just met? He had been drawn to her beauty and charm, but tonight he had seen a new dimension to her, which only added to the mystery and attraction. He reached out a hand to touch her face, but held it just an inch or so above the surface of her skin. Then he cleared his throat, straightened in his seat, and returned his focus to driving.

When the Roadtrek slowed to turn into the hospital parking lot, both Amanda and Cepi came awake quickly, ready to roll. They found parking near the emergency entrance just before two and hurried in through glass double doors, where a young man sat behind a counter, looking at a computer screen. As best Ryan could tell, they were the only ones in the ER. He felt a shiver, like a cold hand on his neck, as he recalled the many desperate and uncertain hours he'd spent in a place like this just a year ago.

The man—a muscular guy with a buzz cut, who looked like a Marine, but wore pale blue scrubs—peered at a screen through frameless glasses and hunt-and-pecked some words on his keyboard. "Reynaldo Gomez. Says here he's up on the third floor in pre-op. The elevator's just down the hall." Then he hollered, as they were already running to the elevator, "Good luck."

They hurried to the third floor, where a nurse informed them that Reynaldo had just gone into surgery. She confirmed that he'd had a heart attack, but she didn't know his condition or the nature of the surgery.

Ryan exchanged concerned glances with Amanda and Cepi. "Is he okay?" Cepi asked the nurse. "I am his wife."

The nurse, a middle-aged woman with a peaceful smile and caring eyes, was just the kind of calming presence you wanted at a time like this. Her nametag said she was Meg. "Dr. Gutierrez is the surgeon, and I can tell you he is very good. Your husband is getting the very best care." She placed a reassuring hand on Cepi's shoulder. "If you'll have a seat in the waiting room just across the hall, we'll let you know as soon as we know anything. There's coffee there."

The next hour passed slowly. They were the only ones in the waiting room, and Ryan suspected that Dr. Gutierrez had been called in from a restful night's sleep. The surgical waiting room was small and windowless, with upholstered chairs that were comfortable enough, but reminded Ryan of the Chevy dealer waiting room they'd been in yesterday. He paged through old copies of *Field & Stream* and *Arizona Highways* but read nothing, paced the hallways, and slurped down two Styrofoam cups of coffee that tasted like it had been brewed the previous morning. Amanda stayed seated, close to Cepi, who continued to clutch her crucifix and pray.

Not that long ago, he had been pacing a similar hospital hallway—didn't they all look alike?—when a sad-eyed doctor had come up to him and said, "Mr. Browning, we did everything we could."

To escape these terrible images, Ryan took himself to midcourt, where he led the full court press. He was about to intercept the inbound pass and drive to the bucket when his fantasy was interrupted. He gasped, as a man in blue scrubs came walking toward them, head cast down.

Chapter 21

Amanda and Cepi jumped to their feet when they saw the man approaching, and Ryan quickly joined them. The man ran his hand through thinning gray hair like he was mentally preparing himself to say something difficult. Sensing that Cepi might need someone to hold on to, Amanda moved in closer to her.

"Mrs. Gomez?" the man said, looking into Cepi's eyes. "I'm Dr. Gutierrez. Let's sit down," he said, gesturing toward the sofa.

"Is he okay? Is he okay?" Cepi clutched her crucifix with both hands.

"He came through the surgery fine, Mrs. Gomez, and I believe his prospects for a full recovery are good. Tonight he—"

"¡Gracias a Dios!" Cepi squealed. Amanda rubbed Cepi's shoulder with little circular motions that silently echoed Cepi's prayer.

Dr. Gutierrez continued. "Tonight your husband was a very sick man. He had almost complete blockage in one of his coronary arteries. What that means is that your husband had a major heart attack, and if the ambulance hadn't gotten to him so quickly, it could have been a different story. We did a procedure called angioplasty, and I inserted a small structure, called a stent, that will keep that artery open."

Cepi was now quiet, mouth open. She continued to clasp the crucifix.

Amanda had put her arm around Cepi's shoulder. "Will he be in the hospital for very long?" she asked.

Dr. Gutierrez looked at Amanda as Cepi rested a hand on Amanda's arm and said, "This is Amanda, my friend." She beamed.

Dr. Gutierrez gave Amanda a quick nod, then said, "I'm guessing we'll keep him in ICU for twenty-four hours or so, then probably on the general floor for another day or two."

Ryan asked, "Will Mr. Gomez be able to go back to work?"

The doctor seemed to mull this over. He looked at Cepi and said, "We'll talk more about this later, but I can tell you this much now. I understand your husband works on a highway construction crew. If his job involves a lot of physical work—which I'm guessing it does—then ..." He paused. "Then it's unlikely he will ever be able to do such work again."

Cepi swallowed hard, then said, "I do not care about that now. Rey is alive, and I thank God for that."

Dr. Gutierrez smiled at Cepi, and said, "Yes, I believe you should thank God tonight. By the way, your husband is now in recovery. He will be unconscious for a while, but if you'd like to see him, then—"

Cepi jumped up. "Yes," she said, then nodded toward Amanda and Ryan. "Can they go in with me?"

"I'm afraid only next of kin can—"

Cepi insisted, "They are my friends. I need them to—"

Amanda interjected, "It's okay, Cepi, we can—"

"No, I want you there."

Dr. Gutierrez said, "I think it will be all right if you all go in, but you can only stay a very short time."

Cepi entered a small glass-walled, dimly lit room that smelled of antiseptic, followed by Amanda, and behind her, Ryan. The bed took up most of the space in the room. Tubes and cords, looking like spaghetti, ran from Reynaldo Gomez to racks of monitors and other electronic devices. It was quiet except for the periodic beeping of the monitors. Cepi covered her mouth with her hand when she saw her husband and gasped, "¡Dios Mío!"

It appeared to Amanda that Cepi might be about to faint. She quickly grabbed Cepi's shoulders to stabilize her, then whispered, "It's okay, Cepi."

Cepi glanced at Amanda over her shoulder, then placed a hand over one of Amanda's hands. Softly she said, "I'm fine now."

Cepi approached the bed as Amanda and Ryan stayed back by the door. She leaned in toward Reynaldo and breathed the words, "Te amo, Rey, con todo mi corazón."

Amanda choked up at Cepi's words, and even Ryan nodded, as if he understood her words as well.

Then Cepi turned to Amanda and said, "Can you say a prayer for my husband?"

Amanda glanced over her shoulder, thinking Cepi might be speaking to someone else. She felt something turn over in her stomach. She licked her lips and said, "Oh, I'm not so good at—"

"Please," pleaded Cepi, softly. "Ryan, you come close too, and let's hold hands."

The three of them formed a semicircle around the bed, and after several moments of deep breathing, Amanda began.

"Dear God," she said, then cleared her throat. After a pause, she continued. "Dear God, we thank you that Mr. Gomez is doing okay now … that he came through the surgery … and, uh … and we thank you that Dr. … uh … Dr. Gutierrez was here to take care of him." After another pause, she said, her confidence building, "And God, we ask you to bless Reynaldo and Cepi." She sighed, then said, "Amen."

"Oh, thank you, Amanda, that was beautiful. And thank you, also, Ryan. I know that Rey is going to get better." Cepi's eyes were wet again, but they were twinkling with a joy that Amanda had not seen before.

Meg, the nurse, stood in the doorway, indicating that they needed to leave. In the hallway, she spoke to Cepi, while Amanda and Ryan stood nearby. "Mrs. Gomez, right next to the hospital we have housing where you can stay while your husband is in the hospital. And someone from your husband's company brought his car over. However, we never got information about health insurance."

"We have no insurance," said Cepi. There was now alarm in her eyes. "My husband was only temporary worker, and I am, how you say, part-time at Walmart."

Meg looked worried, but quickly found her game face. "Cepi, may I ask if your husband and you have papers?"

Cepi looked around at Amanda and Ryan, then back at Meg. "We are both legal, but I don't have any papers with—" She stopped suddenly, a panicked look appearing on her face, but then Meg smiled and laid a hand gently on Cepi's shoulder.

Meg said, in an upbeat way, "This insurance business is very complicated these days, so we're not going to worry about that now, Mrs. Gomez. We'll figure out something."

When Meg had left, Amanda said to Cepi, "We can stay with you until your husband is awake, until you get settled in."

"Oh, no," said Cepi. "I know I will be okay. You go, get some sleep." She gave Amanda a look of pure love, then hugged her.

As Ryan and Amanda began to walk away, Ryan suddenly stopped and said, "Wait here, both of you. I'll be right back." In a few minutes he returned, went straight to Cepi and pressed something into her hand. She looked shocked, shaking her head at a wad of bills Ryan had given her.

In the parking lot, Ryan seemed full of nervous energy. He looked up at the hospital building, let out a sigh of relief, then said, "I think it's a little over an hour to the park. I say let's push on."

Amanda knew he must be exhausted but, sensing his restlessness, she nodded okay.

In the car, he looked over at her and said, "That was a nice prayer you said. I could tell Cepi put you on the spot, but you handled it beautifully."

"Thank you. Yeah, I was kind of unprepared for that." She let out a laugh.

"Are you religious?" He shot her a serious glance.

"Raised Catholic, confirmed when I was a teenager." She was surprised how that came out with such pride. Then she added, "But I haven't been to church in a long time. How about you?"

"Nope. Never have given it much thought."

"Maybe because you're a scientist?"

"I'd say it's more because my parents never had any interest in church. My dad was never home, and my mom just didn't talk about it. I guess the science did sort of replace it though—I mean, for answering the big questions and all that."

They rode in silence for a few minutes, then Amanda said, "You gave Cepi some money. That was very thoughtful."

Ryan seemed to turn gloomy. "Her situation makes me so sad." Then more upbeat, he said, "Anyway, it would be hard to match you tonight in the thoughtfulness department."

"How much did you give her?" Amanda asked, then immediately regretted her invasive question.

"Just a little to help them get by. They're going to have it hard for—"

"I'm sorry I asked. I shouldn't have. You don't need to tell me—"

"Five hundred."

Amanda's jaw dropped. She started to speak, then said nothing.

They rode in darkness, north through wilderness toward the park. Amanda tried to stay awake, to be an extra set of eyes watching the road. But overcome with fatigue, she dozed with her head resting against the window. Occasionally, she would come awake suddenly, worried about Ryan driving so late at night. Yet, even though it was nearly four, Ryan seemed wide awake.

Chapter 22

Ryan was still wired, stimulated by a complex array of thoughts and emotions, ranging from exhilaration to utter despair, when they arrived at Mather Campground, the main campground for the south rim in Grand Canyon National Park, at 4:30 a.m. Amanda stumbled to the bed in the rear and crashed, not bothering to change her clothes. Ryan opened his laptop and, from the driver's seat, wrote a new post for his unpublished blog.

Why do bad things happen to good people who've tried to do the right thing?

I'm coming to see that there is evil in this world, and it is a powerful force. It preys on everyone, good and bad. Like my mother. She was on a noble quest. She had kind things to say about everyone and continued to harbor hopes that I would see the light and draw closer to her. (I wish I had, but that's for another post). She didn't deserve to die, and the manner of her death had nothing to do with her worthiness. It just happened. And I say it was evil. Not that the guy who backed across her in that truck stop in Carson City was malicious—maybe he was, maybe he wasn't. I'll never know.

What I do know is that she died needlessly. If she hadn't died, she'd still be travelling around in this Roadtrek, and maybe I'd have gotten off my sorry ass and joined her for a grand adventure.

Or take Cepi. She seems like the nicest person you'd ever want to meet. But there she is, working late nights at a menial job at that Walmart in Kingman. And now she's got a husband clinging to life in the hospital. It isn't fair. Cepi talks about her faith and holds on to that crucifix around her neck, but I can't see what difference it makes. She still has that stinking job, and her poor husband—if he makes it at all—will be a physical mess for the rest of his life.

I know that theologians and philosophers have written a lot about this, and I've read some of their thoughts. But I'm not sure they have a clue about this subject, either. Einstein said to look for the simplest explanation to a problem. The simplest explanation to this problem is that evil exists. It is real and it is ugly, and I haven't got the slightest idea what to do about it.

He sat back and read the post again. He blew out a big breath, then looked out into the darkness. *Too negative.* For God's sake, here he was in a national park with a beautiful woman. In the light of day, these words wouldn't reflect how he felt. But tonight they did. He slapped the laptop closed with a disgusted swipe, not bothering to power it off, then leaned back and fell asleep.

Chapter 23

"Is this really Kobe Bryant's signature?" Ryan bolted awake at the sound of Amanda's voice. She stood next to him, holding the ball with two hands like she was about to pass it to him, and for a moment he thought she might.

It was light outside, but Ryan had no idea what time it was. Amanda had changed into a long bulky blue sweater, tight black exercise pants, and hiking boots. She had on her Patagonia down jacket. He realized that he was cold.

"Yeah, it really is," he said. He now sat up straight.

"Cool."

"Sorry you had to sleep with the basketball. These vans should come with a basketball shelf."

"There are worse things than hugging a basketball all night. Well, I guess it wasn't quite all night, was it?"

"What time is it?"

"Around seven."

He rubbed the sleep from his eyes with the back of his hand. "So, you like basketball?"

"You kidding? Power forward on the state runner-up team, Wausau East High School, '02." Now she spun the basketball like a top on her index finger, just like the showboaters from the old Harlem Globetrotters had done. She smiled, with her tongue poking out of the corner of her mouth, as she concentrated on the difficult stunt.

Ryan had never been able to master that trick. "That's amazing," he said.

"My high school coach showed me how to do it."

"I knew there was a reason I asked you to come on this trip."

She gave him a mock scowl. "I hope there was more than that."

"You know there was," he said with a smile. He thought she may have blushed a little.

When they stepped outside, Ryan was stunned to see a fresh dusting of snow that made the forest of pines around their campsite glitter like crystal.

"This is beautiful," Amanda said, gasping.

"I think we're not far from the rim. Wanna go see?"

They walked along a trail toward the canyon rim, but just fifty yards from the edge Amanda stopped and grabbed Ryan's arm. "I've been looking forward to this moment for years. What if I'm disappointed?"

Ryan gave her a reassuring smile. "Frankly, I don't think you'll be disappointed at all. But there's only one way to find out." He took her hand in his and urged her forward. "Let's go see."

They stood at the edge in silence. The abyss that stretched beyond them was staggering. Even Ryan, who had seen the canyon several years before, was almost breathless. He had forgotten how magnificent it was. Amanda seemed frozen in place.

Sunlight from the east had still not reached the bottom—down into the narrow inner gorge—and shadows swept across the mile-deep carved walls and cliffs like something no artist could begin to capture, or perhaps even imagine.

Sheer walls, a mile high—built of layer upon layer of various colors and textures of rock, then exposed by the carving of the Colorado River—revealed the process of creation, like a picture history book—stories not written, but sculpted from stone. Each layer was a long story, seemingly endless, as if it would be the final chapter—yet it would be replaced by another story, a newer story. The sheen of newly fallen snow made the scene even more electric, dusting the rocky layers, giving them a white accent, like a grand "Got milk?" magazine ad.

Ryan thought about the approach to the Grand Canyon—through beautiful pine forests and rocky hills and beautiful skies—and how you could believe that you had seen it all. Seen what is most beautiful, most spectacular. Then you come suddenly to this rim, and there it is: nature's statement that no matter what you may have experienced before, no matter what you may have expected, no matter what you believed might be possible, there is more. Perhaps this all meant that, when you think you know it all, when you think you've got it all figured out, there is yet more to know, more to grasp, more that will drive you to your knees.

He recalled the famous MIT physicist Alan Guth, inventor of the inflation theory that describes the universe's development after the Big Bang. Talking about the discoveries of modern physics, Guth said that if we were to imagine the most bizarre universe possible, that universe would still be more dull than the one we actually see.

Maybe that's why visitors cannot take their eyes off the Grand Canyon: because it shows something about our world—something spectacular, mind-boggling, unexpected—that is beyond the limited boundaries of the perceived reality that encases our small, day-to-day, hum-drum existence. You cannot look into the Grand Canyon and not think about big things.

Ryan also thought about the blog post he had written last night, and he cringed. How naïve and small was his understanding of almost anything. He was glad he hadn't shown it to Amanda.

"Oh God, I think I'm going to cry. It is so beautiful." Amanda was still holding Ryan's hand. Then she breathed, "Thanks for inviting me to come, Ryan." She turned to face him, and for a moment he thought she might be about to kiss him, but instead she pulled out her iPhone and took several shots. Then she asked Ryan to join her for a selfie. This time, she put her arm around Ryan for the shot. Then she tapped busily on her phone, probably uploading it to Facebook.

Ryan had lugged his heavy Nikon with him. He took several shots of Amanda against the spectacular backdrop. Composing his shots through the large, clear viewfinder of his DSLR gave him the opportunity to study her face. With the precision spot focusing and metering, he was able to focus on her eyes, so that her face would be in crystalline sharpness, and the big low-f-stop lens enabled him to throw the background out of focus. It would give the portrait a powerful, almost 3-D quality that professionals pursued. The light was still good this early in the morning, when the sun was low—during what photographers call the golden hours. It illuminated one side of her face and caught wisps of her hair, stirred in the light breeze, with a scintillating back light.

Amanda gave him her best customer-service smile when she realized he was focusing on her. But it was the shot he'd snapped just before that he had high hopes for. She was gazing toward the canyon, in awe it seemed, not with a smile but in reverence, and there was a sparkling catchlight in her eyes.

"I think these will be beautiful," he said. "Now, I'm getting hungry."

They stepped into the dining room at the Bright Angel Lodge, right on the rim, and took in the ambiance of the busy restaurant, done up in a rustic national-park-lodge motif— charming, but worn by the millions of visitors who had wandered through. The clatter of dishes, laughter and energetic morning chatter contributed to the good vibe.

Ryan spotted the tall stack of pancakes a waitress had just delivered to a nearby table. "That's what I'm ordering," he beamed. "I hope I can get them with blueberries. I'll justify it as carb-loading for our busy day."

Amanda laughed. "Carbs are good, but what I need now is caffeine."

While they waited, Amanda called the hospital in Flagstaff, but couldn't reach Cepi. She was on hold for a long time. Then, rolling her eyes toward the ceiling, she whispered to Ryan, "I got a nurse, but he wouldn't tell me anything because I'm not family." Amanda left her number with the nurse, then bit her lower lip as she put the phone away, clearly worried.

Chapter 24

Sometimes exaggeration is the only way to capture the truth. As they studied art prints in a gallery near the canyon edge, Amanda explained how the famous Western landscape painters of the nineteenth century, like Thomas Moran and Albert Bierstadt, sought to capture the breathtaking scale of the national parks. But their paintings seemed to many to be too grand to be realistic, and perhaps they were. While their colorful and vast panoramas stirred the imaginations of people trying to survive in crowded, smoke-choked factory cities in the East, some art critics labeled them grandiose, ostentatious, exploitative, unreal. Of course, these critics had never been to the West and could not grasp such landscapes from their tiny flats in New York City.

Amanda turned toward Ryan, who was nodding slowly as he gazed at a Moran print. Then Ryan pressed a forefinger against his chin, clearly giving this some thought, and said, "As a physicist, I'm used to describing reality in terms of numbers and facts. But when you're dealing with a topic as extravagant and mind-boggling as the Grand Canyon, mere numbers and facts just don't cut it. I mean, you can mention all the miles of its dimensions and the billions of years of its creation, but, while these statistics are astounding, they don't take your breath away like actually standing on the rim does."

Amanda laughed. "Confession time. I've always been a harsh critic of Moran and Bierstadt, even though I know their works were instrumental in educating the people in the East and paving the way for the creation of the national parks. I've always found these paintings too—what's the right word?—embellished. Almost caricatures of what reality must be like. Frankly, it always put me off. But that's what you conclude while you're sitting in a classroom in Madison." Then she extended her hand toward the canyon rim, visible through a window in the gallery, and added, "But now I take it all back."

They continued to stroll through art and souvenir shops along the canyon edge, where Ryan bought a magnet for the Roadtrek and Amanda looked through the turquoise jewelry, but found it all to be beyond her budget. Then Ryan said he wanted to visit the Lookout Studio a ways farther along the rim, while Amanda headed toward another gallery to look at Native-American paintings. As she left that gallery, she noticed a woman standing before an easel, right on the canyon edge, and painting with large, quick strokes.

"May I watch for a while?" Amanda asked.

"Sure." The woman smiled, her face shadowed under a wide-brimmed straw hat, but didn't look up from her work. Probably in her fifties, she had long dyed-red hair and wore a colorful Southwestern dress.

Amanda was amazed at how the woman was creating such a magnificent painting right before her eyes, with such quick brush strokes. "You work fast," said Amanda.

"You have to when you're painting the Canyon. The light changes so fast, you've only got two hours at most to capture it."

Amanda shook her head in disbelief. How could one create such art in only two hours?

"It's ironic, when you consider it." The woman shot Amanda a quick glance, and laughed, but quickly returned to her work. "Those rocks out there took four billion years to form, layer upon layer. Then the Colorado River carved the Canyon out in only three million years—just the blink of an eye, really. Then here I sit, and I've only got two hours to paint the whole dang thing." She shot Amanda another quick look, then continued her sweeping, bold brushstrokes.

Amanda watched in silence.

After a few moments, the woman said without looking up, "You married?"

Amanda shrugged. "No."

The woman continued. "I was married." She was quiet for another moment, while she worked in some detail on her painting. "Yeah, but it didn't work out." More silence, then she said, "Heck, 'didn't work out' is hardly the right thing to say—as if my divorce was something that just happened, not something Andy or I had anything to do with."

Amanda looked out at the canyon, then back at the painting developing before her eyes.

Without slowing her work or looking up, the woman continued. "We were lazy—that's what we were, both of us. Then before we knew it, it was too late."

"I'm sorry," was all Amanda could come up with.

"Guess the lesson is: don't sit on your ass, thinking you have all the time in the world. It just isn't fair, but that's the way it is. Four freaking billion years, and I've only got two hours." Now she turned her face, tanned and wrinkled from too much time in the sun, toward Amanda. Her hard look made Amanda avert her eyes. "Don't miss opportunities, dear. The only thing that is certain is that the light will change."

Chapter 25

Ryan checked his iPhone as he entered the Lookout Studio and saw that he'd again been tagged in Amanda's latest post. It was a great photo that would lead the casual observer to conclude their relationship might be more than it actually was. The post said, "With Ryan at the Grand Canyon. Place is awesome! Now on to Santa Fe."

Constructed in Native-American style—out of limestone, probably quarried locally—the Lookout Studio blended into the backdrop of the vertical canyon walls. It was a gift shop and photo studio built out over the canyon edge, surrounded by a low rock-walled terrace that offered observers a great view into the canyon. As Ryan strolled around the shop, amidst the displays of T-shirts, caps, framed prints, inexpensive jewelry, and picture postcards, an old man working behind a counter said, "I see you're sporting some nice Nikon glass there."

Ryan turned toward the man, who was leaning on his elbows over the counter.

"I've had my share of good equipment, too," the man said. His wispy, snow-white hair was combed across a deeply-creased forehead. He wore a crisp white-linen shirt and colorful suspenders like you might see at a beer festival in

Germany. "The photos I took would have made Ansel Adams green with envy." He managed a weak chuckle, then said, "But I've been working here for so long, seeing this amazing canyon every day, that it's sort of all been taken out of me."

Two girls laughed nearby as they debated about which earrings to buy.

The old man continued to speak, even though Ryan had not said anything in response. He gestured toward the crowd of people vying for positions on the observation terrace outside. "They're all snapping their shots for Facebook and Instagram, or thinking about the photo they'll email back home to Ohio, the one that shows that they were really here. Yet all the photos look alike."

A woman asked the man, "Where's the bathrooms?" Without looking at her, he said, "Outside, around the corner." He then looked hard at Ryan with steely-blue eyes that made him squirm. "Ultimately, we are all alike, aren't we?"

Ryan looked around for Amanda, who had just entered the shop and was studying some old black-and-white photographs on the far wall. He took a step away from the counter, but the man continued. "Years ago, I took so many pictures of this canyon. It is simply the most beautiful thing in the world." The old man looked over at Amanda. "Yep, maybe even more beautiful than your girlfriend, there. Yet, after a while, you can't see it any more. You know those exercises where you stare at an object for thirty seconds? Then you close your eyes and you see a certain image?"

Ryan nodded, as he continued to back away slowly.

"Well, sometimes life is just the opposite of that. You stare at the most beautiful thing in the world for long enough, and you become so immune to its power, you can no longer see its beauty. You just sort of go blind, as far as that beauty is concerned. You might as well be looking at a sewage disposal site in New Jersey."

Ryan opened his mouth to reply, but said nothing.

An elderly couple was especially loud in selecting a picture postcard. "I think the one with the big cactus is better, Oscar," the woman said.

"No, we need the canyon sunset shot," the man retorted with conviction.

The old man behind the counter was oblivious to all this as he continued. "Anyway, that's what's happened to me. I look at those tourists outside, and I make fun of them—all excited about the images they want to capture, when they'd be better off just coming in here and buying one of those ninety-nine-cent postcards. Truth is, though, I'm rather jealous of them, because I've lost what they have."

Amanda had now joined Ryan at the counter. The man gave her a long look, then said to Ryan, "Listen to me, don't ever stop seeing the beauty. That's when a part of you will die."

Ryan felt like he should say something, but then the man turned away to help a customer select a T-shirt.

"What was that all about?" asked Amanda.

Ryan shrugged. "He said we should never stop seeing the beauty around us." He looked again at the line of people at the wall outside, then added, "But I'm not sure it was about anything."

Amanda was also looking out the window, beyond the people on the terrace, to a woman at an easel on the canyon edge. "Or maybe it was about everything," she said.

Chapter 26

Amanda and Ryan stood before the sign at the trailhead, just steps away from fine restaurants, where tourists relaxed with margaritas and nachos, and galleries displaying ten-thousand-dollar paintings by the best Southwestern artists. "Caution! Down is optional. Up is mandatory," the sign said. From here, the Bright Angel Trail zigzagged in dizzying fashion from the rim eight miles to the Colorado River, an almost vertical mile below. Another sign added this caution: "Every year over 350 people need to be rescued or assisted due to exhaustion or heat stroke in the canyon." Amanda recalled what she had read at the Lookout Studio, how the temperatures at the bottom of the canyon might be forty degrees warmer than at the rim. So a hiker might head down the trail on a mild sixty-degree morning only to find herself at the bottom in a hundred degrees, with a mile of vertical to climb out.

Amanda hadn't been on a real hike since she lived with her parents in northern Wisconsin. Back then she'd gone on long hikes through the north woods, but none of them were like this, with a mile of elevation change. She tried to recall a time when she'd gone hiking in California, but the best she could come up with were walks on the beach at Redondo, usually barefoot and swaying to romantic music coming through her noise-cancelling headphones.

This looked difficult, not to mention sweaty and dirty. The hike had sounded like a good idea when they were perusing the park brochure, amidst the laughter and clinking of coffee cups, next to the fireplace in the Bright Angel Lodge. Would she collapse in a whining heap halfway back up the climb, humiliating herself—her sweaty, dirty self—in front of Ryan? Would a helicopter have to be dispatched to airlift her out?

She stood with hands on hips and studied the sign, then, brushing blonde hair away from her face, turned to Ryan with an apprehensive look. "So, do you think we have enough water?"

"Maybe in another month we'd need more," he said, nodding as he peered into the abyss. They'd picked up a trail map, some snacks and four plastic bottles of water at the Lookout Studio. "But it's early in the year. Heck, there was snow this morning."

Amanda noticed, however, that the snow had now melted away under the assault of the intense morning sun. Ryan appeared unfazed by the challenge of the steep hike before them. He looked lean and in shape—the muscles in his calves rippled as he walked. He wore a plaid wool shirt over well-worn cargo shorts, and his daypack had clearly seen lots of use. He looked like he could hike all day.

Ryan held the trail map so that they both could study the route. He looked out into the canyon again and said, "I say, let's just go a short ways—maybe down to Indian Garden. The map says it's a little over four miles. Think we can make it down that far?"

Amanda drew a deep breath of the clean, high-altitude air, studied the wild vastness before her, then looked straight into Ryan's eyes. She laughed. "It's not making it down that I'm concerned about." Then she took off down the trail, looking back over her shoulder and teasing, "Well, are you gonna stand around all day?"

The trail—narrow, steep, and long—was literally chiseled and blasted out of the rock of the canyon wall. Amanda had read that mule trains made the trip daily down to the river, and riding one of the mules was said to be a hair-raising experience for anyone with any inclination to acrophobia. She shot Ryan a glance over her shoulder—he was right behind her. He gave her a quick smile, but she was certain he'd been checking out her butt, encased in the tight capri leggings. She grimaced, suddenly worried about his view and wishing she hadn't dropped out of her aerobics class last month.

Heading down the trail was easy and pure euphoria. Each switchback exposed a new vista of red, yellow, and gray hues of vertical canyon expanse that staggered Amanda's imagination. They arrived at Indian Garden—where a spring and a few trees crowded a small plateau—in just over an hour. The sun was now directly overhead, and the sparse shade, provided by what Ryan said were live oaks, was welcome. Sitting together on a large rock, they each had a granola bar, sipped some of their water and watched nature put on a spectacular show before them.

Ryan stood and pulled his camera from his shoulder. He held the big Nikon before him with both hands as he gazed out at the sweeping panorama, turning his head slowly to take it all in. Then he busied himself with the camera, fiddling with various knobs and buttons. After a few moments, he shot

Amanda a self-conscious glance and said, "I don't know why I lugged this heavy thing down here." He squinted up toward the high walls above them, now bright in the morning sun, as if pondering the challenge of carrying the big camera back up to the rim. His hair moved with the soft breeze, reminding Amanda of palms swaying on a California beach.

"It's because you're an artist," she said.

He gave her a surprised look. There was silence for a moment, then Ryan said, "Nobody's ever said that to me before." He glanced out at the canyon, then back at Amanda. "I know this guy. Doug. Sometimes we get a beer. I remember him saying something like, 'Isn't photography just a technical thing? Isn't it just about selecting the right f-stop?' I told him there was more to it than that for me."

He paused, so Amanda gave him a smile that said she wanted him to continue the story.

Ryan turned toward her. "I mean, I'm a physicist. I've taken courses on the properties of light. But for me, light is more than photons."

"What did Doug say about that?"

"He didn't get it."

She gave him a knowing nod, then said, "Maybe you should have told him that saying photography is about picking the right f-stop is like saying that Mozart produced such great music because his piano was well-tuned."

Ryan laughed, as he lifted the camera to his eye and snapped off several shots of the canyon. Then he turned the camera toward Amanda, causing her to immediately gather her hair and pull it back behind her head. "God, I must look like a mess," she said. But she gave the camera her best smile anyway. He took several portraits.

Ryan now faced out toward the canyon again and said, "I can't stop thinking about what that old man at the studio said."

"You mean about appreciating beauty?"

"Yeah," he said. He turned to face her. There was a sunny sparkle in his eyes that made him look wild. She had to catch her breath. "I don't think I could ever grow tired of looking at this."

Amanda wasn't sure if he was talking about the canyon or her, and she felt heat rush to her face. She looked down for a moment, then pulled her iPhone from her pocket. "Now, let me get one of you." She framed his face and that look. This one was not for Facebook.

They polished off another bottle of water, then Ryan looked up again at the three thousand feet of canyon wall above them, using a hand to shade his eyes from the sun, which had now become a furnace. The hike back up would be a much different experience than the hike down.

Amanda stuffed her down jacket and sweater into her daypack and now wore only a white T-shirt atop her leggings. When she'd purchased the purple Osprey pack at REI two days ago, along with the sturdy Merrell hiking boots, she'd been more interested in their stylish looks. Now she recognized them as valuable tools.

As they began the challenging trudge back up the canyon wall, Amanda ticked off each switchback in her head, as if counting them would help draw her closer to the top.

Along the way, they crossed paths with other hikers. Some, carrying large backpacks, were headed down to the Phantom Ranch at the bottom of the canyon. A few hikers struck Amanda as unprepared—little water, poor hiking shoes—and she thought again about the 350 who had to be rescued every year.

One man appeared to be really struggling. His casual loafers were better suited for a morning stroll around the mall, and the white sport shirt he wore over chino slacks was darkened with sweat.

"Are you okay?" she asked him. He was tall, with a ruddy face that should have been lathered with sunscreen. His sweat-soaked black hair looked plastered to his forehead. He carried nothing, as far as Amanda could tell. He looked like a heart attack waiting to happen.

The man paused when Amanda spoke to him, but said nothing.

"Would you like some water?" She held her water bottle out toward him, even though she could see through the translucent plastic that it was now only about a third full, and they still had much climbing to do.

The man turned his face away, as if he didn't want her to look at him, then briskly continued down the trail.

Amanda turned to Ryan with a worried shrug. "I hope that guy's going to be okay."

Ryan glanced at the man over his shoulder and nodded. "He sure wasn't the most friendly character around."

They continued up the trail, stopping only to take pictures, catch their breath at the bend of a switchback, or savor another sip of their rapidly disappearing water supply. Now they stopped again. Amanda wiped the sweat off her forehead with the back of her hand and took the level of the last water bottle down to what was probably the final swig. She focused on the image of the showers back at the campground and the thought of the cleansing water pouring down upon her. Ryan looked to be struggling also. His plaid wool shirt was tied around his waist, and sweat glistened on his sinewy forearms and blotched his faded blue UCI T-shirt.

Ryan took a swallow of water, then said, "Hey, there's our buddy. Looks like he decided to give up."

Amanda turned to look back down the trail. The man who had refused her water was heading back up, moving slowly, but no more than a hundred yards behind them. He looked up toward them, then stopped and turned to look out at the canyon.

"Okay, that's odd." She was quiet for a moment, then added, "But I'm relieved to see he's showing some good sense. I was worried about him."

When they finally made the turn on the last switchback and could see the top of the rim, where tourists were clicking photos of canyon adventurers such as them, they picked up their pace.

"Woo hoo!" screamed Amanda as they stepped out onto the blacktopped canyon rim path. She turned toward Ryan, and they exchanged high fives. "Now that was awesome." Yeah, she was in fact sweaty and dirty, but she couldn't care less at this moment. It was indeed awesome.

Ryan was grinning. "Hey, look," he said, holding up his water bottle. "I still have a few drops left."

By the time they returned to camp, a few shallow puddles were the only evidence that there had been snow. Now, sunshine poked through the canopy of ponderosas, and the forest was filled with the rich scent of pine under the warming sun.

After long swigs of cool water from the van, Amanda said, "I'm heading for the showers. I've been fantasizing about them for the last three hours."

They walked together toward the bathhouse, a few hundred yards away, still experiencing euphoria from the hike. Amanda took note of all the different license plates on vehicles she passed in the campground—it was an old habit from when her brother and she played States on long car trips with her parents: seeing who could identify the most out-of-state license plates. "Good grief," she said, "I've seen fourteen different states already."

"I think everyone wants to see the Grand Canyon," Ryan said.

The shower threatened to quell her euphoria. The gray concrete floor of her stall was still wet from the last user, and at least a half-inch of water stood at the low point of the floor because hair partially clogged the drain. Amanda was thankful that she'd brought flip-flops to wear in the shower. The plastic shower curtain had a peppering of brown dots, probably mold, and the grout between the off-white tiles on the walls was a dirty gray. She tried not to touch the walls—God knows what might be growing there.

But the water felt life-giving, cascading down over her dirty, tired body. She heard a foreign language—perhaps Chinese—from the next stall, accompanied by laughter. She looked down toward the gap at the bottom of the metal partition between the stalls and saw two sets of brown bare feet, one an adult and one a small child's. Most likely a mother and daughter. The Grand Canyon wasn't just a park in Arizona, she thought. It belonged to the world, and today she was a part of it.

Back at the Roadtrek Ryan pulled a couple of Blue Moons from the fridge and offered one to Amanda. They clinked their bottles together in a celebratory toast.

Amanda said, "Ryan, I really had fun today. That's the first—"

"Don't look now," Ryan interrupted, his voice suddenly soft, "but that guy from the trail, he's in the campsite right next to us."

Amanda took another sip of beer, then calmly looked toward the adjacent campsite. Fifty yards away, through the pines, he stood behind his car, but there was no question that he was looking straight at her. Even in the warm, midday sun, she felt a shiver go down her back. She looked back at Ryan, suddenly afraid. "That's weird. Do you think he was following us?"

Ryan also looked concerned. "Maybe I should go over and ask him." He began to move toward the man.

Amanda placed a restraining hand on his arm. "No," she said with urgency. "Don't let him know we're suspicious." She chewed on her lip, pondering, then said, "It's probably nothing." She walked a slow loop around the camp table, then stopped to face Ryan again. "On the other hand, I'm not going to be comfortable as long as he's there. I say, let's just go."

As they prepared to leave, Amanda made the decision to believe that the incident was indeed probably nothing, but she committed the man's car—a gray Sonata with Arizona plates—to memory anyway.

Chapter 27

Amanda nodded with interest as Ryan told her about Santa Fe, but kept her eyes glued to the road—it was her first turn behind the wheel of the Roadtrek. She felt comfortable driving the big van, unlike Ryan had been when they had departed Manhattan Beach. It brought back good memories of driving her dad's big Dodge pickup with the slide-in camper. Nonetheless, the heavy truck traffic on I-40 made for tense driving.

They'd left the campground quickly, but tried to make it look casual so the creepy guy wouldn't know they were suspicious. They'd seen no signs of the gray Sonata after they left the park, and Amanda had stopped checking the rearview mirror an hour ago.

Ryan was obviously excited about heading to Santa Fe—he'd been talking about little else across eastern Arizona and western New Mexico. She learned that for six years Ryan had lived just a half-hour away from Santa Fe in Los Alamos, known for its famous science lab. But at night and on the weekends, to hear Ryan tell it, the streets of his sleepy hometown rolled up, and if you had a passion for world class art, history or legendary sunsets—not to mention great food—you would head down to Santa Fe.

It's called the City Different, he told her, and for good reason. It's a small city—only fifty-thousand residents—yet it has the most art galleries of any American city outside New York and Los Angeles. It has more restaurants per capita than Paris. It's a place where the finest homes are accessible by dirt roads, and the paved streets are in the more middle-class neighborhoods. A place where anthropologists work as waiters. Where Native Americans from surrounding pueblos, untouched by modernity, sell handmade jewelry on the plaza, a block away from trendy bistros where you might sip your latte next to a movie star. Ryan mentioned that he had once spotted Julia Roberts at Pasqual's, a breakfast place near the plaza. It's the second oldest city in the United States, and the only one that has been under the authority of four different governments. And the New Mexican cuisine, based upon the power of the famous regional chiles, raises the daily question for residents and visitors alike: red or green?

"Needless to say, it is a cool place," said Ryan, wrapping up. He was silent for a moment. Then he sighed. "Geesh, I must sound like some encyclopedia. I didn't mean to babble on like that."

Now Amanda shot him a quick glance. "You're not babbling at all. I've heard about Santa Fe all my life, and I can't wait to see it." She was enjoying his enthusiasm—it was boyish and innocent and, yes, it was rather sexy. From a distant AM country station in Gallup, Kelsea Ballerini sang, *If you're gonna kiss me, kiss me like you need it* …. Amanda cleared her throat and returned her gaze to the highway, then smiled as she said, "Anyway, you're kinda cute when you're all excited about something."

On the way—east across I-40 to Albuquerque, then up I-25 to Santa Fe—they passed places where Amanda wished they could have stopped: the Painted Desert, the Petrified Forest, and several Indian pueblos. But Ryan wanted to make Santa Fe for dinner—"I can't wait for you try the food," he had said—so they contented themselves with the striking scenery they saw from the interstate: high cliffs of yellow and bronze and vast panoramas set against a sky that seemed larger than any Amanda had ever seen in southern California.

In a town known for its architecture—with award-winning luxury homes and romantic B&Bs and centuries-old adobe palaces and churches on the historic register—it was hard to find a place to camp. They considered themselves lucky to snag a lackluster site—no more than a concrete pad—in an RV park just south of the historic plaza. But they didn't plan to linger around the RV park anyway. Despite their lack of sleep the night before, the strenuous hike and long drive today, and the late hour of their arrival—it was now eight—Ryan seemed pumped to introduce Amanda to the Santa Fe scene. And she was ready.

That meant the historic Santa Fe plaza. They were in the RV park for no more than ten minutes—Amanda had enough time to change into a flowing white summer dress and open-toed sandals—before Ryan pointed them down a narrow street toward the plaza.

As they stepped out into San Francisco St., bordering the plaza, Amanda stopped and did a slow three-sixty. The sun was setting behind old adobe buildings with rounded corners and exposed rough-sawed roof beams. The few clouds she could see over the rooftops had turned a yellow gold and reminded her of a Monet sunset painting. It produced a complex stirring of emotions in Amanda: maybe it was a mixture of peace and nostalgia with a little joy added in, the gentle ending of a beautiful day. It was the visual equivalent of one of the softer Indie folk pieces from her Pandora collection.

The small town square, where people have gathered since the early sixteen hundreds, wasn't anything special to look at. Grass and a few trees. Footpaths cut diagonals across the square. A monument in the center of the plaza commemorated war dead, not unlike those found in many town squares Amanda had seen in the Midwest.

But this place reeked of history. Ryan pointed to a long white building on the far side of the plaza. "That's the Palace of the Governors," he said. "It's the oldest public building in the country, built ten years before the Pilgrims landed at Plymouth Rock." Then he stopped and looked directly at her. The wild sparkle she'd seen in his eyes this morning down in the Grand Canyon had been replaced by a soft warmth— maybe it was the sunset. "This place is truly amazing," he said. "It's the end of the Santa Fe Trail and, I think, the Royal Road up from Mexico City." Now he turned and looked out onto the plaza. "Can you imagine? Wagon trains arriving from the east circling the plaza in celebration?" Then he pointed to one corner of the square. "And over there is where Billy the Kid once sat in chains, while Pat Garrett grabbed a drink at a local saloon."

On this quiet evening it was hard for Amanda to grasp that the ancient-looking cluster of adobe buildings around her was also an epicenter for fancy restaurants, upscale clothing and accessories stores, art galleries and goggle-eyed tourists by the thousands. She gazed out onto the footpath crossing the square, where a group of teenagers huddled, laughing. Dots of orange flickered from their cigarettes. A couple of them swayed atop skateboards. Her dad would have labeled these kids stoners, but who was she to judge? An old man sat on one of the benches along the footpath, leaning on his cane, looking down toward his feet, ignoring the Monet sunset. This place was an historical must-see, for sure, but it was also the center of a modern city, where people gathered with all the same hopes, worries and fears of people everywhere. She looked at Ryan. "Maybe it is the City Different," she said, "but when you get down to the human level, maybe Santa Fe's pretty much like everywhere else."

Ryan gave her a surprised look but said nothing.

They made their way past the plaza, up San Francisco St., toward the St. Francis Cathedral, now bathed in spotlights at the head of the street. The massive stone-block building looked like a church you'd expect to find in Barcelona or Madrid and seemed out of place among the brown adobe pueblo-style architecture of the city around it. They cut north from the cathedral over to Palace Avenue—named for the Palace of the Governors—and stepped through a low archway—Ryan had to duck—into a small patio of uneven brick that looked ancient. On the far side of the patio, in a low building with a sagging roofline, was The Shed.

Ryan explained that The Shed was an icon for New Mexican food in a city of great New Mexican restaurants. The place was still hopping, even though it was past the dinner hour. Tourists in newly-purchased turquoise and silver snapped selfies and panos, while struggling with the Spanish menu. Locals relaxed with the laughter of friends. They were all here for the food.

Amanda and Ryan didn't have to wait long for a table, and soon they were oohing and ahhing over the legendary red-chile enchiladas, surrounded by the ambiance of laughter and celebration in a century-old hacienda. Ryan described the architecture to her. The high ceiling was supported by massive aspen timbers, called *vigas*. Between the vigas were rows of peeled branches, probably also aspen, called *latillas*. Inset into the adobe walls were *nichos*, small shelves where religious icons and statues were displayed. In one corner was a round *kiva* fireplace, surrounded by *bancos*—benches carved as part of the adobe walls—where several patrons sat, sipping margaritas.

Everything oozed warmth and tradition and antiquity. Amanda could almost sense the presence of the laborers cutting and stripping the vigas and latillas, just as she could imagine the *mamacitas* back in the kitchen preparing these amazing enchiladas from old family recipes.

While they sat back after dinner, waiting for their coffees to arrive, Ryan rubbed his tummy and said, "I guess we should have cooked in the Roadtrek tonight, but good Lord that was wonderful."

Amanda gave him a smile of guilty pleasure. She'd definitely eaten too much.

A young man came to clear the dishes. His stringy blonde hair was combed over to one side, so that he had to keep shaking his head to keep it out of his face. The hair and his great tan indicated a life more dedicated to surfing than developing a career. "You guys visiting?" the young man asked.

"How could you tell?" asked Amanda.

"Oh, I can tell. I'm just passing through myself."

"Oh?" said Amanda.

"Yeah, just picking up a few bucks and hanging out, taking a year off and working my way around the country."

When the young man had left, Ryan leaned toward Amanda and said, "You know, I used to look down on kids like that. Taking a year off from college and heading to Europe with a just backpack and no plans." He pursed his lips as if pondering what that would be like, then added, "I'm sure I said they were irresponsible or afraid to face the reality of life or whatever. What a crock that was. Now I realize that I was secretly envious of them. Kinda wished I'd done that."

Amanda laid a hand on his. "Maybe that's what you're doing now."

"Yeah, but I'm old. I'm—"

"Seriously, Ryan," Amanda interrupted, "you're only thirty-four."

"Yeah, but I'm already halfway to being one of those old retired guys who goes on bus tours with a group from the library." This got Amanda laughing, and soon Ryan was laughing too. "All I'm saying is that I wish I'd done it when I was just a kid."

Amanda knew about regrets. She said, "Maybe it's never too late to have a happy childhood."

The coffee arrived, and Amanda took a sip, then set her cup down when she saw the man over Ryan's shoulder. Almost in a whisper, she said, "Ryan, there's a man over there, and he keeps looking at us."

Ryan casually looked over his shoulder at a slender Hispanic man, probably in his fifties, sitting alone at a nearby table, munching chips and salsa. When the man caught Ryan's eyes, he looked down, busying himself with a paper in front of him.

The memory of the man at the Grand Canyon was still fresh, but now Amanda regretted saying anything to Ryan. She wasn't going to let her paranoia ruin this evening. "Maybe it's nothing," she said.

But it was clear that Ryan was not going to let this pass by unaddressed. He stood and stepped over to the man's table. The man looked up and smiled. If he was nervous about Ryan approaching him, he didn't show it.

"Excuse me, sir," said Ryan, obviously trying to project authority. Amanda was now having second thoughts in light of the man's friendly smile. Ryan cleared his throat. "I thought you were looking at us, and so I thought I'd come over and see if you wanted something ... or if maybe you knew us." They were close enough that Amanda could hear their conversation. She busied herself with stirring her coffee, but kept an eye on them.

"Oh, please forgive me," the man said. "I didn't mean to stare. I live in Albuquerque and I'm up here for work by myself. Love to eat here when I'm in town." The man had sincere brown eyes, graying hair and an easy smile. He wore a white dress shirt open at the collar beneath a pale-blue sport coat. "I guess when I get bored, I tend to watch other people. Again, my apologies. I'm Eric Sandoval. And you are ...?"

Ryan didn't give his name. Instead he said, "I'm sorry to have bothered you, sir. I hope you have a nice—"

"Why don't you and your wife join me for a margarita?" He nodded in the direction of Amanda, who looked back down at her coffee.

"Thank you," Ryan said, backing away, "but I think we'll pass tonight."

When he got back to the table, he said, "Well, that was awkward. He was just a lonely businessman doing a little people watching. Maybe it's time for us to stop being so jumpy."

Amanda nodded her agreement. "And anyway, who would want to follow us? And who would know how to find us?"

Ryan sighed heavily and sagged. "I guess there is a reason I may be over-reacting a bit."

Amanda's raised eyebrows silently said, "Tell me more."

Ryan told her about the termination of his employment, about threats of legal action, about strange phone calls from his former bosses, and about the fear he'd heard in the senior scientist's voice. "So there you have it," he said, forcing a nervous laugh. "Pretty boring, I guess."

"Not boring at all." Amanda licked her lips, then asked, "So what did you do to get them so angry?"

He told her about sending in the two abstracts for presentations at a scientific conference.

Amanda didn't understand what he was talking about. "What do you mean by an abstract?"

"An abstract is just a few-hundred-word summary of a talk you propose to give at the conference about your research. Scientists are expected to do it in their profession. I did it in protest to the repressive policies at Lightyear that prohibited publishing research results. After I sent in the first abstract— and they saw it in the conference announcement—I got a royal chewing out from Rockville. That's when I sent in a second abstract. So getting canned wasn't exactly a big surprise."

"I still don't get it," said Amanda. "I can understand them being upset that you violated some company policy, maybe even firing you, but why would someone be following you now? I mean, they already fired you." She shrugged her shoulders, confused.

Ryan shook his head slowly. "I don't get it, either. I see no way I could be a threat to them. So, maybe I'm off-base about this, but I can't think of anyone else who'd want to follow me." He blew out a big breath. "Like I said, maybe I'm over-reacting."

Amanda let out a small laugh. "So I'm guessing you won't be going to the conference now, huh?"

Ryan laughed too. "No." He scratched an ear with an index finger, then said. "So you must be thinking why am I here with this guy who got fired for breaking company policy and then invited a girl he doesn't know on a long trip." Now he leaned his chair back on two legs and rocked nervously, with a smirk like he was expecting her to tell him what a jerk he was.

"Why do you think you did those things, Ryan?"

He pursed his lips and shifted uncomfortably. "Frankly, I'm not sure. I've never been a person to go very far outside the box."

"Do you think your mother's death might have something to do with it?"

Ryan brought his chair back down onto all four legs. His mouth fell open, as he met her eyes. "I'm not sure." He was silent for a while, then said, "You'd be justified in thinking I'm crazy."

"I like it," she said.

Chapter 28

After the incipient romance in the Walmart parking lot, both Ryan and Amanda were playing it cautious tonight. Ryan was on his best behavior, painfully aware that he had jumped the gun last night—one more wrong move now, and she'd probably be on a Greyhound back to LA. So he helped Amanda hang a sheet between the front of the Roadtrek and the bed in the rear. At ten, she stood and yawned, gave him her Rose Parade wave and said, "Busy day tomorrow. Art museums, here we come!" Then she disappeared behind the sheet.

Ryan found his way to the passenger seat, which he reclined into a sleeping position. He stretched out, fully clothed, and pulled a blanket over himself. Although he'd only had a few hours of sleep the night before, he was wide awake. He didn't understand why. Maybe it was being so close to Amanda, just a few feet away in the back of the van. Or maybe it was being so close to his old home in Los Alamos, a place he'd left not under the best of circumstances.

Old memories threatened to return, but he forced them away with his imagination. *It was the championship game of the Final Four. UCI faced undefeated Duke, and Ryan was guarding their all-American superstar, who would probably leave Duke after this season*

*for the NBA, even though he was just a freshman. One-and-done is what
they called such players, and this one was considered the best in the
country. The game was tied and down to the last minute, and Duke had
the ball. All that stood between Mr. One-and-Done and the bucket was
Ryan Browning. He was coming fast and now he was airborne—*

Ryan let out an audible sigh, then hoped Amanda hadn't
heard it. A basketball fantasy would not rescue him tonight.

Those days at Los Alamos might sound prestigious and
glamorous to someone on the outside, but that's not the way it
was. When he should have been writing computer code,
diagnosing the bugs in new experimental equipment, and
staying abreast of the current scientific papers, Ryan was often
out hiking through the forests, the caldera and the Jemez back
country; skiing at Pajarito Mountain on Wednesday
afternoons; or photographing the spectacular New Mexico
sunsets and the approaching afternoon thunderstorms. It
wasn't that he didn't care about science. It's that science was
only one of the things he cared about.

Ryan was a competent physicist. He'd done well in a
strong graduate department at Irvine and showed enough
promise that his thesis advisor had pulled strings to get him
that internship at Los Alamos that would evolve into a staff
position. But physics just didn't command all his interest, like
it did the truly dedicated scientists, the ones jokes are made
about—the absent-minded, walking-into-the-wall types. The
way Ryan saw it—although he could only articulate this now in
retrospect—was that if physics sought to understand the
natural world, then shouldn't the natural world itself also
command his attention? Shouldn't mountain summits, golden
sunsets, gourmet dinners and beautiful women also command
his attention, just as much as a challenging equation, a new

finding about string theory, the calibration of a sensitive detector?

In a fiercely competitive tech world like the Lab, however, his approach was not the formula for success. Ryan was not, as one program manager had reminded him once, a mover and a shaker. He was conscientious about his work—he reaffirmed that to himself now, as if needing justification—but he didn't put in the long hours that many of his more dedicated colleagues did.

Ryan had busied himself with life in a small town—Los Alamos had only twelve-thousand people, almost all of whom were connected to the Lab. He played basketball in the community league. He joined the astronomy club. He ran a half-marathon. He had a network of casual friends with whom he'd meet for lunch, sometimes accompany down to Santa Fe for a meal, and travel to technical conferences.

These friends were all men, mainly because most of the technical staff were men. This wasn't just a Los Alamos thing; it was the way it was in the world of physics. At the time Ryan got his Ph.D., the number of women among new recipients of physics Ph.D.s was a little over one in ten. He found this tragic. On a practical level, this meant that Ryan rarely met a single woman in his workplace. A real killer for his romantic life.

The problem with Ryan Browning, at least in his own eyes, was that there seemed to be nothing very special about him. Sure, he had a Ph.D. in physics, and people often seemed impressed with that, and in his field he was considered competent, yes, but—God, he thought, here comes another downer—mediocre. And his work at the Lab had always been as an assisting member of the team, not the guy who had the bright idea.

Bright ideas aren't the product of a light suddenly going on, an almost mystical flash of insight or inspiration. Bright ideas—contrary to conventional wisdom—come to those who have worked hard, learned their craft, studied the literature late into the night while others were sleeping, worried about their computer code over perfect weekends while others were backpacking. Bright ideas came to the ones who missed the Saturday-night gourmet dinners at the fancy restaurants along Canyon Road in Santa Fe, in favor of finding the vacuum leak in that critical detector for the next experiment. Productivity in physics comes from genius mixed with sweat.

So Ryan was not the one who wrote the proposals and brought in the new funding, not the one who won the prizes, not a section leader or a group leader or any kind of leader. He had been a follower. Just like his ordinary name, Ryan, he was ordinary.

And so it hadn't been a huge surprise when he was RIF'd—a reduction in force during a downturn in funding that was just polite language for being laid off.

Ryan sat up in the chair and stepped outside the Roadtrek, closing the door quietly so as not to disturb Amanda. Perhaps a walk would help. But as he looked around at row upon row of other RVs crammed together in the darkness onto claustrophobic concrete slabs, he abandoned that idea. He gazed up toward the sky, toward the legendary starry display that the high altitude and clear air of Santa Fe make possible, only to be blinded by the glare from high-intensity security lamps around the RV park perimeter.

He climbed back into the Roadtrek, sat motionless for a few minutes, then reached down and picked up his laptop. Maybe he could channel his dark feelings into a new blog post.

He flipped open the computer, clicked the power button and brought up Word. His fingers were poised above the keyboard, but the only words that came to his mind were those from Amanda: *It's never too late to have a happy childhood.* This brought a smile, but that soon faded. He had nothing else to say tonight.

With a sigh, he set the laptop aside and picked up the road atlas. He turned to the New Mexico map. The borders of the page were filled with his mother's notes. It seemed like she'd been down every road in New Mexico. He chuckled as he read some of the notes, like one about getting lost in a remote pueblo and spending the night outside a sweat lodge, where she fell asleep to the sounds of strange chants and drumming and the odor of what she claimed was burning sage. Then he came to this one:

Tonight I'm in Bandelier, in the national monument campground. I'm not far from where Ryan used to work at the Lab, but he's moved to California now. Makes me feel lonely. But he's never far away in my heart.

Ryan felt his throat close off, and he couldn't get enough air. Then he felt a pressure building behind his eyes. Soon tears began to flow. At first, just a few tears, which he dabbed away with his sleeve. Then large sobs that made his chest heave. He had to fight to keep the sobs inaudible, lest Amanda come out to see what was wrong. He didn't want her to see him cry. He realized, in fact, that this was the first time he had cried about his mother's death. And this brought even more tears.

Chapter 29

They'd taken a meandering route, because Santa Fe is a city whose narrow, winding streets invite meandering. It was just beginning to warm up as they again passed in front of the massive St. Francis Cathedral, on their way to the New Mexico Museum of Art, on the plaza. Ryan knew that Amanda would not want to miss visiting a few of Santa Fe's art museums and its more than 250 art galleries, and this museum was a great place to start.

While the temperatures never get very high at this elevation—7,000 feet—the Santa Fe sun nevertheless brings an especially intense warmth, unfiltered by the lower mile-and-a-half of atmosphere. It had also evaporated the sadness that had accompanied Ryan into sleep last night.

Amanda paused in front of the Cathedral, at the tall bronze statue of Archbishop Lamy, under whose leadership the cathedral was built. She pointed out to Ryan that Lamy was the subject of Willa Cather's *Death Comes for the Archbishop*, which Ryan did not know, despite having lived nearby for six years.

A priest vested in a long black robe, walking a small dog, came toward them. "Good morning," he said with a warm smile.

Amanda immediately went down to her knees—not in prayer or in deference to the priest—but to play with the dog, a Jack Russell terrier. "What's her name?" she asked, looking up at the priest, while rubbing the dog's neck.

"Gracie," said the priest. "She'll let you do that to her all day," he laughed, "so don't say I didn't warn you."

"I haven't had a dog since I left home," she said to Ryan. "Isn't Gracie about the cutest thing you've ever seen?"

Ryan nodded and bent down to give the dog a pat on the head.

"You two visiting or do you live around here?" the priest asked. He was tall and slender, and looked to be under forty. His hair was cut short and he wore frameless glasses. He looked like a scholarly person, the sort of guy Ryan had seen a lot of at the Lab. He wondered if the priest had once been a scientist.

"We're just visiting," Ryan said, suspecting the priest had already deduced that.

"On vacation?"

"We're actually going to wind up at Glacier National Park, but for now I guess you could say we're just sort of wandering."

"Wandering?"

"Well, it's a new thing for me," said Ryan. "I haven't actually travelled all that much."

"Wandering is a great tradition," the priest said.

"Huh?" Ryan was already regretting he'd used the word *wandering*, since it could imply vagrancy or drifting or just being a bum.

"Take the saints of the Church," said the priest, "like Patrick of Ireland or Francis of Assisi." He nodded up toward the church. "In many ways, they were wanderers. They had no home anywhere." He smiled, then added, "So they made their home everywhere."

Ryan nodded. It came to him that maybe the priest was actually describing the last few years of his mother's life.

"There's even a word for it. *Peregrinatio.* It means holy wandering. Wandering with the ultimate hope of drawing closer to God, even if it's not clear how you're going to do that." The priest gave Ryan a friendly smile, a smile that somehow conveyed a sense that he understood or intuited more about Ryan than Ryan had told him.

"Interesting," said Ryan, "but I'm not so sure our wandering is holy."

The priest smiled a patient smile.

Amanda now stood. She'd been taking all this in, while doting on Gracie. "Thank you," she said.

"You two have a nice day. And if you're out in the early mornings, there's mass at seven, in the chapel just behind the church."

Ryan had seldom visited art museums, and he certainly had never visited one with an art historian. His understanding about paintings and sculpture was like his understanding of progressive jazz, French cooking and golf. He appreciated the basics, but he was lacking on the rich layers of finer points. As they strolled through the galleries of the New Mexico Museum of Art, Amanda helped illuminate some of those finer points. He was impressed that she was not a show-off of her knowledge. He'd seen enough of those kinds of know-it-alls in the world of physics. Amanda was different. She was enjoying the art with him, not holding all the answers—although she may have had them—but providing just enough perspective that it enriched his appreciation and made him want more. He was not learning from her so much as he was experiencing it with her. It was a real turn-on.

He'd asked her about the Georgia O'Keeffes, of which this museum had surprisingly few, considering O'Keeffe had lived just north of Santa Fe for so many years. Maybe they were all at the Georgia O'Keeffe Museum, he conjectured, a few blocks away. Amanda was enthusiastic about going to the O'Keeffe Museum next, but she amazed Ryan with the story that O'Keeffe had once offered many of her paintings to the New Mexico Museum of Art, but the gift was rejected by the museum, presumably because of the unconventional and erotic nature of her works. Those pieces, Amanda pointed out with a laugh, became centerpieces of other collections in the East.

Ryan was surprised at the painting in the museum that seemed to move Amanda the most. It was titled *Trinity Site,* painted in 1989 by Judy Chicago. It certainly wasn't one of the most famous paintings in the museum. In fact, it was not normally even on display. The work was relatively small, only 16 by 20 inches, yet Amanda stood enrapt with it for a good ten minutes before saying a word. Then she explained that Judy Chicago was a contemporary feminist artist; Ryan had never heard of her. The painting portrayed a woman—perhaps a Native American woman, perhaps an Asian woman—facing away from a starkly barren desert that looked like the Mojave Desert they had traversed two days ago. But it probably represented the desert at Trinity Site, near Alamogordo, New Mexico, where the first atomic bomb was tested. The woman's arms were raised, as if in prayer. There appeared to be burns on her arms and neck—perhaps from radiation? She was naked, her hair was in a simple bun, and there was an enigmatic look on her face. Maybe it was despair, maybe anger, or shock, or terror. The woman was painted in color, while the desert around her was drab and gray and portrayed with photographic realism.

"What does it mean?" asked Ryan. Frankly, he hated the painting, but he was not about to say that to Amanda. "I don't get it."

"I don't know what it means, either," said Amanda, her eyes locked onto the image of the woman. "That's okay. Art doesn't have to mean something specific, but it should challenge, test, twist, confuse, convict, shock your feelings and your rational abilities, prevent simple or simplistic answers." Now she turned to Ryan. "And this painting does that for me in spades."

Ryan turned his eyes away from Amanda and back onto the painting, as if he could grasp it if he only tried hard enough. "Is it a protest against nuclear weapons?" he asked. With six years at Los Alamos, he should be able to engage a discussion about that.

Amanda seemed to consider his question seriously. "That could be part of it, I guess. But that's too simple of a conclusion, almost a cliché. Sure, New Mexico has played an important role in the development of nuclear weapons, so that's a reasonable conclusion for such a painting on display here. But for me it's not about weapons or war or politics. For me, it's about her."

Ryan now turned toward Amanda, captivated by her words. He gave her a nod that said, "Tell me more."

"What it says to me is all about the value of life, its frailty, its beauty, perhaps its holiness. For me, it's a testimony about love and life and how vulnerable those precious things are in the face of aggression, militarism and hatred." She looked at Ryan, her eyes now pressing into his. "And yet those vulnerable things are ultimately the only protection we have against the ugly things that attempt to do us in."

Ryan was in conflict. Last night at the RV park, they had been so careful to keep it platonic, politely sliding past each other without touching in the narrow confines of the Roadtrek. Now he wanted to pull Amanda down onto the carpet right there in front of Judy Chicago and *Trinity Site*. But he also wanted to hear her speak more about the painting and her passion for art. He wondered if her father, who had pushed her toward being an accountant, had ever seen his daughter, the amazing art historian, in action.

Amanda turned her body away from the painting and toward Ryan. "You asked if the painting was a protest against nuclear weapons. You worked at Los Alamos. I'd like to hear what you think about that."

Ryan took a deep breath, then blew it out hard. "That's a big topic. I never worked on nuclear weapons, but I knew a lot of folks who did." He ran a hand through his hair, then said, "There are a few types at the Lab who like to blow things up." He gave out a hollow chuckle. "But I'd say most of the people who work on nuclear weapons see their work as a way to protect lives. They seriously engage the topic of the morality of nukes, and they don't ever want to see them used." He blew out another breath as he struggled to provide a thoughtful answer to her important question. "I guess one school of thought is that a strong deterrent actually makes the world safer against someone starting a nuclear conflict."

Amanda nodded thoughtfully, looking straight at him with those big green eyes.

"Like I said, it's a big topic." He felt sweat forming on his forehead.

"But how about you?"

"Me?" He squirmed. "I don't think I could personally work on them. I just don't want to be in that business." Good grief, he thought, had he just said something that sounded that stupid?

Amanda bit her lip, like she was thinking this over. It was a lame answer he had given her, but the truth was he had never really thought much about the morality of nuclear weapons. It was a big topic, like he had said, but that wasn't the reason he didn't have an articulate position to present. Quite simply, he had been too busy with his day-to-day existence—worrying about meeting women, the next backpacking trip, what new lens he wanted for his camera— stuff that at this moment seemed shallow and self-centered. He looked down at his feet, wishing he was the deeply thoughtful citizen that Amanda was hoping to hear from now.

Then Amanda asked, "So, why did you leave Los Alamos?"

Ryan swallowed something the size of a golf ball. He produced an insincere smile, then said, "Oh, I just decided that …" He stopped. This could be a key moment in his relationship with Amanda. As much as he was ashamed to admit that he had been laid off, it was important to be honest with her. He was silent, while he searched for the most face-saving way he could find to tell her the truth. "There was a downsizing," he said.

She nodded, but was quiet.

He waited in the silence, expecting her to seek clarification, ask some penetrating question that would finally expose him as a loser. But all she said was, "That's too bad. I guess that must happen even to bright guys like you." Then she added, "I heard you say we're just a half-hour away from

Los Alamos, but I haven't heard you say anything about us going there. Is it because of the nuclear weapons issues?"

Truth was, he hadn't considered going to Los Alamos, but it had nothing to do with nuclear weapons research. The way it had ended—getting RIF'd and being dumped by Melissa—had been a dark cloud that he didn't want to walk back under. Sure, he was over all that, but Los Alamos was the kind of small town where you were always running into everyone you knew. If you needed a quart of milk, you'd better allocate an hour at the market, because that's how long it would take to say hello to all the acquaintances you encountered.

"Ryan?" she queried.

"Yes. I haven't talked about going up on the Hill." That's what the locals called the town, because it's set atop high mesas, formed by an ancient volcanic eruption. "Just didn't think it would be that interesting. So, I—"

"I'd love to go," said Amanda.

Ryan nodded. "Okay, I'd love to take you up there," he lied. "Now," he said, ready to change the subject, "shall we head over to the O'Keeffe?"

Chapter 30

A manda had gotten hooked on art museums early on, when as a child her parents took her to the small Yawkey Museum in her hometown of Wausau, where she was exposed to paintings and sculptures of the natural world. Later, they took her to the art museum in Milwaukee, where she saw international traveling exhibits. It was ironic that her parents—who wanted her to major in something practical, like accounting—had been the ones who initiated the spark in her heart for art.

Art could transport Amanda from a world of constraints, where demands were made, where expectations had to be met, failures reconciled. It elevated her above the realm of plastic customer-service smiles, spreadsheets and bottom lines, BS about synergy and optimizing organizational productivity, hair coloring and the Adams and Richards of this world. Not to mention her own long list of personal shortcomings. All of these things were confining, restrictive, narrow. Art pointed her toward the inexpressible, the ambiguous, the mysterious. The holy. It freed her and injected her with life. It was liberating, just like jumping into an RV and heading out into the unknown with a guy you hardly know.

They turned down Palace Avenue, heading away from the plaza and toward the O'Keeffe Museum, a few blocks west. The cool morning had developed into a magnificent sunny day, the crisp, high-altitude sunlight glistening off the earthtones of the adobe walls and sky-blue wooden doors of centuries-old buildings and modern structures constructed to look centuries old.

The sunlight also shimmered off the colorful attire of Santa Fe women. If she had more money, Amanda could see herself being enticed by the many trendy boutiques offering long skirts, wraps and scarves in the vibrant colors of Santa Fe style. When she paused at one small shop, Ryan said, "Why don't you go in and check it out?"

She gave him a nod that said thank you.

She tried on a long flowing dress, in bright red and purple and yellow, and modeled it for Ryan. Striking a dramatic pose, with her head turned to the side and chin high, she moved her arms above her head and flicked her fingers like she was playing castanets. "Ah, Señor Browning," she laughed with her best Spanish accent, "you want to come to mi casa tonight and drink sangria?"

He shook his head in apparent amazement. "Now that is what I call real art," he said.

She smiled demurely and curtseyed. Then more serious, she said, "I'm afraid all these things are well beyond my paygrade." She returned the dress to the rack.

They strolled on in silence, losing themselves in the beauty of the morning. Then across the street, just a block ahead, Amanda saw Mr. Sandoval, the man they'd seen at dinner last night.

Ryan saw him, too, and he suddenly grabbed her arm. "Let's go around a different block, okay? I just as soon not run into Mr. Sandoval again."

Amanda protested, "I don't see any harm in meeting him again. He seemed like a nice—" She stopped in mid-sentence. Mr. Sandoval now turned, so they could see the man that he had been talking with. And there was no mistake about it. It was the man from the campground at the Grand Canyon.

A minute later, from their refuge just inside the Yellow Burrito Gallery, they peeked out around the edge of the front display window. "Do you think they saw us?" Amanda gasped.

"I don't think so." Ryan was breathing just as hard as Amanda.

"Oh my God, Ryan, I'm scared." Amanda couldn't control her trembling. She could feel her heart in her ears.

"Yeah, me too." Ryan put an arm around her shoulders. "We've got to figure this out."

"Who are they?"

Ryan didn't answer. Instead, he said, "And how did they find us?"

"Should we call the cops?" Now she looked up at him. His eyes were locked on the two men outside, piercing, analyzing. In spite of his words, he didn't look afraid, and this steadied her.

"I don't know. What would we tell them? That two guys seem to be following us? They haven't actually done anything." Ryan licked his lips, clearly trying, like Amanda, to sort this out.

Amanda's breathing was shaky. "You're right, of course." She ran a hand through her hair and held it behind her head, "So what should we do?"

Ryan shrugged. "If they're just criminals following us … no that's not it. Those guys don't look like simple criminals." He turned and paced between large pottery pieces.

A young woman approached them. "May I help you find something?"

"We're just looking," they both replied, almost in unison. The woman raised a curious eyebrow, then returned to a desk in the rear.

Ryan held his head with both hands, like he had a terrible headache, as he paced back and forth. "I didn't tell anyone where I was going. Did you?"

"Of course not. We didn't even know ourselves until we looked at your atlas when we were leaving."

"Then how—"

"Oh hell," sighed Amanda. "I think I know." She bit her lip and looked down. She suddenly felt like crap. "The Facebook posts," she said.

Ryan stopped his pacing and stood facing her. "That could be it. They said where we were going."

"And I tagged you. So they were either looking for you or me, and they were looking at our Facebook pages." Amanda pondered this some more. "But I've got Facebook set so that my posts are seen only by my Facebook friends, and I can assure you those two guys aren't my friends. How about you?"

Ryan shrugged. "I don't know. I don't use Facebook that often."

"Look at your privacy settings," she said.

He pulled out his phone. After a few moments, he blew out an exasperated breath, while shaking his head. "I've got it set to be visible to the public. So, does that mean that anyone could have seen the posts?"

"I'm afraid so."

"But I still don't know how they were able to find us. I mean, the Grand Canyon and Santa Fe are big places."

Amanda's mind was racing. She pulled up the photos she'd recently posted on Facebook, then held one up for Ryan to see. "Here's the answer."

Ryan stared at the photo Amanda had posted from the supermarket parking lot in California, with the caption, "On the way to Grand Canyon and beyond with Ryan." The photo showed the two of them standing in front of the Roadtrek. To make matters worse, the license plate number was clearly visible in the photo. His mouth fell open.

Amanda sagged. "So they knew we were going to the Grand Canyon. They knew we're in an RV, so we'd be in a campground. And if needed, they even have our license plate number. Not that hard to find us." What she didn't say was how she'd only posted the photos to torment Adam. She looked down at the floor, feeling a dark shroud envelop her, replacing the sunny Santa Fe vibe she had been experiencing just minutes ago. Then she looked back up at Ryan. "So you don't have any idea who they might be?"

Ryan scratched his head and resumed his pacing. "They could be the law," he speculated. "Lightyear said they would prosecute me. But if they wanted to arrest me, then why the covert stuff? No, I don't think they are the cops. So that leaves the Lightyear people themselves. Okay, here's what I think. Remember I told you about the creepy call from Robie?"

Amanda nodded, breathing through her mouth.

"He sounded afraid. And he made reference to Julian Assange and—"

"The WikiLeaks guy."

"Yes, and to Edward Snowden."

"The NSA leaker."

Ryan nodded. "So then I suddenly sell my car, abandon my apartment and disappear to parts unknown. Maybe they think I know more than I do, that somehow I can harm them. That must be it. Those paranoid idiots." His fists were now clenched. "Good God, why did I ever have to get tied up with that bunch of creeps?"

"So what do you think they'll do?"

Ryan threw his arms into the air. "I have no idea. Maybe they just want to keep tabs on me. Or ..." He looked down. "God forbid, something worse."

Amanda steadied herself with one hand against a wall and wiped perspiration from her forehead with the back of the other hand. She bit her lip, then sighed. "So, here's one thing—"

"Amanda," Ryan interrupted, "The first thing we've got to do is get you out of here." He bit his lip, and his eyes became misty. He reached out and touched the side of her face with his fingertips. They felt gentle and reassuring. "They're not after you. I'm so sorry I dragged you—"

"Shut up and listen, Mr. Browning." She forced a cute little smile, then said, "You're not getting rid of me that easy. Anyway, if I hadn't posted those stupid Facebook pictures, and the only reason I posted them was to ..." She was unable to complete the sentence. "Let's just say I'm ashamed about that. But here's what I was about to say. The one advantage we have over them is that, as best as we can tell, they don't know we're onto them yet."

Ryan grimaced, then he nodded slowly. "So how do we use that advantage?"

"Well, here's one idea. I post another photo, revealing another destination. But it's not the place we're actually headed."

Now the hint of a smile surfaced at the corner of Ryan's mouth. "Then we go our merry way. Nice, Miss Seward. You are one crafty customer service rep."

Amanda gave his shoulder a little we-can-do-this punch. "So, let's make our post, then let's get the hell out of here."

Ryan posed with Amanda against a gaudy acrylic painting of a giant jackrabbit, as she snapped a selfie. "Where should we say we're headed?" she asked.

"How about Austin? And meanwhile, we'll be headed in the opposite direction."

"Austin it is." She tapped in a message that read, *Ryan and me doing the galleries in Santa Fe. Now on to Austin.* She tagged Ryan and then hit post. As she did, she realized that she hadn't even looked at Facebook for the last twenty-four hours, much less fretted over Adam's likes.

Ryan took her hand, and they walked, almost ran, to the rear of the gallery. He cleared his throat, then said to the salesperson, "Do you have a rear entrance?"

The woman had been leafing through some glossy photos, but now put them down and stood. "I'm afraid it's only an employee entrance, and we don't allow—"

"Thank you," Ryan said, "but we don't have a lot of choice about this." He pulled Amanda toward the rear. They fumbled around several shelves of supplies, some easels stacked against a wall, and past a row of filing cabinets.

The woman shouted after them, "Wait, you can't just—"

But they were already out the door.

Chapter 31

The back door of the Yellow Burrito Gallery dumped them out into an alley, which they followed north, almost at a run, past the rear of several other stores, until they emerged onto Marcy Street, which runs parallel to Palace. They followed Marcy east to a street that would take them back past the St. Francis Cathedral and lead them to the RV park, about a mile beyond.

At the cathedral, they slowed their pace to catch their breath. "I say let's get out of town as fast as possible," said Amanda, panting and shaking.

Ryan nodded, then said, "But they may be watching the Roadtrek. If they are, we don't want to appear to be in a hurry."

Amanda started to speak, then gasped. She grabbed Ryan's forearm in a vice-like grip, while her eyes, suddenly wide with panic, looked up the block behind him. The man from the Grand Canyon was walking their way. Instinctively, they bolted up the front steps of the cathedral, pulled a heavy door open, and quickly slipped in.

"I don't think he saw us, but I'm not sure," Ryan said, once they were inside. They stood with eyes fixed on the door, as if expecting the man to pull it open in the next instant.

Slowly they backed away a few feet, keeping their eyes on the door, then turned toward the front of the church, ready to race toward another exit. A man blocked their way. Amanda let out an audible shriek and Ryan went rigid.

It was the priest they had met earlier that morning. "Nice to see you both again," he said. "And how is your wandering progressing today?" He still wore the black robe he'd had on earlier. He offered a cordial smile, but his raised eyebrows showed that he knew something was wrong.

Ryan and Amanda stood silent, lost for words.

The priest said, "It seems clear that you didn't come in to admire the architecture."

Ryan quickly took in the interior and, even in his state of fear, it almost took his breath away. A high ceiling, supported by Romanesque round arches supported by massive gray-marble columns, rose at least fifty feet above them. Along the sides of the church were tall stained-glass windows. A wide aisle cut through many rows of polished wood pews—past a large basin that Ryan assumed was a baptismal font—up to a high altar, backed by colorful images of people, probably saints. He'd never been in a cathedral before and, except for a few weddings, he'd never even been in a church.

"By the way," the priest said, "I'm Father Jessop. Why don't you come with me and we can find a comfortable place to talk."

They followed Fr. Jessop to a small chapel off to the side of the main sanctuary, where he invited them to have a seat in one of the pews. The priest sat in a pew in front of them, then turned around to face them. His arms were crossed and his body was relaxed in a way that suggested he was settling in to hear a good story.

Ryan told Fr. Jessop everything, shooting occasional glances at Amanda for corroboration or moral support. It didn't take long, as they didn't know much.

When Ryan had finished, Fr. Jessop said, "May I call the police for you?"

"We thought about that, but there hasn't been a crime committed or even the threat of a crime, so what could they possibly do to help us?"

"I don't know," confessed the priest. "You're probably right." He squeezed his chin between his thumb and index finger, as if he were developing some kind of scheme. Then he said, "Okay, here's what I can tell you. First, you are safe here. They don't call this a sanctuary for nothing. So, both of you, right now, take a deep breath and calm down a little." He let out a friendly laugh.

The laughter began to ease Ryan's anxiety, and he sagged more comfortably into the pew.

Then Fr. Jessop said, "I can't offer much practical help, but I know someone who can."

"You mean God?" asked Amanda.

"Yes, of course God, but I was also thinking of Chief Montoya—actually he's the Assistant Police Chief. Maybe there's nothing the police can do for you, but I think Chief Montoya may be able to give you some practical advice." His raised eyebrows asked if that was okay.

Ryan began to refuse the offer—what good could it do?—but Amanda said, "I don't see how it could do any harm. Anyway, I'm not ready to go back out there." She glanced over her shoulder toward the big door at the rear of the church.

Ryan looked at Amanda, then nodded at Fr. Jessop and said, "Okay." After a moment, he added, "But why would he be willing to talk with us?"

"Because he is my friend." Fr. Jessop shared a knowing smile. "And he's also a parishioner of this church. Now why don't you wait here, and I'll go call him."

As soon as the priest stepped away, Ryan said to Amanda, "Maybe we should just slip out the back." He began to rise from the pew, but Amanda placed a hand on his arm.

"I'd like to hear what the policeman has to say. We can't just keep running like this."

Ryan drew in a quick deep breath, pursed his lips and held it, then exhaled slowly, the air coming out in nervous pulses. "You're right."

Within a minute, the priest returned. "He's on his way," he announced, with a twinkle in his eye. Then he sat back down in the pew and once again turned toward them. "You said this morning that you are headed for Glacier."

"That's right," said Ryan.

"I've never been there. In fact, I've never seen a glacier. I've lived in the southwest all my life. But I do know a few things about them."

Ryan glanced at Amanda, then back at the priest, wondering where this was going.

"Glaciers are powerful and relentless, but they move slowly, so slow that you cannot see them move. And yet, they can carve through mountains. Sometimes I think we feel like we're stuck in the place where we'll always be. Maybe it's an uncomfortable place, or maybe it's too comfortable. Maybe it's a boring place, maybe it's a frightening place. And we feel like we're stuck there. Yet, like the glacier, we are moving somewhere else.

"So, you both are frightened today, and I understand that. I wish I could make that fear go away. Perhaps these people are a real threat, perhaps they are not—I certainly hope it's not serious."

Fr. Jessop was trying to calm them down with a comforting little lecture. Ryan let out an impatient breath, but continued to listen.

"But the glacier continues to move. It moves because of gravity, that very familiar thing that is everywhere. Yet gravity is very mysterious."

Ryan wondered again if this priest might have once been a scientist.

"The way our lives move—if we allow them to—is by something that is also everywhere, yet very mysterious. And I believe that is God."

Amanda nodded as Fr. Jessop spoke, apparently concentrating on his words. Ryan had now allowed his gaze to stray up to the high arching beams supporting the ceiling and wondered how people in the nineteenth century, with such primitive technology, could construct a ceiling like this.

Fr. Jessop continued. "You may or may not believe this—I don't know and I'm not going to ask—but that does not change what is true." Now he leaned back and scratched his head. "Okay, so I'm not sure where this metaphor is heading." He laughed. "But I want you both to know that you do not have to be afraid."

Just then, a man came into the chapel with a confident stride. He wore a dark police uniform—gray shirt and black pants, with a black necktie. There was a large brass badge on his chest and a red-white-and-blue patch on his shoulder that read Santa Fe Police. He carried an array of accessories attached to a thick black belt: hand cuffs, a radio, what looked like a night stick, and a large handgun. He looked very official.

Fr. Jessop stood and said, "Amanda and Ryan, I want you to meet Chief Montoya."

They stood and shook hands, as the policeman said, "Art Montoya. And Father, you've got to remember that I'm only the Assistant Chief." Montoya was a short, burly man in his mid-forties, with bulky arms that looked like you wouldn't want to challenge him to an arm wrestling contest. He was fit but with a hint of a gut, which he probably worried about. His round, light brown face bore a few wrinkles and dark, deep-set eyes that were hard to read. If you were on the run from the law, Art Montoya looked like the last guy you'd want to encounter.

"Thanks for coming over, Art. I know you're very busy, but this couple has some problems, and I thought you'd be able to help them know what to do."

Montoya nodded and gestured for everyone to sit back down. Ryan then repeated the story, while the policeman jotted a few notes in a small spiral notebook.

"So, do you know who either of these men is?" The assistant chief had a slow, deliberate voice that indicated caution and discipline. It was deep, almost gravelly. He was a guy who probably was very careful to choose the right words, to say what needed to be said, but no more.

Ryan shook his head. "We don't know either of them. One of the men said his name was Eric Sandoval, but of course that could be—"

"Eric Sandoval?" the policeman asked. "What did he look like?"

Ryan let out a big sigh, then said, "Well, he was sitting down at the time, but I'd say he was tall. A Hispanic man, black hair turning gray. I'd guess he was in his fifties."

The policeman set his notebook down and chewed his lip.

Father Jessop looked puzzled. He asked, "Art, do you know this man?"

Montoya seemed flustered for a moment, then said, "Just wanting a better description of this guy, just in case ... you know ..." His voice trailed off.

Ryan felt a shiver go up his spine. Father Jessop continued to look puzzled.

Montoya now focused his eyes hard on Ryan. "Is there anything you haven't told us, Mr. Browning?"

Something fishy was going on here, and Ryan wanted to get away, fast. "No, sir. We're just on a trip."

Montoya then gave them the promised practical advice. "As you know, there's not much we can do unless a crime has been committed or a direct threat has been made or if stalking can be proved. So, just keep your eyes open. Lock your doors at night. We live in an unpredictable age." It sounded like the pabulum he had probably served up at lunch-hour talks at the Rotary Club.

After Montoya left, Ryan said, "Father, is there a back way out of here?"

"Of course. I'll show you the way. But first, may I say a prayer for you both?" He looked from Ryan to Amanda.

Ryan began to rise from his pew, but Amanda said, "Yes, please do say a prayer." She gave Ryan a sit-back-down look, then added, "And while you're at it, could you also pray for Cepi and Reynaldo?"

As they were leaving the church through a narrow hallway behind the chapel, Ryan said to Amanda, "I wonder why Fr. Jessop was willing to spend so much time with us."

Amanda raised an eyebrow. "Ryan," she said, with a slight bit of admonishment, "helping people is what he's called to do."

But after the past twenty-four hours, Ryan wasn't sure he could trust anyone.

Chapter 32

They drove north from Santa Fe on US 285, the road that leads up toward Colorado, after taking a circuitous route out of town to assure that they weren't being followed. Ryan shook his head slowly and said, "Add one more item to the list of things I can't figure out: it seems clear that Montoya knows Eric Sandoval."

Amanda ran her hands through her hair, gathering it behind her head, like she was forming it into a ponytail. "Maybe, but I'm sure there are lots of Sandovals in this part of the world."

"I hope you're right, and God, I hope all this is behind us for good." He appeared to be gripping the steering wheel so hard Amanda wondered if his hands would leave indentations.

"I certainly plan to stay away from Austin, Texas, for the foreseeable future," Amanda said, trying to generate some laughter. The panic that had resided in her stomach for the past two hours, like a hand grenade with the pin pulled, was finally subsiding. "So where should we go now?"

"Putting some miles between us and Santa Fe, for starters." After a moment, he shot her a deadly serious look, then looking back at the road, said, "First thing we need to do is get you headed back to LA, where you'll be safe."

She turned her body toward him. "There's nothing for me back there. Everything is still up ahead."

Ryan nodded like he understood, although she was certain that he would bring this up again. He gave a shrug of resignation. "You said you'd like to go to Los Alamos."

They had just crested a high hill north of the city and were greeted with a vast panorama. High mountains rose off to the east, and the land fell away to the west, perhaps to a river. Beyond that, a series of mesas, like fingers on an outstretched hand, reached out from another mountain range. "Yes," she said. "You said it's not far from here?"

"About a half-hour away." He was quiet for a while, then said, "I'm sorry you didn't get to see the O'Keeffe Museum."

"I think Georgia would understand," Amanda said. She was determined to move on, but Ryan still seemed to be brooding.

After another long minute of silence, he said, gesturing eastward, "Those big mountains are the Sangre de Cristos."

"Blood of Christ," she said.

He nodded. "They get that name because at sunset they sometimes have a brilliant reddish glow, almost like blood." The diversion from freaking out over Mr. Sandoval and his friend was welcomed. "And over to the west is the Rio Grande, and beyond that, up on those mesas, is Los Alamos. We'll cross that river in a little while."

"It's beautiful," she said. "Where will we stay in Los Alamos?"

Ryan answered quickly. "I was thinking the campground at Bandelier National Monument. It's a beautiful place, with ancient cliff dwellings and amazing rock formations. And it's not far from the town." After a moment, he added, "My mother stayed there once."

"Sounds wonderful," she said. "But I suspect we won't be posting any pictures on Facebook from there." She tried to force a smile, although the thought of her Facebook posts made her want to cringe.

At the small reservation town of Pojoaque, whose major feature seemed to be a large casino, they turned west and drove through open range country, dotted with juniper, toward the distant mesas where Ryan said Los Alamos was located. When they passed the cutoff to the San Ildefonso Pueblo, Amanda spun in her seat to look back at the junction. "Maria!" she squealed.

Ryan almost jumped in his seat at her sudden outburst. "What?"

"Sorry, didn't mean to startle you. It's San Ildefonso, where Maria Martinez lived."

"Oh, sure. She was a potter, right?"

"A great one. Can we go back?"

"Sure," he sighed. Ryan pulled to the side of the highway and prepared to make a U-turn that would get them back to the San Ildefonso cutoff. He seemed a bit annoyed, but maybe that was understandable after the morning they'd had.

"Just for a few minutes, if that's okay," Amanda said, trying to mollify Ryan's apparent impatience. "Maria's work is world-renowned, a unique form of black-on-black pottery that she pioneered. Do you know her work is in the MOMA?"

Ryan raised his eyebrows like he was surprised. "I knew she was famous, but I didn't know that."

The road into San Ildefonso wound through the arid desert setting for about a half-mile before it turned to dirt. Soon they entered a small, quiet village of simple, brown adobe dwellings. Near the center of the village was a large adobe church, the most significant structure in the tiny town, and nearby a sign on a building that housed the tribal government offices pointed to the Maria Martinez museum.

Amanda looked over at Ryan, who answered before she could say anything. "Of course we can go in." He smiled, the first she'd seen from him in a while, as he pulled into a wide dirt parking area.

Stopping at the entrance of the museum, Amanda did a slow three-sixty. Low, earth-tone buildings that could be hundreds of years old were widely scattered around them, and beyond the buildings, high mesas rose in the west. She could have been on another continent, she thought, in another century. She shook her head in amazement. "So this is where Maria got her inspiration," she said, "from this remote place, from these people, from this culture."

Ryan opened his mouth to speak, but said nothing. Instead, he just nodded slowly, as if acknowledging the importance of her words.

The museum was small and sparsely furnished. A few glass cases displayed some of Maria's pottery, a few photos and a brief bio. "Not much here, but it's wonderful anyway," Amanda said. She was in her element.

A young woman introduced herself. "Hello, I'm Tonita. May I help you?"

"We're just looking at Maria's pottery. It's beautiful." Amanda admired the black, glazed surfaces of several large pots, which had a glassy sheen into which intricate patterns were carved. Even Ryan seemed captivated by the pieces.

Tonita busied herself nearby for a few minutes before saying, "Excuse me, but is that a friend of yours?"

"What?" Ryan spun quickly to scan the room.

"He just left," Tonita said. "But he poked his head in for a moment like he was looking for someone."

Ryan bolted toward the door, as Amanda stood open-mouthed. Tonita turned toward her with an alarmed look. "Is everything okay?"

Amanda didn't reply, her eyes locked on the museum entrance through which Ryan had just run.

In a moment he returned, shaking his head. "There's no one there." He let out a loud frustrated breath.

Tonita seemed worried. "I'm sorry. I didn't mean to alarm you."

"What did he look like?" Ryan asked Tonita, his voice filled with urgency.

She shook her head and licked her lips, clearly upset. "I didn't see him very well. He was only there a second. A man. Anglo, I could tell that much."

Ryan sighed and seemed to relax. "It's okay," he said, trying to calm Tonita. "It wasn't anything important." Then he looked at Amanda and smiled. "Good grief," he said, "I've got to stop jumping out of my shoes every time some little thing happens." He managed a nervous laugh, then rested a hand gently on her shoulder.

Soon they were back on the road headed toward Los Alamos. They crossed the Rio Grande at a dramatic spot at the foot of the high mesas. Ryan told her that several John Wayne westerns had been filmed along this stretch of river. Then he pointed to a small ruin on the far side of the river and said, "My understanding is that there used to be a café over there, where Maria Martinez would come up from San Ildefonso and share a meal with Robert Oppenheimer, the theoretical physicist and head of the Manhattan Project."

"Oh my," said Amanda. "I would have loved to have eavesdropped on those conversations."

"Talk about a meeting of cultures: the Native American potter and the Berkeley physicist. I wonder if they had anything in common to talk about."

"Theoretical physics and art. Maybe they had everything to talk about," she said.

Ryan looked over at her and shook his head slowly, then gave out a welcomed laugh. "You say the damnedest things."

From the river, State Highway 4 climbed toward the high mesa tops, where pines and dense clusters of juniper replaced the desert vegetation down by the river. They cut south to the little town of White Rock, then continued up a road so winding that it seemed to challenge Ryan's ability to maneuver the big van.

Amanda knew that Ryan was still thinking about the possible dangers they faced. "Look Ryan," she said with a firm yet caring voice that sought to carry authority, "I know you're feeling responsible for me being in this situation. Maybe you believe I'm in danger because of you. And, yes, I was really scared today. I've never had anything like that happen to me before, and I suspect you haven't either. But I'm a big girl, Ryan, and I can make decisions for myself." Fleeting images of Adam and Richard challenged her conviction about this, but she quickly pushed them away. She crossed her arms to indicate that this was her final comment about the topic.

Ryan bit his lip and rolled his eyes upward, but said nothing. He seemed to be somewhere else, far away from here.

A half-hour later they had found a secluded campsite at Juniper Campground, just inside Bandelier National Monument, and were busying themselves preparing the RV for the night, when Amanda's phone rang. She jumped from surprise—she hadn't expected to have reception out here. "Katy!"

"How are you?" There was a hook in Katy's question that asked so much.

Amanda took a seat at the picnic table, while Ryan continued with the campsite prep. She stammered and couldn't get out a coherent thought before Katy continued. "I mean, I could envision you being held prisoner in some dingy basement as a love slave ... or maybe you two off on a Bonnie-and-Clyde rampage somewhere." This provided Amanda with a much needed laugh.

While Katy told her the good news about her apartment being quickly sublet, Amanda watched Ryan turning on the propane supply and extending the awning to provide shade in the bright afternoon sun.

"So I've been following your Facebook posts, girl. Ryan is cute, that's for sure. Cute in a wild, shaggy poet kind of way, but he's probably not my type." Katy giggled softly, then said, "So those posts were pretty obvious. Probably drove Adam crazy. Have you heard from him yet?"

A mixture of emotions surged through Amanda: glee that Adam might, in fact, have been driven crazy, as Katy conjectured, and a blush of embarrassment, as if Ryan could listen in on the conversation. Yes, the posts had been written to provoke Adam, but they had also gotten Ryan and her into serious trouble. "No," said Amanda, working to show little enthusiasm, even as she felt heat in her face.

Katy apparently bought her sullen monosyllabic answer and moved on. "So, here's the big question. What's he like?"

"Katy," Amanda said in mock protest. "What do you mean, what is he like?"

With a wicked little laugh, Katy said, "I mean, what is he like? You know."

"Geez, Katy, you're a freaking maniac. You know—"

"But a lovable freaking maniac, right?"

"That you are," Amanda laughed. Sometimes Katy was a clown, light, almost giddy, but all that was undergirded by real depth. There was a strong foundation to Katy that people who only knew her superficially probably didn't see.

"So?"

"So what?"

"What's he like?"

"Hey, we've only been away for a few days, so—"

"So you're saying you haven't—"

"No, we haven't and we're not going to any—"

"So it's not that kind of a relationship, huh?"

"I'm not saying that either." Amanda looked over at Ryan again, like she was sizing him up for that kind of relationship. He was now adjusting a plastic leveling block under a rear tire. Today he wore a simple black T-shirt over Levis and rough brown sandals without socks. She watched his biceps flex as he worked the block into position under the tire and as his hair caught the afternoon breeze that had just kicked up. "All I can tell you is that we're having fun."

Katy sounded disappointed not to be getting some juicy news. But she quickly recovered. "So, are you really going to Austin?"

Amanda wanted to be honest with her best friend, but she didn't want to unravel the whole story that made their deception necessary, and she didn't want an off-hand moment of candor to wind up on Facebook, where God knows who would be watching. "We're being pretty spontaneous" was the vague answer she crafted.

Katy was again quiet. One thing Amanda loved about Katy is that she seemed to have the wisdom to know when to probe, really dig at you, and when to be quiet. Finally, Katy said, "You said you're having fun. That's really everything I wanted to hear."

As Amanda headed back to the Roadtrek after the call, she reflected upon their stressful day against the backdrop of this beautiful wilderness. She would put that behind her. Fun, she had told Katy. Fun it would be.

It's difficult to cook a meal together in the confined space of a small RV without bumping into each other. Ryan slipped behind Amanda to switch on the ceiling fan so they wouldn't set off the smoke alarm, while she tossed the stir fry on the stove. She felt him brush against her backside. "Sorry," he said perfunctorily.

Amanda's response may have been involuntary, but it wasn't perfunctory. She let out a little gasp, then was glad she was facing the stove, so he couldn't see her blush.

Later, they sat across from each other at the small table that folded out from under the sink. It was starting to get cold, so Amanda had pulled on her Patagonia jacket. Ryan said, "I want to show you something." He reached down next to the driver's seat and brought out the road atlas and laid it in front of Amanda. "Here, take a look at this."

Amanda began to page through the atlas but quickly stopped. "Oh my God," she gasped, "How come I didn't notice this the other day when we were planning our trip?"

Ryan shook his head slowly.

"Is this your mother's writing?"

Ryan nodded.

"This is incredible." She shook her head in disbelief. "And you just discovered this?"

"Yes. When we were leaving. Here, take a look at this entry." He turned to the New Mexico map and pointed out his mother's entry from Bandelier. She could see that his eyes were misting up.

Amanda read the entry, then looked up at Ryan. "So, she camped here?"

"Yes," he said. He gave Amanda a look of resignation—a look she hated to see. She settled back in her chair and watched him, her face expressionless, as he continued. "But I had left Los Alamos. You know why? I was laid off. I told you it was a downsizing. Right." His voice was cracking a bit. "They said it was a reduction in force due to funding cuts, but I know how the Lab works. They used those RIFs as opportunities to shed the dead wood in the organization. That's how I was viewed. Dead wood. Okay, not very glamorous, but that's my story, that's why I'm not so keen on coming back here."

She wouldn't buy into Ryan's self-absorption. "Have you considered that your mom left that atlas here for you to see? A gift? Maybe it's a long love letter?"

Ryan almost barked his response. "Oh, it's full of love all right. A mother's love that was never returned. Look out the window. It's beautiful, with the sunset flickering through the pines and junipers, the breeze just turning a bit cold. And my mother, alone, sitting here, thinking of me."

"I'm sorry," she said. His mouth was clenched shut and his eyes were puffy and red. She thought he might be about to cry. "Ryan, you said something about starting to get in touch with your mother's death. Maybe that's what this is. If it is, then it's a good thing, and it needs to happen."

"What didn't need to happen was her dying."

Amanda gave him a sad smile.

"I don't know," he continued. "I wasn't sure I'd be able to come here. And now I'm pretty sure I shouldn't have."

Amanda turned in her seat toward the galley and to the metal backsplash above the sink, where the magnet collection was arrayed across the wall. She selected the magnet from Glacier, the one with the mountain goat. She laid the magnet on the table between them and let it lie there for a few moments. Her eyes were cast down, her face without expression. Then she touched the magnet gently, allowing two fingers to move across its surface, tracing out the shape of the animal. Then she removed her hand and put her arm to her side.

Now she looked directly at Ryan. Her face was still expressionless. "You said something about the mountain goat being—and I remember your words exactly—majestic and free. There was something in your voice, something in your face, when you said that. Like you were following a dream." She looked down at the magnet again for a moment, then back at Ryan. "But maybe you don't believe that anymore."

They sat in silence for a while. Ryan stared at the magnet as if he were seeing it for the first time. Then he looked up at her, his eyes wide like she'd just splashed ice water in his face.

Amanda said, "That's why you said you were coming." She paused, then added, "That is why I came, too."

Chapter 33

It had always astounded Ryan that a place so beautiful and historically significant as Bandelier National Monument lay just a short drive away from Los Alamos, where he had lived and worked. It's a place of strange beauty, with steep, rust-colored canyons laced with forests of tall, eerie hoo-doos—bizarre conical rock formations caused by the erosion of the deposits from the volcanic eruptions that formed the region's mesas millions of years ago.

Even more significant was the complex of cliff dwellings built by the ancient peoples, the *Anasazi*, who lived here as far back as the twelfth century.

Ryan had hiked these trails many times, but this morning the canyon that stretched out from the Bandelier National Monument Visitor Center felt fresh and new. They began their exploration of the park with a hike up Frijoles Canyon, following a trail that extended for several miles along a small creek, shaded by pines, and past ancient dwellings carved into the south-facing cliff walls, accessible by wooden ladders and steps chiseled into the rock.

Amanda carried her small daypack, strapped on over a brightly-colored T-shirt from the de Young Art Museum in San Francisco. She wore khaki hiking shorts—revealing shapely legs that Ryan found distracting—and her tough-looking hiking boots over Smartwools.

The despair that Ryan had experienced last night had dissipated with the bright sunshine and the energetic gait of Amanda leading the way up the trail. She seemed set on not missing a thing. Following the hiking guide they'd picked up at the Visitor Center, she led them through the Big Kiva, a large circular stone remnant of an ancient communal gathering place. They stood in the center of the kiva in silence, which seemed like the appropriate response to a lonely place that nine-hundred years ago had been bustling with elders discussing community politics, women busy with workday chores, and laughing children running and playing.

Consulting the guide again, Amanda said, "I think there's a cliff house just ahead." A short walk led them to a wooden ladder and a twenty-foot climb up into the first of numerous cliff dwellings and other archaeological sites along the trail. Ryan followed her up the ladder, ignoring the natural scenery in favor of the muscles flexing in Amanda's smooth calves.

This dwelling was no more than a small, human-carved alcove, which the Spanish called a *cavate*. It was dark inside, and the ceiling was blackened from many campfires long ago, but they were able to make out faint petroglyphs on the cavate walls.

"These dwellings all face south," said Amanda. "I assume that's to collect the sunlight during the cold winter?"

"Exactly," said Ryan, stepping toward the opening and looking up at the rock above him. "I read that the cavates were cut back into the rock with just enough overhang to keep the summer midday sun from reaching the cave interior, but not so much as to prevent the winter sunlight—when the sun is lower in the sky—from warming the interior." He shook his head in a way that showed he was impressed. "These people were the pioneers of modern solar homes."

Turning slowly to take in the interior, Amanda said in a hushed tone, "I wonder what it was like to live here, to raise a family here."

"Yeah," said Ryan. Hands on hips, he looked out again through the cavate opening toward the wall on the opposite side of the canyon. "I wonder what they worried about. I don't think they had too many natural enemies here."

Amanda joined in the speculation. "And the brochure says that the canyon bottom was a fertile place to grow food, and the hunting must have been good." She breathed quietly and deeply, seeming to be profoundly moved by this place. "I wonder if they only worried about work and survival. Or did they think about love and future goals and how their children would turn out. Did they have longings?" She turned toward Ryan with the question.

Ryan bit his lip and nodded but said nothing.

"I suspect they did," Amanda said.

They stood in silence. Ryan's dark thoughts threatened to return, as he thought how there had been life here for hundreds of years. Now there was just this blackened cavate, the only evidence of the people who lived, laughed, cried, worked and died here.

After visiting several other cliff dwellings, they stopped beside the small creek at the canyon bottom. They sat on the trunk of a fallen tree and watched the eddies and bubbles stir, and twigs and leaves bounce across the surface of the busy water.

Ryan said, "I suspect this was an important place for the ancient people. The source of water. And I have seen trout in this creek."

"I wonder if they ever just sat here, like us, and enjoyed the peaceful feeling of this place."

Ryan looked at her. Her eyes were fixed on the creek, almost as if she were hypnotized. "I hope they did," he said.

After they visited several more cavates and a place called *Tyuonyi*, the stone walls of large structure on the canyon floor believed to have been a storage place for food, Amanda turned toward Ryan, placed a hand on his shoulder and said, "This has been great. I want to see some more."

Ryan grinned. "I think I know just the place. Want to go see a waterfall?"

She nodded with enthusiasm.

He led her back past the visitor center and away from the archaeological sites and down a narrow trail into a dense pine forest. After a mile, the trail emerged onto a narrow ledge, where they could hear the roar of water, then zigzagged down the side of the cliff to the base of a high, gushing waterfall.

"They call this the Upper Falls," Ryan said. "It's the same creek that flows through the canyon, but it looks a lot more dramatic here, doesn't it?"

Amanda found a rock to sit on and gestured for Ryan to join her. As he sat down, his thigh brushed against hers, and it made him catch his breath. He wondered if she experienced it as well.

It was cooler down here beneath the shade of the pines, and Ryan noticed the gooseflesh on Amanda's bare arms. "I wish I had a jacket to loan you," he said.

Amanda beamed. "I'll be okay. I've got you to keep me warm." She snuggled closer. He closed his eyes and soaked up the clean scent of her hair. He laid his head over onto hers, his cheek against her hair, and she did not protest.

Finally, Amanda stood and said, "Does the trail go farther?"

Ryan cleared his throat and stood also. He had to refocus his thoughts, then said, "The trail used to go on, down past another waterfall and on to the Rio Grande. It was a beautiful hike—I wish we could go there—but the trail has been closed since the big fire of, I think it was 2011. It was while I worked here. Burned over sixty percent of the park, and then terrible floods followed. Took out the trail to the river." He grimaced and shook his head slowly.

She turned back toward him. "That's too bad. But we've got this beautiful waterfall to enjoy."

Her eyes radiated with life on this perfect sunny morning. "Yes. The waterfall," he said, clearing his throat again.

They sat again on the rock. Amanda opened her pack to pull out some snacks, while Ryan removed a water bottle from his. While they were sorting out the food, Amanda glanced back up at the waterfall. "There are so many clichés about waterfalls, but what word comes to mind when you look at a waterfall?"

Good question. Ryan studied the water gushing over the rocky brink a good seventy-five feet above them. Powerful. Relentless. Eternal. These were words that first came to him. Yes, they were all clichés. But the one word that stuck with him this morning, perhaps a remnant from his sadness of last night, was not a cliché. The waterfall was constant, unstirred and unchanged by the circumstances of the moment, sadness or joy, it was all the same. That was the word: indifferent. He decided not to share this with Amanda. Instead, he shrugged. "I don't know. It's just beautiful."

Amanda nodded. "I think it's somehow nurturing. But maybe that's a cliché, too." She shrugged her shoulders, then handed Ryan a packet of string cheese. "Do you like string cheese?"

He unwrapped the cheese and took a bite. "It'll do for now," he laughed, "but string cheese has never been my favorite. Doesn't have much flavor." He paused, then added, "I know I'm talking to a Wisconsin girl here, who probably actually knows something about cheese, but I always thought string cheese tasted like pencil erasers."

Amanda laughed. "Yep, I'm a cheesehead, all right, but I kinda like string cheese." Then she assumed a look of fake compassion, turned large sorrowful eyes toward him, and said, "Our apologies, Mr. Browning, for not providing you with a fine aged cheddar from one of our cheese factories." Her look dissolved into giggles. "And anyway, what's wrong with pencil erasers? Bet you chewed up your fair share of them back in the second grade."

They shared the laughter, as he studied her beaming face. He then looked back up at the waterfall. Another word came to mind. Romantic.

Chapter 34

They pulled into the Smith's Supermarket parking lot after their morning hike in Bandelier and before heading up the hill, where Ryan had promised to give Amanda a drive-around tour of the Lab before stopping off for a late lunch at the main cafeteria.

Smith's was to be a quick stop to pick up grocery items they had missed at their first shopping stop in the high desert outside LA. But Ryan had just turned the shopping cart up the pasta aisle, when there dead ahead was Melissa—Lab group leader and former girlfriend—comparing items about halfway down the aisle. Ryan stopped in his tracks, then immediately backed the cart out of the aisle.

"Who was that?" asked Amanda.

Ryan sighed as he pushed the cart away from the pasta aisle. "God, an old girlfriend that I don't want to see."

"It ended badly?" Amanda was struggling to keep up with Ryan's fast pace.

"Yeah, she dumped me. So I'd rather not have a nice little chat right now, if you know what I mean." He shot her a sheepish look.

Amanda nodded knowingly. "Do you want to leave?"

"Let's try to get our stuff, then get out of here. I don't want to be a complete wimp about this."

They shopped for a few more items. Then, as they turned up the canned goods aisle, Ryan ran right into Melissa, literally almost crashed his cart into hers.

Melissa hadn't changed a bit. A tailored suit—the kind she had started wearing after her group leader promotion—hung in a dignified way on her angular frame. (She had told Ryan at the time of her promotion that she had to start learning more about power-dressing if she was going to run with the big dogs, literally her words). Her shoulder-length brown hair hung straight in a no-nonsense way. She had an attractive face, with inquisitive and intelligent eyes befitting of a chemistry researcher.

She was with Alan Hixley—apparently the successor to Ryan in the love-life category—who Ryan recalled was another mid-level manager over in Space Sciences or somewhere; he wasn't sure. Hixley was stooped over, examining the labels beneath the display of tomato sauce. He wore a green-striped polo shirt over Bermuda shorts and white socks with Hush-Puppies. All that was missing to complete a Lab-nerd outfit was a pocket protector.

When Melissa began speaking to Ryan, Hixley looked up blankly at him, adjusting his thick-lens glasses, then went back to his tomato-sauce analysis.

"Ryan Browning," she gasped with fake joy, "is that really you?"

Ryan was sure she didn't want to see him any more than he wanted to see her. He nodded. "Melissa, it's good to see you."

At this point, Hixley interjected, "Melissa, the Del Monte is 11 cents per ounce, the house brand is only 8.4 cents per ounce. Easy call, I say."

Melissa seemed to ignore Hixley. "You know, I never got a chance to talk with you after the RIF—that must have been a bummer."

Yeah, it was a bummer, Ryan thought. And you didn't have the chance to pick up the phone and talk? More likely, you were embarrassed to be associated with a loser, now that you were on the way up. He didn't say that. What he said was, "No problem." He blew out a nervous breath. "So, what are you up to?"

"Oh, just group-leadery stuff, you know. Working on the budget and getting some new proposals ready. Performance evaluations for the group. Doing some strategic planning with the senior management." Melissa sighed like the burden of being a manager was a heavy one to bear, then continued. "Trying hard to find a little time to be a researcher after all that." She ended her list of noteworthy accomplishments with a little laugh of superiority. "So how's it been with you? Oh, you did get another job, didn't you?"

Ryan licked his lips and looked around, as if there might be a wormhole he could slip into and reappear in another dimension. He shrugged and began to speak.

Just then, Amanda, who apparently had heard everything in the background, stepped up beside Ryan. She moved in next to him and slipped her arm around him, pulling him close. He could swear she was pushing her breasts out just a little more than normal. "Hey, baby," she breathed, "this some old science buddy of yours? You going to introduce me?"

Melissa's mouth fell open. Ryan could barely contain his laughter. As he was crafting his response, Hixley popped his head up again. "On the other hand," he said, with the same seriousness he probably used in discussing manned missions to Mars, "the Hunts appears to be the densest of them all. Yes, it's 11.3 cents per ounce, but I think we could cut it with water and be miles ahead." He was beaming at his discovery.

Melissa sighed as Ryan said, "Melissa, I'd like you to meet Amanda Seward from Manhattan Beach, California. She's a fine art historian." Ryan stuck the word 'fine' in there for a little more effect.

Melissa, now looking wilted, gave Amanda a brief nod and a quick tight-lipped, I-hate-you smile, then said, "Well, it was nice seeing you today." Without waiting for a response, she busied herself in helping Hixley complete his tomato sauce research.

Ryan was laughing out loud as they turned into the next aisle. "Amanda, you are, what can I say, something else altogether."

She gave him a little punch on the shoulder, accompanied by a sympathetic smile. "Happy to help out," she said.

Chapter 35

Amanda knew that Los Alamos National Laboratory held an important place in American history, but she was learning that it is a strange place. It's set in the middle of some of the most remote wilderness in the country. And that was on purpose. When the government was looking for an out-of-the-way location to develop the atomic bomb, back in the early 1940s, they needed a place where scientists and engineers could work in secrecy, without worrying about outsiders wandering in. The Lab, as locals call it, sprawls over forty-three square miles—the size of San Francisco—of forested mesa tops formed by an ancient volcanic eruption so violent that rocks ejected from the blast have been found as far away as Oklahoma. The place would probably be a national park if it weren't a national laboratory.

The Lab, one of the largest science research facilities in the world, employs ten thousand people with an annual budget of over two billion dollars, and the employees work at far-flung sites miles apart, in buildings ranging from ultra-modern state-of-the-art structures that could have won architectural awards, to old metal sheds the folks who began the Manhattan Project probably designated as temporary seventy years ago.

It's where the atomic bomb was invented, but today the Lab covers the gamut of science research, from biology to computer science to particle physics, while still having a leadership role in the design and stewardship of nuclear weapons. The little town of Los Alamos is said to have the highest concentration of Ph.D.'s in the world.

It was also the place where Ryan used to work. Except for this last item, these were things Amanda learned from gleaning various websites on her phone, from her bed in the back of the van.

After the morning hike and the encounter with Ryan's old girlfriend, Ryan took her on a driving tour—first around the town of Los Alamos, then around the Lab. The town didn't look much different from any other modern small town, other than the stunning backdrop of high mountains to the west. A bank, a clothing store, a movie-theater, a modern library, restaurants and even a Starbucks made Amanda feel like she could have been almost anywhere.

But looks, she knew, can be deceiving. "I'm surprised we're actually able to drive around here. I read that this used to be a secret town."

"Yeah, it's a pretty normal place today, but up until the sixties the town was closed, and you had to flash your Lab security badge just to get in. There's still an old guard tower out on the east end of town, where the entrance gate used to be."

Ryan turned into the parking lot of a strip mall, across the street from a bank and a Subway. A large sign, supported by pillars of stacked flagstone slabs that reminded Amanda of the Lookout Studio at the Grand Canyon, said this was the Bradbury Science Museum. "Better warn you," Ryan laughed, as they climbed down out of the van, "this isn't going to be like the art museums you're used to."

The museum was dedicated to showing off the history of the Lab, especially the development of the atomic bomb back in the forties. Amanda even got to touch a replica of the Fat Man bomb, the atomic bomb built at Los Alamos and detonated over Nagasaki, Japan. As she tentatively touched the yellow metal surface of the big round device, she thought about the Judy Chicago painting they'd seen in Santa Fe and the burns on the woman's arms and the despair on her face. She let out a big sigh, as she felt her eyes growing misty.

Ryan put a hand on her arm and said, "Yeah, this is pretty heavy stuff, isn't it?"

Amanda couldn't take her eyes off the bomb. "How many people did this thing kill?" she asked.

Ryan was quiet for a moment, as he scanned the printed description off to the side of the display. Then he turned to her and blew out a big breath. "It says eighty thousand."

Amanda nodded, unable to say anything. They stood in silence for a while before slowly moving on to other displays.

Despite the sobering reality about nuclear weapons that the museum presented, Amanda found the place fascinating. She was pleased to see there was even a display of ideas in opposition to the development and testing of nuclear weapons. And her spirits were further lifted, as she wandered among the many displays of modern research conducted by the Lab, ranging from development of new medical diagnostics to experimental probes for life on other planets.

The Lab site was just across a high bridge, spanning a deep wooded canyon between mesas. It was not like anything she had expected. She was surprised that so much of this secret place was open to the public and how the people driving around the Lab site looked like employees from anywhere else—maybe First Federal or Johnny Rockets.

She wouldn't remember much about the many buildings that Ryan pointed out on their drive—there were so many of them. He rattled off the names of various organizations that occupied the buildings or the names of experimental facilities—many of them acronyms that only an insider could decipher—where the scientific research was conducted. Finally, he pulled into a parking lot in front of a modern brick building, with three floors of dark windows. He killed the engine, then turned to her and said, letting out a sigh as he did, "This is where I used to work."

Amanda leaned forward to get a better look at the building. "Can we go inside?"

Ryan took a deep breath, then let it out slowly. "No. You'd need a security badge. Anyway ..." he said. "I just ..." He shook his head, then didn't complete the sentence.

Amanda wished she hadn't asked to go inside. It was probably hard enough for Ryan just to bring her here into the parking lot. "Ryan," she said, forcing an upbeat mood, "I know you were in physics here, but I never heard what you worked on."

"Yeah, I probably should've said something about that, instead of just whining." He was avoiding eye contact, and Amanda suspected he was still embarrassed by last night's meltdown about losing his job. Now he looked at her. "I was working on a topic called fusion. Ever heard of it?"

"It means bringing things together, or something like that. Right?"

"Yes. In physics it's about bringing atoms together so that they actually fuse into a new type of atom. And when you do that, energy is released."

"So, in physics, fusion is about producing energy?"

He now turned toward her. "That's right. But it's a very hard problem. The idea is to create energy the same way the sun produces energy. By bringing hydrogen atoms close enough together that they fuse into a helium atom, and in the process, an energetic particle is produced that can be used to generate heat." He balled his hands into fists, then brought them together to dramatize his explanation. He looked like some Nobel-Prize kind of intellectual, giving a lecture on his work.

"And it's special because?"

"It's special because, if it actually worked, we could use sea water as a fuel, since that would be an almost inexhaustible source of hydrogen. You know, H-two-O. And also because it wouldn't produce harmful byproducts like nuclear reactors or coal mining do."

"Sounds great. Why don't we just do it?"

"Yeah. So that's the sticking point." Ryan laughed. "The problem is that it's very hard to make a fusion reaction that's useful. That is, one that produces more energy than it takes to create the reaction in the first place."

"But you said the sun—"

"The sun produces the energy needed to create the reaction by its huge gravitational fields. We don't have a handy energy source like that on earth."

"So has it been achieved on earth?"

"Well, yes, in a nuclear weapon, where you use a fission bomb to—"

"Like the Fat Man?"

"Yes, you'd use that to set off the fusion reaction. Obviously, we aren't going to use devices like that in power plants in somebody's hometown." He laughed. He seemed to be relaxing a bit now, as he got more and more into talking about his old work. Amanda didn't want him to stop. "So far," he said, "limited success has been achieved at big, and very expensive, experimental facilities around the world."

"How do they do it?"

"With giant lasers or magnetic fields."

"And you say it's expensive?"

"We're talking about many billions of dollars. At least that's what the largest facilities, here in the United States and in France, are costing."

"But unlimited fuel and little pollution. Maybe it's worth it, huh?"

Ryan cocked his head and seemed to be analyzing her. There was a new twinkle in his eyes. He reached out a hand and let a finger trail down the side of her face. Then he cleared his throat and, reclaiming his professorial demeanor, said, "The problem with fusion is more than money. There are a lot of technical issues, too." He scratched his chin between his thumb and forefinger, then added, "People thought the fusion problem would be solved a long time ago. But it seems like every time one problem got solved, two new ones were discovered."

"Maybe it's impossible?"

"Some people would say that, but I think most physicists are fairly optimistic that we're finally getting there."

"And what exactly did you do, Ryan?"

"Well, inside that building is a large machine. I won't go into details, but the machine makes plasma." He paused, as if realizing he needed to clarify his words. "A plasma is a super-high-temperature form of matter. It doesn't exist naturally on earth, but actually makes up over 99% of the universe. Pretty strange, huh?"

Amanda didn't completely understand what Ryan was saying, but she nodded. She didn't want to derail his momentum.

"So I worked on experiments to study the plasmas that the machine made, with the goal of better understanding fusion reactions. I helped develop instruments that measured their temperatures and densities and things like that." Then he was quiet. He looked away from her, out the window toward the building where he had once worked.

Amanda wondered what was going through his mind now, but she didn't want to push it.

Then Ryan turned toward her again and said, "We're actually parked in the space where I used to park every day. I used to show up here and go to work in that building, and I thought I would always be doing that. Then one day, I was told I had to leave. And then I thought I'd never come back. So, I hope you understand that it feels pretty weird being here." He let out a big sigh.

Amanda laid a hand on his arm and stroked it gently. "I am really grateful for the tour you're giving me." She leaned over and gave him a soft kiss on the mouth, then pulled back and said with a gentle smile, "I seem to recall you promising me a late lunch. A girl gets hungry out here on the mesa tops."

Chapter 36

Amanda had expected the Otowi Café—a large cafeteria in the central part of the Lab, amidst a cluster of modern glass and steel buildings—to be a gathering place for stereotypical science geeks. She should have known better, because, after all, Ryan was hardly a geek. There were people of all kinds here. A group of laughing young student types, wearing cutoffs and T-shirts with logos for rock groups she'd never heard of, clowned around like high school kids. She wondered if that's what Ryan was like when he was an intern here. Next to the students, an old guy in a musty-looking wool jacket and baggy gabardine slacks that the Goodwill might reject moved slowly, mumbling to himself, probably contemplating dark matter. He looked like he might have known Einstein. And there was everything in between. She heard multiple foreign languages spoken, as people carried their trays to tables in a large dining area, surrounded by windows affording sweeping views of the Laboratory site. As she selected her food items and they waited in the check-out line among this curious collection of people, Amanda wondered if she might be standing next to a future Nobel laureate.

Ryan led the way toward an empty table near a large window, looking out onto a large complex of buildings, almost a city. Amanda took note that he selected a table far from the others, and she understood that he might not want to encounter former colleagues, who might at least make him uncomfortable and at worst rub salt into old wounds.

"Okay, I don't make any claims about the food," he said, with a hollow chuckle, clearly trying to force some levity. "After all, it's still a cafeteria. Better than dorm food, I will say that much."

It was a lively environment, filled with animated conversations and laughter, and it felt good to be here. Somehow, she had expected small groups of dour old men, huddled together and puzzling over scientific documents—grumpy guys who would shoot you disapproving glowers if you laughed.

Ryan breathed out nervously, barely disguising his anxiety, as they took their seats. She was determined to keep the mood upbeat. "It's really fun being here with you, Ryan," she said, then turned her attention to the view beyond the window. "So, what are those buildings?"

Ryan pointed out the library and a large glass structure that housed the administrative offices and parts of the theoretical physics divisions.

"May I join you?" The voice came from behind them, and Amanda could see Ryan tense up. He turned and seemed to recognize a gray-haired man, disheveled in a well-worn sweater, then he visibly relaxed.

Ryan stood and reached out to shake hands. "George, it's good to see you." It was the most animation she'd seen in him since they'd arrived on the Lab site. "I want you to meet my friend, Amanda Seward. Amanda, this is George Thomas. He's one of the best theoretical physicists around here. And he's an old friend."

George Thomas looked to be in his seventies, but his face was smooth and pale, as if he'd rarely been outdoors. He looked frail. But his eyes, a bright blue, were penetrating yet compassionate, as if he not only saw right through you, but also understood and had sympathy for your situation.

"Amanda Seward," Thomas said, seeming to savor the name as he slid into his chair. "It's good to see that Ryan is in the company of high-class colleagues these days." His eyes twinkled, and Amanda took it as a compliment.

"So, uh … Dr. Thomas? You've known Ryan a long—"

"Just call me George, please," he smiled.

"Thank you. You've known Ryan a long time?"

George gave Ryan an appreciative look, then returned his gaze to Amanda. "Sure have. I've always been high on him. Letting him go was one of the biggest mistakes this place ever made."

Amanda could sense Ryan glowing, as he laughingly brushed off the compliment. "George is one of the best minds at the Lab, Amanda, but he's a terrible judge of character."

"Well, I wasn't wrong about you." George Thomas had a constant gentle smile that Amanda found calming. She could imagine that such a disarming smile went a long way in persuading colleagues during heated science debates.

"So you work on fusion, too, George?" she asked.

Ryan cut in. "Actually, George is one of the Lab's last renaissance scientists. Works on fusion, but also works on a lot of other things. He's a Lab Fellow. That means he pretty much works on whatever he wants."

"But of course, like almost everyone around a place like this, I've always been interested in fusion."

"So what do you think, George? Ryan told me that there are still a lot of technical problems." She was doing her best to show interest in something so important to Ryan.

George Thomas nodded. "There certainly are, but it seems like we're finally gaining on it. Fusion has been a deceptive dream, its grasp as slippery as a bar of soap in the shower." He paused as he and Ryan shared an insider chuckle about this. "Back in the sixties, experts were saying a viable fusion energy source was just ten years away. Today, they're still saying that." He shook his head while he laughed. "The brightest minds of the last two generations have worked on fusion."

"Like chasing a rainbow?" she asked.

George seemed to ponder the image. "That's a pretty good way of putting it," he said. "If we ever get there, the pot of gold will be substantial." He then turned his attention back to Ryan. "So, what have you been up to, Ryan?"

Ryan shook his head and looked down. Amanda felt the bite of acid in her stomach, as she anguished for him. He looked up into George's caring eyes and said, "To tell you the truth, it hasn't been all that great. I've been working for a small company in the LA area, working on the flow properties of powders and aerosols, but I'm not there anymore."

George nodded and chewed his lip, but stayed quiet as Ryan told him the whole story. When he had finished, George looked at Amanda and smiled, then turned his gaze again upon Ryan. "I've been around a long time, Ryan, and I've seen a lot of things happen. Just like fusion experiments, episodes in life don't always work out as hoped for. But you need to hear this." He turned again toward Amanda and added, "And you need to hear it too, young lady. Ryan Browning is a first-class scientist, but he's not like some of the others around here. He's a scientist, yes, but he's more than that. Always took a broader view of things than most. Maybe that wasn't appreciated by his bosses, but I think it's just the kind of attitude we need more of." He paused, then added, "Maybe it doesn't matter much what an old coot like me thinks, but that's it."

Amanda thought she could see tears welling up in Ryan's eyes. He nodded and smiled, then reached out and laid his hand on George's shoulder. "It matters a lot," he said.

While Ryan had been telling George his story, Amanda felt a growing uneasiness, and it wasn't because of anything Ryan or George was saying. She turned and glanced behind her to see a man at the next table, looking right at her. He had not been there when they had arrived, so he must have intentionally chosen the table near them. He appeared to be in his forties, thin, with thick, dark hair combed to one side. Probably just another scientist, but somehow this didn't feel right. When their eyes met, the man quickly looked down at a notebook he apparently had been writing in.

Now Amanda leaned toward Ryan and whispered, "There's a creepy guy behind us, and I think he's watching us. Is that someone you know?"

Ryan, trying not to be obvious, turned and looked at the man, then back at Amanda. "He does look familiar, but I don't know who he is. Probably some Lab guy I've seen around." Then he laughed. "There are a lot of unusual people around a place like this. Being creepy is actually pretty normal for a science lab."

Amanda didn't share the moment of levity. She looked back at the man again. His eyes were locked on her again, but then he quickly looked down again at his notebook. She felt gooseflesh on her arms, but turned back toward Ryan and George and resolved to put this behind her.

Chapter 37

You haven't really camped until you've sat around a campfire. There's something primitive and essential about setting the wood, lighting the kindling, and getting a roaring fire going that satisfies primitive instincts. Maybe it's our caveman needs to protect ourselves against the creatures of the darkness or fend off the cold of the night ahead. Or maybe it's deeper. Maybe the glowing coals and crackling sparks connect us in some inexpressible way to our more ancient roots—the fiery moments of creation, the incinerating cauldron from which the stars and our earth and each of us were born. But maybe those explanations, Ryan thought, are too arcane, too obscure.

Maybe it's something more personal—maybe a campfire is a source of shared warmth around which things become simpler, more honest, a place where truths can be told, where truths can be understood.

After leaving both the Grand Canyon and Santa Fe in a hurry—with many things still to see—it felt good to be spending a second night at Juniper Campground. Darkness had fallen and the campground was no more than half full, which created a quiet and isolated environment. They had parked the Roadtrek in an empty part of the campground, as far as they could get from noisy neighbors.

After Ryan laid another piece of wood onto the fire, he sat back in his camp chair and gazed into the flames for a while, then said to Amanda, "So, tell me more about your parents. You said you haven't seen them much."

Amanda poked at the fire with a stick, then said, "I think I let them down."

Ryan leaned forward, his elbows on his knees, and watched the warm glow of the flames dance on her face, still cast down toward the fire. "Did they ever say that?"

Now she looked up at Ryan. "They didn't have to. I was the first person in my family to go to college, and that was after I'd worked for two years after high school as a hostess at a supper club in Wausau." She sighed. "They were so proud that I got accepted to Madison."

Ryan wanted to be encouraging. "They should have been proud, but I've got to say, I bet you were a knockout in that hostess job."

"As a matter of fact, I was." She gave him a smile that could evolve into a laugh, her eyes twinkling with the fire. "And I needed the money for tuition." Then her look turned serious again. "I did well in college, too. They were so excited, even if I was doing my impractical art history thing." Now she poked at the fire some more. "So then I run off, just two semesters short of graduation, heading to LA to live with some guy. They were devastated." There was an emotional crack in her voice.

Ryan shifted his chair closer to her, using the excuse that the smoke was blowing his way. "I can see that, but you did what you felt you had to do."

Amanda gave him an impatient nod, accompanied by an unappreciative smirk. "Sure," she said with a shrug, then continued. "But when Richard left, it just sort of confirmed their suspicions. There was a huge 'I could have told you so' hanging over my head."

Ryan grimaced. "I'm sorry," he said softly.

"Then I was in the dating scene—as far as they were concerned. I think they built their understanding of the single life in LA from reruns of *Baywatch*."

Ryan laughed and that got Amanda going, too.

But then her somber mood returned. "Actually, I went for so many long dry periods without dating at all. A spinster. I thought I'd be an old spinster for sure."

He continued to watch her soft features bathed in the light of the flames. An old spinster was about the last thing that came to his mind. He smiled, encouraging her to continue.

"I think they thought I was just living the wild LA life. That's the way someone who's always lived in northern Wisconsin might see it. But …." She looked at him, and her face was sad. "You realize how many lonely people there are in LA?"

Ryan gave her an understanding nod. He was one of them.

"Wild. I think that's the way my parents see me, especially my dad."

"Your dad?"

"Yeah. He always expected that someday his little girl would bring a man home to meet them; that he and the young man would go off into the den and close the doors; and that the young man would ask for his daughter's hand in marriage."

She was quiet for a second, then let out a soft harrumpf sound and said, "Guess I blew that."

Ryan pursed his lips and fixed his eyes upon her. "You miss them, don't you?"

She looked at him helplessly, her eyes misting up, but she said nothing.

"And they miss you, too," he said.

Chapter 38

Later, as Amanda snuggled into her little nest—that's how she was starting to think of the full-sized bed behind the sheet—she marveled how, after only four nights in the van, it was starting to feel like home.

She wondered if her parents still had the wooden doll house she had as a child. It had a complete set of tiny furniture, miniature dishes, and even curtains and bedding. Living in this tiny space reminded her of that doll house and the fun times she'd had playing house. Yes, this was like playing house.

She looked around at her tiny space, barely larger than the bed itself. Windows on the side helped offset the claustrophobia and provided good air flow. There was plenty of lighting, powered by batteries hidden away somewhere beneath the floor. The wood paneling was a nice touch that made the space feel like it was somehow more than just the back of a van. She rolled up on one side and peered out the window. It was still and very dark. With no moon, she could begin to see stars, first a few and then, as her eyes adjusted to the night, thousands, she guessed. Off somewhere she heard an owl. Then a coyote. And here she was, far from the traffic that never ceased in Manhattan Beach. A wilderness quiet and pure. How did she get to be so lucky?

She rolled onto her back and clasped her hands behind her head. What was going on between Ryan and her? She thought about their campfire conversation, how he listened and drew her out. She was not used to that from a man. And the kisses, those wonderful kisses. She could easily have fallen into that, just gone with the flow, and was about to, wanted to. But she knew she needed to stop him. Going slow, she had said. Yes, she needed to go slow. Maybe not go at all.

What about Adam? Where did he play in all this? Was this trip finally helping her get away from him? Escape his power?

Ryan was so different from Adam. Adam was GQ-good-looking, but Ryan was also good looking—in a different kind of way. What was it Katy had said? A shaggy-poet kind of way? Adam had so many things going for him. With his looks, his talents, his money, he would always be in control, and he knew it. Why had he fallen for her? Maybe that's what was ultimately so attractive about him: that he seemed to have fallen for her, second-most-popular Amanda. That ego medicine had come at a good time in her life, a time when she was low, lonely and uncertain, mostly about herself. Adam made her feel like she was worth something, not because he treated her like she was worth something, but because he seemed to be worth so much. The way that ended should have been no surprise. Her muscles tensed as this thought passed through her mind—like a slow-moving garbage truck, smelly and ugly, working its way down the block—then left.

She scooped up Ryan's basketball from the corner of the bed and cradled it with two hands like she was preparing for a free throw. She wanted to go slow with Ryan for several reasons, which she could articulate now, because she had been thinking so much about them the past two days. First, she wasn't sure she had moved beyond Adam. Would she ever know for sure? Maybe it's that way when you are dumped, because it cuts and it hurts and it takes some of you—your self-esteem, your identity—with it.

But she also didn't want to go fast with Ryan because—good Lord, she'd only known him for a couple of days. There was that—but even more, he was somehow special, or maybe different was a better word. He was not like the confident, slick, and often self-centered men who are so abundant in west LA, men who could have everything they wanted and expected to have it and sometimes got it. With Ryan, it seemed different. He was, should she say it? Shy? In a way he was shy; he was quiet and deferential, respectful, seemed to genuinely care about what another person thought. But maybe he wasn't shy. Good Lord, he'd asked a complete stranger to leave town with him and shack up in a house no larger than a good-sized bathroom. Even Adam probably never would have had the guts or the imagination to do that. But there was even more about Ryan. A sort of simplicity. He was not simple, that was for sure—geez, Ph.D. in physics. She'd never dated a guy with a Ph.D. before. But it didn't seem like that mattered that much to him. He was, how could she say it, old-fashioned? Not in some prudish, corny, out-of-touch, uptight kind of way—no, he was decent in a way that seemed to exist only in old Jimmy Stewart movies.

During that first move, she had seemed to be in such control—good old in-control, ice-water Amanda. Not! She had thought she might faint when he first pulled her into his arms. She had felt tingles shoot down her legs. Felt her physical self and her emotional self go limp. She could not have denied him, if he had pushed it. But he hadn't, and she was glad he didn't, because that demonstrated something about his character. And it demonstrated something about what he thought about her character. And she wanted to live into that.

He was lying in there right now, not ten feet away. She could hear him softly stirring. What if he suddenly pulled open that sheet? What if? But he didn't. And for tonight, she was glad that he didn't.

Chapter 39

In just a few nights, Ryan had gotten used to sleeping in the folded-down passenger seat. At six-two, his head was pressed up against the back cushion of the second-row seat, and his feet hung over the edge of the front seat by a good six inches. Still, it wasn't too bad. There were curtains that pulled around the cabin windows—so it was dark enough to sleep—and the thought of Amanda, there in the bed just a few feet behind him, was a source of comfort. His mind was very capable of producing all kinds of fantasies, where she would suddenly step out from behind the curtain and come toward him, or he would hear her voice, inviting, calling his name. He could also fantasize about just stepping back there uninvited and being received, literally, with open arms.

But he had pushed these thoughts away before they could get too far. He needed to. Dickson was always there to feed him for a give-and-go and an easy two against Ohio State in the Final Four. Sometimes, but not always, this helped. It was becoming clear that Amanda was more than the object for some short-term fling. She was the real thing, someone worth investing in. And that meant showing restraint and letting things develop in accordance with her words that she needed to go slow.

He opened his laptop and laid it across his chest. Maybe he'd work on a new blog post. But in the past few days, he'd lost enthusiasm for his blog. His ideas about the human condition were muddied at best and, at worst, immature and just plain wrong. He had no fresh insights. Maybe at some point he'd show Amanda his writing, but not yet, not until he could be relatively certain that she wouldn't wrinkle her nose funny, like a skunk had just crawled inside and fouled the place. He couldn't bear to be so diminished in her sight.

He pulled the lid down and placed his laptop between the seats. He considered perusing his mother's comments—she's the one who should've been the blogger—but fatigue was now overcoming him. He closed his eyes, and a smile took him into sleep, as he replaced all other thoughts with the image of Melissa aghast, while the ravishing Amanda stood close to him—his little art history honey from Manhattan Beach.

In the midst of deep sleep, a soft click brought him suddenly awake. He knew instantly what it was. Someone had tested the outside handle on the locked passenger door. He bolted upright, his heart pounding like the New York Yankees were taking batting practice on his chest. He couldn't breathe.

Quickly, he stood and turned on the overhead cabin lights. He hesitated briefly before pulling open the curtains to look outside—what if he found himself staring into the barrel of a gun? He started the Roadtrek, turned on the headlights, then pulled back the curtains.

There was nothing there, but then he couldn't see very far out into the darkness.

"What's the ruckus?" asked a sleepy-sounding Amanda, who had just poked her head out from behind the sheet.

"Someone just tried to open the door of the Roadtrek."

"What?" Her voice took on a sudden sound of panic. She moved quickly toward him. "Is there someone out there?"

"I can't see anyone." He looked out through the curtains again.

She leaned down beside him and peered out. "Were you asleep?"

"Yes I was," he said defensively. "But I know what I heard."

She nodded. "I'm not doubting you," she said. "Just trying to understand what happened."

"I need to go outside and take a better look," he said, as the initial panic was subsiding.

"No, don't go out there," she said, taking hold of his arm. "Maybe it's nothing—probably is—but what if it's the people who were following us?"

"I'm not going to hide in here. Anyway, we're not going to get any sleep until we verify that no one's there."

She looked down, with a sigh of resignation.

Ryan found a flashlight, then opened the door and stepped out into the darkness, while Amanda kept watch from the doorway. She had picked up a windshield ice scraper from beneath the seat and held it like a soldier cradling his rifle.

He was barefoot and wore only a T-shirt and sweatpants—his sleeping attire—and the late-Spring chill bit into him.

He panned the flashlight, looking carefully out to the limit of its reach and listening for any telltale sound. There was nothing except the whisper of a soft breeze in the pines.

He clicked off the flashlight, as he entered and locked the Roadtrek, shaking his head. "Nothing," he said.

"Maybe it was just some kids from town, looking for an easy break-in opportunity."

"Yeah, maybe," he said, unconvinced.

"Look, Ryan, we've probably shaken whoever it was that was tailing us. Our Austin Facebook post should have done that. For the record, I'm sorry about being all paranoid about that creepy guy in the cafeteria today. I'm sure that was nothing. And this probably is, too."

"You're probably right," he said. He set the flashlight back on its shelf above the dash, ran a hand through his hair, then said, "Do you think you can sleep now?"

"Only if you give me a kiss." She moved up to him and gave him a soft kiss. Then she put a hand on each side of his face and pulled his face closer. The second kiss was long and passionate. Then she pulled away, as he was leaning in for another kiss.

"Good Lord, we better stop this now," she smiled wickedly. "Just enough kisses to help me sleep, but not so many that I'll be awake all night."

"You're tormenting me, you know that, don't you?" he smiled, not wanting to let her go.

"I know. I don't mean to. But yes, I know." She let a hand brush across his face as she turned and disappeared back behind the sheet.

Ryan stood alone, disoriented. Then he lay back down onto the reclined seat. He looked out the window into the darkness, then pulled the curtains closed. Somewhere out there—probably not far away, perhaps watching them now—was a person who had tried to enter their RV. He lay awake for a long time, thinking about intruders and kisses, neither of which helped him back into sleep.

Chapter 40

Ryan felt sorry for the huge grizzly bear pacing the front ledge of its tiny enclosure at the Denver Zoo, its long white claws clickety-clacking on the concrete surface at the edge of the deep moat that separated it from freedom.

The Denver Zoo is the crown jewel of City Park, a lush square mile in the middle of the city, featuring tennis courts, playgrounds, statues and monuments. It was late afternoon when Ryan and Amanda arrived, after a long but scenic seven-hour drive up from Bandelier. Staying in a metro area of two million was hardly Ryan's idea of a wilderness getaway, but Denver was about as far as they wanted to drive today. They planned to spend one night in the Denver area, then press on toward the Grand Tetons and Yellowstone—another two days beyond Denver—where they would linger for a while before heading on up to Bozeman to visit Uncle Wil.

As Ryan watched the grizzly, he pondered his love-hate relationship with zoos. While other small children were being entertained by *Curious George Goes to the Zoo* and Dr. Seuss' *If I Ran the Zoo*, Ryan was studying *The Encyclopedia of Animals*, a massive tome his mother had given him on his sixth birthday. He would spend hours studying the color photographs and the descriptions, and he was likely the only kid in the neighborhood who could identify a tapir or a pangolin.

His mother took him to the zoo at least once a year, and even back then Ryan was conflicted. He loved seeing the animals up close and learning about them and being part of the laughter and high-energy anticipation: *will the wolves be out today?* It was even more than that. The zoo made him feel connected, not just to other humans, but to all life.

But it was hard to watch captive animals struggling to make do in an artificial environment. It is said that man cannot live by bread alone, but neither can animals. The zoo animals had plenty to eat. They were safe from predators. They were protected from the elements and disease. But even a child could see that the caged animals were suffering.

The poor grizzly's enclosure was probably smaller than Ryan's claustrophobic house in Lawndale. He knew the range of a wild grizzly in Glacier National Park was up to fifty square miles, and he could not watch this bear and not feel sadness.

He wondered if the captive animals bore memories of their natural habitats—vast sweltering savannahs or dense jungles or the rocky ridges above a timberline snow field. Did these memories bring solace in captivity or did they only bring torment?

Maybe the animals troubled Ryan because they were too much like him. *What is my natural habitat?* he wondered. It certainly didn't seem like it was the suburbs of the noisy metropolis where he'd grown up. In fact, he had no memories of a natural habitat—a place where he belonged—only vague longings.

In a sense, he was like the caged animals at the Denver Zoo: vaccinated, fed and safe. Well, maybe he wasn't so safe. The last few days had challenged his feelings of safety. When he raced out the back door of that gallery in Santa Fe, perhaps he experienced something of the terror the springbok must feel when it spots the lion emerging from the high grass. And yet, for Ryan there had been something else. Fleeing danger down ancient streets, with a beautiful woman in hand—as frightened as he had been, there was a part of him that felt fully alive.

He looked over at Amanda, wearing those khaki hiking shorts and a pink racer back tank top on this sunny, seventyish day. She was also fascinated by zoos and had shared her childhood memories of her parents taking her to the Milwaukee Zoo and occasionally to the Brookfield Zoo in Chicago. So, it was no surprise that after their long drive today—she drove most of the way—they would wind up here.

The zoo was packed this afternoon, with almost every adult accompanied by young children. Amanda and Ryan were among the few childless couples there, amidst mothers and a few dads pushing strollers or chasing toddlers and grandparents buying snow cones and stuffed giraffes and generally spoiling their grandkids.

Despite her avowed interest in zoos, Amanda seemed to be more fascinated with the children than the animals. "Aw, isn't that little guy cute?" she said, pointing to a giggling toddler being photographed by his mom atop a plastic rhino. Or, "That is just darling," at the sight of tiny twins in a double stroller, both sporting fuzzy elephant ears.

As they watched a mom with her small son play in front of a lion built out of Legos, Amanda said, "How do you feel about children, Ryan?" Before he could answer, she blurted, "Oh, God, that's an awful question." Her blush was visible even in the bright sunlight. "Forget I said that."

"No, I think that's a fair question," he said, then cleared his throat. "I've—"

Just then a small boy came running down the walkway, arms waving wildly, screaming and sobbing. There was no parent in sight. "Mommy," he wailed, over and over.

Quickly, Amanda ran to the small boy, perhaps three, and knelt down next to him. "It's okay. We'll find your mommy."

Immediately, Amanda was joined by another woman, who also knelt down by the boy. "What is your name, son?" the woman said in a caring way.

Amanda scanned her surroundings, then called out to a man wearing a Denver Zoo employee shirt, "We've got a lost child over here." The man sprinted over, then spoke into a walkie-talkie. Within moments a loudspeaker announced that a lost child was waiting for his parent in front of the native animal exhibit.

"I hate to see a child separated like that," the woman said to Amanda, as they waited for the parent to arrive.

Amanda nodded. "I'm probably the only woman without kids here, so I guess I was able to drop everything and come running."

The other woman laughed. "Me too." After a moment, she added, "I have to confess that seeing all these beautiful kids makes me a little lonely."

Amanda smiled and extended a hand. "I'm Amanda," she said. "And this is Ryan," she added, looking up at him.

"Carol," said the woman. Ryan guessed she was about thirty-five, with long blonde hair framing a pale, delicate face. She looked like any mother you might run into at the zoo, wearing a white turtleneck, blue jeans, and Keens.

An anxious woman came running up the walkway, arms outstretched, with a mixture of relief and embarrassment on her face. "Marcus," she called, while she was still a ways off. Then she scooped her child up into her arms, looked at Amanda and Carol and the zoo employee and gushed, "Thank you so much." By now, a security person had appeared on the scene and asked the woman to show her identification. After flashing her ID, the woman and Marcus disappeared into the crowd.

"It's kind of hard being here without a child," said Carol, now that they were alone.

Amanda nodded but said nothing.

Then Carol added, "Are you from around here?"

"We're travelling," said Amanda.

"Yeah, me too. Where y'all headed?"

"More or less north," Amanda said, "probably up …." She hesitated, then shot a glance at Ryan. "Well, we're not sure yet," she said.

Carol smiled at Amanda and Ryan, as she backed away. "Yeah, I'm headed north, too. Maybe I'll see you along the way." She gave a shy little wave, then left.

Later in the afternoon, just as they got back into the Roadtrek, there was an odd beep from Amanda's phone. "Oh," said Amanda, digging for her phone, "that's Facebook Messenger." She tapped her phone a few times, then read a message. Her lips moved as she read the words, as if she were reading them out loud. Yet, she made no sound.

"Is everything okay?" Ryan asked.

"Yes, fine," she said, pushing the phone back down into her pocket. But there was now an ashen hue to her face, like something terrible had just happened.

Chapter 41

What a jerk she was. Amanda had been cold to Ryan on the way back to the campground, and he didn't deserve it. He'd seemed full of energy after their great day at the zoo, bubbling with enthusiasm about the animals, but after that message, she'd just watched in silence out the window.

Their campsite—in Cherry Creek State Park, just southeast of downtown Denver—was a pull-through site under lush green trees, yet just blocks away from metro traffic congestion and big-city noise. A far cry from the wilderness feel at Bandelier. Amanda now committed to putting on her game face, but she was off-balance, uncertain, freaking crazy.

While Ryan worked to set up the van, Amanda paced. Nearly exploding with conflict, guilt, affirmation and shame, she went over to him. When he turned toward her, she placed both palms on his chest and pushed him back up against the van and kissed him hard on the mouth. When she pulled away, he was wide-eyed, his mouth open. She knew that there were many good reasons to kiss Ryan. But this wasn't one of them. Then she turned and walked toward the restroom.

As soon as she was out of sight of Ryan, she pulled out her phone and read the message again.

You're driving me crazy, Amanda. Your posts make me realize how much I've missed you. I never really considered that we broke up. I want you back in my arms. Adam

She thought about replying, but then decided to ignore the message. It was best to pretend that this never happened. She took a few more steps toward the restroom, determined to move on, then stopped and walked out to a grassy area, where people walked their dogs, and called Katy.

She told Katy about the message, about her being conflicted and completely off balance.

"Oh, Lord," said Katy, "I was afraid that was going to happen." Amanda could hear her exhale an audible breath. Then silence. "So," said Katy, "what are you going to do?"

"I don't know," shrieked Amanda. She could let it out with Katy. She actually threw one arm into the air, palm up, as if in surrender or exasperation or to implore some deity.

"So where does the new guy—Ryan—fit into all this?"

"That's just it. A few days ago, I thought I knew what I hoped for. Now I'm not so sure."

"Say more."

Amanda was quiet for a while. She paced around the grassy dog area and watched an elderly man walk a small Chihuahua. "Come on, Louie, you can do it," he cajoled. She ran one hand through her hair, pulling it to the back of her head. "Ryan," she said. "He's a great guy. Hell, if I let this thing get out of hand, I could get swept away here." She paused. "Yeah, that could happen," she said, as if she were now just realizing that herself. "But I'm working hard to keep the lid on things."

The usually loquacious Katy's response was, "Why?"

Amanda was silent. She paced some more. Now she watched a teenager with a big head-strong Lab being pulled around the walking area. She laughed softly, wondering who was controlling who.

"Why is that?" Katy repeated.

"Huh?"

"Why are you trying so hard to keep the lid on things?"

Another sigh. "I don't know. Maybe I'm just afraid of things getting too complicated. After all, we're sleeping ten feet apart in a van."

Katy laughed. "And the problem with that is …?"

Amanda laughed, too, which she greatly needed. "The problem is I just don't know anything right now."

"Well, you know what I think of Adam," Katy said.

"Yeah, I know," Amanda groaned. "You can't stand him, but—"

"It's not that I can't stand him. He's a hunk for sure, and he's loaded. What's there not to be able to stand? What I can't stand is how you are with him."

Amanda had heard all this before, and she didn't need to hear it again now. "Please Katy, not that same broken record again. I'm not—"

"Oh, okay, I'll shut up, but I thought you called to hear some honest words from someone who cares about you."

Amanda cringed. "I'm just not sure what I want right now."

"Well, I'll just say this and then I'll be quiet. Seems like you'd made a decisive move when you hopped into that RV and headed out to Shangri-La. That you were taking control of your life, that the old Amanda was back. But then you get one crappy text—and I mean it was crappy; I don't recall hearing the word *love* in it—and you're suddenly ready to roll over and jump right back into that mess. I mean, grow up, girl." Katy's voice had raised a few decibels on that last sentence, and Amanda recoiled, actually moving the phone a little farther from her ear. Then Katy said, softer, now sounding almost resigned, "Okay, end of lecture. Sorry to be such a know-it-all."

When they were off the phone, Amanda lingered in the dog-walking park. She watched a middle-aged woman walking a French bulldog. The woman spoke cooing words to the dog. "Okay, Lena, you cute little rascal you, let's do our business, so we can go back and cuddle up." There was such sweetness, such love in the woman's voice. Amanda wanted to cry, but she didn't. What she really wanted was someone to tell her they loved her and take her home and cuddle up.

Chapter 42

Amanda was grateful that tonight was her turn to prepare dinner, and she thought how preparing dinner can be a gift or a curse. When it's no more than something you're required to do when you'd rather be doing something else, when you're boiling pasta and already anticipating how hard it's going to be to scrub that pan later, then it's a curse. But when you're preparing a meal for someone you love, it is a gift. Or—which was the situation Amanda found herself in tonight—when the busy work of preparing a meal serves as a distraction from things that are too painful or awkward to confront, then it's also a gift.

It had now become almost an evening ritual to have dinner either at the tiny table that folded out from beneath the sink or at the campsite picnic table just outside the door. Tonight, with an evening thunderstorm brewing, they opted for the fold-out table in the Roadtrek. Dinner proceeded with a minimum of conversation. Amanda was still caught up in the events of the afternoon, following the text from Adam, and she was certain that Ryan was in a place of uncertainty after that unexpected sloppy kiss. Perhaps he wanted to ask her about that—she wouldn't know what to say. Perhaps he wanted an encore—she wasn't sure how she'd handle that.

And so they munched their way, with shallow chitchat, through their bowtie noodles and brats—your cuisine choices are limited when you're cooking on a two-burner stove top in a cramped space.

As they were finishing their meal, Ryan dabbed his face with his napkin, folded it and placed it beside his plate, then reached behind him and pulled out the road atlas. "Want to take a look at my mother's entries for Colorado?"

Amanda wasted no time in shifting in her seat to move closer to him, aware of the significance of this invitation and happy to have another diversion from her dark thoughts of the afternoon.

They perused his mother's notes, written in small, neat cursive, filling the borders around the edges of the pages of the atlas. Most of the entries were logistical: *Ice on Vail Pass will keep me in Idaho Springs for another day*, and *Now glad I had to stop and get the wipers fixed in Fort Morgan—such nice people.* This one made them both laugh: *Freezing my butt off in Steamboat Springs. Kinda wishing I was on a real steamboat on the Mississippi right now.*

The longest entry was written across the mostly blank space of the southeastern portion of the state:

Although I lived in LA most of my life, I still feel lost in big cities. Denver is no different. It's a big-city base camp for outdoors types: thin, muscular young people in active wear, looking like runway models for the Under Armor collection, driving Outbacks loaded with Yakima racks, bikes, kayaks and skis. There are lots of joggers. They live in older neighborhoods, face-lifted by DIY updates and renovations, adjacent to ghettos full of sad faces slowly being pushed out by trendy new galleries, microbreweries and yoga studios. Like almost any big city, Denver is haunted by the presence of the poor, gathered here, not working so much on burning carbs or finding the best double-black-diamond ski runs as just finding some hope.

They were silent for a while, then Amanda whispered in the near darkness, "Your mother was very thoughtful."

Ryan looked down, then licked his lips, like his mouth was dry, and reached for his water bottle. His hand seemed to be shaking. Finally, he said, "She really saw things." After a pause, he gave out a self-deprecating chuckle and said, "All I did was go to the zoo."

"Sounds like she was a wise woman," Amanda said, then laid her hand atop his. A change of topic would seem to be in order. In an upbeat voice, she said, "I realize that I haven't yet shown you my gallery."

Ryan looked at her with confused eyes, then said, "Gallery?"

"You know, those tubes of art prints that I hauled along? The ones back there next to Kobe's basketball?" She gave him a smile designed to lift his spirits, a smile that could easily evolve into laughter.

Now a smile returned to his face. "I'd love to see them." This probably was Ryan being polite rather than really interested, but she would accept his response at face value.

Amanda led Ryan to the rear of the van, flicked on the overhead light, and set about removing the rolled prints from the long tubes. When she was done, about a dozen prints lay, one atop another, on the bed.

They pondered the first one for a while. Then Amanda said, "It's called *Two Sisters on the Terrace*. It's a pretty famous painting by Renoir, from the Art Institute in Chicago. I went there whenever I could, so my gallery reflects that—it's where I was able to buy prints."

The painting showed a young girl, probably a teenager, with her sister, who's five or six. It's a happy picture. There are flowers everywhere—it's apparently Springtime—and there is a basket with colorful balls of twine on a table before them. Amanda said, "It was a staged picture, a portrait of people Renoir was commissioned to paint. We know the oldest sister was eighteen at the time, an aspiring actress. We don't know anything about the younger girl. What I love is its happiness, its freshness, and I'm sure that's what Renoir was trying to capture. That's what you see when you look at it superficially."

Ryan held his chin between his thumb and forefinger, pondering the painting, as Amanda continued.

"Yet, in the older sister's eyes, there is something more, maybe a look into who she really is. Ambiguity, yes? Something deeper going on than just simple enjoyment of the beautiful environment. What do you think is going on with her, Ryan?"

Ryan scratched his head. "Yeah, I see what you're saying. I love this print, by the way. I'd love to see the actual painting." He said it in such a way that Amanda envisioned him seeing it with her. He looked at her with a nervous, teacher-called-him-to-the-blackboard kind of look, sighed, then returned his eyes to the print. "What I see is a knowing, maybe a loss of innocence, an awareness perhaps that she cannot articulate or understand even, that life—maybe her personal life—is more complicated than she had once thought." He was silent for a moment, apparently lost in thought, before he continued. "While the surroundings are blatantly obvious: beauty and color and life and radiance, I think her eyes say there is something more, something more complex." He stopped and pondered this in silence again, never taking his eyes off the print. Then he said, "And you notice that while the small child is looking directly at the painter, the older girl averts her eyes. I wonder why that is. Is she looking at something else, or has her self-awareness made it too hard to look directly at the painter?" He paused, then shrugged and said, "I don't know, but that's what I see. Maybe that's not right, huh?"

Amanda looked at Ryan with wide eyes, impressed. No, blown away was more like it. "I don't know if it's right or not," she said. "I have no way of knowing what was going through Renoir's mind or the young girl's mind. But there is something, isn't there, that is more than what's obvious. Maybe we want to look at her, to understand who she really is because ultimately we want to understand who we really are."

Ryan chewed on his lip, considering this. "Yeah. So you're saying that maybe what I see could be different from what someone else may see."

Amanda nodded. "Okay, maybe this is far-fetched, and I've never thought about it this way before, but maybe this girl can serve as an intermediary." She stared at the print like she was seeing it for the first time. "By both of us gazing into her life and allowing that to reflect back into our lives, maybe we can begin to understand more about each other by engaging this girl together. Does that make sense?"

"It makes a lot of sense. Good God," he said, "this is really cool. I guess I've missed out on a lot of important stuff in my life." He looked at Amanda with what she interpreted as amazement in his eyes. "I love this," he said.

"You do grasp art. Maybe it's your photography. Maybe it's just who you are." She placed a hand on his cheek, then pulled it back quickly.

"Let's look at some more," he said.

They spent another hour going through the prints and discussing them.

Adam had never talked to her about her gallery.

Finally, Ryan said to her, "I'd like to see some of your painting."

Amanda swallowed to clear a sudden tightness in her throat. She gave her head a quick shake. "I wish I could paint," she said, "but I don't really have the talent for it." Avoiding eye contact, she added, too quickly, "I never thought I had very much to say." She felt his eyes on her, as a bead of sweat formed on her forehead.

"I think you'd be good," he whispered.

Amanda was very aware that they were standing over her bed—in her bedroom, if you could call it that. In less than a week, she had come to think of this small space as her bedroom. And here she was, standing here with this man, this very attractive man.

Chapter 43

S tanding with Amanda over the prints, in the tight
space of the rear of the Roadtrek, Ryan was aware of
more than just her beauty. It was her warmth, her energy, her
intelligence that invigorated him. *My life is very good*, he thought.
In this moment, it is very good.

Later that night, Ryan wrote a new blog post:

New Blog post

I still don't know how to select titles for my blog posts,
but I'll figure that out later. For now, just add that to the
pile of other things I feel clueless about. Why am I even
writing something here that pretends to offer insight to
others, when so often I have such little insight myself? And
yet, tonight that doesn't matter.

Yes, there's plenty for me to weep about. Tonight I
really miss my mother. Her profound writing makes me
realize how little I really knew her. What am I to do?

But then there is Amanda. Beautiful, smart, strong.
The way she handled Melissa, another bad thing that I had
allowed to torture me, showed me that I can move on. And
then the way she pointed me to that magnet, when I was
sinking into self-pity, showed me I can move on. The way

she looks beyond the obvious, like with that Renoir painting. And just her face; yes, just seeing her face.

Bad things happen, but I am learning what to do about it. It is possible to move beyond the pain. And, yes, a beautiful woman helps.

He leaned back in the captain's chair and sighed as he read the post again. He could never post this. It was too personal, revealed too much about his thoughts about Amanda. He selected all the text, then hit delete.

Chapter 44

"Might as well be back on the 405," Amanda mused and Ryan laughed, as they crawled along in the slow-and-go traffic. Fighting the morning craziness on I-25 northbound, from Denver all the way up to Fort Collins, was no fun.

But once they made it to the cut-off to US 287, which angles northwest up into Wyoming, things improved. The road wound through colorful, rocky outcrops, dotted with pines, as it traversed the lower flanks of the Rocky Mountain wilderness to the west. They crossed into Wyoming just south of Laramie, then hit I-80, which runs east-west across the southern part of the state.

This was big Wyoming country. Vast panoramas of high plains with distant snow-capped ranges stretched to infinity and made Amanda feel tiny. She was also feeling tiny because the thought of the 405, which made her tummy clench, brought images of LA and especially the troubling message from Adam. She had hoped for such a message: the wandering lover coming to his senses and crawling back, begging for forgiveness. Katy was right though—the message did fall short in the romance department. Typical Adam. But still. Funny thing was, she had hoped for this message, but now wished it hadn't come. It only stirred things up inside her, like some emotional Cuisinart on the puree setting. She had not replied to the message, and she was hoping to keep its existence out of her mind.

She looked over at Ryan. How long had she been with this man now? Less than a week. There'd been a few kisses, but nothing more. Yet there was definitely more going on here, lots more. In profile he reminded her of an Everest climber she'd seen in *Outside*. His tousled hair could use some styling help, yet its wildness was—let's face it—a turn-on. That patrician nose was the nose of a man looking forward, seeking adventure. The closely trimmed beard capped off the climber image.

She already knew that he was more than an Everest climber, more than a fearless thrills seeker. He was burdened by his mother's recent death, ashamed of his job loss, almost school-boy awkward in the romance department, and he had a genuine—if fledgling—appreciation for art. All this pointed to a man with a deeper, tender side.

Somewhere west of Laramie, but before the cutoff in Rawlins that would take them toward the Grand Tetons, her phone beeped. It was that odd Facebook Messenger beep. She silenced the phone, pushed it deeper into the pocket of her fleece and forced her attention to the passing landscape. But then, begrudgingly, she pulled it out again and read the message.

I'm going crazy without you. Please answer me. And who the hell is this Ryan guy?

She closed her eyes, wishing she hadn't checked the phone. Again she gazed out the window at the expanse of wild Wyoming speeding by. This was vintage Adam—sending texts, while taunting her into picking up the phone and making an actual call, which would show that she was the one who had caved, and the relationship could reignite, with him again in the driver's seat. She considered tossing the phone out the window, be done with it for good. But she didn't. Instead she keyed in a response.

So Bree must be history, huh? And Ryan ... she looked over at him briefly ... *he's just a guy.*

She hit the return key with a forceful tap, then immediately regretted that she had responded. Why bring up Bree anyway? Didn't this make her look jealous and needy? And Ryan—she looked over at him again—was definitely more than just a guy.

Chapter 45

Dark, opaque columns of intense, localized thunderstorms worked their way from west to east across the wide, desolate landscape, on an otherwise sunny day. Watching them—and worrying that they might run right into one—was Amanda and Ryan's main entertainment on the long drive across the high prairie between Rawlins and Dubois, Wyoming.

Ryan pondered the day. If he were still back in LA, he'd be settling in at work about now. But here he was, roaming free across wide-open spaces. He realized he didn't even know what day it was, and this pleased him. "Is this Monday or Tuesday?" he asked. He managed an apologetic laugh. "I usually know what day it is."

"Must mean the trip is accomplishing its purpose," Amanda said. Then she laughed and added, "I don't know either. I think it's Wednesday. Does that sound right?"

"Maybe. Geez. We should both be at work somewhere, but here we are out cruising across Wyoming. That'll look good on my resume." As soon as he said that, he cringed, thinking that being let go from his last two jobs also wouldn't look that great on his resume.

Her laughter stopped, and out of his peripheral vision, he could see her give him a serious look. "Some people might not hire somebody who took a break to travel around the country. But I would."

"And why is that?"

"I think it might show a creative streak, indicate an independent thinker. That's the kind of employee I'd want to hire."

"I'll have to be sure to list you as a reference for my next job search," he said. They both laughed. *Certainly won't be listing Evelyn Rockville as a reference*, he also noted in his mind.

"Maybe resumes are over-rated anyway," she said. "You spend your life developing and tweaking your resume, and then your final version is the one that gets published in the newspaper."

It took a moment for Ryan to get Amanda's dark humor. "Well, now you've got me cheered up." He glanced over at her to see a laughing twinkle in her eyes.

Their luck ran out near Lander. The sky turned so black that the headlights came on and rain poured in such thick sheets it felt like they were submerged. The storm was so intense that they had to pull off the road to wait it out. Parked at the roadside rest area, they could not hear each other speak over the roar of the thunder, which exploded every few seconds, shaking the Roadtrek. They gawked at the power of the storm through windows that were rapidly steaming up. Amanda seemed mesmerized by the wild assault of the storm, but Ryan was mesmerized by Amanda. For the past few hours, while he'd been driving, he could only shoot her occasional glances. But now, with her transfixed by the storm, he could watch her. He studied her in silhouette, with only the tip of her pert nose and the full lips—open—peeking out from the cover of her blonde hair. The pounding of the storm only added to the pounding desire he felt building for her.

"Oh my God, Ryan, this storm is scary," she gasped, then gave him a brief glance. "What are you staring at?" she asked, brushing her hair back from her face and seeming suddenly self-conscious.

He felt a rush of redness in his face and looked down. Then, as sudden as the cloudburst had begun, it ended. Within moments, they were back on US 287, headed into Dubois.

After Amanda took over the driving, Ryan perused the internet to learn more about Dubois, Wyoming. First, it's pronounced Dew-Boys. Second, it looks like a cowboy town, with one striking difference from the countless other western towns that promote a cowboy image: Dubois actually has real cowboys. The picturesque ranching town of nine hundred sits in a wide valley carved by the Wind River, surrounded by the highest peaks in Wyoming. People come here for fishing, hunting and snowmobiling and to just get away from it all. It is also the last town coming from the east before you hit Grand Teton National Park and where they would stop for the night before attempting the drive—another forty miles—over the high mountain pass to the Tetons.

They turned onto Ram's Horn, the main street of Dubois, at sundown and found their way to the KOA, where they were able to get a tent site, large enough to park the Roadtrek, but with no electric or water hookups.

After Amanda changed into a white spaghetti-strap summer dress and white sandals, they strolled out onto Ram's Horn and headed toward the Cowboy Café, which the camp host had recommended as a local favorite for burgers and homemade desserts. The wooden boardwalks and rustic facades on the old wood buildings gave the town a wild-west look.

A rock shop on the corner was just about to close. The place looked run down. In the window, mineral specimens were arrayed in a seemingly haphazard way on unpainted display shelves. A sign that looked like it had been there a long time said the store was for sale for $150,000, including the inventory.

"I love these places," Ryan said. "Took a mineralogy class in college. Been hooked ever since. Wanna go in?"

Amanda gave a carefree shrug, and they stepped inside.

A weathered old woman was emptying the contents of the cash register into a leather bag. "Go ahead and look around," she said. "I won't throw you out for another few minutes."

Amanda admired the cut pieces of amethyst geodes from Brazil, running her fingertips across the symmetric hexagonal shapes. "Some of this stuff is beautiful," she said, holding up a large brilliant-purple crystal for Ryan to see.

Ryan was poking through a box of polished agates. He shot her a quick glance. "Beautiful, yes." She returned a devilish smile. Then he asked the old woman, "Do you have a tumbler?"

She nodded in his direction, while still counting her money.

"What's a tumbler?" asked Amanda from across the room.

"It's a machine," said Ryan, "that smashes rocks together, and in the process they come out polished."

Now the old woman weighed in, while still doing her work. "Getting banged around takes off the rough edges."

Then she looked up. "Works for rocks, works for people, too." She laughed, then looked back down at the money she was counting. "'Course, sometimes people are more like rocks than they'd like to admit."

As they left, Amanda laced her arm in his. "That was fun," she breathed into his ear. "What's next?"

"Let's go see," he laughed. Then he turned serious, hesitating a moment before saying, "I've been thinking some about why bad things happen to people, and I've been a little all over the map about it." He wasn't yet ready to show her his blog.

"What have you concluded?" She looked up at him with interest.

"Well, it's pretty clear that bad things do happen to everyone, and it doesn't matter whether they deserve it or not."

"Okay," she said, in a way that indicated that this was obvious. "And?"

"But that woman's comment about the tumbler made me wonder if maybe bad things can also make us stronger."

Amanda shrugged. "Sure, the old what-doesn't-kill-you-makes-you-stronger theory. Where are you going with this, Ryan?"

"So maybe bad things aren't always bad things in the long run?"

Amanda gave a noticeable wince.

"What's wrong?" he asked.

"Oh, nothing."

"C'mon. What?"

Amanda sighed. "I'm just wondering what an Auschwitz survivor would say about that."

Ryan bit his lip and glanced away. He was glad he hadn't shown her his blog.

Their next stop was a western-wear store. Ryan pulled the Nikon from his shoulder and snapped a few shots of Amanda trying on cowboy hats. She gave him a sexy cowgirl pose—with one hand tipping her hat toward him, and the other placed on her jutted-out hip—as if saying, "Hey, cowpoke, wanna show a lonely girl around town?" They both wound up laughing.

Their wandering finally brought them to the Cowboy Café, a simple, down-home coffee shop, where they both ordered burgers, bypassing the house-favorite bison burger. The place was packed, apparently with locals, and they were treated to a lively din of refreshing conversations about livestock, the snowpack in the high country, and pickup carburetors. Ryan was tempted by the homemade apple pie, but decided to pass when Amanda said she was full.

It was dark when they stepped outside. Traffic on Ram's Horn was now almost nonexistent. The sound of twangy guitars from across the street drew them into a place called The Rodeo. A busy bar ran the length of one side of the room, mostly dark except for the small raised stage in the corner, illuminated by colored spotlights. Two singers, both with guitars, had just finished a song. A cluster of rustic wood tables faced a small dance floor, where a half-dozen couples waited for the next song to begin. Loud patrons, in lively conversations at the tables, seemed oblivious to the music. A low ceiling of acoustic tiles, with water stains visible even in the low light, gave the place a claustrophobic feel.

Amanda and Ryan found a table near the rear and ordered beers when the waitress came by. "This place is perfect," said Amanda. "I just may need to get a pair of cowboy boots before we leave."

A sign in front of the stage said the band was North Plateau, which consisted of a man and woman, looking to be in their forties, with chiseled faces that weren't so much weathered, as worn by the ups and downs they must have experienced over the years. The man, wearing old cowboy clothes, said a few words, which drew a couple of laughs, then they launched into another set of mostly country staples, with a little Beatles, Eagles and Jimmy Buffett mixed in.

Amanda leaned toward Ryan and raised her voice to be heard above the music and conversation. "Do you like country music?"

"I like this," he said.

"Me, too," she laughed. She was silent for a moment before adding, "Maybe we're just country folks who had the misfortune of living in the city."

Ryan nodded. An image of the grizzly bear in its cramped enclosure at the Denver Zoo flashed through his mind. "You could be right," he said.

After a few more songs, the male singer announced a short break to the room that didn't seem to be listening, and the couple stepped down off the stage. "Mind if we join you?" the woman said to Amanda, as they neared their table. She wore a bright pink sequined blouse over tight blue jeans. Her bottle-blonde hair tumbled down her shoulders from beneath a cowboy hat ringed in silver studs.

Amanda shot Ryan a questioning glance. "Sure," she said.

"Glen," said the man, tipping his hat toward them. "And this is Leah."

"Nice to meet you," said Ryan, who started to stand, before Glen held out a hand, palm up, and said, "Oh, don't get up."

"You don't look like locals," said Leah.

"How can you tell?" said Amanda.

Leah laughed. "For one thing, we've been coming here for over twenty years. We've met all the locals."

The waitress brought Glen and Leah ice waters. Glen lit a cigarette and said, "So, you're on vacation. Headed over to the Tetons?"

Ryan nodded. "Do you guys live around here?"

"We live down in Cheyenne," said Leah. "Make the rounds of joints like this all over Wyoming and up into Montana. Been doin' it forever."

"That must be fun," said Amanda. Ryan wondered about the sincerity of her comment. Doing their circuit sounded like a grind to him.

"It has its moments," bellowed Glen, giving Leah a wink and a knowing grin.

"You sound really good," said Amanda, making conversation.

"Well, she does," said Glen, looking at Leah. Up close, Ryan could see that Leah had been a real beauty at one time, but time and probably too many nights in places like this had taken their toll. "She was a finalist on *Idol* not that long ago."

"Glen, you are so full of BS. I never was a finalist. Made the trip to Hollywood though, damn proud of that. And it was back in '02, which is a bit more than not that long ago." She laughed, then took a long drink from the ice water.

"Still, she could've been big," said Glen. "But she had to get stuck with me." He shot Leah a mischievous look.

"You old fart," laughed Leah. "Getting stuck with you was the best thing that ever happened to me."

"So, how'd you meet?" asked Amanda. Ryan thought how she was better at keeping conversations going that he was. A natural-born customer service rep.

"It was a place like this," said Leah. "Laramie. The Spur Club. Isn't that right, hon?"

Glen nodded, smiling as if savoring the memory.

"We both were there alone on a Friday night, just enjoyin' the music. And I see this big handsome cowboy across the room."

Glen leaned forward, as he cut in. "Yeah, but that guy was married, so you had to settle for me." He laughed. Glen had a grizzled look, like he might indeed have been a cowboy at one time. Of course, that was no doubt the image he hoped to project.

"Oh, shut up. You know it was you I'm talkin' about." She'd probably heard that joke a thousand times. "So, anyway, he was pretty shy, so I had to go up and start a conversation."

"And it hasn't stopped yet," Glen quipped.

"You keep that up, mister, and you'll be findin' yourself a new lead vocal." She laughed, then added, "I hear Minnie Pearl's available."

"She's dead," said Glen.

"And you'd be, too, if you ever lost me."

Glen laughed. "That is true, babe, you know that's true."

"So, you two married?" Leah asked, looking from face to face.

"Oh, no," said Amanda, just a little too quickly, thought Ryan.

"Well, be careful. You can see what happens when a couple of lovebirds hook up in a place like this."

Amanda gave Ryan a quick romantic glance. "Maybe that wouldn't be so bad," she said. Ryan was speechless.

"Not bad at all," said Glen. With that, he stood, tipped his hat and said, "Well, nice meeting you kids. Love is in the air tonight. Go grab some of it." Then he looked at Leah. "Okay, babe, guess we'd better get back up there."

When Glen and Leah returned to the stage, Amanda stood and reached out a hand to Ryan. The melodies were mostly two-steps, so Ryan felt confident. He and Melissa had taken a country dance class together—she was into classes— although they had never actually gone dancing. They danced to *Lookin' for Love in All the Wrong Places,* and then Glen did his best to sing *Amarillo by Morning.* He had George Strait's hat, but not his voice.

"By the way," shouted Ryan to Amanda above the loud music, as he spun her around, her white dress swirling, "you'd look great in those new cowboy boots."

She came back fast from the spin right into his arms, up so close that their faces were just inches apart. Then the song ended, but they stood there with faces still close, their eyes locked onto one another.

"Now an oldie for all you old-time cowpokes out there," said Glen. Leah took the lead vocal on *The Tennessee Waltz,* singing in a breathless, throaty way that reminded Ryan of Stevie Nicks. It was slow and romantic, and Amanda immediately moved close into Ryan's arms. She looked up at him with the eyes of someone watching a sunrise or the birth of a child. She ran her fingers gently across his forehead, then rested her face against his shoulder.

When the song was over, they said nothing as they headed for the door, and the hand-in-hand walk back to the campground was in silence. Inside the van, they stood in the near darkness, the only light coming from the dim blue LEDs on the RV's status panel. Amanda looked down in shyness, then quickly back up at Ryan with invitation in her eyes. She took his hand and gently pulled him toward the bed in the rear.

Chapter 46

They tumbled onto the bed, Ryan on top, their mouths locked together. The passionate kisses continued for a long time. Crazy with desire, he drank her in. Then he raised up on one elbow and looked at her. In the dimness, he could see only the sparkle of her eyes and her blonde hair arrayed across the pillow. She nodded yes.

He lowered his face to her again, then began to—

BEEP!

Amanda pushed him away slightly. "What was that?" she whispered.

"Nothing," said Ryan. "Just the RV doing its thing." He lowered his face onto hers again, and—

BEEP!

"That wasn't nothing," said Amanda. "It sounds like some kind of alarm."

"I don't think we need to worry about—"

BEEP!

"Ryan, please check it out. What if it's something—"

"Okay," he sighed, as he sat up on the bed. He looked around the Roadtrek interior for any sign of something wrong. Then he saw a flashing red LED from a small metal box beneath the bed. He'd never noticed it before.

BEEP!

Ryan stepped to the front of the Roadtrek, then fumbled through a cabinet above the dash, where his mom had kept the operator's manual. He was wishing at this moment that he'd spent more time studying it. Amanda came and stood beside him, clearly concerned.

BEEP!

He turned a few pages, then erupted. "Oh, God," he blurted. "That's the carbon monoxide detector. Let's get the hell out of here." He grabbed Amanda's hand and pulled her out through the side door into the night.

BEEP!

"Oh, God," said Amanda. "Is there carbon monoxide in there?"

"I'm not sure," said Ryan, still poring through the manual, angling it up toward a lamppost so he could read it. He jumped, as he noticed a man standing almost next to them. He turned toward the man, an elderly guy wearing a bath robe. He was holding a small toiletry bag and a towel under his arm, apparently headed for the shower.

"Got a problem?" the old man said.

"My carbon monoxide detector just went off," said Ryan.

The man nodded his head. "What kind of sound is it making?"

"A loud beep, every ten seconds or so."

"That's not carbon monoxide. That's the detector telling you your house batteries are almost dead."

"Why would the—" Then Ryan remembered that their site had no electric hookup, and he hadn't turned the propane on when they arrived at the campground. The fridge automatically switched to the house battery when the propane supply was off. He blew out a big breath, then said, "I guess the fridge has been running off the RV-battery power for the last few hours."

"Yep. That'll take your batteries down in no time." The man nodded his head and made a smacking sound, like he hoped this dumb rookie had learned his lesson. "If I were you, I'd turn your propane on, then start your vehicle to get those RV batteries back up."

Five minutes later, the beeping had stopped.

Amanda now sat on the bed, pulling her hair behind her head, doing her ponytail thing.

"Well, that's a relief," Ryan said. "I've never been a big fan of carbon monoxide, but right now I've got to say I'm even less of a fan of carbon monoxide detectors." He produced a shallow laugh, which Amanda did not share.

Ryan took a step toward her. "But let's not talk about that anymore," he said, with his best effort at a romantic mood.

Amanda stood and came toward him. She smiled, then said, her voice soft, "Maybe we should just call it a night." She gave him a quick, sweet kiss, then retreated to the rear, pulling the sheet closed behind her.

Chapter 47

Standing next to a snow bank at the top of Togwotee Pass, at almost ten-thousand feet elevation, Amanda hugged herself, shivering even with her Patagonia down jacket on over her warmest sweater, but Ryan seemed unfazed in just a wool shirt. The van had worked hard on the long, steady climb out of Dubois up to the pass, where they had pulled off to enjoy the spectacular early-morning views and let the van rest before the long downhill roll into Grand Teton National Park. Snowcapped peaks surrounded them in a vast still-winter environment.

Their banter during the ride up the pass had been friendly and superficial, neither of them mentioning the romantic roller coaster of last night. She couldn't be sure what was going through Ryan's head, but she was certainly thinking about it. As Ryan had maneuvered the switchbacks up the pass, she had oohed and ahhed over the stunning landscapes, but her mind was elsewhere. Had last night been the product of a little beer and *The Tennessee Waltz*? Or had it been the evidence of something deeper growing between them? Amanda had adjusted the vent on the dash to let in more fresh air—not because it was stuffy, nor because of the high elevation. It was the wave of unmitigated excitement, as she contemplated what might lie ahead, that threatened to take her breath away.

She watched Ryan snap a series of photos of the snowy scene, turning between clicks to capture the full 360-degree panorama. She'd only known this guy for a little over a week. Could she trust her feelings? After all, you spend a week in close quarters with an attractive man, what else do you expect to happen? And she had to consider all this against the backdrop of her suffering over the Adam breakup—she had heard too much about disastrous rebound flings.

A short drive beyond the pass, they caught their first glimpse of the Tetons, still far in the distance. A girl from the flat country of Wisconsin could easily be wowed by the sight of high mountains, but Amanda had been to Tahoe and Mammoth with Richard and Adam. She'd seen tall mountains. But this was something different. She tried to find words to describe them. Brilliantly white with snow, the Tetons spread across the horizon like a string of giant shark's teeth. Just as sharp and ripsaw-jagged, they were intimidating, jaw-dropping and oddly terrifying. Wild. Beautiful.

She had to remind herself to breathe. Even her preoccupation with her possible future with Ryan took a back seat, at least for the moment, to the sweeping view before her.

They passed through the national-park entrance at Moran Junction, and a few moments later stopped at a breathtaking viewpoint called Oxbow Bend, where the Snake River winds before the spectacular backdrop of Mt. Moran. Photographers lined a small ridge, pointing massive professional lenses on heavy tripods toward the scene.

Ryan moved right in among them and snapped off pictures with his Nikon. Then he called to Amanda to stand at the edge of the ridge overlooking the river, so he could photograph her against the calendar-quality backdrop. He fired off a burst of photos, as she flashed him her best smile. Then he approached her, shaking his head and grinning as he said, "You see that guy over there with the two assistants? That's Hal Walport. He's one of the most famous landscape photographers in the world. I've got a couple of his books. But even with all his skill and megabucks gear, he doesn't have anything as gorgeous as you to photograph."

Then Ryan put his arm around her, as they admired the view together in silence.

They scored a campsite near Jackson Lake, a huge expanse of blue, backed by snowy peaks. Then they continued south along the Teton Park Road to the trailhead for Taggart Lake. Their goal was to find a hike right beneath the most majestic peak in the park—and maybe in the northern hemisphere, to hear Ryan tell it—the Grand Teton.

There were still patches of snow around the perimeter of the parking area, indicating that they could expect snowy travel on the five-mile loop trail to Taggart Lake. Only a few other cars shared the parking lot with them this early in the season, but Amanda suspected that when school let out in another week, the crowds would begin pouring in.

Amanda and Ryan went about their now-familiar routine of getting ready for a hike. Load the day packs with snacks and water bottles; put on hiking boots; check maps. As she watched Ryan shoulder his pack, she shook her head in amazement. Just a week or so ago—she had lost track of the days—her idea of getting outside was sunset margaritas on the deck at the marina. Now she was tramping off into the wilderness, where there might be bears and moose and God knows what else.

While folks in Manhattan Beach were scheduling their next pedicure, she was now sharing public bathrooms and showers—often only marginally clean—and when there weren't showers, sponging off in a sink. While her friends were debating the purchase of a Tempurpedic mattress, she was sleeping in the back of a van. While her girlfriends longed for stainless appliances and granite countertops, she was now using a two-burner propane stove in a cramped kitchen space to prepare meals that she would have recently considered substandard, items that would never appear on a tapas menu. These things that would have appalled her in the past were now just part of her life. And she loved it. She was actually anticipating hikes that she knew would challenge her physically, get her sweaty and dirty—in fact, she now reflected, they reminded her of her best days: playing basketball back at Wausau East. Or perhaps, these were her best days.

Amanda had not been camping since those long weekends as a child with her parents in the upper peninsula of Michigan—in the Porcupine Mountains or the Pictured Rocks lakeshore. She felt a sudden pang of sadness, like a dark cloud passing in front of the sun, as she thought of how seldom she spoke to her parents these days.

The sad thoughts evaporated as she looked up the rocky trail leading off into the wilderness and at the Grand Teton looming above it. This mountain—like a cathedral spire of rock and ice—was surrealistic. It was like something from a fantasy-writer's imagination, unlike anything she'd ever seen. It looked like earth's attempt to reach to heaven, with the intention to present itself to the divine with its most beautiful self. Indeed, it felt like church being here—quiet, yet unsubtle—like God saying, "Yes, I really exist." Amanda could not look up at this mountain and not be moved.

Ryan caught her eye and, with a look of uncertainty, said, "What?"

Amanda went over to him and kissed him on the mouth. "I want you to know that I am having a wonderful time."

Despite the snow around them, it was much warmer here, being three thousand feet lower than Togwotee Pass. Abundant sunshine warmed Amanda's shoulders as they set off up the trail, which climbed switchbacks to the first of several lakes, set against the breathtaking Teton crest high above them.

They stopped for a mid-morning snack at a ledge overlooking one of the lakes and munched on trail mix, fruit and more string cheese. They ate in silence, watching the late-morning sun sparkle off the lake surface, where a light breeze caused small waves to dance on the water and a whispering in the wind-bent pines around them. Wildflowers in reds, yellows and purples carpeted the slope leading down to the water.

As he gazed out across the lake, Ryan said, "Do you have a lot of friends back in LA?"

Amanda pondered this for a moment. "Not really. Just one good friend. Katy. You'd like her."

Now he turned toward her. "Why's that?"

"Well, she's funny and smart. Sees through stuff." She paused. "But I don't really have many other good friends." She was surprised to hear herself say this. After all, what about all the dinners with girlfriends at the marina? What about her colleagues at the bank? But, other than Katy, she could not think of one person she would consider a close friend. "I did when I was in Wisconsin. But the last eight years have been sort of ... what should I say ... bumpy?"

"Bumpy?"

"I mean, I never really felt like I was settled in, or settled down, putting down roots." She was struggling to find the right words, but Ryan's nods confirmed that he knew what she was saying. "I don't think that's just an LA thing, but maybe it is. I just always felt like where I was or what I was doing was only temporary. Which was funny. Because sometimes I felt like I was stuck and things would never change. Does that make sense?"

"Yeah. Too much sense." He gave out a forced chuckle.

"How about you?"

"Sorry to say I don't really have any close friends." He shook his head sadly as he said this. "I've only been back in LA for two years. Guess I've been a bit of a hermit during that time. In Los Alamos I had some friends, but I guess even there we were never close. Not sure why that was."

"Maybe that's a guy thing? I've read that a lot of men have a hard time finding close friends."

Ryan nodded like, yes, that described him. Then he looked out at the lake again for a while, before turning back to Amanda and saying, "I wonder if you can have community while you're travelling. Okay, this is crazy. Maybe. I mean, we've already run into interesting people on this trip, even if we only knew them for a short time."

"You mean like Cepi?"

"Yeah. It's kind of odd. I only knew her for a few hours, and yet it seemed like she was more of a friend than some people I interacted with for years. I wonder why that is."

Amanda wondered too. She said, "And Fr. Jessop. And maybe even Leah and Glen from the bar in Dubois."

Ryan rubbed his chin with his thumb, then pursed his lips, but said nothing.

Amanda continued. "And I met this woman, a painter, on the rim of the Grand Canyon. Only talked to her for five minutes. But it was important." Now she turned fully toward him. "So maybe you're saying that, while a lot of superficial friendships can't equal one good one—like with Katy—there may be deeper friendships with people we meet even briefly, and all those can add up to something significant. I'm remembering something Fr. Jessop told us about St. Patrick, I think, and maybe St. Francis. He said that they had no home anywhere, so they made their home everywhere. Remember that?"

Ryan nodded. "Good stuff, Miss Seward. But you're getting me to thinking about physics here."

"Oh?" She laughed. "Tell me more." She enjoyed seeing him light up when a physics topic came up.

Now he shifted his whole body toward her, his knee brushing hers. "Okay, this could be way off base," he said. "Probably is. But in physics, there's an important theorem that might apply here. It's called the ergodic theorem."

Amanda raised her eyebrows. "Ergodic theorem? Definitely didn't study that in high school."

"It's really important to a branch of physics called statistical mechanics."

"Okay," she said tentatively. Then she laughed. "I'm anxious to see what you do with this."

"I'm gonna get technical here for a second, but then you'll see where I'm going. The theorem says that for a large number of particles—like the molecules bouncing off each other in a gas—that the average of some property for the whole system, like the average particle speed, at one instant is equal to the average over a long period of time of just one of the particles." He paused to see if she was following him.

Amanda nodded. "I think I understand." Maybe. "Keep going."

"So what if we apply this to the large number of people in the world—instead of gas particles—and we consider a property of this large number of people, like the relationships between people—"

"You've got me there, Mr. Wizard. Say more."

"Okay, I admit this is a stretch and maybe wrong. I'm sure one of my old physics professors would throw me to the wolves for something like this. But maybe the theorem is saying that on a road trip like we're on, if we pay attention to all those brief friendships, that they are equivalent to a small number of long-term friendships."

Amanda was loving this. "Geez, that's pretty cool." She licked her lips and sat up straighter. "So..." She dragged the word out. "Maybe wanderers like us can find community, even if they only meet people briefly before they move on."

"Yeah, maybe." He laughed and shrugged his shoulders. "So we need to be paying attention, I guess." He now touched her cheek with a finger and let it trail slowly down to her neck. A shiver went down her body. "But maybe I can say all this only because I'm here with you."

Amanda felt heat flow into her face. She began to lean forward to kiss him, but then she saw it over his shoulder. A bull elk stepped from the trees, no more than twenty yards from them, then stopped and stood motionless at the edge of the steep slope leading down to the shoreline.

It was huge—its shoulders perhaps higher than her head. The elk had a thick, luxurious fur coat, dark brown around the shoulders and under its belly, but a light reddish-tan on its back. The enormous antlers, with their velvety covering, were frightening and probably dangerous—a lethal weapon that stirred her instinct to flee. But the antlers were also delicate and beautiful, like the free-flowing design from an artist's brush—almost reverent, like slender hands lifted in prayer. Mixed with her fear were awe and an odd sense of connection—but maybe not odd at all. Maybe it was the sacred link that bonds all living things together.

Amanda silently gestured to Ryan to turn around, and she heard a soft gasp as he saw it too.

She could not breathe. They sat transfixed, motionless, then Ryan slowly reached for his camera and grabbed several quick shots before the elk, unconcerned with their presence, sauntered off down toward the lake.

"My God, that was amazing," Amanda whispered.

Ryan nodded, then looked into her eyes. He leaned over and kissed her. Her arms enveloped him and pulled him to her, then down onto the warm flat rock on which they sat. They lay there in each other's arms for a while, before Amanda gently pushed Ryan away. She looked around, expecting to see another hiker. "Not here," she said.

Ryan looked like a man who'd just been sentenced to the gallows. Then he nodded in compliant surrender.

It was early afternoon when they got back to the van and began to make their way back to their campground, taking it slow to take in as much of the staggering scenery as possible. Just south of Jenny Lake, Amanda spotted a sign for the Chapel of the Transfiguration. "Turn in here," she said, pointing toward a narrow side road. "Let's check that out." A short drive brought them into a parking lot—nearly full—next to a small rustic log church set against the Teton backdrop.

Two tour buses waited with their big diesels idling, as lines of photo-hungry tourists had to share a narrow path to the chapel. Amanda and Ryan made their way into the tiny church—just a log cabin, really. It looked old.

The chapel was illuminated entirely by the brilliant light streaming in from a wide window behind the rough-cut wooden altar. The window looked out upon a panorama of the Teton crest. It was like being in a chapel looking out to a cathedral.

A woman next to them said, "I was here for a service last summer, when the biggest darn moose I'd ever seen walked right past that window. The priest was in the middle of her sermon, but then noticed that the people had become distracted." The woman paused to laugh, apparently building up to her punch line. "She turned to see the moose, then—not missing a beat—turned back to us and said, 'Well, you can listen to me talk about the beauty of creation, or you can all come right up here and witness it firsthand for yourselves.' Then we all went up around the altar and took pictures of the great moose."

Amanda stayed at the altar rail for a while, gazing out the window to the rugged mountains beyond. She thought about the great elk they had seen. Maybe she would get lucky again. Then she looked down at the altar rail and ran her fingers over the smooth wood surface. How long had it been since she had stood at an altar rail? Were there answers for her here? Were there answers for her anywhere?

Chapter 48

The place was beautiful all right, thought Ryan. For Amanda—now silent at the altar rail—perhaps it was more than that. Perhaps it offered her something spiritual—maybe a connection with the old days she had told him about, back in Wausau, when she went to church. For Ryan it was a beautiful little building, but just a building.

And it presented him with a significant technical challenge. The most advanced, high-tech photography gear—such as the big Nikon digital that hung from his shoulder—falls far short of what the human eye can detect, especially in high contrast light like the inside of the chapel presented, with the bright light pouring in through the altar window, adjacent to the dark wood of the interior. He knew that most of the people now snapping shots with their phones were doomed to be disappointed with the results—either the scene through the window would be exposed perfectly and the interior—including dear Aunt Suzie, who posed at the altar rail—would come out too dark, or Aunt Suzie would be perfectly exposed and the scene through the window would be washed out. Such a wide range of contrasting light was one of the greatest challenges a photographer may face and will almost always spoil the efforts of an amateur.

Ryan knew there were ways to deal with this. Use flash—but he had left his flash unit in the Roadtrek—or, take a sequence of shots at varying exposure settings and combine them later with software, but this was more effort than this photo opportunity seemed to warrant. Furthermore, there were just too many other visitors filling the small space for him to capture the beauty of the place.

He shrugged, as he conceded defeat, and was ready to leave, but Amanda wanted more time at the altar rail. Ryan waited outside in the sunshine, snapping off a few exterior shots of the picturesque little building, trying to frame his shots so that there would not be too many tourists in the scene.

"Is this a thin place?"

A young man with long hair was looking right at Ryan, his eyes expecting an answer.

Ryan began to speak, but stopped when he realized he had no idea what the man was talking about. Then he noticed that the man was looking beyond him, and he turned to see a small woman, no more than five feet tall. She wore a black nun's habit that looked like wool and must have been very warm on this sunny day. She leaned over a walker-cane, one of those metal canes with four feet for extra stability—he thought they were called quad canes. She was very old.

The young man asked again, "Sister, is this a thin place?"

The old woman smiled at the man, then tilted her head up at Ryan and smiled at him, too. You could tell by the pattern of the many wrinkles in her face that she had smiled a lot in her life. Her eyes looked hazy, perhaps from cataracts, and Ryan wondered for a moment if she was blind. But then she looked right into his eyes and held her gaze for so long that

Ryan squirmed. But she was not judging or appraising him. It was like her eyes were a welcoming doorway opening to him, accepting him, inviting him—a stranger—to be a part of this moment.

Then she began to speak, so softly that both Ryan and the young man had to lean in to hear her. "Is this a thin place, you ask." She touched an index finger to her chin, as if pondering the question. "Hmm."

"Yeah," said the man. "Like Lourdes or Iona or Sedona. I mean, this place is so beautiful." He looked back and forth between Ryan and the nun.

The nun said, "A thin place is a place where the separation between heaven and earth is small."

Ryan must have winced. She gave him a smile that acknowledged his skepticism and said it was okay. But then she looked at the young man and said, "Thin places are not just physical locations—rock and water and sky. I believe they are located wherever hearts have ached and longed. Where pleas were made, where God was begged, where knees were bent and spirits that were broken were healed." She paused, then added, "So a thin place is not just a place, a piece of ground. It's ground that has been soaked in prayer."

The young man was silent, his lips parted for words that never came, as if he were too surprised to speak.

Then she turned slowly toward the chapel in a sequence of small steps, repositioning her walker-cane before each step. "I suspect this is such a place," she said.

The young man beamed and said, "Thank you." Then he turned and disappeared into the crowd of tourists.

Now the old nun turned toward Ryan. "I see you have a nice camera," she said.

Ryan nodded and shuffled his feet, suddenly self-conscious about being the owner of an expensive material object before this woman who probably lived near the poverty line. He licked his lips that had become suddenly dry.

"The talk of thin places and your nice camera equipment remind me of a time I spent in Iona," she said.

"I'm sorry," said Ryan, "but I don't what Iona is."

"That's okay," said the nun, the smile never leaving her face. "Most people don't. It's a small island off the west coast of Scotland. It's where St. Columba established an abbey in the sixth century."

Ryan didn't know who St. Columba was, either, but he decided not to ask. He nodded, as the woman continued. "So, today, there are fewer than a hundred people who live there, but the restored abbey is there, and many pilgrims from all over the world come there to pray."

Ryan shifted his weight from one foot to the other, then glanced toward the door of the chapel to see if Amanda was coming out yet, but there was no sign of her.

"I remember one day when I was walking toward the abbey, along the shore." She closed her eyes for a moment, as if she were imagining the scene. "There were many irises growing along the shore, and in those irises, you could hear the song of the cornrake—that's a tall shore bird that is occasionally seen on Iona."

Ryan wondered where this story was headed.

"The cornrake has an amazing song—sounds like running your fingers along the teeth of a comb." She looked like she was hearing it right now. "It's beautiful. But on this day I was there, you could not see the birds." She stopped and studied

Ryan's face, causing him to wonder what she was seeing in him.

"That morning along the shore, there were photographers with their expensive super-telephotos waiting patiently to photograph the cornrakes emerging from the irises. They were wearing their professional camo outfits and had their long lenses mounted on big tripods."

Ryan was beginning to be engaged in the story. He could envision himself there with a big telephoto lens, too. He smiled at the little woman, but said nothing.

She continued. "When I returned to the path along the shore, after my prayer time at the abbey, the photographers were getting ready to leave. I could tell they were frustrated. I asked one of them what was the matter. He grumbled something like, 'Darned birds, they never came out.' They all left without photos of the cornrakes, and they seemed miserable. Can you believe that? Such a beautiful day in such a beautiful place, with the lovely irises and the call of the cornrakes. And they were miserable."

Ryan nodded again, but remained silent.

"I wonder," she said, "what you are holding out for." She paused as she continued to study him. Perhaps she was expecting a response from him, but he could not come up with anything to say.

"Are you holding out for scientific proof—the digital photograph of the cornrake, like those discouraged photographers? Or might you be able to find joy in hearing their song and knowing they are there—close by—among the beautiful irises?"

He thought about his preoccupation with photographing the interior of the chapel and realized he could scarcely recall what it looked like. He'd always argued that photography helped a person to see things better because you concentrated on the light. But maybe it was possible to be blinded by the camera, too. Maybe that's what set the great photographers apart from the mere practitioners of photography, like him— the ability to really see.

And this was true in physics, too. There were many capable practitioners of physics but only a few great physicists—many who could skillfully manipulate equations or calibrate sensitive detectors, but few who could actually get inside a problem, really grasp what was going on. He recalled the time he had met Neville Mott, the great theoretical atomic physicist who wrote a famous textbook and even had physical phenomena named after him. There were many scientists who could calculate what went on inside an atom, but it was said of Mott that he could actually think like an electron coursing its way through an atom. Maybe for Mott, the atom was a thin place.

Maybe this was what the nun was getting at. You needed to reach for something beyond the concrete, beyond the obvious, if you wanted to experience what was going on in nature. Maybe doing that was easier in what she called a thin place. He wondered what Amanda would say about this. Was this also true for painters? He suspected it was.

The nun had now left him, as she slowly made her way toward the entrance of the chapel. Ryan looked around, suddenly feeling claustrophobic and closed in by the press of the crowd of tourists. He moved away from them, off the entrance path, toward the edge of the chapel property, enclosed by a rustic split-rail fence. There he spotted a patch of purple wildflowers. He knelt beside them. His instinct was to pull the Nikon out and switch the lens to its macro setting.

But he didn't. He moved in closer. He touched the petal of the flower, its surface like velvet. It felt like he imagined the velvet of the bull elk's antlers might have felt. Then he studied the leaves of the wildflower. They were amazingly complex—veins carried nutrition throughout the leaf structure in an intricate pattern, like a network of canals irrigating a farm.

He closed his eyes, and for a moment he was transported far away from the crowd of noisy tourists. He was on a beach. A soft ocean breeze washed his face. And the haunting music from the cornrake calmed his soul.

Chapter 49

Just as Amanda emerged from the chapel, a man came toward them, led by a large chocolate-brown Labrador retriever. The energetic dog was trying to strike up friendships with everyone it passed. As they came near, Amanda immediately went down to a knee and welcomed the dog into her arms.

Images flashed through Ryan's mind like a highlight reel: Amanda racing to comfort the lost child at the zoo; reaching out to help Cepi; offering water to the man on the Bright Angel Trail; stepping up to save him in his encounter with Melissa. A lump in his throat caused him to swallow hard.

When Amanda rejoined him, she was beaming. "Someday, I'm going to get a dog like that," she said. "Maybe if …" She paused, as her gaze shifted to across the crowded pathway. "Ryan, isn't that the woman from Denver?"

Ryan turned toward the direction Amanda was looking. He saw no one he recognized.

"Of course it is," Amanda said. "Carol—I think that's her name. The one who ran up to the lost child with me at the zoo. That's odd that we would see her again."

Ryan nodded.

"Carol," shouted Amanda across the crowd.

The woman turned and, at first, didn't seem to recognize Amanda. Then a second later, a smile burst upon her face, and she hurried toward them.

"I can't believe it," the woman said with a big grin. "But you said you were headed north, so I guess this shouldn't be a surprise. This is a popular place. I'm sorry, I don't remember your name."

"Amanda. Amanda Seward. And this is Ryan Browning." She laced her arm in his as she said this.

"I'm Carol Shepherd. Well, it's good to see you again. I thought about you after that day at the zoo, about how it's a good thing a few women without children are there to help with lost kids."

Amanda seemed to stiffen slightly at this, but said, "I guess we all love kids."

Just then Ryan's phone rang. Annoyed, he pulled the phone from his pocket and checked the ID. He was immediately cheered. It was Uncle Wil. He raised his phone toward Amanda, and gave her an I-need-to-take-this-call nod as he stepped away from them.

"Hey, Ryan," said a deep gravelly voice, "when are you gonna get your ass up here?"

Ryan laughed. "Well, we're in the Tetons right now, so I'm guessing we'll make Bozeman in a few days."

"We?" Uncle Wil sounded curious.

"I'm travelling with a new friend, Amanda. I think you'll really like her."

"Ah ha, I hope this is something romantic. You've been a little deficient in that department, as I recall."

Ryan chuckled. A little deficient? An understatement. He hadn't seen his uncle since his mom's funeral, but that long two weeks with him in the hospital waiting room had provided plenty of time to discuss Ryan's love life or lack thereof. "I think it just may be," he said, looking over at Amanda, who was still chatting with the woman from the zoo.

"Good for you, Ryan. Can't wait to meet her. Hey, reason I asked about your ETA is because I'll be going out of town in a couple of weeks and wanted to make sure I didn't miss you."

"And I can't wait to see your place, after all I've heard about it." Ryan had never been to Bozeman.

As he was about to click his phone off, he noticed a popup message saying there was a Facebook comment on a post he was tagged in. He clicked on the message, which brought up the picture Amanda had posted from Santa Fe. There were many likes, but only the one new comment. From Adam somebody, it read: *When you comin' home to me, babe? Glad to hear this Ryan dude is "just a guy."*

It felt like someone had kicked him in the gut. He could barely breathe. He looked around, half expecting that Amanda was watching this, but she was still occupied with Carol Shepherd.

There was five seconds left when Dickson fired the inbound pass to him. They were down by one. He looked up court, but all his team mates were covered. He would need to drive the length of the court and score. Was there time? He drove hard, crossed midcourt, left two defenders flat-footed in the dust, then—

"So, I'm just heading out," Carol said to Amanda. "Maybe we'll run into each other again along the way, huh?"

"I would like that," said Amanda, as Carol turned and left. Then she looked at Ryan and said, "Seems like a good woman. But still, it's funny that…what's wrong, Ryan? You look pale."

Ryan's initial shock at the Facebook comment was now turning into something else. Rage? Was he just a fool who was letting his heart get out ahead of his brain? Finally, he found words, but they only came out in short bits. "So, I'm just a guy?"

"What?" Her face immediately reddened. "No, Ryan, that's not …." She pulled out her phone and frantically scrolled. "Oh, God," she wailed. She looked back at Ryan, who was now turning away from her. He felt her hands on his shoulders, trying to pull him toward her, but he resisted. "Ryan," she pleaded, "please look at me. Give me a chance to explain. I deserve that."

Ryan turned slowly toward her. She took his face in her hands, but he could not allow his eyes to focus on her face. "Look at me," she said, shaking his shoulders. "I had a life before I knew you, and I don't have to be ashamed of that."

"So why was he waiting for you to come home?"

Now Amanda paced. "I told you that there's nothing for me back there," she said. Then she turned back toward him. "Ryan, listen …" Her voice was faltering. "Please …" Then she stopped. Suddenly, she grabbed his arm and gripped it so tight, he could feel the bite of her nails. "Oh my God," she gasped. Her voice had gone from pleading to panic.

Ryan looked at her face, but her eyes were now fixed on the parking lot. "What?"

"Look. It's Carol getting into her car."

Ryan had to scan the busy lot before he saw the car. "So?"

"Ryan, it's the car."

"What car?"

Amanda was breathing hard, her eyes wide in what seemed like terror. "The Sonata with Arizona tags. It's the car from the campground at the Grand Canyon."

Chapter 50

Ryan drove the Roadtrek back to their campsite—where else were they to go?—probably breaking park speed limits, while their conversation bounced wildly from one panicked question to another, with few answers. "How did they find us?" "Who are they?" "What do they want from us?" "Are we in danger?" "What should we do?" Against this panic, Amanda felt the issue of the Facebook comment stirring down deep in her gut, like she'd swallowed rat poison and was now waiting for its deadly effects to take hold. How could Adam sink this low? Posting his message to her as a comment to a post in which Ryan was tagged—including the demeaning "he's just a guy"—to be certain that he would see it.

Now they paced anxious loops around the camp table and the fire ring. Amanda had not seen Ryan so worked up. He pressed his palms to his head, like he was fighting the mother of all migraines. Was it only about the Carol Shepherd incident and their safety? She tried to keep him focused. "Obviously, the Austin ruse didn't fool them," she said. "So, either they have followed us or they've planted a tracking device in our vehicle."

They both turned toward the Roadtrek. "It probably isn't inside; we've kept the thing locked," Ryan said.

Without further words, they both circled the RV, looking for anything that wasn't an obvious part of the vehicle, peeking into vent holes, under flaps, behind the bumpers, inside the wheel wells. Ryan crawled under the van with a flashlight, and Amanda could hear him cursing. "There's so much stuff under here, all this wiring and plumbing." He muttered another obscenity, then said, "I think that's the generator, and there are the water tanks." He continued to mumble about the various components of the RV, as he crawled around for another ten minutes. Then he crawled out and stood, brushing dirt from his clothes and shaking his head. "I can't see anything suspicious under there."

They stood silent, staring at the RV, as if some new clue would jump out at them. Amanda laid a comforting hand on Ryan's arm, but he pulled back. She looked up at him. "We'll be okay," she said, unconvinced herself. "If they wanted to harm us, they would have done it already. For some reason, they're just watching us. Maybe it's your old company, making sure you're not up to something that will hurt them." She knew she was talking too fast. "Anyway, I'm sure that when they see that you're not—"

He seemed almost in tears. "I need you to leave. I wanted you to go earlier, and I should've stood my ground. It isn't safe for—"

"I'm not going," she said defiantly. "My place is here with—"

"You need to go. They're after me."

She felt her face flush. "I don't want to go."

Now he took a step back from her and gave her a cold look. "You know you need to go back to Adam," he said. His eyes pounded into her.

She felt tears welling up, and she tried to fight them back. She was not going to manipulate him with tears. He was too good for that. She was too good for that. "Ryan, listen to me, please ..." She tried to approach him, to hold him, but he stepped back quickly, with his hands up like stop signs.

Ryan now turned and stepped quickly to the edge of the campsite, then looked down. His arms were at his sides, his fists clenched. Now, he looked up, as if searching the sky. He let out a low wail, then said, loud and deliberate and slow, "I don't want you here anymore."

Chapter 51

Why we love sunsets is a mystery. If that love is inherited from ancient ancestors, it doesn't make sense. Sunset signals the onset of darkness, the time of danger when predators and enemies begin to stalk—sunset should prompt terror. Or, if a day is a metaphor for a lifetime, then sunset should indicate the end of that life, the bittersweet and all-too-soon conclusion of all our struggles and hopes. Yet, day after day, around the world, people stop to watch the sunset. Sunset is universally a time of quiet reflection, awe, peace.

Ryan tried to consider the sunset objectively, as he walked from his campsite at the Madison Campground, just inside the west gate of Yellowstone National Park, down to a wide grassy meadow, where a fly-fisherman teased the waters of the fast-flowing Madison River. Orange flashes from the fading sun danced off the swirling water. Fir-covered mountains rose on all sides of the meadow.

But the stunning sunset view only intensified Ryan's despair and threatened to restart the tears that had flowed so freely over the past two hours.

After their crisis in the Tetons and after his definitive pronouncement—"I don't want you here anymore"—Amanda had seemed to quickly accept that it was over, and they had set about getting her on a plane back to LA. She had boarded a late-afternoon regional jet out of the West Yellowstone Airport that would get her into LAX late, after a layover in Salt Lake City.

It had been a long, quiet and awkward two-hour drive to the airport, and it had cost a bundle for the last-minute ticket and the excess baggage charges—Amanda had refused to let Ryan pay. Periodically, he'd shot glances over at her. Several times he started to speak, but was unable to find words. Her body was turned toward the door.

They had driven north, through a vast portion of Yellowstone National Park that had been burned by the disastrous 1988 fire. Mile after mile of new-growth pines and spruce, only twenty or thirty feet in height, could not hide the tall, blackened spires a hundred feet taller, an ugly reminder to Ryan that some wounds take a lifetime to heal.

After hitting the drive-thru at a Mexican fast-food restaurant on the highway leading north out of West Yellowstone toward the airport, he had dropped her off. He did not wait until the plane took off, and the last he saw of her she was striding proudly down a hallway toward the boarding area, carrying the three mailing tubes of her gallery under her arm. As she'd made a turn into the hallway that would take her out of his sight, he'd thought he'd seen her pause, thought she was about to turn around toward him, but she hadn't. She never looked back.

He had remained distant from her until that moment—he had to; it was the only way he would get through this. When she had disappeared from his sight was when he'd fallen apart.

Now he turned from the sunset and the river and walked slowly, head down, back to the campground.

Almost every site was occupied in Madison Campground, and Ryan had been fortunate to get a place without a reservation. A father tossed a Frisbee to two small children. A young couple was busy setting up a tent. Another young couple strolled hand in hand toward the river. An elderly couple was preparing their dinner over a camp stove. Everyone, it seemed, had someone with whom to share this beautiful place. Tomorrow these people would set out on adventures to see geysers, catch a glimpse of an elk or a bison, purchase souvenirs at the Old Faithful Lodge, hike to waterfalls and mountain tops and wildflower-filled meadows.

He could not hold the thoughts of Amanda at bay. At stressful times like this, Ryan often turned to a basketball fantasy for escape, but the only images that his mind would generate now were from their campsite in the Grand Tetons. He had turned away from her. He had had to turn away—he couldn't look at her when he said, "I don't want you here anymore." It was the biggest lie he'd ever told.

Chapter 52

"Darling, are you okay?" The woman had a Southern drawl that oozed kindness and nurture—the kind of voice Amanda needed to hear. She had been sobbing almost continuously since boarding the plane, her head in her hands, so lost in her sorrow that the flight attendant had to tell her twice to fasten her seat belt.

Now she looked up at the woman in the seat next to her, middle-aged with gray hair pulled back behind her head. Warm eyes bathed Amanda from behind gold-wire-framed glasses. She had the tailored look of a businesswoman. Amanda shook her head through sobs to say that she wasn't okay.

"Is there anything I can do for you?" The woman laid a hand gently on Amanda's arm.

Amanda choked back her sobs to speak. She drew a deep breath, wiped her eyes with the back of her hand, blew her nose into the tissue the woman offered, and said, "I just broke up with …" She paused for a moment to pick the word that best described Ryan. "My boyfriend," she said.

"I'm so sorry, darling. That must hurt."

Amanda nodded. "God, it does," she said, then swallowed hard, fending off another sobbing fit.

The woman shook her head slowly and bit her lip, as her eyes moistened with sympathy. She extended her arms toward Amanda, who buried her face into the woman's shoulder and allowed the caring arms to envelop her.

The tears had subsided by the time Amanda stepped off the plane at the Salt Lake City airport, but now she felt faint. She found a bench near the gate to gather herself.

She pulled out her phone and called Katy, a call she didn't want to make. She couldn't bear to rehash the events of the day, but she needed a ride from the airport and a place to crash tonight.

Katy said yes, of course she'd pick her up. Then there was an awkward silence before Katy said, "I'm so sorry to hear you're coming home. I had such high hopes for this new guy."

"I did, too." Amanda wanted to keep the conversation brief—it would be so easy for the sobbing to begin again—but she knew that Katy would insist on details.

"So I saw Adam's asshole comment on your post—pretty clear why he did that—so I'm guessing this is about that?"

Amanda sighed. "Yes ... I mean, I'm not sure. I sure didn't handle that very well. But, Katy, there's a lot more to this. I can't go into it all now, but we were in trouble. There were some people following us."

"Oh my God, you mean like criminal types?"

"I don't know, but probably yes. Look, I don't know a lot, but Ryan wanted to me to leave."

"Because it wouldn't be safe? So he still—"

"No, I'm afraid it's final. He said he didn't want me there anymore. Didn't leave me a lot of options." She surprised herself at how objective she sounded, when objectivity was something she had no handle on at all right now.

Now Katy was quiet. Amanda hoped the conversation might be over. She was feeling more faint, even queasy. *Was it that Mexican food at West Yellowstone?*

But then Katy said, "Okay, I know you want to keep this call short, but I've gotta say this. You'd better not be considering going back to that jerk Adam. He's—"

"Please Katy, I don't want to go into—"

"Please hear me out on this, Amanda." Her voice was firm and insistent. "This is a critical time for you. You run back to him and you'll be back on the path to being that woman you were becoming. You know, that pathetic woman who sits at dinner, gazing all lovey-dovey with that reverent look, while Mr.-I'm-so-wonderful goes on and on about his many accomplishments. That woman who's—"

"Katy, please don't—"

"That woman who's learned to be in an almost perpetual state of hysterical laughter at all his jokes that aren't funny. That woman who's come to not expect that he will actually ask you how you're doing or laugh at one of your jokes. Okay, end of rant, but, Amanda, you were in danger of becoming that poor woman."

Amanda chewed the inside of her cheek, looking away at the hustle-bustle of travelers coming and going. She didn't need a lecture right now.

After the call, Amanda made her way slowly to the bathroom. The nausea was getting worse. Maybe this was just emotions. She splashed cold water on her face, and that helped. Then she studied the face in the mirror before her, evaluated it the way she would assess a painting. Who was this woman? What made her tick? What could she see in that face?

Her initial reaction was to be appalled at the mess of her hair. She'd done nothing with it since their hike this morning at Taggart Lake—*My God, was that still today?* It seemed so long ago now. She pulled a brush from her carry-on and worked it through her hair, without much success.

The face in the mirror looked old. There was darkness under her eyes from exhaustion and too much crying. But the eyes showed no emotion. They seemed defocused, lifeless. Perhaps ashamed. Defeated. She tried to recall a painting that evoked such feelings, but she could only think of photos she'd seen of battered women.

She splashed more water on her face—it was the only thing that made her feel better. She began to worry about making it to LA without throwing up.

Chapter 53

Ryan didn't make it back to the Roadtrek. A crippling wave of intestinal distress had almost doubled him over and sent him hurrying to the closest campground bathroom. Now on his knees on a cold concrete floor, inside a narrow stall enclosed by graffiti-covered gray metal walls, he was too miserable to worry about niceties like when this public toilet might have last been cleaned or how his violent retching might be grossing out other users of the bathroom.

After one siege, he leaned in exhaustion against the metal wall separating the stalls, breathing hard and feeling relief that his body told him was only temporary. It must have been the fast-food place. He wondered if Amanda was okay, if she had somehow been spared. How awful it would be to feel like this on a plane. He wished he could be there, even in his diminished state, to comfort her if she were ill.

From outside the door he heard several kids laughing—no doubt his distress would be fueling much juvenile campfire humor this evening. Then there was a voice. "Hey buddy, you okay in there?"

"Yeah, I'm okay." He tried to sound calm and collected, like his puking had been no big thing. "Got some food poisoning I think. I'll be all right." Then another wave of distress seized him—like a golf-ball-sized knot in his stomach, swelling to the size of a basketball—and he was over the toilet once more.

"Hey buddy," the voice said after the siege subsided, "that doesn't sound good at all. Sure I can't help?"

It was all Ryan could do to speak. "I wish I knew what you could do, but I think this thing has just got to work itself out."

"Yeah, I know. We've all been there. Look, buddy, I'll check back in a little while, okay?"

What Ryan wanted most right now was to be left alone.

Awhile later—perhaps an hour?—Ryan was able to stumble out of the stall and make his way slowly back to the Roadtrek. The helpful man had never returned, for which Ryan was grateful. He collapsed into the passenger seat and lay his head back.

Maybe he fell asleep, he couldn't be sure. He didn't know what time it was, but he felt somewhat better. It was now completely dark. Through the windshield all he could see was the flicker of a few distant campfires. He saw the road atlas stuffed between the seats and pulled it out. He turned to the Wyoming map and read his mother's entries. Like the other entries he had read, most were logistical: *Got an oil change at Fairfield Chevrolet in Rock Springs—the nicest folks*, and *Worrying about the blizzard forecast for tomorrow—need a place to hunker down.* Then he saw one that made him smile: *Should make it up to Bozeman tomorrow. A good visit with Wil is just what I need.*

He read about half the entries, but then one entry caused him to close the atlas and let it fall into his lap: *Wyoming is such a vast and empty state. On nights like this, it doesn't help me fight the loneliness.*

He was breathing through his mouth, unsure whether another intestinal attack might be coming. He felt like he was standing on a floor of cellophane above the abyss. He stood, holding onto one of the cabinets, then turned and stepped slowly toward the rear of the Roadtrek, where he soaked a towel with cold water and dampened his forehead. Then he noticed the sheet still hanging against the wall at the rear of the RV. On other nights she had been on the other side of that sheet. He closed his eyes and imagined her there now, waiting for him to pull the sheet aside and come to her. A huge sob welled up inside him. With one swipe he ripped the sheet from the rod that supported it, crushed it into a ball, then buried his face in it and wept.

He threw the sheet to the floor and turned forward. He had to get a handle on this. He thought about his mother's sad entry about her loneliness, but then he recalled her other entry, the one about visiting Wil.

Chapter 54

Her eyes were locked on the small white bag in the seat-back pouch in front of her. This was the first time she'd ever studied one seriously. What do they call these things anyway? Her friends called them barf bags. She picked up the bag and examined the writing: *For motion discomfort. Call flight attendant for disposal.* She looked around anxiously at the passengers next to her. She had a window seat; there were two people she would need to climb over, and the pilot had not yet turned off the Fasten-Seat-Belt sign. But she needed to head back to the bathroom now. She began to speak to the young man seated next to her, who was already asleep, but it was too late. She grabbed the barf bag, then pulled it to her face, as she leaned her head down between her knees.

When she was finished, she felt better, but, God, was she humiliated. She quickly sealed the bag and pushed the flight attendant button, as she looked around at the other passengers sheepishly. To her relief, the young man next to her was still asleep.

Now she felt a churning low in her stomach and a sudden sweat break out on her forehead. She took a deep breath, then pulled down the folding tray table and leaned her head down and moaned, "Please God, no. No. No."

Somehow Amanda made it to LAX, thanks largely to a helpful flight attendant who got her to the bathroom in time and offered consoling words through the door, while Amanda succumbed to full-blown food poisoning. With her body folded up into the small confines of the airline head, in between sieges she worried about Ryan. Had he been afflicted with this same malady? She couldn't imagine a worse place to endure the onslaught of food poisoning than in the small bathroom of the Roadtrek or a campground bathroom. She wished she was there to comfort him.

She was feeling a little better by the time she got off the flight in Los Angeles, and was able to make it to the baggage claim area under her own power. As she made her way through the crowds, the noise and the bright lights, another wave washed over her, and this had nothing to do with food poisoning. Last night she had danced to *The Tennessee Waltz* in a cowboy town in the middle of nowhere, spent the night in a van with a guy she had begun to really care about, then headed out the next day into a wild range of jagged peaks and bull elk. And now this. The wave that washed over her was a wave of resignation.

She stared off into the middle distance, focused on nothing, waiting for her bags to come around on the carousel, when her phone's ringtone jolted her to attention. It was a number she didn't recognize. "Hello?" she said.

"Amanda, I so glad to talk with you. This is Cepi."

"Cepi," Amanda shrieked. "It is so good to hear from you. How is Rey?"

"He is home now. Feeling good. I thank God every minute for this."

"Oh, Cepi, that is such good news." Amanda didn't want to ask about the insurance situation or what Reynaldo's employment future was looking like—she suspected these issues were still unresolved. "I am so grateful."

"I thank God for you, too, Amanda. You are very good to me. And Ryan too."

"Yes," Amanda said, but couldn't find additional words.

"My friend Amanda. Mi Amiga Amanda." Cepi laughed.

Amanda realized that the first smile she had experienced since the Grand Tetons was now breaking onto her face. "And you are my friend, Cepi. You are a woman of great courage. And love."

There was silence on the other end, and Amanda suspected her words may have touched Cepi. Then Cepi said, sounding choked up, "Yes, I know about love, and I also know about bad things. I know when you get love, you hold onto it. Never let go."

Now Amanda was choked up, too. Hold onto it. Never let go. "That's beautiful, Cepi."

"How is Ryan? He was very good to me."

Should she tell her? "He is fine," she said.

"He is very good man. You be good to him, Amanda. He love you very much. I can tell."

Amanda opened her mouth to speak, but all that came out was a whimper.

Chapter 55

The drive from Madison Campground to Bozeman followed a dramatically scenic route along the rapids-filled Gallatin River, a famous fly-fisherman's destination, where *A River Runs Through It* was filmed; past the ski-resort town of Big Sky; and up into the broad valley, ringed by peaks still snowcapped, that contains the thriving city of Bozeman, Montana. Bozeman is the home of Montana State University, where Uncle Wil taught European History for over thirty years before recently retiring. Ryan knew that the MSU Bobcats fielded a basketball team that usually fared well in the pretty-good Big Sky Conference. Unlike Irvine and its UCI Anteaters, Bozeman really does have bobcats, not to mention mountain lions, grizzly bears and moose.

Ryan knew what to expect. Uncle Wil had described his place in detail during those endless hours in that hospital in Carson City. It was a log ranch house, with a few acres—enough space to have a couple of horses, a goat, a dozen or so chickens, two large dogs that had the run of the place, and a huge vegetable garden. Wil called it his ranchette, because it wasn't big enough—at least by Montana standards—to be considered a ranch.

Since Ryan got such an early start—unsurprisingly, he slept little—he was in Bozeman by mid-morning. Uncle Wil opened the door on the third knock and greeted Ryan with a hug. "Dang, it's good to see you, nephew," he said. "Get your sorry butt inside here." Then he looked beyond Ryan with a confused look and said, "So where's the new girlfriend?"

Ryan looked at his feet, as he said, "She went home."

"Went home? Dang it, Ryan, I thought you said things were heating up. What happened?"

Ryan was still looking at his feet. "It's a long story."

"I know it's a little early, but is this a better-get-out-the-good-Scotch kinda long story?"

Even in his sorry state, Ryan had to laugh. He grinned at Wil and said, "I think it may be."

Wil was big shouldered and rangy—no sign of the gut you see on many men in their sixties—with wavy, gray hair, well-worn Levi's, scuffed-up Redwings, and a light blue denim shirt under a leather vest, unbuttoned at the neck to reveal a tuft of gray chest hair. He had dressed this way for as long as Ryan could remember. He looked like he was ready for the roundup, the Marlboro Man without nicotine: a man who knew how to rope a calf, handle a shotgun and draw to an inside straight. In other words, he completely fit the Bozeman scene. It was hard to imagine this guy lecturing on the Tudor dynasty, but maybe that's what made him such a popular teacher.

Wil went to a counter behind him, then returned with a bottle and two glasses, larger than normal whiskey glasses. He gestured for Ryan to take a seat in one of the red-leather, brass-riveted upright chairs around a low rough-wood table, then set the bottle and glasses on the table between them. It was the Oban Limited Edition.

"I gave you a bottle of this stuff, didn't I?" Wil poured generous amounts into each glass.

Ryan nodded. "Good stuff." He took a healthy swig, let it do a rich, warm smolder in the back of his throat, then set the glass down, ready to begin.

Wil sat back, relaxed with one leg crossed over the other, and seemed to give Ryan his full attention.

When he had finished, Ryan sagged back into the chair, spent.

"So you're tellin' me that you sent her away to protect her from these bad guys, but used the old boyfriend as the reason?"

"That's about it."

Wil scratched his head, pulled at his chin, then said, "Seems to me, you're either a true hero, Ryan." He paused to take another sip of the Scotch. "Or you're about the biggest dumbass I've ever seen."

Ryan shrugged.

"So, why don't you just call her?"

Ryan expelled a troubled breath. "I can't. Not with the way it ended. It's over."

Wil chewed his lip like he was pondering this carefully. "So tell me, Ryan, how do you know these dudes weren't following her?"

The thought that they might be following Amanda seemed unlikely, but in fact was a possibility to which Ryan hadn't given much consideration. If that were true, then he'd just sent her off alone and unsuspecting. He could not allow himself to dwell on that now. "I don't know for sure, but I'm pretty certain it's something from my last job that's following me."

Wil stood and walked over to a tall cabinet, opened a glass door, and removed a double-barrel shotgun. He held it up, pointed it toward a far wall and aligned his eye with the sight. Then he picked up a soft cloth and carefully wiped down the barrels with gentle, polishing strokes. While he did this, he said to Ryan, "So, I'm kinda hopin' these bastards are stupid enough to show up around here."

Wil didn't allow Ryan to sit around and mope. He put him to work almost immediately—even with a glass of Scotch in him—helping with chores around the ranchette: moving newly delivered bales of hay for the two horses, running the riding tractor-lawnmower over a wild acre of grass-like vegetation that Wil called his lawn, and doing some long-overdue Spring window cleaning.

In mid-afternoon, Ryan sagged onto one of the hay bales and wiped sweat from his forehead. Wil came over from where he was repairing a stretch of fence around the corral and put one Redwing up on the bale, adjusted his sweat-stained Stetson, and said, "Am I keeping you busy enough, nephew?"

"Holy crap, Uncle Wil, you're kicking my ass is what you're doing."

Wil laughed. "Good," he said. "You know what they say. You don't have time to be depressed when you're working your butt off."

In the late afternoon, Wil set the coals for a cookout in a large brick barbeque pit at the edge of the shaded patio behind the house. Then he and Ryan settled in with a six-pack of Madison River Ambers. The sun was setting behind them, and a reddish alpenglow was beginning to bathe the western flanks of the Bridger Mountains to the north.

Wil said, "Seems like a couple of smart fellers like you and me ought to be able to figure out who these bad guys are."

"I don't know. I've already given it so much thought, and I can't come up with anything, other than it's got something to do with my former employer. They were royally ticked off about my antics in sending in those two abstracts."

"Following you half-way across the country seems to be a real stretch from just being royally ticked off." Wil stroked his chin thoughtfully, then said, "Do they do any classified work? I mean, does this have anything to do with some secret crap?"

"As far as I know, Lightyear didn't work on any classified things. Certainly, nothing I worked on was classified."

"So that rules out the possibility that they were selling secrets to some unsavory enemy?"

Ryan shrugged. "I'd guess it does."

"Or maybe they thought your conference abstracts were leaking some insider commercial information that a customer was paying for?"

"It could be. I did have to sign nondisclosure agreements, which, of course, I intentionally disregarded." Ryan took a swig of beer. "They said they would prosecute me for that, and maybe they will—I did worry about that for a while—but that's hardly a reason to be following me."

Wil got up to check the coals. "Yeah," he said over his shoulder, "that doesn't seem quite right. Say, I think these coals are about ready. You want to grab those T-bones next to the kitchen sink?"

Once the steaks were on, Wil sank back into his patio chair. He ran a hand through his silver mane, then drummed the top of his head softly with his fingers. "Lots of things don't add up here. I mean, if they wanted to harm you, then why haven't they done it yet?"

Ryan shook his head. "Maybe it's not Lightyear after all. I mean, they really are a small company. We saw at least three different people tailing us, and God knows how many we didn't see. Could a small outfit like Lightyear do that?"

Wil looked out at the sunset pinkness that was now becoming twilight. "Or maybe Lightyear had a big-time customer who does have the resources?"

Ryan nodded. "So why haven't they done anything yet?"

Wil got up to check the steaks. While he poked at them, he said, "Maybe they're just trying to scare the crap out of you." He loaded the steaks onto a large platter and brought them to the table between their chairs.

"If that's true, then they've certainly achieved their goal," Ryan said, trying to make this a laughable thing.

Wil forked a steak onto Ryan's plate. "I hope you like your steak medium-rare 'cause that's what you've got."

They ate in silence for a while, as night fell, then Wil said, "So, Ryan, don't mean to be a downer here, but you've got a lot going on right now. Might as well name it for what it is— getting fired, losing your girlfriend, being chased by mysterious bad guys. That should be enough for anybody, but you're also driving around in your mother's old van. I think that might depress the poo out of me."

Ryan finished chewing a bite, shook his head slowly and produced a nervous laugh. "When you put it like that, you old silver-tongued rascal, maybe I should be depressed. But, you know, I actually am enjoying driving the Roadtrek." He set his fork down, then put his hands together, steepling his fingers. "She left this road atlas in the RV. I should show it to you."

"What's so special about it?"

"Well, she wrote all these notes in it, on almost every page, as she travelled around the country. It has a lot of her thoughts." He gazed off into the encroaching darkness. "Sure makes me wish I'd spent more time with her." He paused then added, almost choking up, "I think she was lonely."

Wil looked away, too, and seemed to be almost choking up himself. Then he looked back at Ryan. "I never said this to you before, certainly not while we were doing that vigil in the hospital—we had other things on our minds then—but I'd say your mom was lonely most of her life."

Ryan felt his throat tighten. He nodded his head slowly with grim acceptance.

Wil continued. "That no-good father of yours was the main cause. Leaving you and her alone all those years. She kept herself occupied with raising you and keeping busy with chores. Never saw her relax and enjoy life. She never was a stop and smell ..." He paused and closed his eyes, a smile on his face, like he was recalling some memory. Then he continued. "No, she was a stop-and-*prune*-the-roses kind of girl. When your father left—as traumatic as that was—was the day your mom got a new lease on life."

Ryan said slowly, "I just wish I could have been there for—"

"Oh, gimme a break," interrupted Wil. "Don't say stuff like that. She knew you were busy, like young folks are, trying to get your life moving ahead. She was a smart girl—she understood that. So don't go moping around like—"

"I mean, I just—"

"Look, Ryan, here's what you need to know. Your mom understood and she loved you deeply, more than anything else." He paused, then, with a devilish twinkle in his eye, said, "Except for maybe that darned van."

They both laughed, but Ryan felt little relief. Tormenting images of his mother and Amanda—flickering reminders of what had been lost—danced in his brain, and it seemed like the darkness that was filling the big Montana sky was also filling his heart.

Later, Ryan sat up in the double bed in Wil's guest room, staring at the screen on his laptop. The room was simple and homey, like the rest of the house. A natural-finished wainscoting, made of vertical one-by-fours, gave the room a north-woods-lodge look, as did the ceiling—tongue and groove supported by a large, rough-finished glulam. The windows were old—Ryan guessed the house was built in the fifties. He decided to write a blog post entry, but he didn't know where to start. He was becoming more and more convinced that he would never actually publish any of this stuff. He gazed at the far wall, where an old schoolhouse regulator clock tick-tocked noisily, chronicling how his life was passing—measuring what had been lost—as he sat and did nothing. He wondered if Amanda might be watching a clock somewhere, thinking of him—their lives connected by the same seconds passing, the only thing they now shared. He whimpered out loud, then cursed himself and began to type.

New Blog post

In my last post I said it's possible and important to be strong and move on beyond the failures in your life. What a crock. I now know that sometimes terrible things happen, and there's absolutely nothing you can do about it. Being around good people like Uncle

Wil helps, but ultimately the pain is still there, and there doesn't seem to be anything you can do about it. I do not understand why there is so much misery in this world. I know the average person living in Somalia or freezing to death on a winter street in Chicago would probably laugh at my situation, but since Amanda left, I just don't know what to do with myself. Maybe I did the wrong thing in sending her away. I could just dial her number and beg her to come back. But there is still a danger. Isn't there? I wish I could see her face, the smiling face that I will never see again.

He set the laptop aside and studied the room again. A guest room, a temporary overnight accommodation, and yet it was at the moment his only home.

He was an orphan. But even orphans have orphanages. He had nothing.

Chapter 56

The bleak thoughts that had followed Ryan into sleep had now retreated to the perimeter of his consciousness. When he shared this at breakfast—oatmeal and English muffins with some kind of amazing berry jam—Wil had given him an understanding nod and said, "It's good to hear the wolf's no longer at the door, but it seems like he's still in the yard." Wil had a way with words.

Wil scrubbed the oatmeal pot, while Ryan loaded the dishwasher. "So, sometimes I stop by a little service down at the church," Wil said, as he rinsed the pot. "Let's go do some chores, then why don't you come into town with me?"

Ryan was quickly crafting an excuse. "Oh, I don't usually—"

"It's only a half-hour or so, then we'll go grab some lunch. I hadn't noticed that your dance card was especially full today." Wil shot Ryan a quick grin.

"Sure. That would be fine," sighed Ryan.

St. Anne's Episcopal Church, one block off the main street of Bozeman, was essentially a large A-frame, its front dominated by a tall triangle-shaped window facing the street and a small, simple cross at the peak of the roof. There were only a dozen or so cars in the large parking lot. "Just a few folks show up for the mid-week services, really informal, and nothing is expected of you," said Wil, obviously trying to allay Ryan's misgivings about being here.

Inside, they found themselves in a large sanctuary that would probably seat several hundred, but Wil steered Ryan toward a small chapel off to the side, where about a dozen people were now gathering. Everyone was quiet, either sitting—apparently in contemplation—or kneeling in prayer, as a man about Ryan's age played soft melodies on a flute.

Wil gestured Ryan into one of the pews, then excused himself for a moment, leaving Ryan sitting alone among these strangers. He shifted uncomfortably in the wooden pew, as he surveyed his surroundings. Next to him was a tiny elderly woman, with a deeply wrinkled face and short, thin white hair. On his other side, a middle-aged businessman type, in an expensive-looking suit, had just slid in next to him. In the pew in front of him, a young mom was busy with an infant and keeping a toddler mollified with picture-story books. Next to her a skinny, tattooed young woman with long purple hair sat quietly, looking up toward the small altar. A young couple down the row looked like college students. Beyond them sat a disheveled young man, his clothes dark with dirt and his hair matted and shaggy. Ryan guessed he was homeless.

Ryan lifted his eyes from the people around him, not wanting to be caught leering. The chapel was not much larger than Uncle Wil's living room, finished simply, but with well-cared-for oak trim and an arched, wooden ceiling. Colorful stained-glass windows around the edges of the room featured various scenes, which Ryan assumed portrayed bible stories. The altar—set behind an oak rail—was draped with white linen. Two lighted white candles in brass holders sat atop each end of the altar. All in all, it reminded him of a modern version of the little rustic chapel in the Grand Tetons—that beautiful place where his life had taken a nosedive. And that made him uneasy.

Ryan looked around for Uncle Wil, who had now taken a seat a couple of rows back. When their eyes connected, Wil gave him a relaxed smile and a gentle nod, which helped a bit to alleviate his mounting anxiety. He would have liked Uncle Wil to be next to him, but his row was already full. Ryan closed his eyes and allowed the soothing flute music to calm him.

When the music stopped, everyone stood, and Ryan opened his eyes to see a woman—the minister, he assumed—in a white robe and carrying a book, walk slowly to the front of the chapel. She was probably in her forties, with short brown hair, showing streaks of gray. She greeted the small congregation with a friendly smile and bright blue eyes that twinkled behind frameless glasses. She invited the people to follow the service in the prayer book, which Ryan found in a small rack in the pew-back in front of him.

The minister read words and the congregation made responses, which Ryan followed in the book. One sentence struck him right up front, as everyone said together: *Almighty God, to you all hearts are open, all desires known, and from you no secrets are hid: Cleanse the thoughts of our hearts by the inspiration of your Holy Spirit* .... If such words were true, then everything about him was being laid open—along with everything about the white-haired old lady, the businessman, the young mom and her kids, the purple-haired girl, the college students, the homeless guy, and Uncle Wil. This thought made Ryan squirm, but it also strangely comforted him.

After a person from the congregation read some passages from the bible, the minister gave a short talk and some prayers were said. Then the minister extended her arms in welcome and said, "The peace of the Lord be always with you." The people responded, "And also with you." Immediately, everyone stood and greeted one another, including Ryan. They treated him no differently than anyone else. The little white-haired lady extended her hand in greeting to him—it was small and cool—and said, "Peace be with you." The businessman-type gave him a strong handshake. The young mom's handshake was soft and warm, the purple-haired girl's handshake was bony and limp, the homeless guy's hand felt calloused and rough, the college couple both had smooth, cool hands that probably spent a lot of time at computer keyboards. Even the minister came by and shook his hand. This all felt surprisingly authentic.

Then everyone sat, while the minister prepared some vessels on the altar, then said more words, to which the people made responses. At this point, Ryan was no longer following the book. He was just listening.

Then the minister invited everyone to come forward for communion. The people stood and began a slow, quiet procession up to the altar rail, while the young man with the flute once again played soft music. Ryan was unsure what to do. Perhaps he was unqualified, perhaps an outsider like him was unwelcomed. Weren't there things he had to do to prepare for this?

He looked back at Wil for a clue, and Wil gave him a smile and gestured him forward. He was still uncertain about this. Then he looked up at the minister, who apparently sensed his uncertainty. She extended a hand toward him and mouthed the word, "Come." He followed the white-haired lady to the rail and knelt beside her. Moments later, the businessman knelt on the other side of him. He cast a quick glance down the rail and saw the young mom with her two kids and the purple-haired girl and the homeless guy all kneeling together with him. Farther down the rail, beyond the two college kids, he saw Uncle Wil kneel.

He'd never seen anything like this. It was like everyone was here: the ones who'd made it alongside the losers, misfits and outcasts—the victorious and the beaten, side by side, focused on something beyond themselves. He didn't know what that something was, but it felt good. And somewhere in that group was him.

It was as if he was—at least for this brief moment—not an isolated speck, alone and misunderstood, trying to figure it out all by himself, enduring his suffering alone, but part of something bigger, part of everyone there. He was old and young, he was dirty and clean, he was poor and wealthy, he was broken and healed.

He recalled the words the minister and the congregation had just said. Words about remembering the past and looking toward the future: a connection in time, telescoping all history—past, present and future—into this moment. A rational part of him tried to analyze, justify, explain this. But he couldn't, and for now he didn't need to, so he just let it go.

Maybe the destination of all his searching, all his unarticulated longings, was here at this wooden rail. He grasped it tightly, like it was the safety bar on a roller coaster. He was trembling. Then he felt a hand on his arm. It was the old woman next to him. She looked up at him with such confidence and acceptance that he nearly lost it, and it took all his discipline to hold back his tears.

When the minister passed by, he held up his hands like he saw others do, and the minister pressed a piece of bread into his hands and said, "This is the Body of Christ." He placed the bread in his mouth and swallowed it. He had no idea what this meant.

Yet, something had happened. Oddly, Ryan Browning, Ph.D. physicist, didn't need to be shown data or a mathematical proof—he just needed to be in this moment. His thoughts were not something that he could describe, not something to be typed into a blog post.

It was a feeling—a holistic but wordless unification— more silky and complete than any three-pointer ever could be.

What was that something? Maybe it was an illusion. Or maybe what was happening was something he had always longed for—perhaps it was even wired into him—a cosmic embrace, an affirmation from the universe that he was okay.

And in that cosmic embrace he saw faces flash before him: Cepi clutching her crucifix and Dr. Gutierrez coming down the hall in his blue scrubs; the old man at the Grand Canyon mourning his lost appreciation for beauty; Father Jessop talking about glaciers; Judy Chicago grieving the suffering woman at Trinity Site; the nun talking about thin places. They were all at this rail with him.

Then he saw his mother's face. It was not the face of a dead woman, nor the face of a woman abandoned. It was the face of love—a mother's love mixed with the knowledge that she was loved. And he saw Amanda—though she was far away, at this moment she was right here with him.

He stood to return to his pew, still fighting back tears. He felt dizzy and needed to rest a hand on the altar rail to steady himself. The others turned to look at him. "I'm sorry," he said quietly. He felt a hand on his arm, then another and then another. An arm came around his shoulder.

Maybe it was true that he had nothing. But maybe he had everything.

The minister offered a closing prayer that he did not hear. Then it was over.

As Ryan left the chapel, Wil was waiting by the door. They walked to Wil's big Ford pickup in silence. Inside, Wil said, "So, how was it?"

Ryan shook his head slowly, knowing that Uncle Wil, of course, knew exactly how it was. "I think I'll need some time to process it." He blew his nose into a tissue, then added, "You kinda set me up for that, didn't you?" His shaking had just now subsided.

"Well, I ...." Wil paused.

"I mean that's fine—better than fine, actually—but you could have let me know what I was getting into."

Wil shrugged, then, while keeping his eyes on road, said, "So tell me Ryan, what's your favorite food?"

"What's that got to do with—"

"Just tell me. Take a second to think about it if you need to, but tell me."

Ryan shrugged. "Okay I'll play." He sighed, then said, "I guess broiled salmon."

"Broiled salmon, huh? That's a fine choice. So tell me what broiled salmon tastes like."

"You're crazy, you know that, don't you?" Ryan was laughing now.

Wil was undeterred. "Just tell me, please."

Ryan exhaled dramatically to signify impatience. "Well, I'd say it's flaky ... and mild ... with a distinct flavor ... geez, Uncle Wil, you know I can't describe it."

"So if you wanted someone to know what it tasted like, what would you do?"

"Duh, I'd just take them to a seafood restaurant," said Ryan, shrugging.

Wil nodded, then looked over at Ryan with a grin. "I rest my case."

Chapter 57

In the late afternoon, Wil poured two glasses from the Oban Limited Edition and handed one to Ryan. "So, here's your dram."

Ryan nodded a thank you, then studied the glass. "So, just how much is a dram anyway?"

"It's a measure of a pouring of Scotch."

Ryan nodded. "Yeah, I know. But how much is it?"

"Does it need to be a precise amount?"

Ryan shrugged. "Well, if it's to be a useful unit of measure, I'd say yes."

"It is a useful unit of measure."

"But how much is it?"

"Well, some say twenty-five milliliters, some say thirty-five." Wil paused and savored his first sip. "But the Scots say it is a pouring of whiskey, whose actual volume is determined by the generosity of the pourer." He smiled.

Ryan was confused.

Wil added, "I'd say that's a useful measure. Wouldn't you agree?"

Ryan smiled. "Guess I'd have to agree that it is." He paused, then added, "But quantitative measurement has its place. Surely you'd agree with that."

"Of course." Wil gave a little nod, like this was obvious.

"I mean …." Ryan pursed his lips, crafting his response. Finally, he said, "Science provides specific answers to things. And many times specific answers are needed."

"Of course," Wil said again.

Ryan continued. "Take for example …." He was searching for just the right example. "Take the water in a tea kettle boiling on the stove. Why is it boiling?"

Wil laughed. "I want to see where you're going with this."

"Well, there is a specific answer that's not open for debate." He hesitated, as he offered a quick, satisfied smile. "The water's boiling because there is a heating element on the stove that's pumping heat into the kettle, and it has imparted enough energy into the water to raise it to the boiling point." He steepled his fingers with the satisfied look of a prosecutor completing his closing arguments.

Wil nodded slowly. "Hmm. Yes, that's certainly correct." He took another sip of Scotch, then waited for a few moments before saying, "But the water also could be boiling because someone wanted a cup of tea."

For a moment Ryan was stumped. "That's a good thought," he conceded. He started to say more, but took a drink of the Scotch instead.

Later, in the guest room, Ryan took a few reflective moments, closing his eyes. He saw the nun from the Chapel of the Transfiguration, the little woman who taught him about the cornrakes and thin places. He could see her face like she was standing before him right now. Then he began to type a new blog post. *Just let it rip*, he thought. *Don't overthink, just react.* He chuckled. *Let your writing be determined by the generosity of the pourer.* Quickly, he realized that he was writing his post in the form of a poem and that brought an unexpected smile to his face.

Physicists, they say, probe the secrets of the physical world.
They measure things unseen,
correlate mysterious forces and energies,
And speculate on hidden truths;
Uncover and discover;
Give explanations and do definitive experiments
That turn myth into fact and magic into equations;
Music into acoustics
And thoughts into magnetic fields.
Beauty is data to be analyzed
In a microsecond of computer time.
Love is a chemical reaction,
And life is an electric circuit.
Some do not see the forest for the trees, it's said,
And some cannot see the trees for the branches
Or perhaps the branches for the lichen on the bark.
But the lichen are only molecules
And the molecules atoms and the atoms nuclei and electrons.
The physicist can see the electron
And sometimes understands it pretty well.
He can measure every important property,
And, indeed, can marvel (in his moments of romantic zeal)
At its fuzzy beauty and that it's neither here nor there.
But what does this have to do with forests?

He leaned back and read it again. He wasn't sure if he liked it, but maybe he did. Maybe it was the first good thing he had written.

Chapter 58

The next morning, Ryan tapped on the front door with a foot. After a moment, he tapped again. The door opened and a confused Wil stood there. "Oh my God," said Wil, "what the hell have you gone and done now?"

"I just had to," said Ryan, grinning. He set the large puppy down on the floor and let it run into the living room. "Oops," he said quickly, "guess I'd better not do that. I'm sure he's not housebroken." He set out after the scampering pup.

"Well, it wouldn't be the first time a dog took a leak in this house," laughed Wil.

Ryan scooped up the puppy and brought it back toward the front door, where the surprised Wil still stood. "Got him down at the shelter. He's a Golden Retriever, at least mostly a Golden, they thought. No papers or anything."

Wil leaned in closer for a better look. "I'd guess he's three months old maybe?"

Ryan shrugged. "They didn't know. He was found out on some county road. Apparently, he'd been dumped, but I mean, how could anyone dump something that looks like this?" He held the golden-yellow pup up closer to Wil, and the pup immediately lapped Wil's face with a wet pink tongue.

Wil recoiled and wiped his face with the sleeve of his denim shirt. "Good God, young-in, you are a friendly thing, that's for sure."

"So I hope it's okay if I keep him here for a while."

"Of course. We'll have to introduce him to Alpha and Omega though," Wil said. Alpha and Omega were Wil's two big Labs that mostly ran around outside. "Shouldn't be a problem. They're a lot more accepting of others than I am." He laughed.

"I haven't had a dog in a long time," laughed Ryan. "You're gonna have to give me some pointers."

"Between me and Alpha and Omega and this little slobber factory, you'll get all the pointers you need. Bring him on in here, and let's get him settled in."

Ryan carried the dog toward a sunroom in the rear of the house.

"So, important question: what are you going to name him?" Wil asked.

Ryan pursed his lips. "Good question. I don't know. I think for now, I'll just call him NoName."

"NoName?" bellowed Wil. "That's not a good name for a dog."

Ryan shrugged. "It's all I've got for right now."

Wil gave Ryan a puzzled look. "Okay," he said, with a hint of skepticism. "NoName it is."

NoName looked up at Wil with intelligent eyes, like he knew exactly what was going on. He was now wriggling in Ryan's arms, so Ryan set the dog down, and he scampered to the corner, where he squatted and peed on the brick floor.

Wil looked at Ryan with raised eyebrows. "Okay, lesson number one. Better go get some newspaper." Then he laughed.

Ryan grimaced, then started to look around for newspapers.

"One more question," said Wil, now standing with hands on hips and giving Ryan a serious look.

Ryan turned. "Yeah?"

"Why would you be wanting to get a dog right now anyway?"

Ryan looked down, then back up at Wil. "It's what she would have wanted," he said.

Chapter 59

At sunset, they sat out back in the patio chairs again. No steaks tonight. Wil had microwaved some frozen concoction and Ryan had made a salad. After dinner, they relaxed, while NoName dozed in Ryan's lap.

"Beautiful sunset we've got tonight, nephew," said Wil. "Just seeing it kinda makes you feel grateful."

"Uncle Wil, I never took you for a religious type."

"Why's that?"

Ryan struggled to find words that wouldn't be insulting. "I mean ... uh ... you're an academic ...."

But Wil clearly understood what Ryan was driving at. "Well, first off I don't consider myself a religious person. I go to church and I believe in God, but I'd say I'm a person of faith rather than a religious person."

"Fair enough. But how then do you reconcile faith in something you can't see, that can't be proven scientifically, with your academic background?" Ryan now remembered how Wil would go off to the chapel at that hospital back in Carson City, and how he had readily welcomed the prayers of the hospital chaplain.

"I know where you're coming from, nephew, but there's no conflict for me. First of all, my faith in God stands up to any intellectual inquiry I have. And it needs to. You can't or at least shouldn't believe in something that's just patently wrong or can't stand up to rational questioning."

Ryan nodded his head. "That's been the stumbling block for me, I guess. I can't just seem to make sense of it."

"Have you done much reading about the subject?"

"Well, I confess I haven't."

"That doesn't sound much like an intelligent inquiry to me."

"Touché." Ryan laughed.

"I hope you'll read what some of the more thoughtful scholars have to say about the relationship between science and faith."

Ryan nodded with interest, and he leaned forward as Wil continued.

"I'm talking about writers like John Polkinghorne. The guy was a top theoretical physicist at Cambridge University."

"I think I've heard of him." Ryan, suddenly more engaged in the conversation, scooted his chair closer to Wil.

"Yeah, he occupied the same endowed chair that Stephen Hawking had. So the guy's not a slouch. Anyway, Polkinghorne's also a Christian pastor."

Ryan's lips parted, as he listened.

"I've got some of his books back in the library. Hope you'll take a look." Now Wil cleared his throat and crossed his leg, like he was getting more comfortable. "So," Wil said, "have you ever considered where all this came from?" He waved his arm in an all-encompassing way, suggesting that he was talking about the whole universe.

"I would say that there are laws of physics. Equations that govern the behavior of the universe."

Wil nodded his agreement. "But Hawking raises the question in his book, *A Brief History of Time*—you ever read that?"

"A long time ago, maybe."

"Anyway, Hawking raises the question, so if there are equations that describe the universe, then who was it who breathed fire into the equations to give them an actual universe to describe?"

Ryan licked his lips, as he pondered Wil's words.

Wil continued. "And Polkinghorne takes it one step further, asking just where did those equations come from in the first place?"

Ryan smiled helplessly and shrugged his shoulders.

Then Wil said, "But there's more to all this than just intelligent inquiry."

Ryan raised his eyebrows. Uncle Wil was holding court, and Ryan was soaking it up. He was getting a glimpse of why his uncle had been such a successful teacher.

"For me, faith must be able to withstand intelligent questioning, like I said. But the real draw for me is that faith is more like a love affair than an experiment."

"Oh?" Ryan shifted uneasily in his chair.

"Yeah. Faith involves both the heart and the mind. Both are essential. I think it was Feynman—one of your guys—"

"Richard Feynman," Ryan interjected, "the great Caltech physicist who discovered quantum electrodynamics."

Wil nodded. "Feynman was an agnostic himself, who always emphasized the use of scientific reasoning."

Ryan had read some of Feynman's famous papers—after all, the guy was a Nobel laureate.

"Yet, Feynman conceded that the most important questions don't lend themselves to scientific answers."

"You mean, like questions about relationships?"

"Exactly. Take that girl of yours, for example."

Ryan nodded, then looked down. As controversial as the relationship between science and faith was, it was a preferable topic to Amanda right now.

"You've clearly got some strong feelings for her, and you've got some strong opinions."

"I guess I do," he said softly.

"But I suspect that spreadsheets and equations and lab experiments have very little to do with any of those opinions."

Ryan chuckled nervously. "You're right, of course."

Now Wil looked out at the evening sky. "It would seem like you had a strong reaction to that church service."

"Yes, that's true."

"So, feel free to analyze that. In fact, you must analyze that. Make sure it's not hysteria or stupidity—the way you should in a relationship."

Ryan nodded.

Wil reached over and patted Ryan's knee. "Look, I don't want to sound like some know-it-all with all the answers. There are a lot of things I don't understand. I'm just telling you how it's been for me. So, use that great brain of yours, but use that heart also. Which by the way is also pretty great." Wil, who had been so serious, now grinned. "And don't let some interminable analysis stand in the way of enjoying the relationship."

Ryan nodded again, and now he turned his attention to the beautiful twilight sky as well.

They sat in silence for several minutes, then Wil said, "So, what are your plans, Ryan?"

Ryan took a deep breath and shrugged. He started to speak, but Wil cut him off.

"I mean, you're welcome to stay here as long as you want. It's really good having you around, and you're probably safe as long as you're here."

Ryan stood and stepped to the edge of the patio, still holding NoName. He looked out to where the sunset glow had now faded off the peaks north of the city. The temperature had taken a sharp drop as the sun disappeared, probably ten degrees in twenty minutes, and they'd have to go inside soon. "I've been thinking about that," he said. Now he turned and faced his uncle. "When I arrived here, I thought I'd eventually head back to LA. Not that there's anything there for me anymore, but it's the place I'm familiar with. My enthusiasm for the Glacier thing had just sort of dissipated at that point."

Wil nodded. "I could see how you'd feel that way."

"But the longer I've stayed here, the more I began to realize that's not the answer."

Wil now rose also and walked over to the edge of the patio, where Ryan stood. He also looked out into the darkness, although there wasn't anything to see. "While you're working through options, let me put another one on the table for you."

Ryan turned toward him, but said nothing.

Wil continued. "I don't know about your financial situation, but I assume that at some point you're going to have to get a job."

Ryan sighed. "You're right, of course. I haven't got much socked away. Mom's bills pretty much knocked me flat."

"I figured," said Wil. "So anyway, I'm thinking that the physics department here at State is always looking for some qualified adjunct help."

"You mean like a temporary position?"

"Not necessarily. The adjunct professor slots are filled as contractors. So no tenure track or anything like that. And you'd probably get stuck with the big survey course sections, which can be a lot of work. And because it's a contract position, they have to be renewed every year." He looked at Ryan with raised eyebrows. "But the pay's not too bad, and if you worked out, then the renewal each year is pretty much a formality."

"I've never taught before, you know."

"Sure, but you're an accomplished physicist, at least in my book. Ph.D. from Cal, staff scientist at Los Alamos. You've got a lot to share with these kids."

"Sounds pretty good, I've got to admit, especially since I have no other options right now. But aren't those jobs pretty competitive?"

"Yeah, they are. But if you have an insider friend going to bat for you, it can be a lot easier." Wil grinned.

Ryan felt tears welling up once more—damn, he'd cried so much the past few days—as he looked at Wil. Here was the only family he had. "You'd do that for me?"

"You kidding, nephew? Does old *ursus arctos* defecate in the understory? Seriously."

"That would be really nice," Ryan said, then gave his uncle a hug.

Wil said, "Now let's not get all gushy here." He laughed.

So did Ryan. Then he turned away and walked to the other edge of the patio. "Like I said, the longer I've been here, the more I've come to realize something."

Wil nodded, "And that is?"

"I think I need to finish out the Glacier trip. The trip has always been sort of a tribute to my mom, but it's more than that. It's also about me."

"I get the tribute part, yes I do. Tell me more."

"My track record at finishing things hasn't been so good lately. I didn't cut the mustard at Los Alamos. I was drifting in my new job at Lightyear. Then Mom died, and that made me start seeing things differently. I think I sent those abstracts in because of her—Mom sort of woke me up to the fact that I can't just drift, and I can't let fear hold me back. And then I launched out on this trip, asking a girl to go with me, one I'd only known for fifteen minutes."

Wil smiled and nodded approvingly. "Sounds like you've gone straight from the kiddie pool to the high dive. I like it."

"So I want to complete the trip, even if there are those shadowy figures pursuing me."

Wil placed hands on both of Ryan's shoulders and looked him squarely in the eye. "There's real hope for you, nephew. I'm an old man, and it's taken me my whole life to learn that I cannot let fear rule my life. Because that is no life at all. You've learned it at a much younger age."

"Thank you, Uncle Wil," Ryan said softly. "When I'm done I may want to call you about that adjunct position, if the offer still stands. It does sound perfect, I've got to admit."

Wil nodded. "The offer will always be there."

"Thank you again, Uncle Wil, I—"

"I've gotta say one more thing, Ryan, and it's this. If you hit the road and in fact you find yourself in a tight spot, just give me a holler. I'll load up the gun rack in the back of the F250, and I know these Montana roads like I know my own spit. I can be wherever you need me to be before you even know it." He now looked into Ryan's eyes with a serious piercing stare that evolved into a big grin.

"I'll do that," said Ryan.

Just then the doorbell rang, and they both jumped. "Who'd be coming around here this late?" wondered Wil. He looked at Ryan. "You stay here."

A few moments later, Wil called out to Ryan from the house. "You might want to come in here, nephew. I'm looking at the prettiest girl I've ever seen, and I think she's here to see you."

Chapter 60

Most of our lives go by in a sequence of uneventful episodes, like an unfunny sitcom that no one ever watches. Those times creep slowly. We think they will never end, that nothing will ever change. The cliché we use is that we are stuck in a rut, but the reality is that sometimes we feel we are stuck in a deeper hole—our own grave, from which we will not emerge.

But Ryan knew that once in a while, there may be a transition moment when everything changes. He had studied the phenomenon of phase transitions in grad school—the sudden process when a material instantly transforms into something completely different. The phase transitions most familiar to us are the ones that water undergoes—from liquid to vapor at the boiling point, or even more dramatically, when it goes from liquid to solid at the freezing point: when the amorphous, continuous medium we call liquid water suddenly crystallizes into one of thirty-two solid structures, when dull water takes on the beautiful sparkle of ice.

As Ryan stepped toward the door—before he could see her—he sensed that he was on the brink of a phase transition in his life. A moment when suddenly his life would never be the same again. He could hardly breathe. It felt like Kobe had just made a slam dunk in his chest.

Amanda stood in the doorway and, like Uncle Wil had said, she was the most beautiful woman he had ever seen. She wore the familiar Patagonia down jacket over those sexy blue jeans she'd worn on the first day of their trip. Ryan began to speak, but he could not find words.

Finally, Amanda said, "I've been travelling all day. You gonna invite me in out of the cold?"

Wil pulled the door open wider for her to enter.

Her eyes were locked on Ryan. She stepped closer to him and placed a single finger gently on his chin, as if touching him to see if he were real.

Ryan finally found words. With his eyes moist and his body trembling, he cradled her face in his hands and said in a shaking voice, "You shouldn't be here." He took a deep breath, then blurted, "I'm a guy who's been fired twice, and I'm being chased by people who may be dangerous."

Amanda shook her head like she expected to hear this crap. She smiled, then said, "That doesn't matter. I'm just a girl from Wisconsin who dropped out of college." She paused, let out a little laugh, then added, "And I'm not a blonde—my natural hair color is brown."

Wil, who had witnessed this exchange, cleared his throat audibly, then said, "So now we're trying to see who can out-do who in the self-deprecation department. Just cut it out, would you? Dang it, I've known Ryan all his life and there's no finer man anywhere. So Ryan, you just shut up." Then he looked at Amanda. "And Amanda, from what I've heard from Ryan, you're one class act."

They both stared at Wil with open mouths and big eyes, like scolded children.

"And anyway," Wil said, "what the hell's wrong with Wisconsin?"

This got everybody laughing.

"Now you two get in here," he said, gesturing toward the living room.

"Not quite yet, Uncle Wil," said Ryan. He stepped toward Amanda, tipped her chin upward and kissed her softly on the lips. Tears flooded Amanda's eyes, but as she began to speak, NoName came bounding into the room and right up to her. Her jaw dropped, as she scooped the pup up into her arms. "Oh my, who is this little sweetheart?"

"I call him NoName for right now, because he doesn't have a name, but you can call him anything you want."

"You mean he's mine?" asked Amanda in disbelief.

Ryan nodded, as NoName licked Amanda's face. She moved the pup away from her face enough to look at Ryan, then said, "I know what I'm going to call him. Bozeman."

"Never heard of a dog named Bozeman before," said Wil. He then added, "Oh, and I'm Wil." He extended his hand toward Amanda.

"I figured," said Amanda, grabbing Wil's hand and flashing him an appreciative smile, before returning her gaze to Ryan.

"Why Bozeman?" asked Ryan. It was all he could come up with.

"Because that's where I found all this love."

Ryan smiled. "He's awfully easy to love, all right."

Amanda put a hand around Ryan's neck and pulled him closer to her. "I'm not talking about the dog, you big dummy."

Then they were in each other's arms. How long this went on, Ryan couldn't say. At some point, they separated, but only by a few inches, as they made their way toward the living room.

"So, how did you find this place?" asked Wil.

"It was easy," smiled Amanda. "I knew you had worked in the history department at Montana State, and I knew your first name was Wil. So I just called up the department and said I was a history major from Madison—not too much of a stretch of the truth—and I was supposed to call Dr. Wil ... uh ... Dr. Wil ...." Amanda said this with wide-eyed, comic ditziness, while Wil and Ryan roared. "And the receptionist just filled in your last name. With a little help from the internet, it wasn't hard after that."

"God, Ryan, she's smart, too. How the hell did you get so lucky?"

"I really don't know," laughed Ryan, shaking his head. He felt light-headed.

"Let's get you something to eat," said Wil.

"Oh, thank you," she said. "I'm famished."

"And what about luggage?" asked Wil.

"Oh yes, in all the excitement I forgot," she said. "It's still out on the porch."

Ryan started for the door, but Wil held up a hand to stop him. "I'll take care of this," he said to Ryan. "You stay here and make sure she doesn't get away again."

As he made the first trip back in from the porch, Wil said, "Amanda, you'll have the guest room that Ryan has been sleeping in. Sorry, Ryan, but it looks like you get the couch." He looked from one of them to the other. "What?"

Ryan and Amanda both laughed, and then Wil joined in. It was clear to all of them that the couch would not get much use tonight.

Chapter 61

Amanda held the big coffee mug with two hands, just below her chin to let the rich aroma waft up and over her face. Sunlight streamed into the kitchen, where she and Ryan sat on stools around a massive butcher-block preparation table in the middle of the room. The kitchen was the only modern room in the house, and it was geared for serious culinary work. A big eight-burner gas range, like the ones Amanda had only seen on the Food Network, sat under a huge stainless vent that looked like it could suck up a house. Built into another wall was a tall walk-in fridge. Counter and storage space abounded, all illuminated by bright pendant lamps.

Wil had been outside for the past hour, tending to the animals and giving morning greetings to Alpha and Omega. Amanda and Ryan had offered to help, but Wil had said, with a sparkle in his eye, "You've got more important things to do to this morning." They didn't put up much of a fight.

Most of their conversation was spoken with their eyes. At one point though, the dreamy love evaporated from Ryan's eyes, and he said to Amanda, "I'm still worried about the people following me, and the danger you may be in by being here." She watched the deep concern return to his face.

She had known this conversation would take place—that it must take place—and she had rehearsed what she would say. She was ready. Amanda looked him hard in the eye before she spoke, making sure he realized how serious she was about this. "I know there may be danger, and I came to realize that's why you sent me away—it was out of your care for me," she said. "That's why I came back. If there is danger, then I want to face it together, with you."

Ryan began to speak, but no words came out.

"So, do you still want to go to Glacier?" she asked with a twinkle in her eye.

"Do you?" he asked.

"Yes, I do," she said firmly. "We've got to go see that mountain goat." Her mouth upturned slightly at the corners with the hint of a smile.

Awhile later, Wil came in from out back. They heard him stomp the dirt off his boots on the back porch, then he entered the kitchen, pulling off worn leather gloves and tossing his Stetson up onto a rack by the door. "Beautiful day out there, you guys," he said. "Anybody up for a horseback tour of the countryside?"

Amanda was interested. She looked over at Ryan, who said, "You've only got two horses, Uncle Wil. Why don't you take Amanda out riding and show her around?"

Out at the stable, Wil said, "Amanda, I want you to meet Thunder and Lightning."

Thunder was a big brown grade horse. Lightning was black. "I only rode a few times as a kid. I really don't know much about horses," Amanda said. "Is it okay to pet them?"

"You bet," laughed Wil. "They'd be hurt if you didn't. Just give them a rub on the nose."

Amanda giggled as she rubbed the noses of both horses.

While Wil got the horses saddled, he said, "Thunder and Lightning are both old timers, like me." He let out a deep laugh. "I'll put you on Thunder because she's probably a little easier to ride. Got her name because she's always slower than Lightning, always gets there a few seconds later."

They rode out through a back gate into wide-open, slightly rolling range country, carpeted in tall grasses, still green on the first day of June. Dense stands of spruce were like islands in this vast sea of grass. Amanda watched as a slight breeze washed shadowy waves across this sea. In the distance, the tops of high mountain peaks were still covered in snow.

Wil pointed up to the distant mountains. "Ever ski?" he asked.

"Just a couple times," Amanda said. "I'm really a beginner, I guess."

"Bridger Bowl's right up there. You can be up there in a half-hour from my place. Good place to learn."

"That would be fun." Horseback riding and skiing. After last night, everything felt new today, everything felt possible.

They trotted side by side for a while, Thunder seeming to sense Amanda's unsteadiness and going easy on her. They stopped at the brow of a hill to survey the view, a grand expanse of wilderness, and were silent, the only response possible to this grand vista. Then Wil turned toward Amanda. "You know, Ryan's just about the best there is," he said. "I want you to really know that. But then, I suspect you're already figuring that out for yourself."

Amanda beamed.

Then Wil said, "He probably hasn't told you this—he wouldn't, I suspect—but his mom's hospital bills cost him a bundle. I offered to help—I'm only a teacher, don't have that much, but I could have helped. But he said no. And so he shouldered the whole cost, must have been well over a hundred grand. Just about broke him, I suspect. But he did it without complaining. He did it out of responsibility. Out of love. That's the kind of guy Ryan Browning is." He continued to look at Amanda for a moment, then he turned back toward the view.

Amanda had no words. She felt like she was floating.

They were silent for another minute, then she said, "Were you ever married, Wil?" She had turned Thunder so she could look directly at him.

He shook his head. "Nope. Guess that just wasn't in the cards for me."

Amanda nodded but said nothing.

He continued. "Sometimes I think about it. But things just don't always work out the way you once thought they might." He shot Amanda a warm smile that said he appreciated her asking about him. "But all my critters do a pretty good job of keeping me occupied." After a pause, he said, "So what about you? What's your story?" His eyes were filled with curiosity.

"Whew, that's a tall topic for the morning. Let's see. Born and raised in Wisconsin. Went to Madison for three years. Art history, which I love. Dropped out to follow some loser out west, then went through quite a few years of bad choices and bad luck, especially with men." She gave out a big laugh, rather amazed how she could laugh about this now. It was like being able to talk about the stormy sea, after you're safe upon the shore.

"So, how come you never finished that college degree?" he asked.

"I wanted to," she said, hoping she wasn't sounding too defensive. "I checked into UCLA's department, but so few of my credits would transfer, I'd have been set back at least a year. Then, I had to work full time to support Richard—that's the guy I followed out west—so my dreams of going back just faded away." She took a deep breath, realizing she had quit breathing, something she did under stress.

Wil held the inside corner of his cheek between his teeth, giving her words careful consideration. "Sometimes I think big mistakes turn into big breaks. If you hadn't come out west, you'd have never met Ryan."

Amanda gave him a penetrating look. "Yeah, guess you never know," she said. "Ryan asks me out of the blue to go to Glacier with him, after I've known him for like fifteen minutes, and I said yes." She paused, then laughed. "Guess we're both a little crazy."

Wil's eyes were on her, the smile still on his face. "Crazy in love is what I'd say."

Amanda felt herself blush. She started to craft a response, but then just grinned instead.

Wil said, "You know, you could come on up here and finish that degree—they've got a good art department here, with an art history major. And you might want to put in some part-time hours at the little art museum in town. That could all be made to happen, you know."

Amanda swallowed hard and gave Wil a long, serious look. "That sounds pretty wonderful," she said.

He nodded and said, "Think about it." Then he turned his gaze back out onto the wide open range.

That night, the Montana Ale House, a popular brewpub in downtown Bozeman, was packed. They sat around a high table in the midst of the pandemonium. It had looked like a long wait, but the hostess was one of Wil's former students, and remarkably they were seated right away. In fact, it seemed like everyone there knew Wil—not surprising when you considered that at one time he'd probably had almost every one of these people or one of their kids in his classes.

Their conversation came in small installments, separated by greetings from people stopping by the table. "It would probably be safest for you to stay here for a while," Wil said between visits. "Gotta say, I could easily see both of you winding up in Bozeman on a long-term basis. And I hope you know that I wouldn't mind that at all." Now he looked from face to face, then looked away for a moment, as he flashed a big cowboy smile and waved at a couple of students across the room. When he turned back to them, he said, "But I'm sensing that you want to hit the road. That old van, it seems, has got wandering dust built into its transmission, and it just makes you want to go." It was hard to tell in the dim light, but there seemed to be mistiness in his eyes.

Chapter 62

"Straight up to Canada," grinned Wil, stretching a hand toward the north, as if that provided useful travel information. "That's how you get to Glacier."

Ryan had already entered their destination into Google Maps, but he patiently listened to Uncle Wil's instructions anyway.

"Get your butt over to Helena, but don't stop there. Up the interstate a bit, but don't stay on the interstate like most folks do. Cut over to 287, then 89, take that all the way up. Stop in Choteau for lunch. Elk Grill Inn—a good place. Then on up the road until you hit the turnoff into the Many Glacier Valley, just ten miles this side of the border." There was a gleam in his eye, as he talked fast. "Prettiest place on earth. When you're sittin' there on the deck of the Many Glacier Hotel, sipping a Going-to-the-Sun IPA, think of me."

Ryan and Amanda nodded, then each gave Wil a hug. Ryan looked around at the beautiful country stretching out from Wil's ranchette. "Prettiest place on earth, huh? It's gonna have to go some to beat this."

"Keep thinkin' that," said Wil.

They waved and Ryan honked the horn as they pulled out, Ryan driving and Amanda next to him with Bozeman on her lap. It was a bright, blue-sky morning as they headed toward I-90, which would lead them onto the route that Wil had described.

"I could see living here someday," said Amanda.

Ryan nodded. "Me, too." Then he grinned at her. "But the winters are a tad cooler than LA."

Amanda laughed. "Hey, you're talking to a northern Wisconsin girl. I know about cold winters."

Ryan shot her a quick glance, enjoying the fantasy of Amanda in tight ski pants, a puffy parka with a furry collar, and fuzzy earmuffs.

She looked down at Bozeman, already napping in her lap. "We're going to have to get Bozeman a kennel," she said with concern. "It's not safe for him to ride like this."

Two hours later, Ryan carried a new puppy kennel out to the Roadtrek from the Kmart, just off I-15 in Helena. Amanda had her arms full of doggie food and treats and other canine essentials. As he loaded the last of Bozeman's stuff into the side door of the Roadtrek, his phone rang.

While Amanda climbed into the RV to get Bozeman settled into his new digs, Ryan checked the caller ID. He was not up for a call right now—preferring no further delays to getting up to Glacier with this beautiful woman—and his inclination was to ignore it.

He didn't recognize the number. It was from the LA area. He sighed and took the call.

"Is this the blogger deluxe?"

Ryan groaned. Doug Bartles. "Hello, Doug," he said.

"So I haven't heard from you since we were at Lydia's the other night."

Ryan was quiet. *Geez, that seems like years ago.*

"Wondering what you thought of the news."

"About what news?" Ryan sighed. He shouldn't have taken the call. He looked over at Amanda, working with Bozeman, and at snowcapped Montana mountains in the distance beyond the blacktop of the Kmart parking lot. He had better things to be doing right now.

"You mean you don't know?"

"Spit it out, Doug." He could visualize Doug pushing his frameless glasses back upon his nose and perhaps salivating, savoring his possession of what he considered juicy gossip.

"About your old company. Lightyear, right?"

This got Ryan's attention. "I haven't heard anything, Doug. What's going on?"

"I can't believe you haven't heard."

Ryan blew out an impatient breath. "I'm listening, Doug."

"About the head guy. Robie. Is that his name?"

"Yes, what about him?"

"Well, I heard he put a bullet through his head."

When the call ended, Ryan stood frozen in place. He felt like a balloon had been inflated inside his chest, pushing out the space for air. Amanda poked her head out the window. "Is everything okay?" she asked.

"I can't believe it," he said, shaking his head. "My old boss at Lightyear just killed himself."

Amanda climbed down out of the RV, hurried to Ryan's side and put an arm around him. "Oh my God, Ryan, I'm so sorry."

"Damn," breathed Ryan, running a hand through his hair, "It must have been soon after I talked with him. I thought he sounded strange."

"There's nothing you could have done about it."

Ryan wasn't so sure this was true. Did his misbehavior have something to do with Robie's suicide? Surely his sending in those two abstracts and his subsequent termination couldn't have been that high up on Robie's screen. He pulled out his phone again and Googled Nils Robie. It didn't take long to find the newspaper account, from the *Long Beach Press-Telegram*.

Dr. Nils Robie, 54, was found dead this morning at his home in Palos Verdes Estates. Tentative cause of death was by gunshot wound. Robie was the president of Lightyear, Inc., an R&D company in Redondo Beach, and a former chief scientist at the U. S. Naval Research Laboratory in Washington, D. C. He is survived by two adult children in Washington, D. C., and a sister in Boston. Police are treating the death as a suicide.

Ryan climbed into the Roadtrek, then turned to Amanda. "I don't know what to think," he said. He felt dizzy.

"Did you know him well?"

"Not very well," he said. He took a huge breath, then blew it out with force. "I've never known anyone who committed suicide." Then he shook his head. "There are too many things that don't fit together. All these people following us, then Robie's death. Could they be connected in some way?"

Amanda shrugged and looked troubled. "What do you want to do?" she asked.

"I don't know. My first response is to contact somebody, but I don't know who to contact and, if I did, I don't know what I'd say."

She reached over and gently stroked his cheek, but said nothing.

"I'm scared, Amanda. I'm scared that I've pulled you into something that will harm you, and I just can't stand the thought of that."

Amanda grabbed Ryan's arm tight and shook it gently, like she was trying to shake some sense into him. "Ryan, listen to me," she said, looking him hard in the eye. "Nobody's forced me to be here. I'm here because this is where I want to be. Yes, I would say that this is where I belong." She paused for a moment, while continuing to look hard into his eyes, like perhaps she could see his soul. "For what it's worth, I'm not going to let this drag me down, because I am where I belong. I am with you, and we're going to Glacier to see that damned mountain goat. Now, I say, put this sucker in gear and let's go."

Chapter 63

The welcome sign at the edge of town said it is the "Gateway to the Rocky Mountain Front," and high mountains looming off to the west supported that claim. Amanda observed that the other signs they saw as they drove through the small city of Choteau, Montana, displayed more pictures of elk and trout than either people or buildings. Other than that, the small downtown section of Choteau looked to her like many small towns in northern Wisconsin—it even had a classic late-nineteenth-century stone courthouse in the middle of the commercial strip along US 287. The town seemed larger than its advertised 1,600 inhabitants, probably because they had just driven many miles through wide-open, rolling range land with distant mountain vistas and the near absence of any sign of human presence.

They would have passed right by the Elk Grill Inn, if Uncle Wil hadn't recommended it. It was a low-key place in a forgettable little building on the main street, but the many cars and a dozen or so Harleys parked out front told them that this was a good place to stop.

Inside, things were simple. A loud and laughing clientele occupied simple ladder-back chairs around plain, Formica-topped tables. It was hard not to feel good here. As Amanda perused the plastic-laminated menu, where their allegedly famous ribeye steak was featured, she felt a pulse of excitement surge through her. She was on the road again with Ryan, out in the middle of nowhere, and Glacier was just a few hours up the way.

And it seemed like the dark cloud of Nils Robie's death that had hung over Ryan for the last few hours was beginning to clear.

Amanda laid her menu aside, as Ryan pushed the plastic salt and pepper shakers to one side, then reached across the table and took both of her hands in his. "Sorry to be such a downer," he said, as he gently stroked her hands. "You are simply wonderful, and I can't think of any place I'd rather be than right here with you." Those seeing eyes bathed her, and it felt as if the cartilage in Amanda's knees had just turned to Jello.

She had spent too much of her life missing out on the joys of the present, brooding instead about the past—the mistakes and wounds and missed opportunities. And she had worried about the future, which often stretched out before her like a dull continuation of the past.

Right here in this place—this obscure, wide spot in the road that most people had never heard of—she felt centered, full, alive. The demons of the past—the preoccupation with Adam being just the most recent example—had dissolved, and maybe this shaggy-poet lover across the table from her and the big Montana sky had something to do with it. Adam? Funny how that had tormented her for months, and now it was firmly over, replaced by a sense of peace.

Could she learn to live fully in the moment? To be centered on the precious gift of life in the now? As Ryan's hands enfolded hers, gently, she was convinced the answer was yes. Sure, she understood that there were problems facing them. Those people who were following them were probably still out there. That run-in with Carol Shepherd, on that God-awful afternoon that precipitated her break-up with Ryan, proved that there was still danger awaiting them. But at this moment, she could push that problem off into the future with the other unknown problems that would come her way—such is life—and live now, here, where there was love and joy. Not to mention famous ribeye steaks.

After lunch—they both opted for salads and resisted the ribeyes—when they were headed for the door, one of the Harley riders from the large gathering at a big round table in the corner ran up to them. His hand was raised, as if he was trying to flag them down.

Ryan's first response was to ignore the man—he was probably gun-shy from their recent encounters with strangers—but the man called out, "Hey, you two."

Amanda stopped and turned toward him. He was a burly man, probably in his early fifties, but it was hard to tell, because he had an unshaven, scruffy look—his beard and hair were gray. "Sorry to bother you," he said. "I see you're both heading out. I just wanted to ask you about your van. It's a Roadtrek, isn't it?"

The man wore the leather pants and jacket of a Harley rider. Earlier, Amanda had noticed that all the people at his table—there were both men and women—had the word "Crowns" written on the backs of their jackets, in that jagged font that motorcycle clubs like to use. Above the word was a large golden crown.

Ryan seemed to relax. He began to speak, but the man interrupted. "Oh, I should've introduced myself. I'm Jake, from Minneapolis. Our club," he gestured toward the group, "the Crowns—we're all retired dentists." He let out a big laugh.

Ryan and Amanda introduced themselves. "Yeah, it's a Roadtrek. About a '96," Ryan said.

The man stepped over to the window and looked out toward the van. "It's a beauty all right. What kind of mileage you get?"

"Tell you truth, I haven't kept track."

"Me and Nancy. She's right over there." He gestured back toward the table again. Nancy had curly hair piled up under a pink bandana, surrounded by huge hoop earrings. She wore a black Harley jacket just like Jake's. "We're thinkin' of getting one like that someday. Nice rig."

"We're enjoying it," Amanda said, giving Jake a big smile.

"You know, I've been workin' my butt off all my life. Finally concluded it's time to live a little."

Riding your Harley through the Montana boondocks certainly seemed like living a little to Amanda. "Sounds like good advice," she said.

"You know what they say," he continued. "The secret of happiness is to have time, energy and money." The man paused to let that sink in. "The problem is, when you're young, you have energy and time, but no money. When you're in your middle years, you've got energy and money, but no time. And when you get old, you've got money and time, but no energy." He let out a big laugh, looking from Ryan to Amanda, expecting them to be laughing, too.

Amanda manufactured a courteous laugh and Ryan managed a weak smile.

"So, here we are," Jake said, "in that place where we've still got a little of all three. So I don't want to be wastin' it."

Amanda and Ryan both nodded.

"So we're gonna get one of those Roadtreks, Nancy and me." He looked out the window again. "Bet folks are stoppin' you all the time to talk about it. Just noticed a guy givin' it the look-over a few minutes ago."

Ryan twitched, like he'd just received an electric shock. "What guy was that?" he asked. Amanda could tell that Ryan was working hard to keep his voice calm.

Jake peered out the window again. "Don't see him now. He was peekin' in all the windows. Sure seemed interested."

As they headed out to the van, and before Ryan could say anything, Amanda took hold of his arm and stopped him. She looked at him with piercing eyes, but was silent for a moment before saying, "Okay, I know what's going through your mind. Look, Ryan, I know there are people who have been following us. Maybe this guy is one of them. Maybe not. People check out RVs all the time. I say, it's probably nothing. And I will not … do you hear me, Ryan Browning? I will not let this ruin our beautiful day."

Ryan cradled her face in his hands, then smiled at her. "You know, I really like having you around," he said. "I will not let this ruin our beautiful day."

Amanda bit her lip, as she felt her eyes misting up.

Chapter 64

Ryan had felt a python's grip of fear on his soul after the shocking news about Nils Robie and the disturbing event at the Elk Grill Inn. But he would not go down without a fight. As they drove north, he looked over at Amanda with an appraising look. Here, he thought, was the really big news about his life. Compared to having her with him, being pursued by unknown stalkers was just a flyspeck on the back wall of the tool shed. He chuckled to himself—these were words he'd heard Uncle Wil use, and they provided a moment of calmness for him now.

He recalled Amanda's encouragement and admonishment back in the parking lot in Choteau and the look in her eyes. It was a look of strength that said something about the power of love, a look of compassion that said, "I know what you are feeling." A look that said, "I trust you and I'm counting on you." He needed to decide to not be afraid. He needed to suppress his anxiety and be here for her. Fully present. Not just a hollow shell of a man, shaking on the inside.

In his mind he saw the old woman who sat next to him at the church service in Bozeman. And there, on his other side, was the businessman. He saw the young mom and her babies, the girl with the purple hair, the homeless guy, the college students, the minister—he didn't know any of their names. Yet, he felt their presence with him now.

But there was more about that church service, something greater. The minister called it God. Whatever it was, it was powerful and beyond him, but also with him, beside him. It seemed like it would be with him beyond this moment— perhaps throughout all his life and all his failures and joys— from mountaintops and a mother's love to a depressing surgery waiting room. And it would be with him in his future, whatever that might be. He couldn't understand this, and he was uncertain if he believed it. There was no rational physicist's explanation. Oddly, he didn't need one. All he cared about was what it meant—that he didn't have to be afraid.

He would decide to not be afraid and he would do it not just out of his own strength, though it had to start there.

He looked over at Amanda again, as they first saw the jagged carved peaks of Glacier in the distance. And he felt his fear gone, evaporated—the chains that had bound him had been ripped away. He didn't know what the look on his face conveyed, but it must have been pleasing to her. Her mouth fell open like a child's, when she first sees the presents under the tree on Christmas morning. If he had to describe it in a word, it would have to be joy.

Ryan didn't need Dickson to feed him the ball for a long three-pointer. What he needed was not fantasy at all. Everything he needed was here.

Chapter 65

T he mountains of Glacier are young. They are not eroded, they are carved. They were not formed by sandpaper, but gouged by an axe. They are not worn down like me, they are new.
(Entry by Ryan's mother in the margins of her road atlas)

"And you should be prepared for an encounter with a grizzly bear." The man behind the counter wore the neatly pressed green uniform of a national park ranger. He gave them a friendly smile, as if they were the only people he'd spoken to all day, even though he'd probably relayed the same spiel to a dozen people in the past hour.

"Oh?" said Amanda, feeling her heart move up into her throat. They'd come into the visitor center at St. Mary, the first major park entrance coming from the south, and they'd asked about campgrounds, hikes and where one might go to see a mountain goat. Amanda's spirits had soared as the ranger had pointed out several good hikes and showed them the campgrounds on a large map pressed beneath glass on the counter top. Then he made his comment about grizzly bears.

"There are several hundred of them here on the east side of the park, so your chances of seeing one are pretty good." The ranger was in his fifties with thinning gray hair, but he had the wiry look of someone who'd spent his fair share of time out on the trail. "Usually," he said, "they'll be far away—they don't want to run into you any more than you want to run into them." He now paused and looked from face to face. "But on switchbacks or where the trail passes through thick vegetation, it's easy to surprise one. They haven't been out of hibernation for long, so the sows and their cubs are scouring the hillsides for food, just like you'd be if you hadn't eaten all winter."

Ryan nodded and leaned forward on his elbows, apparently wanting to hear more.

"If you startle one, she might fake a charge, which can be really scary, but most likely she won't attack." He scratched his chin, then added, "If you get between her and one of her cubs, though, it could be a different matter."

"So what do we do if we meet one?" Amanda said. She pressed her palms flat onto the counter, and she was aware that they were sweaty.

"The main thing is to make lots of noise as you're hiking along—sing songs or talk loud—give them plenty of warning that you're there. If you see a griz on the trail, stay calm, if that's possible, and try to back away slowly. Don't run. They can go thirty miles an hour, so trying to run away is a bad idea."

Ryan looked at Amanda with a big smile, obviously trying to project bravado but betraying a bit of apprehension.

The man continued. "And you'll want to purchase some bear spray."

They'd seen the aerosol canisters of bear spray, a mace-like pepper spray, for sale at the entrance to the gift shop— fifty bucks—and had winced from sticker shock.

"Yeah, it's expensive," grinned the ranger, "and you'll probably never use it. But if you need it, you'll be really glad you've got it." He pulled out a demo canister from beneath the counter. "This thing will send out a stream of spray out to thirty feet for about seven seconds. So don't fire it until the bear gets within thirty feet." He held up the can, released the safety pin and pretended to spray. "Then empty the can." He laughed as he added, "That probably won't be the only thing that gets emptied."

Amanda glanced at Ryan to see if he was blushing, too, then sighed. They would have to fork out the fifty bucks. "You've been very helpful," she said to the ranger.

"Thanks," he said. "This is my first week of the season. Things really pick up after Memorial Day around here, so the Park's just gotten staffed up. Always an exciting time."

"It must be fun being a ranger," she said.

"It is. Actually, I'm a seasonal ranger. Just do this in the summer—been doing it for fifteen years now. Rest of the year I teach high school over in Kalispell."

As they headed to the van with their maps and brochures and newly purchased bear spray, Ryan said, "You know, being a seasonal ranger up here would be pretty cool."

"I'd love that," Amanda said. "We have to have find jobs at some point." She laughed, then stopped abruptly. She hadn't meant to presume that they would need to find jobs together. Or that they'd be living together. Or that .... She cleared her throat, then added, "It's not like we have an endless supply of cash."

"I'll have to check with my customer service rep about that," Ryan said, straight-faced. Then he stopped right there in the parking lot and pulled her to him. After several long kisses, he said, holding her at arm's length and bathing her with his eyes, "Gotta say, I'd like to see you in one of those ranger outfits."

It appeared that a storm was moving in, as dark clouds poured over the ripsaw-contoured crest to the west, like some eerie brew oozing over the lip of a witch's cauldron. The peaks looked menacing up there, where the Going to the Sun Road climbs up over Logan Pass, where they'd heard that snow drifts still blocked the highway, even at the beginning of June.

They pulled the van into a site at the St. Mary Campground—only a mile up the road from the visitor center—just as the sun was setting behind those thick clouds, reddening them like the glowing coals of a dying fire.

They had hoped to make it to the Many Glacier Valley tonight—about twenty miles up the road and only ten miles from the Canadian border—but the ranger had informed them that the campground there was full. If they got an early start tomorrow, they could get a site there and still have plenty of time for a long hike.

The storm never materialized and, as darkness fell over the campground, just a few campfires crackling in the distance competed with the astounding array of stars that were now beginning to appear.

They gazed at the sky in silence from their camp chairs around the fire, after Ryan had prepared a simple meal of spaghetti, canned green beans and sliced tomatoes. This was nothing like the LA night sky: contaminated with the reflected glare of city lights off polluted air, landing lights of planes on approach to LAX, and the floodlights of police helicopters scanning suspicious areas. As astounded as Amanda was by the stars, she was more captivated by the flicker of the campfire dancing in Ryan's eyes. It gave him an adventurer look, like he might indeed be a starship captain, navigating to distant galaxies. She sat up straight and said, "Tell me how many stars are up there, Ryan. You're a physicist. You know stuff like that."

"Yeah," he said, and it sounded like it was more from awe at the cosmic spectacle above them than in response to her question. He was silent a bit longer, then said, "I don't think I've seen this many stars, not since I used to go backpacking up in the Sierras. How about you?"

"This makes me remember those cold clear nights up north in the U.P. on camping trips with my mom and dad and my brother."

"So you asked me how many there are." He let out a gentle sigh, then said, "The number is going to stagger you."

Amanda leaned toward him. "I'm ready to be staggered," she said.

"Okay. So, the number of stars we can see tonight is perhaps ten thousand."

"Hmm," she chuckled, "about the same as the attendance at a Lakers game."

"Yeah, close. So it's quite a few. And yet, all the stars we can see tonight are just a small fraction of the many billions of stars just in our own galaxy, the Milky Way."

"Wow. So, all the stars we can see are from just one galaxy?"

"Yep. If we had binoculars, we could catch a peek at Andromeda. That's the next nearest galaxy."

"So, how many galaxies are there?"

"Maybe a hundred billion."

"Dear God."

"Here's one way to visualize the number of stars in the universe. On this clear night, the number of stars we can see is about equal to the number of grains of sand that can fit into a tablespoon."

"Okay."

"The number of stars in the universe is more than the number of grains of sand in all the deserts and beaches of the world."

She shook her head. "No way," she said. She was silent for a while, then asked, "So just how big is the universe?"

Ryan leaned forward and laid a new log on the campfire, then sat back and said, "Well, the known universe is about ten billion light years across, but keep in mind that there may be many universes, perhaps even an infinite number."

Amanda chewed her lip. "Ten billion light years? I have no idea how big that is."

"I don't either." Ryan laughed. "It's a distance too big for anyone to fathom. But, here's an example that might help." He sighed. "Let's say you want to build a spaceship to travel to the edge of the universe."

"I'm ready," she said. "Do we leave tomorrow?"

Ryan laughed again. "You and I'll have the best accommodations, I promise." He then continued. "Okay, so we're going to travel across the universe." Now he stood and began pacing around the fire, like a professor thinking on his feet in prime lecture mode. "The first thing we'll need is a spaceship, a really fast one." He paused and turned toward her. "About the fastest way we know for getting from one place to another is on a jet airliner, right?"

"Okay," she said.

"A jet airliner can fly around the earth in, what, about 48 hours?"

Amanda nodded, then shrugged. She pulled her feet up onto the chair and hugged her knees. She grinned like a little girl ready for a bedtime story.

"That won't be even close to fast enough for our journey. So, let's assume we could have a spaceship that travels around the earth in just one hour. This would be really fast, faster than the rockets we now send into space. But even that's not fast enough for our needs. Let's go for a spaceship that can fly around the world in one minute. That would mean changing time zones every three seconds. Can you imagine that?

"But even that's too slow, way too slow," he said, his arms now waving wildly, as he was getting into the drama of his story. Now he stopped and placed a forefinger to his lip. "Hmm. How about a spaceship that can fly around the world in one second?" Then he turned and stared at her, as if expecting her to respond, but he continued immediately. "Well, have I got a deal for you. My buddy down at the used spaceship lot can get us a little unit that can fly around the earth eight times in one second! Now that's really honkin'. We'll take it."

Amanda squealed in delight and pressed her palms together in a praying position, like she was about to applaud.

Ryan went on. "Next, we need a crew for our trip across the universe. This will be an extensive trip, no doubt, so we'll need a substantial crew. Okay, let's see …." He stared off into the darkness, as he rested his chin on his balled fist, pretending to be in deep reflection. "I say we hire the entire population of LA, millions of people, to be our crew! It's a big crew, yes, but with the Lakers and the Dodgers and all of Hollywood, we'll at least be entertained during our flight."

Amanda laughed as she shook her head. "This is too much," she said.

"So, we have a space ship that can fly around the earth eight times in one second, and we have the entire population of LA as our crew. Now we need to make some flight plans. Being fair-minded starship commanders, I say we allow every crew member an opportunity to be the captain of the ship for a while. That's only fair, don't you think?"

Amanda nodded, still laughing, "I'd say that's only fair."

"So for our journey to the edge of the known universe, how long do you suppose each crew member will have to serve as captain? One minute? One hour?" He stopped and looked at her, as if expecting an answer.

Amanda shrugged, grinning. "I know you're going to surprise me."

"Yep. The answer is that each person would be at the controls for two thousand years! So, if the ship had departed earth at the time of Christ, the first person at the controls would just now be handing it over to the second person. And only by the time the whole population of LA has had a 2,000-year turn at the wheel, would we be arriving at the edge of the universe."

She shook her head, her mouth falling open. "Ryan, that was freaking amazing. Where did you read all this?"

"Well, the numbers are well-known, but I came up with the illustrations."

Amanda shook her head in disbelief. She was silent for a moment, then said, "I think I'm beginning to understand what George Thomas was saying about you back at the Lab."

Ryan didn't respond. He stood with hands on his hips, gazing up into the night sky for a good minute. Then he turned back toward Amanda. "Do you remember reading Whitman in high school?"

"Yes," she said in a soft voice. A physicist talking about poetry on this starry night. She licked her lips and squirmed in her chair.

Ryan glanced at her, then back up at the night sky. He began.

"When I heard the learn'd astronomer,
When the proofs, the figures,
were ranged in columns before me,
When I was shown the charts and diagrams,
to add, divide, and measure them,
When I sitting heard the astronomer where he lectured
With much applause in the lecture-room,
How soon unaccountable I became tired and sick,
Till rising and gliding out I wander'd off by myself,
In the mystical moist night-air, and from time to time,
Look'd up in perfect silence at the stars."

Still gazing toward the sky, he gave out a self-conscious laugh. "Geez, I can't believe I still remember that poem."

Amanda could barely breathe.

Ryan turned back to her and said, "When you think about how big the universe is, it's awfully easy to feel small."

Amanda pondered this for a while, then said, "Yet, here we are, sitting here on this glorious night, able to watch all this and appreciate the scope and majesty of it all. Small, yes. But definitely not insignificant."

Ryan sat down next to her. The flicker in his eyes from the campfire was now even more intense than before.

Chapter 66

They let the campfire die, yet remained in their chairs, watching the sky and talking about the universe and their place in it, as the coals grew dim. What they didn't talk about was that tonight would be their first night in the Roadtrek since their reunion in Bozeman. Tonight they wouldn't be needing that sheet that separated them anymore. And yet, Ryan felt awkward. Why would this be different from last night in Uncle Wil's guest room? He wondered if Amanda was thinking about it, too.

But her mind seemed to be elsewhere. "So, what are you working on late at night on your laptop?" she asked.

This shook him out of his thoughts about sleeping arrangements, and he wanted to brush her question away. His blog was in such preliminary form that he didn't want anyone to see it, especially the person whose opinion mattered most to him. But he needed to be open with her. His honesty with her was more important than preserving his dignity. "I'm working on a blog," he said. "It's still in a very rough-draft form."

Amanda sat up straighter, clearly excited. "What's the URL? I want to look it up."

"I haven't published it yet."

"You haven't published it?" She sounded skeptical.

Ryan felt a bead of sweat on his forehead. He began to craft the explanation of why he hadn't published it, one that would make him sound less uncertain about his convictions, less tentative about putting his opinions out there, less afraid. But what he said was, "No."

"Oh," she said. She pondered this for a moment, then said, "So then it's like journaling?"

Now Ryan felt even more defensive. *Journaling?* Good Lord, journaling, he assumed, was just one rung above keeping a diary. What he was doing was not that, not something that love-struck teenage girls do. Or was it? He felt deflated, regretting that he'd allowed her into this private place in his life. "Well," he said, trying not to sound apologetic, "I think it's a little more than journaling."

"Can I see it?"

She sounded enthusiastic. But what if she hated it? "Sure," he said with a light air. "But it really is in rough-draft form," he added, wanting to keep her expectations low. He took her hand and led her into the Roadtrek. He invited her to sit in one of the captain's chairs, while he flipped open his laptop and opened the folder that contained his entries, then handed her the laptop. He swallowed a lump back into his throat and had to consciously subdue his nervous squirming.

Her eyes were glued to the screen, as she quickly clicked open the first blog post.

Ryan couldn't stand to watch. He looked out the window, feeling vulnerable and exposed, as if he were reading his eighth-grade essay at the school assembly, naked.

"Uh huh," she said, as she paged onto the second post.

Uh huh? What does that mean? Does that mean it was so deep that she's reflecting on its meaning? Or does it mean that it's such a steaming pile of BS that there was nothing else she could say?

Finally, she set the laptop down and looked at him, expressionless.

He licked his lips and forced himself to meet her gaze.

Amanda reached out and touched his arm. Then she said, "I want to give you a helpful response, not just an attaboy to make you feel good."

He nodded. *I would settle for an attaboy,* he thought. *Here it comes.*

"And that means I've got to think about this some more. You've written about things that are at the core of being a human."

He nodded again.

She continued. "What's good about this is that you're going through a process—maybe you could call it a growth process—as you understand more about important topics, more about yourself."

He laid his hands out on the small table in front of them with his palms open and upturned, determined for her to see how relaxed he was.

"You're not a philosopher or a seminary professor," she said, "and that's obvious. But that's also what makes it good. It's raw, it's real."

Ryan remained silent. His anxiety was beginning to subside.

"What this shows, in my opinion, is that you are very deep for even worrying about such important things." She bit her lip. "But what do I know? I think you should definitely publish this." Then she was quiet. Her eyes probed his. She had finished her appraisal.

Shows that you are deep were the only words that stuck with him, the only words that mattered. *I think you're wrong*, he wanted to say, *you're the one who is deep.*

Amanda stood and moved toward him. She wrapped a hand around his neck and pulled him back toward the bed.

Later, he fell into a deep sleep in her arms, in the double bed in the back of the Roadtrek—a more romantic place than any boutique hotel in Paris. Dreams overtook him, pleasant dreams of the day they met.

It was that first day at the bank, while he was waiting in line. He would soon be meeting Amanda. It was a surrealistic scene. Instead of the glass and oak paneling, there were paintings hung around the interior of the bank—the portraits from Amanda's gallery—and under each painting there were words written in his mother's handwriting. He looked around at the others in line with him. The little lady—Rose—with her white hair tied in a bun was in front of him, the guy behind him writing in a notebook, the—

Ryan bolted upright, thrashing.

Amanda came awake immediately. She tried to put her arms around him, but he was moving too wildly. "Ryan," she gasped, "what's wrong?"

"I saw him," he said, still fumbling between the real world and the world of his dream. He was drenched in sweat. He looked at Amanda, finally beginning to ground himself in reality. "I know where I saw him."

Amanda now got her arms around Ryan, holding onto him like she was trying to corral delicate China on a toppling table. "It's all right. We're safe here together," she said. She reached overhead and switched on a light. "Saw who?"

Ryan was breathing hard, like he'd just finished running a fast break. "The man we saw at the Los Alamos cafeteria."

"The weird one who sat behind us?"

Ryan nodded, while wiping the sweat from his face with the sheet. "Yes."

"Where did you see him?"

"He was standing behind me in line at the bank on the day I met you."

Amanda's arms slid from around him and her hands now grasped his shoulders firmly. She turned him toward her and looked at him hard. "Are you sure?"

"Yes, I remember him now. He was standing right behind me, writing in a notebook. I said something to him, but he didn't look up. He said something like, 'No problem, buddy,' and then—" Ryan stopped in mid-sentence. He put his hand on his forehead, and breathed, "Oh, God."

"What?"

"When I was sick in the bathroom in the campground at Yellowstone …"

She rested a hand on his arm, and gave him a sympathetic smile.

" … A guy kept asking me how I was doing. He kept calling me buddy."

"Did you get a look at him?"

"No, he was on the other side of the bathroom door. I'm not sure the voice was the same, but that's odd. If it was the same man …" He didn't finish the sentence.

Chapter 67

Ryan stepped out of the Roadtrek into a sunny morning. Bird songs came from nearby trees, and a hawk soared overhead. The only other sound was a rushing stream not far away. The smell of frying bacon wafted from a neighboring campsite. The troubling dream and the realization about the man from the bank had kept them awake for a long time. It's strange how even little things are magnified in the middle of the night. The knowledge that this man had been following them all the way from the bank in Manhattan Beach was no little thing. Even so, it seemed ridiculous to be afraid on such a beautiful day.

He fired up the Coleman stove and heated a pot of water for coffee, while Amanda got dressed. He sat on the edge of the picnic table and gazed up at the high mountains around them. The high, chiseled faces on the peaks testified to the power of the glaciers that carved these deep valleys during the last ice age, nearly twenty thousand years ago—only a heartbeat ago on the scale of geologic time.

Ryan knew he had a choice. He could cave into his fear. Yes, he'd come to a decision just yesterday about not being afraid again. But fear is a disease, like a plague that can recur just when you think you're on the road back to health. No one would blame either of them for being afraid. As someone had said—probably some meme on Facebook—it's not being afraid that matters, it's what you do next that matters.

But what would they do if they gave into fear? Flee? To where? Live in panic, worrying about the next knock on the door, the car that just drove down the street a little too slowly? Or you could move ahead, in spite of your fear.

Ryan had no job, almost no money, and a host of people following him. That would seem like a sorry state of affairs. But there was another side of the ledger sheet, too. He did a slow three-sixty, his jaw dropping at the scenery around him. He shook his head in awe. And the most amazing woman he'd ever known was just a few feet away. Yes, he had a choice. And he was going to choose to live. *Isn't that what the mountain goat would do?*

Amanda emerged from the Roadtrek just as the coffee was ready. She had on those sexy, khaki hiking shorts again and a powder blue T-shirt. She tilted her nose into the air and extended an arm, with her hand dangling limply, like an heiress greeting her lowly servant. "I'll have my coffee now," she said in a snooty voice, then burst into a giggle.

Any thought of fear evaporated in the morning laughter of this woman.

Ryan would have liked to linger in this special place, but they had to make it to Many Glacier if they would have any chance of getting a campsite there. The ranger had advised them to arrive early, since the campsites are first-come-first-served, and folks start queuing up by six to get a place. As it was, they wouldn't make it before nine, but surely that wouldn't be too late. They didn't have a back-up plan.

They poured coffee into insulated travel mugs and packed the stove. Then, after taking Bozeman out for a quick morning walk, they climbed into the Roadtrek and headed north. Just fifteen minutes south of the Canadian border, they turned west onto the narrow road into the Many Glacier Valley. Now, each turn revealed increasingly greater vistas of jagged icy peaks, and patches of gravel on the sketchy road caused the dishes in the Roadtrek cabinets to rattle.

They entered the valley at the spectacular Many Glacier Hotel—it looked like a huge, nineteenth-century Swiss chalet—perched on the shore of a long, deep-blue lake, backed by rugged peaks on all sides. The road dead-ended just a couple miles farther up the valley at the popular campground.

Ryan and Amanda pulled in right at nine, but immediately encountered a 'Campground Full' sign at the entrance. They shared frustrated grimaces, but continued on into the campground until they reached a large RV, where a sign said the camp host resided.

An elderly couple was chatting with a camper under the RV's awning.

With their most friendly faces, Ryan and Amanda approached the couple, who they assumed were the camp hosts. Amanda carried Bozeman in her arms. Maybe, just like hotels, 'full' did not always mean 'full.' Maybe the sign had not been updated since yesterday. Maybe they had a site that had just been vacated.

"Good morning, sir," said Ryan. Amanda wore her most polished customer-service-rep smile. "We've just come a long way and were sure hoping to get a campsite here for tonight."

A carved shingle by the door of the RV said this was Roy and Emma Randall from Clear Lake, Iowa. They both appeared to be about seventy. Roy was a big, burly guy with a red face. He stuck out a beefy hand to shake and said, "Good morning, folks." He seemed to be in morning visiting mode and in no apparent hurry to worry about finding Ryan and Amanda a campsite. Emma and the other camper also turned to greet them.

"We don't need anything special," Ryan said, gesturing toward the Roadtrek. "We're self-contained."

"Yeah," mused Roy. "Nice rig. Sometimes I wish we had something a little more manageable." He nodded toward his big motorhome. "But Emma's got to have her amenities, you know." His eyes flashed from under a wide-brimmed Tilley hat.

Emma laughed. She looked like the stereotypical Iowa grandma, who should be baking cookies for the grandchildren. Ryan thought it was pretty cool that instead she was out here working among grizzly bears in Glacier National Park. "Oh, Roy, you know you like your big flatscreen," she said.

"Anyway," said Roy, turning back toward Ryan, "I'm afraid the campground's full. Sorry about that, but you need to get here before seven usually." He shook his head slowly, as if sharing in their sorrow. "This is one of the most popular campgrounds in the country. I'd say find yourself somewhere to stay tonight, then be here early tomorrow. You can go to the KOA, back on the main highway, but that'll set you back sixty bucks." He turned back to Emma and the other camper. "Where else could they go?"

The other camper, a scrappy looking guy in his thirties, now weighed in. "I'd just find some wilderness road—and there are a few of them around here, back off the main highway—and park there for the night, then be back here around six tomorrow. That's what we did last night. Just make sure you don't camp on Indian land or inside the Park boundary."

"We've got a fair number of folks leaving tomorrow, so you'll get a good spot then," added Roy.

Emma said, "Won't you folks stay for some coffee? Just put a new pot on."

Maybe there'll be cookies, too, Ryan thought. He exchanged glances with Amanda, then said, "Thanks, but I think we'll head out for a hike, then go find that wilderness road."

Roy reached over and scratched Bozeman's head. "What will you do with your pup while you're out hiking? They're not allowed on the trails, you know, and you don't want to leave him in your RV—it could get too hot."

Ryan looked at Amanda, bit his lip, then looked back at the camp hosts. "Hadn't thought about that. Guess we could leave him in the van with the AC on—would have to leave the generator running, I guess."

Roy adjusted his Tilley hat, scratched his chin between a thumb and forefinger, then said, "I've got a better idea. Why don't you just leave him here with us while you're out hiking? That way, you don't have to worry about the AC conking out. And old Rhonda will keep him entertained." He nodded toward a large Golden Retriever sleeping by the door of the Randalls' RV.

"Thank you so much," said Amanda. "We'll get his crate and food out of the van."

Ryan and Amanda were ready. They knew that Many Glacier was a hiker's paradise, with trails to a dozen famous destinations radiating out from this valley. One could select from a spectacular menu of hikes, each with its own unique offering: trails that take you up to a high mountain pass, or a sapphire blue lake choked with icebergs, or a high alpine tunnel that cuts through a knife-edge ridge above timberline. But Ryan and Amanda decided on the hike to Grinnell Glacier, which climbs for five miles up onto a glacier at the headwall of a steep canyon. The ranger had advised them that snow would likely block most of the trails in the higher terrain this early in the season, so they probably wouldn't be able to go all the way to the glacier. But the scenery would be gorgeous in any case. And while the area is popular with grizzlies, there also would be an excellent possibility of seeing a mountain goat up close.

From a parking lot just a mile from the campground, the Grinnell Glacier trail contoured through dense forest around two large glacier-sculpted lakes toward a steep canyon, before climbing up one flank of the canyon just beyond the headwaters of the second lake. Here, Ryan and Amanda emerged above the tree line into more open country, with a dotting of trees, rocky outcrops and dense thickets of head-high vegetation. The glacier, still high above them, sat in a bowl beneath the vertical headwall of the canyon.

The open hillsides were covered with huckleberry bushes, producing berries that make great jams, fillings for pancakes, and there's even a local huckleberry beer. But at the Visitor Center, they had read that huckleberries are a favorite food of the local grizzly bear population. Because they're mostly vegetarians—as opposed to the Alaska bears that eat salmon, for example—the bears in Glacier only attain a weight of around four-hundred pounds, whereas their meat-eating counterparts may reach eight hundred. "That's still plenty big enough for me," Amanda had told Ryan.

Surely it was too early for the huckleberry plants to have berries on them, they rationalized, so perhaps there would be no grazing bears along the trail.

As the trail climbed the north wall of the canyon, each switchback brought more stunning scenery into view. Below them a deep canyon fell away, like the bottom had dropped out of the earth. One misstep here and you'd have plenty of time to reflect on your error before hitting something hard. At the bottom of the gorge, Grinnell Lake, a deep green from fine suspended particulates—called glacial flour—from the glacier high above them, looked like the jewel in an emerald brooch. Across the canyon, they watched a waterfall cascade down a cliffside that must have been a thousand feet high. Then their eyes were drawn even higher, to the sheer face of a mountain another two thousand feet above. It was so inspiring, you wanted to dance with your arms in the air; it reminded Ryan of a scene from *The Sound of Music*.

But instead, they made noise to alert bears by singing *Ninety-nine Bottles of Beer on the Wall*, and one can't sing that song for very long before concluding that being mauled by a grizzly might be preferable to having to sing another verse. They only made it to eighty-seven before a change of song was mandated. While they continued up around a switchback, Ryan boldly began belting out *Amarillo by Morning*, which he remembered from the bar in Dubois. He thought he sounded pretty good, but he made it only a couple of lines into the song—"Amarillo by morning, up from San Antone, everything that I've got is just what I've got on"—before he couldn't recall the next lines. So he hummed. They both broke into laughter.

Then Amanda, holding her fist up beneath her chin like a mic, projected her best MC voice: "And now, live from

Nashville, let's give a big Grand Ol' Opry welcome to Miss Amanda Seward." Ryan turned, and while walking backward, applauded enthusiastically and managed a high-pitched whistle. She then launched into *Lookin' for Love in All the Wrong Places*, which they'd also heard in Dubois. "Lookin' for Love in all the wrong places, lookin' for love in too many faces...." She stopped, just like Ryan had, also unable to recall the next lines.

"Miss Seward," Ryan said, "I do believe you have a bright future in country music." But the laughter was gone from Amanda's face. "What's wrong?" he asked.

"That song. I think it might have been written about me." She exhaled hard, in disgust.

Ryan stopped and looked at her, but said nothing. She needed to talk.

She put her hands on her hips, looked out across the broad deep chasm to the east and the high snowy peaks beyond. Then she said, "I was definitely looking for love in all the wrong places."

"We all have," Ryan said, immediately worrying that this may have sounded like he wasn't taking her seriously. He shrugged and added, "At least I have."

Amanda shook her head. "Yeah, but I was still doing it two weeks ago." She let out a self-deprecating laugh.

Ryan wanted to put his arms around her. In fact, the sheen of perspiration on her face and bare arms was a turn-on. He chided himself for his lust, when she had something important she needed to talk about. He remained quiet.

"All those selfies I posted on Facebook. They were just to make an old boyfriend jealous." She shook her head, looking down.

"It's okay, Amanda." He took a step toward her. "I can't say I'm disappointed about how things have worked out." He manufactured a chuckle, but she didn't laugh.

"I got that text in Denver saying he wanted me back. I didn't know what I wanted." She looked up at him helplessly.

Ryan nodded.

"When you sent me away, I thought I deserved that, and so I didn't put up much of a fight." She shook her head slowly. Her words were coming out only in short bits. "When I got back to LA, it seemed like the natural thing to do would be to go back to him. Good old strong Amanda. Can't be without a man for one day."

He thought she was about to cry.

"But I got a call from Cepi, and she made me realize that there was something more between you and me, something real."

He took another step toward her.

"It was only then that I realized you had sent me away because you were afraid for me." She looked hard into his eyes. "I never went to see Adam—that's the old boyfriend. In fact, I never contacted him at all. Because I knew what I really wanted. And it wasn't him." She blew out another breath. "I just came back here. Took a chance that you'd take me back."

"And I'm so glad you did," he said and touched the side of her face gently with his hand.

She nodded, then blubbered, "I know, but I just had to tell you." Then she was in his arms.

"Amanda, I—"

"What's that?" she gasped. Ryan heard it, too. A loud rustling from the dense, head-high thicket above them. Still clinging to each other, their eyes were now locked on the foliage, but they could see nothing moving.

Ryan's hand slid down to the canister of bear spray strapped to his belt. "Let's be quiet," he whispered.

They waited another moment, but heard nothing.

Ryan swallowed hard, as Amanda clung to him, her fingernails digging into each arm. "Let's just continue up the trail slowly. The ranger said that bears don't really want an encounter with us."

They continued hiking, never taking their eyes from the head-high foliage up to their right. After about a hundred yards, they stopped again and listened. Suddenly there was a rustling in the opaque wall of green just above them, not ten yards away. It was something large.

"Oh, God," breathed Amanda. "It's following us."

Then it was quiet again.

"I don't understand this," Ryan said. He stepped toward the foliage and with one hand peeled back some branches to better see into the interior. He held the bear spray canister in his other hand, his thumb over the safety pin.

"Be careful, Ryan," Amanda cautioned in a worried voice.

He peered hard into the thick vegetation, but he couldn't see far. No sign of an animal nor any motion. He stepped away from the foliage and turned toward Amanda. "I didn't think a bear would stalk us."

Amanda looked up at him. "Maybe it's not a bear."

They both jumped, as there was motion from just beyond them up the trail. A figure appeared, then another. Two hikers were coming down the trail.

"We just heard something large moving in the bushes," said Amanda. "Did you see anything?"

A couple, probably about their ages, stopped and looked into the foliage with them. The man rested his hand on the bear spray canister fastened to his belt. "Haven't seen anything. Do you think it was a bear?"

Ryan shrugged. "I don't know."

"Why don't we hike back down together?" the woman suggested. "There's safety in numbers, they say. Anyway, the trail's blocked with snow just a quarter mile ahead."

"Good idea," said Amanda. Then she turned to Ryan. "I feel a little silly, I guess." She gave him a quick peck on the cheek that said everything's okay. But when she pulled back, the look in her eyes mirrored his feelings completely. Everything wasn't okay.

Chapter 68

"It's Kobe for three!" Ryan hollered, like he was doing play-by-play coverage, as he lobbed a high pass to Amanda.

"Intercepted by Seward," she retorted with excited laughter, leaping to grab the pass. Amanda gripped the rough leathery basketball, enjoying the hard pebbly feel that separates a quality game ball from a rubber playground ball—this was not a toy you'd find in the sporting goods department at Walmart. It took her back to those exciting game days at Wausau East. She fired a hard pass to Ryan, while Bozeman bounded back and forth between them, following the path of the ball, leaping and barking like there was a bird that he might snatch from the air.

The clearing where they played, next to the Roadtrek, was a half-mile down a dirt road just north of the Many Glacier cut-off, near the tiny town of Babb. It was the perfect place to spend the night. Babb itself was just a general store, a sagging old motel and a bar. It wasn't clear why it was even on the map. But the spot they'd found to camp was perfect. Open country with a sprinkling of pines. Good visibility in all directions allowed the early detection of bears, gray Sonatas or any other unwelcomed species.

"I wish I could have seen you on your old high school team," Ryan said, as he attempted a behind-the-back pass, then had to chase the ball down when it careened wildly in the wrong direction.

"Me, too. I wasn't the leading scorer or anything, but I wasn't bad. Good on defense, that was me."

"Well, Miss Seward, in this commentator's humble opinion, you are nothing less than an MVP." He had to jump to catch a high pass. When he came down, he said, "So, do you still follow basketball?"

"Yeah, sort of. But I don't really watch games unless I'm channel surfing. Mainly I liked playing it." Their passing was fast and energetic, and they both were breathing hard as they talked.

"Me too," he said. "So, what did you get out of basketball?"

"Hmm." She held the ball for a moment before passing it back. "Well, it's challenging."

"That's for sure."

"And it's hard to think about anything else when you're playing it."

Ryan nodded.

"Then there's the sense of being part of a team." Amanda was into this now. "I mean you really need the support of others. And you need to support them."

"Yes," Ryan agreed. "And you need to be bold and be out there taking risks. But also share."

Amanda laughed. "Yeah. Don't be a ball hog." She certainly never had been a ball hog back in high school, she thought. If anything, she should have been a more aggressive shooter—she had a good jump shot—but she was always more of a supporting member of the team. Supporting others and not going for it herself. Maybe that had been a theme for her whole life. She pushed that thought away with the memory of what it felt like on the infrequent occasions when she had sunk a long jumper.

She held the ball and walked over to Ryan. "You know how it feels when you hit a long shot?"

Ryan nodded with enthusiasm. "Yeah, so perfect. Like everything fits together—every part of your body and mind working together in one coordinated flow."

Amanda nodded. "Holistic, I'd say. Everything working as one."

"Then, when it doesn't work …." He said it seriously, then broke into laughter.

"There is that," she said. "You have to get over it. Quick. You can't be brooding over that shot you just missed."

Ryan's brow furrowed, and the hint of a frown replaced his laughter. "As hard as basketball is, it sure seems a lot easier than real life."

Amanda nodded. "No kidding."

"So what do you do when life gets hard?"

She had a ready answer. "You go on a road trip." She delighted in seeing the smile return to Ryan's face. "Anyway, you can't stay on the basketball court."

"Sometimes I do," Ryan said.

Amanda squinted, trying to understand what he meant, but she waited for him to continue.

"Sometimes, when I'm in a difficult situation, I tend to drift off into a basketball fantasy, I guess as a means of escape. Does that sound creepy?" His mouth showed a smirk, like he was ashamed.

Amanda placed a hand on his shoulder. "Not at all," she said, looking hard at him. "Maybe you're just practicing for the way life ought to be. Teamwork. Grace. Flowing. All that."

Ryan's eyes widened as she spoke, with something that looked like relief. He nodded slowly. Then he said, "Yeah, I guess I love everything about the game. Even love the sounds and the smells of the game."

"Like shoes squeaking on the hardwood?" she asked.

He grinned.

"And the smell of the leathery ball?" she added.

He laughed. "I thought you were going to say the smell of sweaty gym socks."

This triggered something deep inside Amanda, and she broke into involuntary giggles. She covered her mouth with her hand, as if she could somehow hold her laughter in, but it was out of control, like a runaway semi on the downhill side of the pass. Happy tears flooded her eyes. She felt herself turning red. She should have felt embarrassed.

It must have been infectious, because now Ryan had the giggle fits, too. She had never laughed like this with a man. This was like the kind of laughter she shared with Katy, usually after a Margarita, or with her girlfriends back in high school. Right now she was as giggly as a teenage girl, and it felt juvenile, silly, and cathartic. It was wonderful.

She thought about the way she normally laughed, especially around men: perfunctory, controlled, insincere—something she did because it seemed expected. It was almost an act of apology, of submission—the kind of laughter that had drawn Katy's criticism, criticism she had rejected because it was so right on target.

As she and Ryan shared the giggles, Bozeman barked, seemingly wanting to be a part of the action. This caused more laughter as they collapsed into each other's arms.

Later, around their campfire, they shared drams of the Oban Limited Edition, which they hadn't touched since that first night in Kingman. The night was quiet, except for the distant hoot of an owl. They were quiet also, watching the flames dance as the wood glowed red, crackled and sent sparks up into the darkness.

Finally, Ryan said, "Sorry again to have burdened you with that awful dream I had last night."

Amanda stared into the fire. "You didn't burden me at all. It was important that you remembered about that creepy guy."

"I've been doing some thinking about fear," he said, "and I've concluded that I can decide whether I'm going to allow fear to control me."

She straightened and looked at him. "We've had some legitimate things to be afraid of. And anyway, I certainly don't see you as the fearful type."

Ryan smirked with raised eyebrows like he didn't agree.

"Not sure why I'd remember this now, but my priest back in Wausau liked to say that perfect love casts out all fear. I think he was talking about God, but it surely means that the more we love, the less we have to fear."

He looked into her eyes. "I went to church a few days ago. With Uncle Wil."

"Oh?" She was surprised. After a moment she said, "What was that like?"

"It was amazing. I'm still not sure what to make of it, but it deeply moved me."

She nodded with interest.

"I felt something like ... geez, I don't know how to express it. It's like there was love all around me, and that it was okay to let it go, I mean let go of my emotional burdens. And I did."

She laid a hand on his arm. "Do you think you might want to go again sometime?"

"Would you go with me?"

She swallowed back something that felt like a sob. "Yes."

Chapter 69

Later that night, after Amanda had fallen asleep, Ryan lay awake on his side, looking at her. She was on her side too, facing toward him, just inches away, breathing softly. Her blonde hair lay arrayed across the pillow, like a beautiful cornucopia poured out for him. He leaned forward and studied her skin in the dim near-darkness and the way the narrow, delicate strap of her nightgown cut across the soft skin of her shoulder. He longed to touch her again. He reached out his fingertips and allowed them to hover over her skin, but then withdrew them, not wanting to disturb her peaceful sleep.

He rolled onto his back and gazed into the darkness above him. He exhaled a soft breath, as a thought about his blog came to mind—how it had been an outlet for his negativity and doubt and how it had seldom expressed joy. Certainly not like the overwhelming joy he felt at this moment.

Ryan had just fallen asleep, when Bozeman let out a low growl from the foot of the bed.

"Bozeman, it's okay," Amanda whispered, sounding half asleep. He was probably having a bad dream.

But the low growl continued. Then came the unmistakable sound Ryan had heard at the campground in Bandelier. Someone tested the locked side door of the RV.

Ryan and Amanda both bolted upright. They sat in the darkness, listening. He realized that she was trembling. He was, too. It was quiet for a moment.

Suddenly the Roadtrek shook and there was a sound like someone had hit the side of the van with a sledge hammer.

They both jumped up off the bed. "What the hell was that?" cried Ryan.

He flicked on a light, just as another ear-drum-piercing slam hit the van. In the same instant, the interior filled with an explosion of what looked like sawdust. Then the lights went out.

It was gunfire.

Chapter 70

Ryan had heard that your life passes before your eyes when you die. He had not known if that was true or not, but at this moment it did seem as if time had slowed down. What must have been just a few seconds seemed to last forever, allowing him time to reflect, almost in a detached way, on their situation. The gift of time did not seem to be adequate for him to craft a plan, however, to figure a way out of this situation that seemed like certain death. His reflection was objective. *This is it. This is how it will end.* Just when his life had seemed to unexpectedly fill with hope, with love, it was all coming to a sudden end. He and Amanda and Bozeman were one in this, their lives to be extinguished in a flicker of time. There was time to grasp this fact, but no time to feel the loss nor to be angry nor to be sad. In fact, there was no time at all.

Again the Roadtrek shook as another shot smashed into it. Then another and another. Instinctively, Ryan grabbed Amanda and pulled her to him. He looked around frantically for a way out, but there was none. The impulse to flee the van was a bad idea. It could take them directly into the gunfire. But they were sitting ducks here.

He considered racing to the front, starting the van and driving away. *Where are the keys?* But just then another shot exploded the windshield. He would be in plain sight up front, an easy target.

There was not time to talk this over. He pulled her roughly down to the floor. Then he slid them both quickly across the floor to the door of the refrigerator. *Isn't there a compressor or heat exchanger inside that thing?* It had mass. And right now, mass was what he needed between them and the shooter. Ahead of the refrigerator was a food cabinet, where canned goods were stored. More mass.

He covered Amanda's body with his, and she clasped Bozeman to her chest under them both. He tried to shift his body to the side from which the shots seemed to be coming, anything that might shield her. His thoughts were on surviving the next few seconds, not anything beyond that.

More shots, each one like a bomb going off. How many had there been? Five? Ten? He held onto Amanda for dear life, but she was not moving. He did not know if she'd been hit. There was no time to ask.

Then the shots stopped. Now there was nothing but silence and the ringing in his ears. He instinctively took an inventory of his body. He was alive. This much he knew, but he also knew that he was awash in adrenalin, which could mask an injury.

Beneath him Amanda twitched. "Are you okay?" she cried.

"Yes. Are you?" He now felt a sharp burning sensation in his leg, below the knee.

"I think so," she said.

They lay there in the silence, with no place to go. Only now could he begin to think about what might happen next. Certainly, someone was outside with a weapon and they intended to kill them. And there was no way out.

"Dear God," he cried. "Help us."

Then he heard a loud, commanding voice. "Ryan Browning, Amanda Seward. Come out. Right now." After a moment of silence, the voice boomed again. "Come out, now."

They were trembling in each other's arms. "What should we do?" cried Amanda.

Ryan tried to sort through their options, but his brain felt jammed by panic. There were probably only seconds to decide how to respond before the gunfire resumed.

"We have no choice but to go out," Ryan said. He suspected that as soon as they appeared, they would be gunned down. But at least they would be in the open, and maybe there would be a second of time, as the shooter sized up his targets. If there would be any way to make a break, being in the open was their only chance. Maybe he could create a diversion that would allow Amanda to escape into the darkness.

Ryan peeked through the window in the exit door but could see nothing. Pitch black. He paused, using the few seconds he guessed they could afford before the gunfire continued. With one arm, he held her close in the darkness, while he ran his free hand frantically across the shelves around him for anything that might help. A weapon. Something that could create a diversion, a moment that might allow Amanda to escape. His fingers trailed across a metal cylinder. *The bear spray.*

He would be shot for sure, but before he was taken down perhaps he could squeeze off a pulse of the bear spray, providing enough time for Amanda to flee. He grasped the canister and had to trust his memory in the dark on how the safety pin and firing mechanism worked. His finger found the plastic safety clip and released it. His trigger finger slid into a ring that would enable him to point the nozzle, and his thumb came down against the lever that would fire the spray of mace. He lowered the canister to his side so that it might not be immediately visible to the shooter. He was ready.

Before pushing the door open, he said, with surprising calmness, "When I give you a push, you run."

She held him tighter but said nothing.

"Okay?" It was more a command than a question.

Still nothing. Then she said, "Ryan, I love you."

He turned toward her. His words came out in a gush. "Amanda, I love you, too."

Ryan stepped out first, with Amanda directly behind him. Suddenly, a bright light flooded them and made it difficult to see. But what he could see was unmistakable: the barrel of a large handgun, pointed in their direction, grasped two-hand style by Carol Shepherd.

Chapter 71

"Move away from the van," a voice, a male voice, boomed from behind Shepherd. "Now."

Ryan quickly raised the bear spray canister toward Carol Shepherd and with his other arm prepared to push Amanda off into the darkness. He brought his thumb down onto the firing lever, but then he stopped. Carol Shepherd's gun was not aimed at them at all, but on two people lying motionless on the ground beside the van.

"Get away from the van now," the voice demanded again. "The propane or gas tanks may be punctured. This thing could explode. Do it. Now."

Ryan lowered the canister, then stumbled away from the van, Amanda clinging to him from behind. With his ears still ringing and his pupils trying to adjust to the bright light, he almost toppled over as he moved. He was trying frantically to process what was going on, but he was functioning about as well as a blind man crossing the Santa Monica Freeway.

Then a man stepped out from behind Carol Shepherd and lowered his large flashlight. It was the man from Santa Fe, Eric Sandoval.

"Ryan and Amanda," he said, his voice now softer and surprisingly calm, "it's nice to see you again. Are you injured?"

Ryan's first instinct was to flee with Amanda into the darkness beyond the van. But for the moment, he stood frozen in place. He said nothing.

Amanda managed to say, "We're okay."

Sandoval flashed a badge, which Ryan could not make out, and said, "We're FBI." He then nodded toward a man standing over the two people on the ground. "So is he. That's Rudy Kucera. I think you've met him also." It was the man from the Grand Canyon. He glanced their way and nodded, then busied himself again with the two people on the ground.

Amanda had now stepped out from behind Ryan. She looked at Sandoval with glazed eyes. "What happened?" Her voice was amazingly steady and objective, considering their situation. Ryan remained silent, still doubting he could trust what Sandoval was saying.

"You are lucky to be alive. Those two on the ground just tried to kill you both. But I'm happy to report that this episode is finally over."

"Why?" asked Amanda.

"I'll get to that. Right now we're trying to stabilize this situation. State troopers are on the way, but we are out in the middle of nowhere, so it may take a while."

Ryan returned his attention to the two people on the ground. They lay flat, face down in the darkness, with arms out over their heads. What looked like an automatic weapon lay on the ground, not far away. One seemed to be injured, and Kucera was tending to him.

The other person now squirmed a bit, and Carol Shepherd—still holding the handgun in a two-handed, police-style grip—barked, "Don't move. I will shoot you."

But the person's face had raised just enough that Ryan could make out the features. There was no mistaking it. It was the face of Evelyn Rockville.

Chapter 72

Eric Sandoval had handed Amanda a blanket when she emerged from the van. She now pulled the blanket tighter around herself, not just for warmth against the cool night air, or modesty—she had been wearing only a nightgown—but mainly as a shield, a sanctuary of sorts, from the mind-shattering chaos around her. Ryan had on a T-shirt and pajama bottoms. For Amanda, who had always been concerned about how she looked, what Ryan and she wore right now was the last thing on her mind.

"Look, I know you two have been through a lot, but I want to assure you that you are safe now." Eric Sandoval had a deep, calming voice, an experienced voice that had no doubt issued comforting words many times in similar situations.

"So here's the one-minute summary. I'll tell you more later and, anyway, you probably don't want to hear it all now." He looked from Ryan to Amanda with caring eyes. In a steady, almost pastoral tone, he said, "Ryan, your old company, Lightyear, was involved in some very dirty things. Dangerous things that threatened our national security. We've only been on to them for a few weeks, ever since your first abstract was published."

"What?" Ryan looked at Amanda with eyes full of questions, then back at Sandoval.

"I'll explain later. Anyway, that got us onto Lightyear, and what we found was very interesting." He now looked over at Rockville and the man on the ground. "That lovely pair murdered Nils Robie, and they were going to kill you, too. Almost succeeded, I'm sorry to say."

"But wasn't that a suicide?" Amanda asked.

"The police initially thought it was a suicide, but we had just come onto the Lightyear case, so we were primed to look closer."

"But why would they want to kill us?"

"We'll go into that more later, but we think they saw you as a potential threat. You published the abstracts, then left town in a hurry, heading for Canada. Perhaps heading out of the country with information you could supply to their competitors or enemies or—"

"But we were only going to Glacier," said Amanda, almost with a whimper.

"That's apparently not what they thought. When you're panicked, as they were, you sometimes act before you have all the data."

"Who's the other guy?" asked Ryan.

"A real piece of work. Rence Booker. Mob connections. We've known about him for a long time."

Amanda was certain this was the man who had been watching them in the cafeteria at Los Alamos. "Is he dead?"

"No. Carol took him down while he was spraying your camper with gunfire. If she'd wanted him dead, believe me, he'd be dead."

"Oh my God, you're hurt," Amanda gasped. She had just noticed blood seeping from Ryan's calf.

Ryan looked down and seemed surprised to see the injury. Sandoval bent down to take a closer look. He touched a sharp wood fragment, apparently part of the Roadtrek interior that had been blown loose from the gunfire, protruding from Ryan's calf. "It doesn't look serious, thank God. We'll get this taken care of as soon as the medical guys get here."

From out of her peripheral vision Amanda saw it. Evelyn Rockville, who had been motionless, spread-eagled in the dirt, suddenly flipped—with surprising speed—and spun to her knees. Somehow she had reached the weapon—Agent Kucera had fallen short as he'd dived toward her—and it was now in her hands, aimed directly at Ryan.

It all happened too fast. There was no time to speak, no time to think, only react. There wasn't time to grieve the dreams that would never come true—the man going into her father's den, closing the doors, and asking for her hand in marriage; pushing her toddler on a swing at the playground; endless adventures with Ryan. She opened her mouth, but no sound came out. Pure instinct is all that can be relied upon when there isn't time for anything else.

Amanda spun, pivoting on one foot—the power forward from the '02 state runners-up at Wausau East High School threw her body in front of his, like a basketball player setting a screen. Those amazing reflexes, quick and decisive, took her directly into the line of fire.

Chapter 73

Physicists like Ryan know that most important events occur on timescales that we cannot grasp. The development of the universe and the processes of evolutionary biology and the carving of the Grand Canyon and the aging of a lover's face relentlessly alter what we call reality, but they are too slow for human senses to detect. The vibrations of an atom, the reactions of molecules that we call chemistry, and the bullets speeding from an AR-15 on their way to a loved-one's flesh can change what we believe to be true, but they are too fast for humans to detect.

It could not be changed or prevented. It could not be rescinded or turned back. No intervention could be made. No time to emotionally or rationally respond, no time for terror or grief, no time to analyze or consider how things could have been different. Certainly no time to raise the bear spray canister. Only time to observe—a fraction of a second that would change his life forever.

And so Ryan watched without time for reaction, helplessly, as Amanda threw her body between him and certain death.

Rockville fell toward them onto her elbows, the gun trained toward them, as practiced as any combat veteran. The first shots went wide before she found her balance.

As fast as some things may be—like the shots from an assassin's weapon—other things may be even faster. Other eyes besides Amanda's saw the almost instantaneous unfolding of events. As Evelyn Rockville turned her weapon toward Ryan—determined it would seem, when it would later be reviewed, to eliminate the witness who had undone her evil life—Carol Shepherd also saw the unfolding horror. She, like Amanda, also responded to the threat on instinct, with practiced and conditioned responses that would be needed when there wasn't time to think. Almost instantly, she spun toward Evelyn Rockville, the handgun grasped in two hands, a single shot fired just as the spray from Rockville's automatic weapon had begun. A single shot was enough. Suddenly, Rockville was down, motionless on the ground.

In the struggle between good and evil that Ryan had so fruitlessly pondered, it often seemed like evil triumphs over good. But not always, maybe not even at all in the ultimate scheme of things. And certainly not today.

Chapter 74

"Coffee's not bad here," Eric Sandoval said to Carol Shepherd. He looked relaxed in the straight-back wooden chair. With one leg casually crossed over the other, his white dress shirt opened at the collar and his graying hair combed neatly to one side, he looked about as nonchalant as an old man on the front porch, getting ready for an afternoon nap.

The five of them—Ryan, Amanda, Eric Sandoval, Carol Shepherd and Rudy Kucera—sat around a large oak table next to a tall window with an expansive view of Swiftcurrent Lake, in the dining room of the Many Glacier Hotel. It had been a long night. After the state police and their medical teams hauled Rockville and Booker away and tended to Ryan's injury—which was minor—the FBI agents had taken them to the hotel, all five of them ironically sharing the cramped space in the gray Sonata that had previously struck fear into Ryan and Amanda. The hotel was fully booked, they had been told, but it was amazing how influential three FBI agents could be in finding rooms when there apparently weren't any. The Roadtrek would be towed to an RV repair shop in Great Falls.

"Yes, the coffee's pretty good," replied Carol Shepherd, adding some cream to her cup, "but I'd say you earned it, Eric."

Amanda and Ryan had slept well for a few hours, surprising after the trauma they had experienced. But maybe that was the predictable result when the body's full supply of adrenalin has been depleted. Bozeman—who Ryan had smuggled into the hotel under a blanket—had no sleeping problems at all. And now Amanda was hungry, as she and Ryan perused their breakfast menus.

"So I'm guessing you two might have a few questions," said Sandoval.

"Yeah, about a million," Ryan said.

"Well, I can't tell you everything, you understand, because there will be a criminal case here ...." He paused, then gave them a tight-lipped smile. "But the way I see it, this is just some friends having breakfast in a beautiful place out in the wilderness." He stopped to survey the view for a moment and watched a kayaker make her way across the lake. "So fire away."

Amanda spoke up. "I want to know how they found us. I mean, we posted that Facebook note saying we were going to Austin and all."

Sandoval nodded patiently. "Well, it was easy, actually. We believe they did begin to track you by reading Ryan's Facebook page, where you had tagged him. But later they relied upon this." He looked over at Rudy Kucera, who held up a plastic baggie. Kucera laid the bag in front of Ryan and Amanda for their inspection. Inside was an iPhone and a portable battery pack.

"A poor man's tracking device," Kucera said. "Buy an iPhone using false ID for the contract, plant it on the vehicle you want to track, then use the Find Your Phone app to always know where the vehicle is located. Battery will keep it alive for a week or two."

"But we looked all over the van," said Ryan.

Kucera smiled. "You must not have looked on the roof, right behind the fan exhaust, where it wouldn't be visible from the ground."

Ryan shrugged. "No, we didn't." He paused, then said, "So you used a tracking device, too?"

"No," said Sandoval. "We have to respect the legal rights of citizens, so we had to do it the old-fashioned way. We followed you. That's why it took so long for us to get to you last night. You threw us a curve ball by heading up that dirt road in the middle of nowhere. We lost you for a bit."

Sandoval took another sip of coffee. "By the way, I recommend the omelet. I saw a woman eating one over at another table. Looked good." Amanda glanced back down at her menu. She smiled at the thought of Sandoval noticing what other people were eating. She suspected he was pretty good at noticing what was going on around him.

Ryan blew out a big breath, then said, "So tell me what you can about Lightyear and that mess."

Sandoval set his coffee cup down. "Yeah, that's quite interesting." Just then the waiter came and took their orders. Sandoval interjected, "Breakfast is on the U.S. taxpayers this morning. That's the least they can do for you." He gave them another tight-lipped smile, which Amanda figured was probably about as close as Sandoval ever came to a real laugh. Even though he seemed relaxed and casual, for him this was still all business.

When the waiter left, Sandoval continued. "Lightyear is what we call an aggregator. We've run into a few of them over the years."

"Aggregator?" Ryan looked puzzled.

"An aggregator like Lightyear collects unclassified information, data and ideas from many sources—government agencies, private industry, universities, whatever. A bright mind like Robie's synthesizes these pieces—each, perhaps, relatively unimportant by itself—into something valuable, something that may be important to national security. Because Lightyear and similar companies hold no security clearances, nor work on anything classified or sensitive, they can fly under the radar of national security agencies." He paused to take another sip of coffee and check the progress of the kayaker on the lake. Then he continued. "Robie was the genius, who out of resentment toward the Federal government was the brains behind the operation, but it was Evelyn Rockville—who had worked for him at the Naval Research Lab—who ram-rodded the organization, had the founding idea and exploited Robie's hate and made the contacts with customers in Iran and Syria and other places."

"Iran and Syria? Oh, God," said Ryan, looking suddenly pale.

"Yeah, that's not something you'll want to post on Facebook, mind you, so just keep that to yourselves. Remember, we're just friends having breakfast this morning."

Ryan and Amanda nodded like obedient students before the principal.

Sandoval continued. "Because of his past experience, Robie had many contacts in government and industry. He could easily pick up contracts, just small ones, from a lot of places. He would do paper studies for them, augmented by a small amount of research that our tech guys tell us wasn't really so important. Sorry Ryan, don't take it personally."

Another smile. "It was only for gaining access to their customer's corporate knowledge. Then Robie would package all the pieces into something that was more than the sum of the parts—driven by hate. All orchestrated by Rockville, who knew how to use mob and overseas connections."

Ryan shook his head in dismay.

"Rockville wormed her way into the Naval Research Lab, initially at a low-level position, then apparently set her sights on Robie. They had an affair, and she probably fueled his anger at the institution. When he left, she went with him. Then later, she took up with Rence Booker. Maybe Robie found out about that, maybe he was finally feeling guilty about what Lightyear was doing or maybe he was scared because your abstracts might bring them down—which of course, they did. Anyway, Rockville and Booker saw him as a danger to their schemes, and he had to go."

Ryan's mouth was open, like he was breathing hard. He leaned forward toward Sandoval. "So, how did my abstracts play a role? I mean, like you just said, they weren't all that important, technically."

Sandoval nodded. "The Bureau has a team of tech guys who read the abstracts for most scientific conferences. You might be surprised at how much good stuff about what we call critical technologies we find there. We had no idea about Lightyear's work until we saw your abstracts. Dissemination of powders and aerosols. Come on, Ryan. You advertised it as aiding the applications of herbicides and fertilizers for agriculture." Sandoval raised an eyebrow to suggest that Ryan should have known better.

Ryan looked embarrassed. Amanda gave him a reassuring little punch on the shoulder. She knew he didn't want to be seen as gullible or naïve in front of her.

Now Sandoval leaned forward. "So, here's where it's really important. You want to fly a plane, or a drone, or a missile over a battlefield or a town in Iraq and spread biological or chemical warfare agents and you want the poison to be optimally dispersed. You don't want your plane returning to home base, still loaded with that poison because it got stuck in a holding tank because some nozzle got clogged with it. And you don't want your missile to come down on its target, and because you didn't do your dispersal engineering correctly, you only contaminate two acres." He now leaned back and smiled. "Anyway, that's how the tech guys explained it to me. Hell, I'm just a field ops guy—I'm the one who goes and catches the bad guys—how would I know?"

"So they were afraid I might be heading out of the country to contact a competitor or spill the beans?"

"I think so," said Sandoval. "As evil as they were, they weren't pros. We suspect they initially thought that firing you would solve their problems. But then you took off, and we suspect they panicked. When it appeared you were heading into Canada, they apparently believed they had to strike." Then he leaned toward Ryan and his face softened. "So why did you send in those abstracts?"

Ryan chewed his lip, seeming to craft his answer. "I'm a scientist." Sandoval certainly already knew that. "And scientists have a code of ethics. We're honest about our work, we don't cheat, and—unless the work is classified—we share our results with the world." Ryan looked over at Amanda, who was glowing. "And that's what I did, whether or not Lightyear liked it."

Sandoval rubbed his chin between his thumb and forefinger as he considered this. "That's the answer I was hoping I'd hear." He looked from face to face at the table, then said, "I believe that Ryan Browning is something of a hero."

Ryan sat up straighter. Amanda felt a surge of pride for him. It was a code of ethics, after all, that motivated his actions, not the angry knee-jerk reaction of a disgruntled employee. Yes, he had been fired, but he had also helped bring down an enemy of the country. Ryan looked at Amanda again, and their eyes remained locked for a while—their looks were solemn, not needing an overlay of smiles or laughter.

Then Amanda turned back to Sandoval and asked, "But why would they try to kill us in such a violent way?"

"Well, I can only speculate about that," said Sandoval.

Carol Shepherd cut in here. "I might interject that Eric's speculations are seldom wrong."

"Thanks, Carol. Anyway, an execution-style killing would seem to be Booker's style, given his mob heritage. If you had a partner out there, this would send them a strong message. If you were selling info to a foreign competitor, the execution would send a strong message. Stay away. Even so, we didn't expect they'd try something so Al Capone-ish, so crude, so violent." He shook his head slowly. "We would have never let them get so far."

Kucera added, "Rockville and Booker were some tough bastards."

"Yes, they were," agreed Sandoval. He now turned and looked out the window again, watching as the kayaker made it to the far shore and was pulling her boat up onto the sand. Then he turned back, gave a quick smile, and said, "But then, I guess, so are we."

Chapter 75

As they left the dining room—down a rustic hallway leading into the huge lobby—Carol Shepherd walked alongside Amanda. She looked like a suburban mom who'd just popped into Starbucks after dropping her kids off at school. She wore a pink sweatshirt with a Glacier National Park logo—had she just bought that at the gift shop here in the lobby?—over blue jeans and Keens.

"Those people you shot last night." Amanda cleared her throat and realized she was stammering. This wasn't the kind of conversation she was used to having. "Will they live?"

"Yes, they'll be fine. I didn't intend for my shots to be fatal."

"How could you know for sure?"

Shepherd stopped and looked directly at Amanda. "Some people are good at tennis, others are good at quilting. I just happen to be really good with a Glock 22."

"Oh," Amanda said meekly. She swallowed something that felt like a lump in her throat, then said, "You saved my life last night. I'm really grateful for that."

"You're welcome. I'm sorry you had to be placed in such danger."

"So they were following us all along?"

Shepherd nodded. "They approached your RV in Bandelier. You knew about that. We were watching, too. If your door had opened, we'd have been all over it. But it didn't, and they didn't press it at that point."

Amanda's mouth fell open. "So that was them in the campground?"

"Yep."

"And you were there, too?"

"Yep."

"Why didn't you just grab them then?"

"We didn't have all our ducks in a row yet. We'd only been on the case a few days."

Amanda shook her head, as she realized that they had apparently been in physical danger all along the way. "Then we saw a creepy guy at Los Alamos. Was that Booker?"

"It was. We think it really cranked up their fear when you went to Los Alamos—all the high security, national defense experts and so on. We're dealing with amateur paranoid people here, but very dangerous ones who could have done a lot of harm to our country."

"You were there too?"

"Not us personally, but we've got lots of colleagues around that place." She laughed. "The Lab's not a good place for criminals to try something."

Sandoval had been speaking with the clerk at the hotel desk, but now rejoined them. "Yeah, we've kinda made this whole trip with you. Rudy—he's from the Phoenix office—had you in Arizona until you saw him in the campground. By the way, you really kicked his butt on that hike you went on." He again gave that smile that was his closest thing to a laugh. "So we got called in then—Carol and I are from Albuquerque."

"So then I saw you in Santa Fe," Ryan said.

Sandoval nodded. "It was my intention in Santa Fe for you to see me. I was hoping to start a conversation, maybe learn more about what you were up to. You publish those abstracts, then leave suddenly, close out your bank account—we didn't know what the hell you were doing."

Ryan retorted, "Eating New Mexican food, as I recall."

Sandoval nodded again. "Then Art Montoya told me how you'd seen Rudy and me."

"The police chief?"

"Assistant chief, he always reminds me." Again, the smile that was almost a laugh. "But yes. He's an old friend. That's when we knew we had to hand the ball over to Carol."

Carol looked down, then said, "But I almost compromised the whole case. I was following you both that morning at the Denver Zoo. You should have never seen me. Then there was that lost kid." Carol bit her lip and looked at Amanda. "I couldn't just stand there. I guess there are some things that trump being an agent."

Amanda placed a hand on Carol's arm, and it seemed like the sharpshooter agent's eyes might be misting up.

Sandoval looked at Carol. "Like I've said before, Carol, that's what makes you such a good agent. Yeah, you're about the best shot in the whole Bureau, but you also haven't forgotten how to be a human being."

Then he turned to Ryan and Amanda. "By the way, you two, we've got you a rental car. Parked out front. Afraid it's just a subcompact, but it ought to hold you until your RV's fixed." Sandoval handed Ryan the keys. Then he said to them, "One more question. Just why were you headed toward Canada?"

A big smile came across Amanda's face. "Like I said, we weren't headed to Canada. We were coming here."

"Why?"

"We came to find a mountain goat," Amanda said. Ryan smiled and nodded, as he put an arm around her shoulder.

Sandoval looked puzzled for a moment, eyebrows raised. Then he shrugged and said, "Okay."

Chapter 76

From their room at the Super 8 in Great Falls, Ryan and Amanda had been checking the internet regularly for reports on the attack. On the second day, a small article appeared in the *Great Falls Tribune*, deep in section two of the paper, reporting vandalism involving gunshots fired at an RV outside Glacier National Park. No names were given. There were no reports of injuries. The article said an investigation was underway. It was obviously the efforts of the Feds, probably with support from the local authorities, to keep this as quiet as possible while they continued their investigation.

Still, Amanda worried that her parents might have learned about the attack. After the *Tribune* article, she called them, while standing in the parking lot of Up North RV Sales and Service, not far from their motel. While the phone rang, she watched Ryan, at the opening of a nearby service bay, talking with a mechanic who was working on the van.

Her mother answered, and soon her dad was on the line, too. How long had it been since she'd spoken with them? It seemed like forever. They asked where she was calling from. "I'm in Great Falls, Montana," she said. They seemed to have no knowledge about the attack, and she certainly wasn't going to tell them about it. Not yet.

There was silence on the other end.

"I'm on a camping holiday," she said. After a moment, she added, "With a friend."

Her parents did not inquire any further about the friend, no doubt assuming the worst. Too many reruns of *Baywatch*, Amanda thought.

They asked her when she was coming to see them. Amanda bit her lip, as she looked over at Ryan, who was now looking under the van with the mechanic. "I don't know," she said. Then she added, "I want to come soon." Her mouth felt suddenly dry.

After a period of awkward silence, Amanda said, "Mom, Dad ... I miss you."

There was now more silence on the other end, and Amanda began to regret that she had said this. Then her dad said, seeming to be stammering, "Oh, Amanda, we miss you, too."

Amanda felt tears well up in her eyes. There was more silence, then she said something she had not said to them for a long time, although she'd never stopped feeling it. "Mom and Dad, I love you so much."

She could swear she heard a gasp on the other end. *Was that her mom?* Then, almost in unison, she heard them say, "Oh, darling, we love you, too."

Amanda swallowed hard and had to lean against a big fifth wheel to steady herself. When the call was over and Amanda felt like she could breathe again, she covered her face with both hands and sobbed.

When she had pulled herself together, she called Katy and pretty much told her everything. She began by telling her about the reunion with Ryan.

"So, this sounds pretty serious," Katy said.

"Yeah, I think it is."

"So, has the big-L word come up yet?"

"Geez, Katy, you don't beat around the bush, that's for sure."

"Well?"

"As a matter of fact, it has."

Even before Amanda had completed the sentence, Katy squealed. "Oh, my ... I'm so excited." She was talking fast, then she squealed again, which made Amanda beam. "So when's the wedding?"

"Katy," Amanda said, with false admonishment, "you are so bad. As usual."

"Well?"

Amanda looked over at Ryan again. He was now leaning over and studying the bullet holes along the side of the van. "Katy, come on," she said. "You're embarrassing me now. There are no plans for a wedding. We've just barely—"

"I'll be maid of honor, of course. Won't I?"

Amanda looked around nervously, as if Ryan might be listening in. "Katy, you are too much."

Then Amanda told her about the attack. It was the only way she could get her off her wedding fixation.

There was silence on the other end. Then, a solemn Katy said, "Oh, God, Amanda, are you okay?"

"Yes, we're both okay. It was terrifying, but that episode is now behind us."

Katy seemed to recover from her interlude of sympathy quickly. "So, how come I haven't seen any selfies on Facebook, with the caption, 'Me and Ryan, after surviving a siege of automatic weapons fire?'" Katy was still her old self.

Amanda laughed, shaking her head, as if saying, "No, I do not know this person." Then she said, "I think I'm pretty much done with Facebook, at least for a while. I want to concentrate on what's right in front of me." She was watching Ryan again, who had left the mechanic. He was now with Bozeman, playing tug-of-war with an old sock.

After Amanda had finished her calls, Ryan came toward her, carrying their puppy. "How are your folks?" he asked.

"They're fine. They haven't heard anything about what we've been through. I'll want to tell them at some point, but not yet. Not until I can see them face to face."

Ryan nodded.

"And I called Katy, too. She's as insane as ever. Did you ever reach Wil?"

"No, but I keep trying. Wish he'd get a cell."

Behind them, brakes squealed, causing them both to jump. They spun around to see a large pickup come to a sudden stop near them and a man jump out. It was Wil. Ryan and Amanda exchanged shocked looks.

"Good God in heaven," Wil shouted, even before he got to them, "I should've never let you guys leave." He looked from face to face. "Are you both okay?"

"We're okay," said Amanda, as she gave Wil a hug.

"You've been all over the news."

"Really?" said Ryan.

"Well, actually, I only saw a little article this morning about gunshots fired at an RV in Glacier. Didn't take a genius to figure out who that was."

"I'm really glad to see you, Uncle Wil," said Ryan. "Sorry if we scared you."

"Scared me?" Wil laughed. "You fried my pacemaker. Well, if I had a pacemaker, you would have." Now they all laughed.

"How'd you find us?" asked Amanda.

"Wasn't hard. Made a couple of calls."

"But Montana's a big state," said Ryan.

"Only in square miles, nephew." Wil gave a sly smile, then added, "'Course it didn't hurt that the police chief of Great Falls was one of my students."

Ryan shook his head, laughing.

Then Wil said, "You don't have to tell me the whole story, of course, but I figured it was something pretty big. I just mainly had to make sure you were okay."

"You deserve to hear the whole story," said Ryan. He looked around. "Let's find a private place to talk."

They all sat at the dining table in a big Winnebago. Ryan left out no details. Maybe Eric Sandoval wouldn't approve of him telling the whole story, but Ryan wasn't going to hold anything back from his uncle.

Wil shook his head slowly. "Good Lord, I am so grateful that you guys are safe. I just can't get my arms around the thought of you two in that van, with all that ...." He paused, choking up, then collecting himself, he grinned. "Hey, it's not every day we have somebody here in Montana breaking up a gang of traitors."

Amanda smiled. "Thank God, the FBI was on to them. It would have been a different outcome."

Wil nodded slowly. "So the old van got shot up? They going to be able to fix it?"

"Let's go take a look. It's just on the other side of the lot."

Wil walked around the outside of the van, which looked just fine, except for a blown-out windshield and about a dozen holes that looked like they'd been made with a half-inch drill by a sloppy craftsman. Wil trailed his fingers over the holes, blew out a troubled breath, then shook his head. "Lordy, I don't know how you survived this."

"It was Ryan's quick thinking," Amanda said. "He hid us in the only safe place in the van. Saved our lives." She beamed with pride toward Ryan.

Ryan was shaking his head. "But you were the real hero, throwing your body in front of me when Rockville got her hands on the gun."

"That was just instinct," she said softly, looking up at him with love in her eyes.

"Wow, you two are something else, altogether." Wil said, shaking his head with incredulity. "Why don't you come back down to Bozeman and get yourselves back together?"

Ryan looked at Amanda. "We're not quite sure what we want to do yet," he said. "It's all still too unreal."

Wil gave them a serious nod, which broke into a grin. "I figured. You have had a few distractions lately. Gotta say, Ryan, your mama would be very proud of this adventurous son of hers." He bit his lip, as he nodded his appreciation. "And she would have been amazed by you, Amanda."

Ryan looked down, as if suddenly self-conscious. Then he looked up and said, "You don't know how good it makes me feel to hear you say that." He then looked at Amanda, who moved close to him.

"I suspect you'll be seeing us again soon," Amanda said.

"I'd like that," Wil said. "Now, one more question. Anybody here interested in lunch? I know this Italian place downtown."

Chapter 77

"Do you think we have PTSD?" Amanda asked. They stood together at the entrance of the C. M. Russell Museum in Great Falls.

Ryan began to laugh, but he quickly suppressed it, realizing this was a serious question. "I don't know." He shrugged. "Maybe we should, but I feel okay. At least I think I'm okay." He laughed nervously. "How about you?"

"I think I'm okay, too. No nightmares yet. But isn't PTSD kind of sneaky? I mean, how do we know if we have it?"

"I'll watch you and you watch me." He shrugged again, then added, "But I guess we're going to be doing that anyway." He smiled, as he gently ran a fingertip down the side of her face. "Meanwhile, I think coming here is just what we needed to do."

The C. M. Russell Museum was in an odd location for a world-class art museum. First, it was in Great Falls, hardly a center of the arts. But also, it sat in a middle-class residential neighborhood, not unlike Ryan's old hood in Lawndale. Yet, here there was an unparalleled collection of western, cowboy and native American art, much of it by the famed painter Charlie Russell himself.

After two hours of wandering through the vast collection, Amanda and Ryan found themselves sharing a banana split at a Dairy Queen a few blocks away.

Amanda swallowed a bite of ice cream, then slowly pulled the plastic spoon from between her lips in a seductive way. "I've never studied western art, but I'd always heard of the Russell. I loved today," she said.

Ryan nodded. "I especially loved the paintings of the Indians on the plains. There was something so wild and free and raw about those paintings."

"Oh yes. The one of the hunting party when they first saw the Lewis and Clark expedition coming up the river?"

"I liked that one, too," said Ryan.

"It felt like I was really there with them," she said, "confused and uncertain, probably afraid, challenged, and maybe anticipating how their lives would never be the same again." She took another bite of the ice cream. "I found the whole experience of the museum soothing."

"Like ice cream," he laughed, as he loaded another bite onto his spoon. "So, why do you find art soothing?"

She set down her spoon and touched her chin with her forefinger, giving this some thought. "Maybe because art usually touches upon the deeper things. It makes me feel challenged, yet safe. Does that make sense?"

"I think it does. Sometimes science did that for me, I mean it still does, but lately I've been struggling with some of this."

"I saw that in your blog, the poem about the forest. I loved that, by the way."

Her comment and the love in her eyes as she said it caused him to almost lose his train of thought.

"I'm not so sure that science and art are all that different in that regard," she said.

"Say more."

"Well, I remember studying some of Dali's paintings. Especially his wonderful *Christ of Saint John of the Cross*. Have you seen it?"

Ryan shook his head no.

"It's in the Kelvingrove Museum in Glasgow. I'd love to go there some day."

Ryan laid a hand on her arm in a gentle way that said he'd like to go there with her.

"Anyway, it shows Christ on the cross, high above a lakeshore, where fishermen are tending to their boat. Probably represents the transcendence of God above the daily life of humanity."

Ryan nodded his interest.

She continued, "Dali said that the symmetry of the image of Christ represented the symmetry of the nucleus of the atom. Not sure I understand that, but apparently this came to him in a dream. And the proportions of the Christ in the painting were also based upon some mathematical principle. Dali said that the image to him represented the unity of all things."

Ryan shook his head slowly. "So, you're saying that for Dali, there was a unity between art and science and mathematics?"

"Apparently so. And for him, it all pointed toward Christ."

They were both silent for a while.

Then Ryan said, "I want to learn more about art."

Amanda looked pleased, then said, "You are an artist, Ryan. You are a very serious photographer."

"Thanks. I still have a lot to learn."

She smiled at him, and her eyes seemed watery.

"I want to take good pictures," said Ryan. "Capture what I see. That doesn't always work out. It seems that painters have a real advantage. They're not constrained by the reality of the light and the way things are. They can paint what is in their imaginations."

"I would agree," she said. "Reminds me of a comment that Matisse once made. *I do not literally paint that table, but the emotion it produces upon me.* But I think that photographers and painters are both seeking to capture truth. If it's not about truth, then it's not very interesting. You photographers have to work with the limitations of the light. The painters have to work with the difficulty of translating the images their imaginations produce into brush strokes. Either way, it's challenging."

"You just said something really important. They both must point to truth. I really like that. Truth. That indeed is soothing."

"You know what?" she said.

"What?"

"I really enjoy talking to you." Now she turned her gaze to the busy street scene outside the window of the DQ. Ryan looked also. There was considerable traffic, which seemed odd, being in the middle of Montana. It felt more like the LA burbs. Near the window, an old man puttered along in a motorized cart. Along the sidewalk, a teenager sped by on a skateboard. In the parking lot, two girls in tank tops and shorts balanced cups of ice cream while looking at their phones. It was a summer scene: green trees and blue sky and a few puffy white clouds.

Amanda turned back toward Ryan. "There's absolutely nothing unusual going on out there. Yet, everything seems so alive. Special. Beautiful." Now she looked out at the afternoon scene again. Then, she gently pushed the banana split aside and took both of Ryan's hands in hers. Her eyes were on fire. "You make me want to paint," she said.

Chapter 78

"That old bucket of bolts seems to be built like a battleship," Ryan mused, when they picked up the Roadtrek the next day.

The windshield and a couple of interior cabinet doors had been replaced and the bullet holes in the body patched. The latter was accomplished with dollops of epoxy that didn't quite match the body color. In light of the age of the RV, they had opted to forgo more expensive body work, which would have set them back a bundle. Minor electrical repairs got the lighting system working again, but the other electrical and plumbing systems were intact. The gas and propane tanks had not been hit.

"A battleship, yes," said Amanda. "It certainly has been in a battle." She shook her head as she laughed. "I hope you never have to sell that thing. It will be hard to explain all those globs of epoxy on the body."

The only item that had incurred serious damage was the refrigerator, which was completely destroyed by two bullets that had been stopped by the compressor. It would cost a thousand bucks to replace it. Since their RV insurance policy did not spell out coverage for gunshot damage—and had a high deductible anyway—Amanda and Ryan decided they would use the dead fridge as a closet and pick up an ice chest for forty bucks at REI.

"Sell it?" Ryan feigned incredulity. "Why would we ever want to sell this beauty?" He shared her laughter. "Anyway, think about it. How many Roadtreks are there that have survived automatic weapons fire?" He stepped over to the van and stroked it gently, like he was touching the fine finish on a Corvette. "I tell you, this thing is priceless."

Ryan understood that their laughter was a balm much needed to heal the trauma they had endured.

Stepping inside the van felt like coming home. Sure, Ryan had only spent a couple of weeks in the Roadtrek, but they had been the most important weeks of his life. Amanda must have shared his feelings. "Welcome home, my darling," she said.

While they had waited for the van this morning, Ryan and Amanda perused the entries from his mother's road atlas. Many brought laughter, some were bittersweet. But one caused Ryan to gasp and fight back tears.

Today I bought a new magnet at Swiftcurrent store. It's a picture of a mountain goat at sunset. He is a noble animal, at peace. Gentle and pure, unafraid. It reminds me of Ryan.

Amanda gripped his arm as she read the words. "So, I guess this means we have to go back to Glacier," she whispered.

In three hours they were back at the St. Mary Campground, on the east side of Glacier. They were barely settled in when a ranger, making his rounds of the campground, stopped at their site. "Hey folks, thought you'd want to know. Just heard the good news that the road up to Logan Pass has opened for the season. Not all the way over to the west side, but it's open up to the pass."

Amanda looked at Ryan. "So what are we waiting for?"

At just under seven thousand feet elevation, Logan Pass was the high point along the famed Going to the Sun Road, connecting the east and west sides of the park. A visitor center sat atop the pass, which commanded spectacular mountain views in all directions. Driving the road up to the pass from St. Mary was an adventure in itself—the most challenging mountain drive that Amanda and Ryan had yet made. The road snaked through tunnels, clung to narrow ledges along steep mountain walls with thousand-foot drop-offs, and offered jaw-dropping views of distant glaciers and waterfalls.

The sunny days of early June had so far made little impact on melting the heavy winter snowpack at the top of the pass. The cleared walkways around the visitor center were narrow channels carved through six-foot-high walls of snow.

However, the trail heading south from the visitor center, toward Hidden Lake, climbed an exposed ridge, where the combination of stiff winds and intense sun had removed most of the snow. Here, there were patches that were clear, where short alpine grasses were already beginning to turn green. It was beside such an area, near a rocky ledge that looked out over the wild terrain to the east, that Amanda and Ryan dropped their day packs beside a fallen log and settled in to enjoy a snack.

Small pines, sparse and scraggly here near timberline, surrounded them like weary soldiers sagging after a long march. Above them loomed a high peak with a near-vertical face. Ice choked the narrow shoots on the face, and a waterfall poured down one sheer wall from a high snowfield.

Ryan had just poured himself a handful of trail mix, when a mountain goat stepped up on a high rock, not twenty feet away. They froze in place. It was a large animal, with long winter fur, white as the snow. The goat had a beard, long tufts of white hair dropping from each side of its jaw, giving it a Fu Man Chu appearance. Its eyes were so dark, it was impossible to tell if it was looking at them. Its curved, sharp black horns protruded a good ten inches from its head. Although the animal was large and equipped with horns that could be a formidable weapon, and its eyes were hard to read, it had a look of tranquility about it, a bearing of dignity.

Amanda rested her head against Ryan's shoulder. She whispered, "Just like your mother said, Ryan." She took his hand. "It's you."

Ryan's jaw dropped, as he gaped at the majestic creature. Then he leaned forward to see better. "Maybe it's not me after all. Actually, I believe it's a female."

They were silent.

Then a small calf appeared next to the mountain goat, a tiny thing, possibly a newborn. It moved in and up underneath its momma's belly. "Oh, dear God," breathed Amanda, "that is so beautiful."

A rustling behind them caused them to jump, which considering their recent experiences, wasn't so surprising. Ryan instinctively moved his hand to the bear spray canister on his belt. They turned to see another mountain goat appear. It was a male. It stepped out onto the rocky ledge, then stood motionless, looking directly at them.

Ryan thought his heart might stop. He wanted to pull the Nikon from his pack and get a photo, but he was unable to move. All he could do was watch. Then the male stepped quietly toward the female and the calf.

The three mountain goats stood there for a moment, still apparently oblivious to the presence of Amanda and Ryan—or so unafraid that they did not care. Then the three of them turned toward the steep rocky drop-off, so surefooted that it seemed like they were dancing. They leapt across a narrow fissure with agility astounding for such large animals, and disappeared down the nearly vertical mountainside.

"A family," said Ryan.

"Yes," whispered Amanda, "a family."

That afternoon, back at their campsite, Amanda studied park literature they'd picked up at the visitor center, while Ryan wrote another blog post. It didn't take long to write it, but he realized that it was by far his most important.

New Blog post

So much has happened since my last post. I must confess my head is spinning, and it may be a while before I can make sense of everything. About all I can say at this point is that Amanda and I have now experienced the full ugliness of evil firsthand. And yet we are alive today because there is so much good in this world: the dedication of those FBI agents, for one, but also the sacrificial nature of love, which Amanda demonstrated without hesitation.

I'm not sure that evil can ever be eradicated. People like Eric Sandoval and Carol Shepherd are taking a pretty good crack at that, but I suspect they'd be the first to admit that there will always be evil in the world. But what can you and I personally do about the evil and suffering in the world? I am convinced—my head is not spinning about this part—that the only answer to evil and suffering is love. Maybe this is not news to you, but it is to me. Here's the point: to love is not to deny the existence of evil or turn away from suffering, but to more and more engage it with the fearlessness that love creates. And I am also becoming more convinced—okay, this is a big thing for me to say—that there is a holiness, maybe a God, that keeps supplying us with that love.

Chapter 79

Amanda stood before the mirror in the tiny bathroom of the Roadtrek. She leaned in and studied the woman she saw. She wore no makeup. The hike this afternoon in the dry, windy air atop Logan Pass had left her hair a mess.

If this were a portrait at the Art Institute, what would she have to say about this woman? She pondered that for a while. Clearly this was a woman who was not conforming to the expectations of her culture—a world demanding perfect grooming, a world in which a woman worried about the right hair conditioner. Her hair today was doing just what it wanted to do, and that made her smile. She noticed that the brown roots had become more evident in the past two weeks, and she had not tended to this. Nor did she intend to. Not only did her lips not display the perfect gloss, selected with professional consultation from the cosmetics department at Nordstrom, but they were chapped from many days hiking in the high country.

What about the eyes? They looked different than she remembered. Gone was the look of frailty, the look that someone might be about to criticize her or see through her façade. These were eyes that cared little for façades. They were honest eyes. Calm eyes. But there was more about them than that. What was it? She studied them for a while, not posing, not trying to display some manufactured emotion, but allowing them to be transparent, allowing them to reveal who she really was. Yes. These were the eyes of love.

This was who Amanda Seward was, someone she'd always longed to be. But she had never been able to overcome the demands upon her—or at least the perceived demands—to be the affirming, always cheerful, agreeable party girl, the one who was always trying to please, the one who desperately wanted to fit in, to be accepted, the one who instinctively laughed at a man's jokes. The one who, if she could just improve herself a little more, might be loved by someone. The one who was always second-most popular. What she had now become, in just a few weeks, was astounding. It was nothing less than her true self.

She smiled at the image in the mirror, as if greeting a friend she had not seen for a long time. She extended a finger and touched the finger reaching out toward her. "Hello, Amanda," she said out loud. "I am so glad you are here."

Later that night, they sat around the dying coals of the fire with their camp chairs close together and Bozeman snoring on Ryan's lap. "So, yeah," he said, "we're going to have to find jobs one of these days."

Amanda realized that this could be a critical moment in their relationship. This talk about jobs. Was Ryan implying that he wanted them to be together when they found new jobs? After all, she'd only agreed to go to Glacier with him; there had been no talk about what might lie beyond that. She decided to play it lightly. Feigning surprise, she said, "What? You mean we can't be unemployed forever?"

"Well, of course, with that big wad of cash I have, that could be a possibility." He laughed. "Not."

"But don't forget all the money I have," she said. She put a finger to her nose, like she was totaling up the vast amount. "Oh wait," she said, "I hardly have any more than you. Dang, I guess we'll have to get jobs after all."

"Seriously, Bozeman looks like a pretty attractive place," Ryan said.

This sounded like he was including her. "I think Wil would like that," she said.

"Yes," Ryan said softly. "I'm not used to having family around that seems to care so much for me."

"You never had a father, Ryan." Amanda laid a hand on his arm. "And Wil has never had a son."

Ryan looked at her, his mouth open, but said nothing. He stood and leaned over the fire, then poked at the embers with a stick. He turned toward her, cleared his throat, and said, "So then, I'd still like to do some more traveling after Glacier. What about you?"

She stood and stepped toward him, then gave him a long kiss. She pulled back just a bit and said, "This afternoon I read that there are fifty-eight national parks—so we've barely made a dent." Then she turned and faced toward the high, triangular peak, visible in silhouette against the starry sky behind St. Mary Campground. She spread her arms, like she was preparing to give the peak a hug. When she turned back toward him, her hands on her hips, she said, "I'm ready."

After Ryan had sloshed water on the last orange glow from the coals and Bozeman had his last walk of the day, they headed into the Roadtrek.

In the hallway, she said to him, "So, where do you want to go next?"

He brushed the hair from her face and gently trailed his fingertips along her cheek. "Actually, I was thinking about the back of the van."

She gave him a devilish look. "I mean after that."

"Well, I've never been to Wisconsin."

Amanda felt her face flush. "And why would you want to go there?"

"There are some people I want to meet."

"Oh?"

He looked at her with questioning eyes. "If it's okay with you …." He paused.

She could hardly breathe, but she managed a nod that said, "Go on."

"There's a den there that I plan to enter. And I will close the doors. And there will be a discussion."

Amanda swallowed hard. "Oh? And what will you say?"

"You really want to know?"

"Yes, I do really want to know."

He took her by the hand and led her toward the rear of the Roadtrek. "Why don't you step into my office here, and we'll talk about it?"

If you enjoyed The Mountain Goat, please consider
posting a customer review at Amazon or Goodreads.

Acknowledgements

It is a pleasure to acknowledge the excellent editorial work of Nicole Klungle. I am also grateful to Bill and LuAnn Dorsey, my sister Patty Trainor, and my wife Mary for their careful readings and very helpful critiques of early drafts of the book.

I wish to thank the Rev. Canon Stefani Schatz and the Rev. Joe Duggan for introducing me to the Isle of Iona, Scotland, where part of this book was written. Portions of this book were written while I served as a prayer resident at the Bishop's Ranch, Healdsburg, California. Part of the story was inspired during my residency as a summer chaplain, Chapel of the Transfiguration, Grand Teton National Park. Much of this book was written on my laptop, while camping across the West—in a Roadtrek, of course.

Thanks to Lucas Trainor for technical assistance in post-processing the cover photograph.

I have been blessed to be inspired by the wonderful art collections at the Kelvingrove Art Gallery and Museum, Glasgow, Scotland; the Art Institute of Chicago; the New Mexico Museum of Art, Santa Fe; the Georgia O'Keeffe Museum, Santa Fe; and the C. W. Russell Museum, Great Falls, Montana.

I am grateful to the scientists of Los Alamos National Laboratory, with whom I served for many years, for teaching me about scientific inquiry, research ethics and integrity, and the excitement of scientific discovery.

We should all acknowledge the beautiful national parks and monuments of America. This book touched upon Grand

Canyon, Bandelier, Grand Teton, Yellowstone and Glacier, but there are over fifty others worthy of extended visits.

The communion scene was inspired, in part, by the accounts of first communions in *The Seven Storey Mountain*, by Thomas Merton, and *Take This Bread: A Radical Conversion*, by Sara Miles.

Thanks to Mr. Dave Drager, Advanced Camper Sales, Milwaukee, Wisconsin, who has taught me so much about Roadtreks.

Some of the quotations about science and its interaction with faith are from my book, *Grasp: Making Sense of Science and Spirituality*. Ryan's final blog post about love as the answer to evil and suffering was inspired, in part, by the helpful article by Steven Paulikas, *New York Times*, June 27, 2016.

Finally, I again thank my wife Mary—my Amanda—who has continually encouraged me throughout the course of this project.

About the Author

Jim Trainor is the author of five books.

He is both a physicist (Ph.D., Univ. of Calif.) and ordained Episcopal priest. He has served at some of the world's top research centers and has authored over sixty articles in physics. He has also served as a parish priest to congregations in New Mexico, Texas and Wisconsin. He is active as a speaker on topics in science and spirituality.

Jim grew up in LA and has lived much of his life in the West. He now lives on a lake in central Wisconsin with his wife Mary. They have three grown children. When not at his desk writing, he's hiking in the wilderness or paddling his kayak across a lake.

More information on Jim and his books at

www.JimTrainorAuthor.com

Also by Jim Trainor

ISBN 978-0692307342

Terror waits in the north woods

For Wil Weathers, who's lost his job and his girlfriend, a backpacking trip might just be a cure for the blues. But while waiting for a late-night bus in a small northern Wisconsin town, Wil finds a body. When he returns with help, in the form of the attractive Sally, the body has disappeared. Come up north, where Wil and Sally now find themselves the target of unknown killers and on a collision course with an eco-terrorist gang preparing to destroy the lives of millions.

ISBN 978-1490936789

Karen hopes that Maui will rekindle the firs in her marriage. But the flames that engulf her are of betrayal and murder, from which there may be no rescue.

The Sand People takes us to beautiful Maui, amidst posh beachfront resorts, then draws us deeper into the Maui most tourists never see: rural onion fields, the county jail, a funeral and a run-down bar far from the beachfront glamour. It blends laughter and tears in grappling with issues that plague our lives: broken relationships, addiction, shame and death -- and pointing toward the victory of hope over failure.